MW00776504

PROFESSOR CHARLATAN BARDOT'S
TRAVEL ANTHOLOGY TO THE MOST (FICTIONAL) HAUNTED BUILDINGS IN THE WEIRD, WILD WORLD

(2021 EDITION)

HARARE, ZIMBABWE

OKAVANGO DELTA, BOTSWANA

KIMBERLEY, NORTH CAPE, SOUTH AFRICA

0 100 200 300 400 500

Miles

Fiction Written by Eric J. Guignard

Doorways to the Deadeye (JournalStone, 2019)

Last Case at a Baggage Auction (Harper Day Books, 2020)

That Which Grows Wild: 16 Tales of Dark Fiction (Cemetery Dance Publications, 2018)

Anthologies Edited by Eric J. Guignard

After Death... (Dark Moon Books, 2013)

Dark Tales of Lost Civilizations (Dark Moon Books, 2012)

The Five Senses of Horror (Dark Moon Books, 2018)

+Horror Library+ Volume 6 (Cutting Block Books/ Dark Moon Books, 2017)

+Horror Library+ Volume 7 (Dark Moon Books, 2022)

Pop the Clutch: Thrilling Tales of Rockabilly, Monsters, and Hot Rod Horror (Dark Moon Books, 2019)

Professor Charlatan Bardot's Travel Anthology to the Most (Fictional) Haunted Buildings in the Weird, Wild World (Dark Moon Books, 2021)

A World of Horror (Dark Moon Books, 2018)

Exploring Dark Short Fiction (A Primer Series) Created by Eric J. Guignard

#1: A Primer to Steve Rasnic Tem (Dark Moon Books, 2017)

#2: A Primer to Kaaron Warren (Dark Moon Books, 2018)

#3: A Primer to Nisi Shawl (Dark Moon Books, 2018)

#4: A Primer to Jeffrey Ford (Dark Moon Books, 2019)

#5: A Primer to Han Song (Dark Moon Books, 2020)

#6: A Primer to Ramsey Campbell (Dark Moon Books, 2021)

#7: A Primer to Gemma Files (Dark Moon Books, 2022)

The Horror Writers Association Presents: Haunted Library of Horror Classics Edited by Eric J. Guignard and Leslie S. Klinger

Vol. I: The Phantom of the Opera by Gaston Leroux (Sourcebooks, 2020)

Vol. II: The Beetle by Richard Marsh (Sourcebooks, 2020)

Vol. III: Vathek by William Beckford (Sourcebooks, 2020)

Vol. IV: The House on the Borderland by William Hope Hodgson (Sourcebooks, 2020)

Vol. V: Of One Blood: or, The Hidden Self by Pauline Hopkins (Sourcebooks, 2021)

Vol. VI: The Parasite and Other Tales of Terror by Arthur Conan Doyle (Sourcebooks, 2021)

Vol. VII: The King in Yellow by Robert W. Chambers (Sourcebooks, 2021)

Vol. VIII: Ghost Stories of an Antiquary by M.R. James (Sourcebooks, 2021)

Vol. IX: Gothic Classics: The Castle of Otranto by Horace Walpole (Sourcebooks, 2022)

PROFESSOR CHARLATAN BARDOT'S
TRAVEL ANTHOLOGY TO THE MOST (FICTIONAL) HAUNTED BUILDINGS IN THE WEIRD, WILD WORLD

(2021 EDITION)

EDITED BY
CHARLATAN BARDOT AND ERIC J. GUIGNARD

ILLUSTRATED BY
STEVE LINES AND JAMES GABB

DARK MOON BOOKS
Los Angeles, California

Edited by Eric J. Guignard
Interior layout by Eric J. Guignard
Cover design by Eric J. Guignard
Maps by Eric J. Guignard
www.ericjguignard.com

Cover art by Andreas Rocha: *Abandoned* (2019)
www.andreasrocha.com

Interior illustrations by
Steve Lines: www.rainfallsite.com
and by James Gabb: www.sketchingdaily.wordpress.com

First edition published in November, 2021

Library of Congress Cataloging-in-Publication Data
Professor Charlatan Bardot's travel anthology to the most
(fictional) haunted buildings in the weird, wild world (2021 edition) /
edited by Eric J. Guignard.

Library of Congress Control Number: 2021943395

ISBN-13: 978-1-949491-50-0 (hardback)
ISBN-13: 978-1-949491-48-7 (paperback)
ISBN-13: 978-1-949491-49-4 (e-book)

DARK MOON BOOKS
Los Angeles, California
www.DarkMoonBooks.com

Made in the United States of America
DMB 10 9 8 7 6 5 4 3 2 1

(V091521)

This anthology is dedicated as always,
and with love,
to my family—
Jeannette, Julian, and Devin.

And also to the ghosts
and ghost makers
around the world.

And to Steve Lines (1957–2021).
Artist, Author, Musician.
R.I.P.

Beyond Haunted Houses . . .

TABLE OF CONTENTS

The weird, wild (and ghostly) world we live in . . .

PREFACE
BY ERIC J. GUIGNARD

I AM A FORTUNATE INDIVIDUAL.

Lucky, blessed, privileged, if you will. I am fortunate to be father to two wonderful children. I am fortunate to have a home, and my health, and to be able (generally) to pursue what I want, which, certain teeth-gnashing frustrations aside, is surely better than the alternate. I am fortunate also to have the honor to collaborate on this anthology with the world's leading travel documentarian in international architectural paranormal investigations, Professor Charlatan Bardot, PhD, EdD, EJG.

I first met Professor Bardot at a convention of paranormal scholars (although I, myself, lack the estimable credentials of my peers). After a meet-and-greet dinner of agents and academics, I found myself seeking sanctuary in the darkest hotel bar for a gin and stogie. Charlatan was there—Charles to his friends (of which I now count myself amongst)—and we discussed some of the finer points of an erudite colleague's earlier panel relating to possessed architectural abodes.

I confessed I wasn't much of a believer, indeed finding the very subject of "haunted houses" to be hysterically overwrought and a rather tired trope. At that, Charles laughed. "Houses," he said, "are the least likely of structures to be haunted." He lifted his tumbler in salute. "It is other building types you must pursue."

And as he then regaled me with tales of haunted (non-house) buildings the world over, I realized the lack of such a guidebook to exist for the average traveler-reader to explore. Charles and I decided thereupon to rectify that neglect, of which we have been engaged for the past eighteen months in doing.

In closing, and after learning much of the weird, wild (and ghostly) world we truly live in, I have since come to realize I am a fortunate individual in another regard: I've never had to endure a true haunting. I hope to remain so fortunate for the remainder of my life, and in whatever may occur afterward.

Midnight cheers,

—Eric J. Guignard
Chino Hills, California
December 21, 2020 (Winter Solstice)

Welcome.

INTRODUCTION
BY CHARLATAN BARDOT

A S THE SAYING GOES, IT'S BEEN A LONG AND WINDING road, and one that extends around the world, past haunted temples, restaurants, hotels, hospitals, bridges, lighthouses, bookstores, markets, theaters, and all other building types ...

Except for houses.

There may be claims for hundreds of haunted houses, thousands, houses in every nation, in every climate and region, haunted houses in every town, including (most presumably) the one in your very own neighborhood. But this book is not about those, for haunted houses I find to be stale. Mundane. And more likely than not to be disproven as result of some hysterical superstition. But besides, I wish to chart the unexplored, the study of *other* manufactured structures, for who else is there to lead such charge? No one before has attempted to investigate, to record and map the stories of non-house-haunted buildings around the world.

I grew up in Taunton, Massachusetts, which is the geographic center of the Bridgewater Triangle, considered the "foremost vortex of unexplainable paranormal activity" in the American northeast. The Triangle includes Hockomock Swamp, where has been seen Bigfoot, demon panthers, and even flying Thunderbirds. Throughout the rest of the triangle are multiple documented cases of poltergeists, aliens, cryptozoological animals, and other inexplainable oddities. Tauton's own State Hospital has been site of a litany of Satanic and cult rituals. The town of Fall River is on its outskirts, where "otherworldly" forces are said to have driven Lizzie Borden past the brink of madness, and you know what she did with her infamous axe. The Bridgewater Triangle even borders the weird and terrifying geography that author H.P. Lovecraft used as setting for his most prominent works, now known popularly as "Lovecraft Country." Truth, indeed, is much stranger than fiction.

When I was a boy, I chanced upon an ancient stone in the woods of West Bridgewater, placed underneath a decrepit wood bridge, and overlaid by moss and vines. The stone is still there (look it up!), and legends and theories of it abound. See, the stone has an inscription carved into it, the author unknown, although it's purported to have association with a heretic religious sect that communed with spectral deities. The inscription reads as thus:

All ye, who in future days,
Walk by Nuckatesset stream
Love not him who hummed his lay
Cheerful to the parting beam,
But the Beauty that he wooed,
In this quiet solitude.

The rock has since become known as Suicide Stone because those who read the stone often hear ghostly voices, and many have taken their life on that spot. Environmentalists point to the term "whispering pines" as being the natural cause of the sounds, explaining the phenomena as wind blowing through filament-like pine needles. Paranormal investigators—myself included—have found the source to be infinitely more preternatural and imbued with the metaphysical.

On face value, and what I was told as a child, was that the inscription referred to the lush landscape surrounding the area. It's certainly a lovely notion, but it's untrue. Since the naïveté of childhood, I've come to understand the much more ominous message. Taken in terms of existence, "Nuckatesset stream" may be substituted for any passage we venture by, whether river, road, or metaphorical life journey. Most damning, however, is the capitalized "Beauty," which is *not* the ideal of visual pleasure we think of today, but rather is reference to a much older idiom, a Macedonian dialect anglicized from the word "Вевету" which means Evil Deity ("Darkness") of worlds outside our own.

Now knowing *that*, reread the poem . . .

And understand, what is whispered in the woods of West Bridgewater can be heard even when there is no wind blowing through pine needles.

That is but one anecdote (I've many more) that set me on the path to become the most renowned and beloved travel documentarian in the world of paranormal architecture (*Journal of Architectural Paranormal Times*)!

I have studied and hold degrees in Global Transcendence Theory; Law in the Occult; and Civil Planning for Metaphysical Manifestations (amongst multiple other academic, legal, and/or honorary distinctions). I've travelled to every nation and territory on this planet. I've seen and experienced catastrophe, divinity, abhorrence, acceptance, awe, and understanding on both this plane and beyond. All that to say, I tell most strenuously to you, dear reader, as I tell every first-year student: We truly live in a weird, wild (and ghostly) world.

Haunted buildings have become my namesake, the epitaph my headstone will someday proclaim. They are the confluence of man's industry and that remnant remaining after man's demise. Buildings have boundaries. Form. Design. Concepts ghosts are drawn to, for spirits have no form themselves. Consider abstract fettles left to float in nether-limbo, an oblivion that has no end, or else perhaps they may find such perch in the tangible, in memory of what once was. Counter to common supposition, hauntings are often not diabolical, but pragmatic—water in the state of evaporating—or in other cases as messages, cautionary tales from beyond, the search for closure or redemption. Snapshots of quiet grace left for reminisce.

I have attended the Orang bunian at Malaysia's Kapong Theater. I have investigated the crimson portals in Transylvania's Hoia-Baciu Forest. I've bare-knuckle fought the "Warden of Deprivation" at Philadelphia's Eastern State Penitentiary; debated the merits of bodily possession with the ghost of David Alléno at La Recoleta Cemetery; and levitated with goat-faced djinns at United Arab Emirates' Jazirat Al Hamra. These and hundreds of other encounters and escapades have I done, and I conclude this brief introduction with final comment that there is nothing beyond the bounds of possibility. And this Travel Anthology attests to that.

Whether sweet or tragic, beautiful or beastly, the following stories of haunted buildings are presented by authors with voices and experiences as diverse as the ethereal entities that flit daily through our lives. They speak to things that may transpire against our will, our choices, our *knowledge*. Curious things left pining, left willful. Thus wonder as you read each account if they speak to things as real in their lives as in your own imagination . . .

For that is where the greatest hauntings occur.

In the hereafter, as in life, I remain yours,

—Professor Charlatan Bardot, PhD, EdD, EJG
Taunton, Massachusetts
June 20, 2021 (Summer Solstice)

ENTER O LIBERTINE,

AND BEHOLD WHAT LIES

WITHIN AT YOUR

PLEASURE AND PERIL . . .

EUROPE

The last outpost of the Evros river delta before
the Turkish border, the "no man's land."

OH MAN'S LAND

FEATURE ENTRY ↑

STRUCTURE TYPE: MILITARY OUTPOST
LOCATION: FERES, GREECE
LAT./ LONG: 40.9682° N, 26.3111° E
BUILT: CIRCA 1915
GROUND ELEVATION: 95 FT. (29 M.)
WRITTEN BY: NATALIA THEODORIDOU

TRAVEL GUIDE NOTES

OPENING STORIES SET the tone for anthologies, and I've always considered carefully that for the casual reader, the first few pages of reading will instill an impression that is most likely going to linger with them for the rest of the book.

If the first story is funny, will there be humor in all the following selections? If the first story is gory, will there be blood splatter for all that ensues? If the first story is beautiful and emotionally resonant, can the same be said for all the others?

I say yes.

For such is the contemplation of this kickoff selection by Greek author Natalia Theodoridou, which sets the much-pondered opening tone. It's a quiet ghost tale, rich in detail, vibrant yet melancholy, thoughtful, ephemeral. Haunting in an honest sensibility.

For the death of family may be the greatest loss we ever experience, and its absence never goes away. Family by blood, by choice, or by circumstance, it matters not when a bond of devotion is formed. It matters not to the pain when that bond is cleaved.

And it matters not when you'd do anything to see them again in "Oh Man's Land."

—Charlatan Bardot

I SALUTE A GROUP OF JOGGING SOLDIERS AS I MAKE MY way to the outpost at the far end of the camp. They respond with the appropriate deference and carry on sweating in their uniforms, their boots slapping the ground. It's as hot today as it was back then, that first time. The cicadas are raising hell, crackling in the heat. If I close my eyes, my head feels light, I lose my bearings.

I can see the top of the outpost now, white as bone under the sun. My old legs seem like they're about to buckle so I give them a moment, take my cap off, rest my palms on my knees and breathe in the fire and dust that's coming up from the ground. The soles of my shoes burn.

Then I put my cap back on and start walking again, my mind drifting, unmoored.

IT WAS A peculiarly warm night. The "German number" shift usually had us bundle up with the night cold of the small hours, especially when our watch was at the last outpost of the Evros river delta before the Turkish border, the shooting range, then the "no man's land." I'd made the mistake of looking up the location online earlier that day. *Egnatia outpost. Address unknown, number unknown, city unknown.* No wonder the outpost's nickname was Oh Man's Land. I asked how it came about and the more seasoned soldiers mimicked the usual dialogue: *"Where are you posted?" "At the Egnatia." "Oh, man."*

2–4 a.m. was a brutal time to be awake, even in summer, even for someone as young and resilient as I was back then. But that night, the air felt viscous. There was no breeze, just a humid hand that made the roots of our hair ooze water, our skin loose and clammy, a strange, feverish shiver in the teeth.

I was supposed to keep watch with a new recruit named Leventis so I, the more experienced one, seeing how I had made it through half my mandatory service, waited for him outside the dorms. The path to the last outpost was treacherous, the ravine yawned too close, and it was always better to navigate that route with two pairs of eyes than one. After a few minutes, I gave up and made my way there alone.

The outpost was near the deepest gaps in the ravine, but you could still hear the water gurgling below. It was a simple structure, like most outposts: a small, squat box set on a barred platform and propped up on steel legs. A tin roof, a rusty ladder. The barbed wire of the camp's edges was visible from the outpost window—no real window, just a cutaway on the thin white

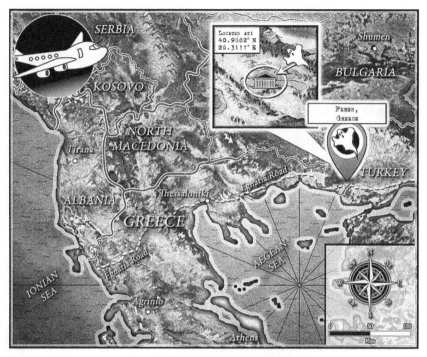

HAUNTED FERES, GREECE

wall, like a gouged eye. Beyond the wire, a tiny chapel, inaccessible through the camp and right on the edge of the ravine, but well preserved, with its candles always lit, though no one ever saw people visit it, and nobody could tell you which path would take you there and spare you a death by a steep, mouthless fall into the deep.

When I got to the outpost, the other soldier was already there.

He stood up as soon as I stepped in. There was something heavy in his demeanor, as if he'd already kept watch for a while. "What took you so long?" he asked.

"Are you Leventis? I was waiting for you, back at the camp."

He looked at me with a dark eye. "Oh, man. Sorry. I was posted here. I didn't know. I'm Costas."

"Alexandros."

"Welcome to Oh Man's Land." He laughed.

We shook hands. I remember it well. His were cold and dry, the skin cracked. Mine sweaty.

I noticed he was wearing a jacket, a solid khaki, not the usual camo. "Aren't you dying in that?" I asked. "It's sweltering in here."

He shrugged. "I don't mind."

We settled against the outer wall with the stars for a roof and shared a smoke. There is a special bond that comes from sharing these small hours with another body, under the naked sky. I've felt it since then, again and again, but never as strongly as that night.

We could both sense it, like an animate thing, growing between us, but we papered over it with small talk, as we are wont to do. Where are you from, what do you want to study, what job are you going to do when you're released.

"I'm thinking of staying on," I said. "Take the exams."

"Ah," he sighed. "A professional military man. I never got the appeal." He rubbed his shoulder as he pondered the riddle of me. "You from a military family?"

"Far from it. My father was dismissed for health reasons. My brother was a conscientious objector, even."

"Was?"

The cicadas paused for a moment, letting the question hang in the air.

"How did he die?" he asked again, sparing me the answer.

"He drowned in a river."

"We have a river here, too," he said.

"Yes."

"On purpose?"

"Yes."

He took another cigarette from the breast pocket of his jacket, lit it, and offered it to me.

It tasted stale, like old paper, or like nothing at all.

WAS I REALLY surprised the next morning when I found out Leventis never showed up for his watch? That there should have been no one else out there at the outpost with me?

I still wonder why I wasn't, sometimes. And what would be the point of lying about that, these days, after everything?

The next time I was posted there, I reassured my tired watch-mate that it was okay if he napped, and promised I would wake him up well before the next shift arrived. He also asked me to alert him if anything strange happened.

He didn't mean visitations from friendly spectral soldiers, of course.

Costas appeared as soon as I settled outside with my back to the cool wall. His cigarette was already lit and hanging from the corner of his lips as he approached. He sat next to me, the smoke from his ghost cigarette drawing rings that he blew like small lassos toward the flickering stars.

"So you know, now," he said, and I nodded.

"It explains the weird uniform," I replied. They hadn't used those in the army for decades, and it was too warm for the season, anyway. "Was it cold when it happened?"

He nodded. He opened his jacket and showed me the bleeding wound there, on the side of the heart. Then, he pointed at the edge of the camp, toward the no man's land.

I looked, but all I could see was the empty field, glowing faintly under pale light. "I can't see anything."

"Look," he instructed. "You're not looking."

So I did and, finally, I saw.

The tall figure awash in moonlight, standing alone near the wire. On our side? Or on the other? And was wire enough to tell them apart?

The figure raised his arm and waved. In camaraderie, I thought. In haunting. Costas waved back.

"You see, I had a brother, too," he said.

"What happened?"

"The army ate him like it eats us all." He paused. "Like it will eat you, too, sooner or later."

I asked and learned about it after that. The soldiers on either side of the border would sometimes exchange small gifts: cigarettes, feathers, pretty pebbles from the river. Costas and Selim had become friends—more than friends; brothers, even, fingers sliced and pressed together to mix their blood.

Then an incident in the Aegean spread tension across the entire border. Someone made a mistake; a shot was fired. Then another, and another. Costas and Selim had killed each other. "Oh, man," everyone who knew them had said. "Oh, man."

I WASN'T SENT to the outpost again after that. I don't know if my shift-mate had heard me talking to someone outside and reported it, or if it was chance that spared me. There were rumors about me, regardless; was it my shift-mate that started them, or something mumbled in my sleep, or, perhaps, something in my face, the corners of the lips, the eyes? Others went and often came back muttering about strange lights in the night, the sound of digging, the smell of old cigarette smoke in the air. I never said anything, neither confirmed nor denied the rumors. People picked on me, and there was even that time with a sheet and some woo-woo sounds in the night meant to scare or ridicule me, or both. I still said nothing. Laughed at their jokes, shared my cigarettes, man, oh man, such a good sport.

When my mandatory service was over, I passed my exams and was sent to Corinth, then Crete, then Lemnos. I went wherever without protest, to all the postings no one else wanted. I never had to shoot anybody. I lingered near rivers in my free time, hoping for a glimpse of my brother's ghost walking into the water, his pockets full of stones. He never indulged me.

When I heard a young man had killed himself with his rifle at the Egnatia outpost, I put in a transfer request. It was easy; what senior officer would ever choose to go to the border of their own accord? Only drifters and daredevils, running from ghosts, or chasing them. They said the boy who took his own life had been stationed at the outpost every night for an entire week. He spent his last hours rambling about a figure in no man's land with a hole in the middle of the forehead.

I KNEW THEY had ordered the outpost blocked off, but I had to see for myself.

Now, finally here, under the unforgiving light of the sun, it is worse than I imagined: the windows bricked, concrete poured to fill the interior so no one could use it as a hiding place. But then why does it feel more like a tomb, a mausoleum meant to keep someone in rather than out? When I asked why they did it, they told me it didn't seem right to tear it down.

"Why not?" I had asked.

"Oh, man," was all they would say, with a shrug. "Oh, man."

WITH TIME, I almost feel happy here, or at least content. I rarely leave the camp, driving to the city only for necessities, never for company. I often wonder what happened to Costas. At night sometimes I sneak out of the unit and visit the dead outpost. I light a cigarette and wait, breathing in the cool night, though I've long quit smoking. He never graces me with his presence. I put my ear to the wall and listen for his shuffling steps, his deep sigh, but there's nothing. I think of him palming his bleeding heart, alone. Was he trapped there? Or set free?

I do see his brother across the field, though. He stands there under the lenient moonlight, the ghost of a bullet hole in his head. I raise my hand; in greeting or farewell, I'm not sure. In camaraderie, maybe, in haunting.

He doesn't wave back.

DID YOU KNOW?

NATALIA THEODORIDOU is a World Fantasy Award-winning author, a Nebula Award Finalist, and a Clarion West graduate (class of 2018). Natalia's stories have appeared in venues such as *Clarkesworld*, *Strange Horizons*, *Uncanny*, *Fantasy & Science Fiction*, *Black Static*, *Nightmare*, and *The Dark*, and have been translated in Italian, French, Greek, Estonian, Spanish, Chinese, and Arabic. An immigrant to the UK for many years, he has recently returned to Greece. For details, visit www.natalia-theodoridou.com or follow @natalia_theodor on Twitter.

ENGLISH MARTYRS UNDERGROUND STATION

BY LAURA MAURO

THIS station is gone now. It was swallowed by fire in the summer of 1993; you watched from the train window as flames lapped at dust-streaked tiles, at leather shoes, and you can still taste the smoke in the back of your throat. It was flooded in 1979; tunnel-mouth drowned in black water, depthless and cold. It was bombed during the Blitz, and the screams of terrified refugees still echo in those long and empty halls, those rubble-choked platforms. It died quietly, alone, unused, and only time bears witness to its slow decay. It was never there to begin with. This station is gone now.

A truly anomalous, or phantasmal, station

LAURA MAURO was born and raised in London and knows all its most eerie corners. She is a British Fantasy Award-winning author of short stories and her debut collection *Sing Your Sadness Deep* was published by Undertow Publications in 2019.

* FILE UNDER: *Haunted Underground Station*

GHOST STOP

BY EKATERINA SEDIA

A regular visitor at the stop on Sadovoe Koltso

O N Sadovoe Koltso, near Sukharevskaya, there is a curious bus stop: one of those old glass kiosks untouched by modernization and Mayor Sobyanin, with the listing of routes hopelessly smudged into obscurity. It's just as well, because no bus stops here. Well, almost none.

Every February 29th, ten minutes to midnight, an old yellow Ikarus bus pulls up, the likes of which haven't been seen since the early aughts, and its doors sigh open. A single passenger disembarks—a rust-colored, grinning stray dog, with cocked ears and curling tail like an ostrich feather. It wags and sits, almost prim, tongue lolling, as the bus pulls away. And from the nearest snowdrift, a bluing, clear like spring ice, hand flops open, and melts slowly but not before a ghostly dog tongue slides, quick, from the wrist to the bruised fingertips.

EKATERINA SEDIA is a Moscow transplant currently residing in the eastern US. She wrote several critically acclaimed novels, and shares her life with her husband and two dogs. She teaches biology at a state university.

* FILE UNDER: *Haunted Bus Stop*

She knew what was up there, silently accusing her . . .

FISH TALE

STRUCTURE TYPE: INDOOR FISH MARKET
LOCATION: KUNGSHAMN, SWEDEN
LAT./ LONG: 58.3603° N, 11.2593° E
BUILT: CIRCA 1892
GROUND ELEVATION: 39 FT. (12 M.)
WRITTEN BY: EUGENIA TRIANTAFYLLOU

TRAVEL GUIDE NOTES

I F, AFTER DEATH, we humans can produce ghosts, so too must other lifeforms—mammals, birds, and even fish. For is it any less that another living creature may carry within it the same soul revenant as does mankind? And is it any less that in spectral transformation, it may feel the same despair or loss of self as those wraiths of lingering mortals? Surely the phrase "Ye too, shall weep" cares not for taxonomy, and so it is with the great Jutland Fish, the mythological denizen of Sweden's briny deep, and its ignominious demise.

Author Eugenia Triantafyllou has lived across Europe via Sweden, Greece, Finland, etc., and writes often of ghosts and gloom and beautiful transformation. She extends such themes in the following, as we come to know the fisherwoman Hanna and her family in an uncommon "Fish Tale."

—Charlatan Bardot

T HE GREAT FISH HANNA HAD KILLED STILL FLOATED around the fish market's ceiling like a buoy in the sea. Reminding everyone of what she had done. Two scrawny boys no more than fifteen, new additions to the Fish Church, could not peel their eyes away from the sleek fish innards. Just like any other newcomer.

"In the Fish Church, fish is your god," Old Thomas said to them waving his knife. "So treat fish with respect."

He took the knife and sliced the belly of a herring like cutting through butter. The guts bloomed and spilled on his lap. Then he whispered something to the boys and glanced at Hanna.

A monstrous tangle of entrails hung above their heads. And farther up was the gutted Jutland Fish, carved and dripping with blood. Its eyes white with death. Only, the fish was not really there. Hanna had sliced it up a year ago and been damn proud of it, for a little while. A short-lived joy.

Its ghost had appeared in the Church—the name of their famous market—one day and she never looked above eye level again. There was no need to. She knew what was up there, silently accusing her. Just like Old Thomas did.

The boys crossed themselves and clutched tight at the little wooden fish charms. All the fishermen wore one when they fished the open sea, but now all the fishmongers had one too. Because the sea had come inside the market the day she had helped her husband kill that fish.

The boys did not look up again. Hanna knew their brothers and fathers. They were all fishermen. They knew the curse was her doing. Hers and her husband's. They scattered like mice when she looked at them, each to their own menial task.

Hanna could not sell anything but eels now, no matter how hard she tried. She did not dare go into the sea to fish them out herself after Jonas was gone. There was no boat that would take her even if she did dare. She was tainted. A kind of taint that spread everywhere. The sea, the Fish Church, and slowly, the city. All she could do was count on the few fishermen who felt sorry for her—no, not her, her children—and would give her eels to sell. Sometimes small herrings too if she were lucky. The scraps. But they were good enough.

As afternoon closed in and there was not much to sell on any stall, besides old fish and sour oysters, Hanna packed the few fishes she kept for the family and slipped between stacks of old nets, coils of rope, and crates half-filled with fresh fish and seashells, dodging fishmongers and patrons.

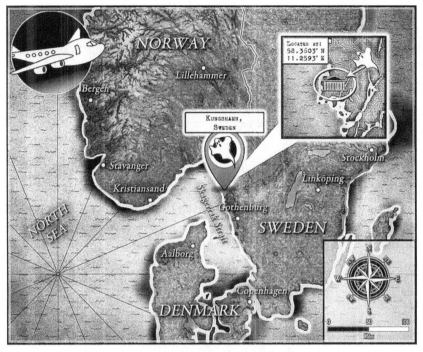

HAUNTED KUNGSHAMN, SWEDEN

The Fish Church had tall archways and an immense ceiling that filled with light. One could believe God himself was hiding up there. What else could this building be then but a church in its own right? Only, instead of whispered prayers there used to be boisterous laughter coming from the fishmongers as they tried to coax patrons to buy their wares. There'd been noise and the smell of fresh fish in abundance, and sometimes music too. But that was before the ghost fish had etched itself in the market's canopy. Now the laugher—if there was any—was cut short once people raised their eyes. So the fishmongers kept their heads low, and the patrons shuffled from stall to stall, eager to get out of there the moment they finished their errands. Day by day the crowd dwindled even though the fish market was the biggest one for miles around. Hanna could see the place becoming deserted soon. One of those beautiful buildings left to rot little by little, soon to be nothing but detritus and bad memories. The haunting would be still trapped inside of course. But that would not make the sea fertile again. It wouldn't break the curse.

Old Thomas had made up his mind about what would bring things back to the way they were and didn't let a day pass without telling her.

"Boats came half-empty again," he whispered from the shadows by the door.

This stopped Hanna for a moment but she did not have the time or patience to answer to a man who had rallied the fishmongers against her. She leaned close, close enough so only he could hear her say, "Go drown."

She saw the man's face flush.

"Come to your senses, woman," he said.

It is you who should be drowning, he didn't say. He very well meant it though.

THEY WANTED HER dead, the fishmongers. The fishermen too. After the curse had settled upon their village like a thick sheet of ice on the waters, and after the ghost of the Jutland Fish could not be exorcised from the fish market, they offered to toss her into the Skagerrak and let the currents carry her body all the way to the North Sea. They said it kindly at first, like she would feel obliged by their courtesy and accept. She had three children to feed, they knew that. The whole village would care for them since her husband was gone too; her oldest son Lars was on the cusp of manhood. Old Thomas offered to find him a job on a trawler until he got his own boat if she'd throw herself in the sea.

As if she would let her son near water again.

The sea had it out for her. For her whole family.

The cobblestone streets were a maze of planks, carts, and wagons, and Hanna walked by the canal. The smell of brine mixed with the scent of wild roses coming from the hill. In times like these, Jonas would have brought his catch from the trawler and Hanna would get first pick. That's how Jonas had convinced her now-dead father—along with some big words about their future—that he might be worth something as a husband. Later, when she became his wife, she would negotiate with the other fishmongers her husband's catch while their babies grew inside of her. Three of them in total.

The water lapped against the canal walls in soft tame waves. It looked as harmless as any other day but Hanna knew better. She stood a few feet away from the dock. Even in the middle of all the noise she could still hear the ghostly sound that fish had made when Jonas dropped it at her feet, and everyone else around her had recoiled. She'd been pregnant with their last one, their daughter. How her flesh prickled when she'd touched the fish's scaly body. It'd been strangely soft. Like an animal's hide or a baby's skin.

"What in the name of the Lord is this?" she'd asked.

In all her life she had not seen a fish like that. It had looked like a basking shark, the way its jaws gaped open as it struggled for breath, but it had the flat head of a skate and barbells like a catfish.

Jonas had beamed. "It's the Jutland Fish."

For a moment she could have sworn she had stopped breathing for good. Jonas' dreams had always been big but ever since he'd gotten his own boat, they'd grown to the size of a minke whale, or the size of the Jutland Fish. She remembered cursing herself for not recognizing something she had never seen before, but heard so many stories about. Jonas had stood there, smiling. His fists resting on his hips as if something very important had been accomplished. Something nobody else in the terrified group of people that surrounded them could appreciate.

She should have stopped him. She should have yelled and insisted he take it back to the archipelago while it was still alive. Where creatures like this belonged. But something in the way he had looked at her, a wild joy mixed with pride, made her hesitate. Jonas had always dared to go where others couldn't and then kept going still, and she loved him for it. Her sense had faltered and she'd followed along. She'd wrapped her arms around the fish's long, slippery tail and Jonas had grabbed the head, and together they'd brought the fish inside the Fish Church, between rows of stunned faces.

They had laid it on the wooden bench in the back. It'd still been alive, still moving like the baby inside of her, when Hanna grabbed her serrated knife and made the first cut. She'd sawed into its flesh, and it had felt like sawing into her own belly. Its glassy eyes had shone like green marbles under the oil lamp before turning bone white. Jonas' tongue had been full of promises of the rich people from the capital that would pay good money for the fish, and how he would earn some respect.

The fish had bled like a heart. Hanna's belly churned and she wanted to be sick. She thought she'd heard a small whimper, not from herself but from the fish. She'd felt her own teeth pressing down on her tongue. *It's in your head* she'd told herself.

"I'll take care of this myself," she had told Jonas. "I know what I am doing."

He'd nodded and trusted her with the job, but there was a feeling of wrongness in everything. He'd then left with the boat and never came back. It was the sea taking what it was owed, the fishermen said. But still that was not enough for the sea. This was only half the price. The other half was Hanna herself.

She could not sell the Jutland Fish either. After Jonas died most of the fisher folk turned their backs on her. They avoided looking her in the eyes for fear they would bring the wrath of the sea upon their heads. Nobody had helped her sell the butchered fish. It had remained in the market tucked under a basket until its stench made Hanna bury it under the hill that overlooked the market. Its blood had stained the place it was cut up, had steeped into the ground it was buried in and bled like an open wound. Before its flesh started to rot completely, and as the boats were coming back with half the catch, its spirit had started to materialize out of thin air. The ghost had found a new sea between the wooden beams of the roof.

SHE FOUND HER son Lars sitting on the jagged rocks next to the pier. She yelled for him to leave. Her limbs went numb every time she saw him talk to the fishermen. She knew what they were asking of him but she did not know what he replied.

Lars pretended he could not hear her and helped the men unload their catch. At twelve, his heart was already full of the promises his father had made. Lars used to spend his days fixing his father's nets, scrubbing the boat clean. Now he did not know what do with himself. It was too late for him to go to school, and Hanna would not let him get his foot wet in saltwater. At first he was obedient; their grief brought them together. But in the months that followed, her wishes turned him bitter. He grew impatient with the new job she found him as a shoemaker's apprentice.

When he finally came down he would not meet her eyes.

"Did you go to the workshop today?"

"No, ma'am," he answered.

"You will do well to be on time tomorrow morning," she threatened, and started for the cottage.

Lars stood still.

"I am getting on a ship by the end of the month," he whispered.

In her mind Hanna was already running to the pier to pull him out of the water, pale and cold, or worse yet, he was gone forever like his father. No trace of him anywhere. No body to retrieve. And in the end it still wouldn't be enough because the ghost wanted *her*. Nobody else could pay off her debt.

"Don't get tangled up in their promises," she croaked.

But it was too late. Lars' ears were plugged with the fishermen's songs. He could not hear Hanna.

"I know that I can't stay here. I am not good at being idle." His gaze swung over to Hanna, pleading with her to understand, and then he ran to the pier back to his friends.

NICOLAS, HER MIDDLE one, sat at the kitchen table, feet dangling in the air, studying the alphabet. His baby sister was asleep in the crib. Nicolas took on the task of caring for her when Hanna had no choice but to work. When he saw Hanna he leaped from the chair and rubbed his face against her dress. All alone in the house his only comfort was his baby sister. It was too much for a child his age.

"Thank you," Hanna whispered to him, and he curled like a ball in her arms before she headed for the kitchen.

The noise woke the baby and so Nicolas picked her up as Hanna stirred the pea soup, singing a sea song under her breath. There were three children and a woman inside a small cabin, yet there was so much space between them ever since Jonas got lost at sea.

When she had not obliged the fisher folk—did not welcome the sea in her lungs like they expected her to—the shunning started. But they could not force her. She would have to want to throw herself at the vastness and appease whatever it is they believe had been angered. So they eventually got tired of that too and now all she got was turned backs and betrayed stares. In a way she was in exile. She was exiled from the minds and the hearts of people.

And now they wanted her son out in the sea.

Lars returned as she was about to turn off the oil lamp for the night. In the half-darkness his face looked ghostly already. How could he trust the people who wanted her drowned and who blamed her for every bad thing?

But he was still not fully a man and when she opened her arms he fell into them like he was still five years old.

"Old Thomas told me he'll take good care of you," he said softly.

Her jaw clenched. Lars did not trust those men but followed them only because he wanted to sail away. He thought he was saving her. That he could offer himself instead of her to the sea.

Stupid, stubborn boy.

Old Thomas had no right to ask her twelve-year-old son to give himself for a family mistake, cruel fate, or whatever it might be. He had no right to lure him in with promises of honor. Of righting a wrong. Just like his father used to do. But it was too late to change his mind now.

"I will be safe. I will be back," Lars promised and hugged her. "I won't let the sea claim me."

"No," Hanna said. "No you won't."

He was a tall boy but in her arms he became as small as his brother. Hanna held him tight. Her son was tortured by this life as much as she was. He could not bear the shame and would avoid visiting her in the Fish Church at all costs. The ghost unnerved him because it showed him how his father had failed them all. So she kept him there, in her arms. Her mind was already made up.

If it was the sea he wanted then the sea he would get. But she would make all the promises the fishermen and his father gave him right. The sea would be harmless for him. She would make sure of that. And if she had to face the Jutland Fish by herself, then she would do it. Tomorrow.

HANNA WASHED HER face with a cloth dipped in cold water and dried herself on her apron. She stood by the kitchen window. It was past five yet Lars had already left for the pier, preparing himself for his first voyage. She sat down at the table with a small glass of brännvin in her hand. The salty air winded in through the open window, carrying with it the sound of the gulls.

She put on her best dress and started for the fish market. The street was busy and gloomy as if everyone already knew what she had set her mind to. When Hanna arrived at the Church she caught a glimpse of the fish's tail sloshing in invisible waters up in the roof. She had to remind herself not to run. To walk slowly. She kept her eyes low and focused on finding the old man.

She found him bartering with some of the fishermen for their catch. Whatever bargain it was they were striking, they did not look happy with it. Still, the old fishmonger and the fishermen stopped talking once she approached and they drew closer together as if an unvoiced agreement happened in an instant. She was always the greater evil.

"Let me guess," Old Thomas said. "You came for the boy?"

"I am ready," she said twisting the folds of her dress with her fists.

The old man's face dropped. This was not what she expected.

"I tried to stir the boy away from the sea. We all did," he said at last. "Not his sin to pay."

For a moment the world rippled around her.

"Well, you didn't try hard enough."

How could she trust these men who wanted her dead and gone? How could she believe Old Thomas didn't fill her son's head with dreams of sacrificing for his family only to make her come here and offer herself? But his intentions didn't matter anymore than her son's innocence mattered to the sea since he had her blood running through him.

She felt a current of air above her that smelled like the deepest of seas. Like the Jutland Fish smelled when it first laid at her feet writhing. She shivered, and her anger dispersed in her own fear. She could taste her terror like brine at the tip of her tongue. There was no going back now. Lars was too stubborn to stay away whatever the men did or did not tell him. She knew her son well.

"What are you going to do with me?" She asked, and she hated that her voice came out smaller than she intended, more girl-like than woman-like.

The world rippled again. The building rippled. The ghost, she was certain, was hovering right above her.

"This is not for me to decide," Old Thomas said and bowed his head, confirming her fear.

People were already whispering her name. *Hanna, Hanna, Hanna*, they chanted under their breath. She tried not to think about the fact that she had no plan except confronting the ghost and the wrath of the sea. What would all these people do after she had drowned? What stories would they tell her children? *A witch, a slaughterer, a curse bringer.*

But there he was, Lars, her son. Half-hidden in the crowd gathering inside. A head among many, but she could see his wide eyes and the hurt in them as if he stood mere inches from her. The fisher folk surrounded his body with theirs, blocking his way. Seeing him made her heart quiet inside her. He would be safe now and he would make sure to tell her story to his siblings and tell it well.

"It is time to listen to what the ghost has to say," the old man said to her as the last of the fisher folk kept coming inside the Fish Church.

He touched Hanna's chin with one calloused finger and gently led her eyes upward.

"Look up, daughter."

And she did.

The creature she met was not vengeful or angry. It carried sadness for all the wasted time it had spent away from the sea. Sadness for the pain that Hanna had caused. *I am sorry*, she thought, and she already knew she was forgiven. As the world rippled, her body followed. It bent out of shape and twisted inward. It became a crescent moon covered in glittering scales. Her face felt raw and elongated, her mouth stretched, impossibly wide, seeded with new rows of teeth.

And then she was on the cold floor struggling for breath and begging for saltwater. She felt the air stinging her gills. Could they hear her pain? The ghost dove from the roof and came straight at her as if trying to show her something. Then, two soft, warm hands reached from the sea of air and picked her up. She could almost remember that face. It was the face of a loved one. Someone familiar and true. Someone she knew in another life and maybe shared the same blood.

"Let's get you to the water," his voice said.

Soon there were more hands touching her. Some were small and soft and quivered, unsteady under the weight of her torso. Others were bigger and calloused but led her steadily to where she had to be. All of them held her with tenderness and passed her from one to another with quiet reverence.

Soon the building was gone. The walls were gone. The crowd of people was gone and she could hear the beating of another heart like hers. A fish heart. She heard another and another. Ten, twenty, a hundred hearts in various sizes beating in the same rhythm as hers.

"It will be alright," she heard someone say.

Then the warm hands of the loved one tossed her into the water.

Water was all around. Above her, below, shifting in light and shadows, bubbling with sunlight under the waves, drawing her toward their gentle ebb and flow. The water was her home now, her memories, her story and her ending. Her eyes opened once more to the loved one's face hovering above her. He watched her from the edge of the pier.

She caught the boy's gaze one last time as the water closed above her head.

Something stirred in the deep water. She was not alone. Another fish that she recognized as her mate was waiting for her to find him at last. Their bodies brushed against each other. She had been found.

The sad memory of a curse slowly faded from her mind.

Did You Know?

Eugenia Triantafyllou is a Greek author and artist with a flair for dark things. She currently lives in Athens with a boy and a dog. She is a graduate of Clarion West Writers Workshop. Her short fiction has appeared in *Uncanny*, *Strange Horizons*, *Apex*, and other venues. Find her on Twitter @foxesandroses or her website https://eugeniatriantafyllou.wordpress.com.

THE NORTHERN LIGHTS EXPERIENCE

BY JOHANN THORSSON

THERE'S a circle of stones by the side of the road, arranged as if for seating. No one knows where they originated—the stones have always been there. For a while the site served as a Northern Lights viewing stop for tourists, but was abandoned after repeated disappearances of those tourists.

Stop, but don't stay long

People still go there, ignoring the warning signs. Couples visiting the country, following old maps.

They sit in the winter chill and stare up as the lights dance, a bright green curtain against the starry darkness. The northern lights steal all attention, and visitors don't see the other people sitting with them now. The silent people, staring open-mouthed into the sky, eye sockets stretched into black pools that reflect the shimmering lights of the sky.

And another car is later found, abandoned.

JOHANN THORSSON is an Icelandic human writer, most often found with a book in one hand and a beer in the other.

* FILE UNDER: *Haunted Roadside Viewing Area*

Whatever the woman is shouting, none
of the televisions lets out a sound.

STILL HUNGRY

FEATURE ENTRY 3

STRUCTURE TYPE: DEPARTMENT STORE
LOCATION: LIVERPOOL, ENGLAND
LAT./ LONG: 53.4024° N, 2.9722° W
BUILT: CIRCA 1970
GROUND ELEVATION: 230 FT. (70.1 M.)
WRITTEN BY: RAMSEY CAMPBELL

TRAVEL GUIDE NOTES

WHEN ONE CONSIDERS the most well-lauded and prolific horror authors in contemporary days, a few names must invariably come to mind: Stephen King, Anne Rice, Clive Barker, and, of course, "Britain's most respected living horror writer" (*Oxford Companion to English Literature*) Ramsey Campbell.

I've read Ramsey's work for decades and was overjoyed to be granted an advance copy of the latest Primer book by my co-editor Eric J. Guignard, giving study and introduction (if hardly needed) to Ramsey's work, via *Exploring Dark Short Fiction #6: A Primer to Ramsey Campbell*. I was also overjoyed to receive the following original contribution from Ramsey for this anthology-tour guide.

As with most of us, we suffer the drudgery of daily labor, and often therein lies the balance of doing "what we were hired for" and doing "what is right." One is certainly an objective parameter, while the other is somewhat *subjective*, and just as likely to waver, especially in the case of Bertram, when reality seems to slowly unhinge, revealing certain hungers, both in the physical sense as well as the emotional. Revealing what occurs when that point of no return is crossed, and you are "Still Hungry."

—Charlatan Bardot

“BERT.”

"No, it's Bertram."

"Yeah, whichever. Pregnant woman and a girl in trackies just come out of food and they've bought nothing. Now she's sending the kid off and I'm betting that's a decoy. You check the mother."

Bertram is in women's clothing, a joke that became one more of the things Jane couldn't stand about him. Stacks of flattened jumpers flank him while he locates the customer. She's bonily thin but frontally swollen, and the idea of ascertaining how genuine her condition is dismays him. He's making his casual way between two ranks of headless dresses when someone clutches at his left hand. "Mister, can you help me find my mam?"

She's in a grubby rumpled track suit that must have started out bright green, not an outfit Bertram would have chosen if he and Jane had ever succeeded in producing a child. She looks about six but short for her age. Plumpness dulls her pale face topped with unkempt mousy curls, and he's ashamed of thinking that her small cold moist hand feels like tripe. "That's the kid," his earpiece says. "Keep hold of her."

He feels shifty for pretending to be helpful. "What does your mother look like?"

The girl's stare summarises how unreasonable adults are. "Like me, only bigger."

It's true, even of the garish track suit. The woman is dodging at speed through a crowd of empty coats, and Bertram takes a firm grip on the child's hand as he heads his quarry off. "Excuse me, madam, I think this is your daughter."

He's in time to block the mother's escape from an aisle of nightdresses. "There you are, Lucy," she complains as her pallid pudgy face struggles to find lines with which to sketch a frown. "I said not to go where I can't see you."

Bertram's earpiece intervenes. "Keep them there, Bert. Management's on the way."

He used to tell Jane the device made him feel like a robot. Sometimes he longs for the strength of one, but just now he wishes he were as emotionless. He doesn't realise how resolutely he's grasping the child's hand until the woman says "You can let her go now, mister."

There's no point in fancying he can save the child. As he releases the hand he says "Stay there for a minute, please. Somebody would like to speak to you."

"Got no time now. Luce, you run."

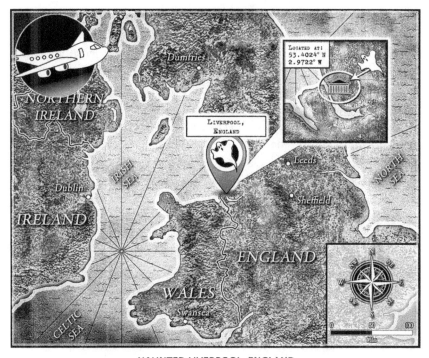

HAUNTED LIVERPOOL, ENGLAND

Though the child looks bemused by the change of direction, she darts around Bertram. When the mother makes to follow he stretches out his arms on both sides of him, entangling his fingers in the embroidery of a nightdress. "You let me look after my little one," she protests and stoops to dart past him, which dislodges an item from her bulging midriff—a sleeve that dangles over her stomach. Bertram's instincts override prudence, and he gives the sleeve a tug, dislodging not just a child's track suit with the price tag still attached but a miniature avalanche of bars of chocolate.

"You keep your hands off me," she cries, sounding far too much like Jane before she left him, and then turns conversational. "You're not going to arrest me, are you, hon? I only did it for the little one. I'm all she's got. We had to leave her dad."

Bertram isn't paid to be sympathetic. That's a manager's job if it's anyone's. He's about to detain her with a neutral comment when she says "Lucy, go on when you're told."

As Bertram glances back to see the girl hesitating by the exit, her mother shoves a rack of nightdresses aside and sprints through the gap. He makes a grab for her but misses, and as he chases her several men who have just entered the store block his way. "Let her off, feller," one says. "She's got a kid."

If Bertram follows her into the mall his occupational insurance won't accompany him. As she and her daughter vanish into the crowd he unhooks the phone from his belt and warns his colleagues in the other shops. Annie from the food department is clearing the sweets into a plastic basket, and hands him the dropped track suit. "You could take it upstairs if you liked, Bertram."

On the top floor he finds Mrs Deacon in Babes And Bigger. Her smile of eager helpfulness subsides when she sees Bertram isn't a customer. "What are you doing with that?" she says across the counter.

"You didn't see it being stolen." When Mrs Deacon makes this and her resentment plain he says "Were you talking to a little girl at all?"

"As a matter of fact I was. She seemed quite a pleasant child."

"That's how her mother distracts people while she's stealing."

"That can hardly be the child's fault, can it, Mr Bertram? Perhaps some of us have more of a feeling for children."

"It's just Bertram, and I didn't get the chance." As he spreads the crumpled track suit on the counter he feels as if he's trying to erase the girl. "We all make mistakes," he says in a bid to placate Mrs Deacon. "I could have. The woman sent the girl to make me think she needed help."

"It's a pity you couldn't respond, then."

He did his best, and nearly says so. Even if he let his marriage down, he's better at his job. The glass lift in the middle of the store lets him look out for suspicious characters as he descends, but he has seen none by the time he reaches the ground floor. He's among the televisions, several aisles of windows on luminous landscapes, when Mr Chalfont finds him. "Bertram," the manager says, though he makes that sound quite a task. "Just keep your eyes on the job."

"I dealt with the situation as soon as control tipped me off."

Mr Chalfont's face is etched with lines like a sketch of stress completed by its features. "I'm talking about now," he says, "while you're listening to me. I just hope there won't be any comeback from your actions earlier."

"What kind of comeback?"

"You're well aware you have no business touching customers."

"She wasn't a customer, she was a thief."

"She was still entitled to the proper treatment. She could sue for being searched in public. It might go against the store, especially when a child's involved."

"But I found the stolen goods on her. We must have that on tape."

"The angle makes it look as if you could have been planting them."

"I hope you know I never would have."

"It doesn't matter what I think. You'd better hope it doesn't matter what anybody else thinks either," Mr Chalfont says and burdens Bertram with a stony look.

He runs a mistrustful finger along the top of every screen he passes on his way to the lift, which elevates him saintlike. Bertram is leaving the televisions behind when the glowing landscapes are replaced by a shaky vista of a station platform, and he halts before he quite knows why. The mother and daughter he failed to apprehend are on the underground platform with their backs to an oncoming train.

Whatever the woman is shouting, none of the televisions lets out a sound. Where is she declaring she won't go? Bertram thinks she could be saying jail, but her lips shape a different word. She takes the child's hand in both of hers, a gesture he can't help finding ominous. He wishes he could intervene, but he had his chance. She releases the small hand and lifts her daughter into her arms. Hugging her with a fierceness Bertram imagines he feels, she leaps in front of the train.

The back of his fist bruises Bertram's lips, trapping a dismayed gasp. The falling bodies seem to hover almost supine—perhaps the image from the phone that filmed them has been slowed down—before the train hits them. It carries them forward until they're dragged under the circular saw of a wheel, and Bertram looks away. How can television show such details, especially at this time of day? Presumably the broadcast is a newsflash someone neglected to edit. He doesn't glance at the screens again until they recover their landscapes, and then he makes for Desmond, who's in charge of the department. "Did you see them?" Bertram says and finds his voice has grown as shaky as the rest of him. "I had to chase them out for stealing."

Desmond gives his resolutely bearded squarish head a puzzled shake, perhaps since the items in his section are too cumbersome to steal or, given his lack of emotion, because he didn't notice the report the televisions somehow picked up. The silenced shout and the suicidal leap replay themselves in Bertram's skull until it's time to head for home. The trains are just reverting to their schedule, and staff in yellow jerkins patrol the platforms. In his apartment, which he's rented since Jane kept the house, he listens to the local radio while he dines on the remaining half of last night's pizza from Stow That Dough, but there's no news of the deaths. He was planning to watch the kind of action film Jane would have complained throughout, only now he finds it hard to concentrate. He pauses the film to listen to each newscast, and is ready for bed by the time he hears that a homeless woman and her daughter—Bridie and Lucy Darwin—were killed by a train. He shouldn't have expected the media to report the woman's words, and he lies awake in the dark trying to deduce them. At last he lurches out of a jerky sleep, having grasped her final word. It feels as though he has just heard her say "Not going to starve."

He's glad to see the dawn, and at first he's glad to go to work. Mr Chalfont is letting staff in like a resentful doorman, and Bertram tries not to feel ashamed to say "Did you see we won't be sued? That woman and her child I had the trouble with, they were killed by a train."

"Then I very much hope it won't be associated in any way with us."

Bertram feels more accused than ever, and retreats to the control room. As he hangs his padded coat up, the security monitors shift their viewpoints with a concerted flicker. Did he glimpse a small shape scurrying down an upward escalator? "Caught short, Bert?" Cy calls as Bertram hurries out, a question undeserving of an answer.

The glass lift shows Bertram nobody at large except staff, but what's that mark on the floor of a frozen foods aisle? It looks like a trail of earth. He has to go down on his knees to identify the substance—a scattering of chocolate. The wrappers of several bars in the racks placed by the tills to tempt children have been bitten through. "I think we've got mice," he says.

He's addressing Annie, but Mr Chalfont hurries over to mutter "Keep your voice down. Just clear this up, Ann, and Bertram, you see to tracing the problem."

The intermittent trail leads to the escalators. Is there an infestation somewhere underneath? Bertram sees crumbs of chocolate on the restless metal treads, and finds traces on the next higher escalator. He thinks he can distinguish increasingly faint marks all the way up to Babes And Bigger, where he halts by a gathering of children's track suits. "Mrs Deacon, can you page Mr Chalfont? He'll want to see this."

Once arrived, the manager peers where Bertram indicates and then stares at him. "What am I meant to see?"

"Those are bites, aren't they? It's where the trail ends."

"I see no trail." Mr Chalfont scrutinises Bertram while saying "I'll look for the culprit myself."

The trouble is that Bertram can no longer make the trail out either, and although the marks on several track suits look like bites, they're larger than any rodent could make. If they represent a manufacturing fault he's surprised they weren't noticed, but it's not his job to insist they should be. As Mr Chalfont takes the lift down, Mrs Deacon says "Try not to let him upset you, Mr Bertram."

"I'm more upset about the woman and her child I told you about. She threw them both under a train."

"How can you know that?"

"They showed it on television yesterday afternoon."

"It wasn't in our paper last night. My dad likes me to read the local news to him."

Perhaps a caprice of the network transmitted the video directly from somebody's phone to the televisions—the railway station is nearby, after all. As Bertram searches for the trail he followed, a track suit slithers off its hanger beside him. He wasn't aware of brushing against it, and when he picks it up by its gaping neck an object seems to writhe inside the left arm. Has he captured the perpetrator of the trail? He shakes the suit, but nothing emerges before the arm grows flat, and he restores the outfit to the hanger, an action that feels like clothing childish shoulder bones. There's no sign of the trail anywhere, and he wonders how much Annie cleaned up. "Get out, whatever you are," he whispers, and the store opens its doors as if it's expelling the problem.

It's letting in the public, coming to life. Not everything is lively yet; the televisions have been switched off overnight, and the black rectangles remind Bertram of graves large enough for children. No doubt that's because of the incident they showed him, which makes the inside of his skull feel as dark as the television screens. He grows tense as Desmond powers them up, and has to fend off an insistent mental image of a small face with a stained mouth, or at least with the remains of one, until every screen glows with a landscape.

He needs to watch the customers. Just now they feel like company as well, but why should he have the impression he's being watched? There are the security cameras, but the scrutiny seems more personal. He's on his way out of the furniture department, having guided a young couple to the cots, when a sight in one of the mirrors high up on the walls halts him. Someone far too pale is lying in a bed.

As soon as he locates the intruder he tries to laugh at his mistake. The white shape poking from beneath a quilt is an empty pillowcase. Did somebody forget to put a pillow in it? Bertram is making for the bed when he hears a rustle suggestive of rodents. His foot has caught a wad of cellophane, the wrapping from the pillowcase. As he retrieves it he glimpses movement, and could imagine the pillowcase or whatever it hides has begun not just to breathe but to hint at outlines reminiscent of a face, though one that's unappealingly incomplete. No, the pillowcase is still lying flat on a pillow. He crumples the cellophane in his fist, only to feel as if he's squeezing out some unwelcome moisture, surely only his own perspiration. He shies the wad into the bin behind the deserted counter, just as the phone at his belt vibrates. Carl is calling from the Espouse Scouse shop. "Lad in a baseball cap on his way to you. Looks like a scally to us."

From the lift Bertram sees a lanky youth stuffing a cap into a hip pocket as he dodges into the store. Bertram follows him through Count On Our Computers and Phones Alone and stays well behind him on the escalator, but when he arrives at the next floor the fellow is waiting for him. "What are you creeping after me for?"

Bertram is distracted by a reflection of the escalator he just used. It looks as if a small figure is rising at his back, not borne by the escalator but wrung from between the ascending treads. He twists around to see the escalator is unoccupied. "Expecting reinforcements?" the youth says. "What's your actual problem?"

"Just doing my job, sir."

"I'm not it. Just tell me what I've done wrong."

Bertram reassures himself he can't really be seeing ill-distinguished fragments scattered over the next highest escalator, especially since they appear to be moving. "I saw what you hid in your pocket," he blurts.

"Right, my hat. I brought it in."

The activity vanishes off or into the escalator in the mirror as Bertram demands "Why didn't you want to be seen with it on?"

"Because you people don't like anybody wearing hats in shops." The youth drags the hat out of his pocket. "Take a good look," he says. "Not yours. I bought it in Greece."

It's a canvas trilby, not a baseball cap. Bertram is preparing to apologise when the mirror shows him a man in such a cap sidling behind him to dash down the escalator. "Bastard," Bertram protests and clatters after him, too late. The shoplifter sets off an alarm as he flees into the mall, and Bertram glares at the mirrors that surround him. "Playing games, are we?" he snarls, and stares at customers who stare at him.

The mirrors have refrained from performing any more tricks by the time Mr Chalfont calls him into the office. "I've had a complaint about you, Bertram."

"If it was the fellow with the headgear, I was warned to look out for someone like him."

"Like won't do. You need to be one hundred per cent certain what you're seeing."

Bertram tries to shut his thought up, only to mumble "Not much chance of that round here just now."

"I strongly advise you to make sure there is." Mr Chalfont presses his lips thin as if to squeeze more words out. "And the customer says you swore at him."

"Not him, the real thief."

"Who you allowed to escape with his loot."

"I'm sorry about that. I was distracted."

"I trust you aren't blaming the gentleman you falsely confronted." When Bertram doesn't risk answering, Mr Chalfont says "If this is about the lady who committed suicide, it can't be allowed to undermine our security. I'll be having eyes kept on you, Bertram."

Bertram thinks he senses them, even once he heads for home. Someone he can't locate is eating chocolate close to him on the platform and then on the train. The smell and taste follow him to his apartment, where they put him off his dinner and invade his concentration on every film he tries to watch. They accompany him to bed despite how fiercely he brushes his teeth, and the fear that they're omens of worse keeps twitching him awake.

At the store in the morning he heads straight for food. A chocolate bar in a shredded wrapper lies on the floor by a checkout desk. Why haven't the cleaners done their job? Perhaps the culprit waited until they'd finished so as to leave the evidence to taunt Bertram. Although Mr Chalfont let him in, Bertram thinks better of showing him. He bins the item and follows the trail he's sure has been left for him.

It leads not much better than invisibly to the escalator and vanishes in the toy department, where Bertram searches the aisles for further mischief. He's abandoning the quest when a mirror catches two objects rearing above a block of shelves behind him. They're hand puppets, and since one is larger than the other he can't help taking them for a parent and child. As he twists around they slump on the shelf, and the contents drop to the floor with two soft thuds. He stalks around the shelves, but the linoleum is bare. He fumbles the mouthpiece of his headset closer as he murmurs "Did you see that?"

"I'm seeing nobody but you, Bert, playing whatever you reckon you're playing."

"I'll catch you," Bertram vows. "I'll show them." He doesn't know how loud he spoke or who may have heard. He avoids Mr Chalfont while he ranges about the store in search of his tormentor. He has seen no further signs of a trespasser by the time the public is let in. Customers are a distraction now, and perhaps they're helping to conceal an interloper too. While he spies on anyone who seems remotely suspect, that kind of miscreant isn't his primary concern. He's sure a small invader is lurking somewhere in the maze of aisles. A glimpse of someone less than adult in Have Some Scents, a department where children surely have no business, sends him to sneak up on the intruder, only for the little girl to complain "Mummy, that man's watching me."

"Just doing what I'm paid for, madam."

"Then find somewhere more appropriate to do it," the woman says and adds an almost physically ferocious look.

Bertram turns to the mirrors, losing sight of her and her child. He rides up and down in the lift to survey the floors, even when he sees Mr Chalfont scowling at him. The ruse shows him nothing he's determined to find, and he sets about roving the floors. As the escalator returns him to the top floor, a mirror lets him see an intrusive shape in Babes And Bigger.

It has appeared at the entrance to an aisle of track suits, wavering as though its composition is unstable. It's the size of a child but a good deal less shapely. Bertram would like to take it for an improperly assembled mannequin, but its eager restlessness gives him no chance, and he tries to see as little detail as he can. On the other hand he needs to catch the malefactor while there are witnesses, and Mrs Deacon is talking to a woman at the counter.

As Bertram turns towards the aisle the figure shambles askew into it. It's heading for the women, who watch Bertram sprint into the aisle. "Got you this time," he shouts, only to snarl in disbelief. His quarry has escaped in a number of directions, apparently unseen by anyone except him, and he's grasping the shoulder of the girl who previously complained about him. "You won't trick me this time, you little bitch," he declares louder still. He should have released the girl first, especially since Mr Chalfont has come to find him.

BERTRAM RETURNS TO the store just once. The crowd in the mall stares at him and stays well clear. Perhaps the stale smell of chocolate repels them, unless they can see what's holding his hand. He stumbles close enough to the doors that they flinch aside. "Go in," he whispers urgently. "That's where you ought to live." He appears to be alone in watching a scrawny form, imperfectly recomposed, dart through the gap between the doors just before they meet. He's letting out a gasp of relief when it turns into a shriek, and he flails his arm so desperately it feels dislocated. He's still holding a hand.

Did You Know?

RAMSEY CAMPBELL was born in Liverpool in 1946 and now lives in Wallasey. The *Oxford Companion to English Literature* describes him as "Britain's most respected living horror writer." He has been given more awards than any other writer in the field, including the Grand Master Award of the World Horror Convention, the Lifetime Achievement Award of the Horror Writers Association, the Living Legend Award of the International Horror Guild, and the World Fantasy Lifetime Achievement Award. In 2015 he was made an Honorary Fellow of Liverpool John Moores University for outstanding services to literature. PS Publishing have brought out *Phantasmagorical Stories* in two volumes, a sixty-year retrospective of his short stories. His latest novel is *The Wise Friend* from Flame Tree Press, who are in the process of publishing his Brichester Mythos trilogy.

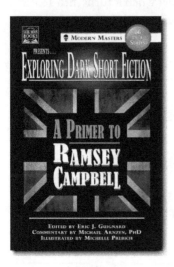

THE HOUSE OF STRAWBERRIES

BY ALESSANDRO MANZETTI

TEN miles from the famous Miramare Castle in Trieste, Italy, going up the hill northward and leaving the sea behind you, can be found a gate with the imperial insignia of Maximilian of Habsburg, Archduke of Austria and Emperor of Mexico. If you climb over the gate (always closed) and walk the snake-shaped path, you will arrive at what they call the House of Strawberries, where in the second half of the eighteenth century the Archduke bedded his lovers. This

Silent apparitions at the west side window

manor is still painted in Pompeian red, and every Thursday a woman dressed in red, with worms in her hair, appears at the west side window. Each time you'll see a different woman, all with their mouths sewn with a gold thread. They say those are the lovers who had been killed by the Archduke and buried under a strawberry field behind the manor. Silence is golden.

ALESSANDRO MANZETTI is a two-time Bram Stoker Award-Winning author. He Lives in Trieste (Italy). You can find out more at: www.battiago.com.

* FILE UNDER: *Haunted Manor*

Where we'd once stood in summer sunshine,
there is suddenly none . . .

IN OUR SEASON

FEATURE
ENTRY 4

STRUCTURE TYPE: MILITARY BASE CIVILIAN
LIVING CONDOS
LOCATION: KEFLAVÍK, ICELAND
LAT./ LONG: 64.0032° N, 22.5532° W
BUILT: CIRCA 1962
GROUND ELEVATION: 6.5 FT. (2 M.)
WRITTEN BY: TAMARA JERÉE

TRAVEL GUIDE NOTES

IT'S BEEN SAID that the greatest fears are of the unknown, and while that is certainly true on a conventional or social scale, I think often greatest *individual* fears relate more to experiences we've actually suffered, that to remember a past trauma and then consider having to repeat that pain or torment again, can be emotionally debilitating.

Worse, for some, is to suffer such conditions that are cyclical, which has the potential to create a frightening dread liable to hang forever in the back of your mind, knowing something is soon to be coming, a building, grinding panic of dwindling time—such is Seasonal Depression (Seasonal Affective Disorder), that by lack of sunlight during dark winter months, mental ailments are triggered, leading to fatigue, hopelessness, and worse.

Talented author Tamara Jerée takes the stages of seasonal depression to a new, surreal level as she travels to Iceland with her girlfriend, and to a building that never warms . . .

One may hope, as with all seasons (though there is no guarantee during the weather of "haunting") this too will pass, especially when "In Our Season."

—Charlatan Bardot

W E STEP OFF THE PLANE TOGETHER, BUT WHILE she is coming home, I have never been farther away from my own. No one in the airport—or in the town where we settle into our hotel—looks like us. Rós squeezes my hand, has nothing but reassuring smiles. Her mother's side of the family is here. I've never met them, but I have seen the family reunion photographs.

Here, in summer, the sun barely sets. She warned me about this before suggesting our trip. I am a brittle insomniac. I haven't dreamed in months. She massages lavender oil into my skin at night, and now whenever I think of the plant I am transported back to our bed where I lie awake with my restless thoughts. Better though, to face sleeplessness in the land of midnight sun than to endure its near-lightless winters. Rós would never risk a winter trip to Iceland, not with me.

The hotel is nice—a short walk from the sea. I know the sea. I've lived near beaches. But this is not Florida. The sand here is volcanic black and tangled with slimy red plants; mountains rise forever at our backs. After a sleepless jetlagged night, Rós asks me what I think of this coastal town with its brine perfume and cold fishermen, its colorful rooftops dotted among the sharp landscape. I think she is asking what I think of *her*. I answer in my limited Icelandic vocabulary, and she smiles.

Over a breakfast of skyr and oatmeal, Rós asks how I would like to begin our vacation. Hot springs? Hiking? She confesses that she's been curious about the now-abandoned U.S. military base, a neighbor to her hometown of Keflavík. Her mother had worked in the school cafeteria on the base, serving food to rowdy American children on the weekdays. As a child, Rós thought this was very impressive and asked her mother all about what life was like on the other side of the gate. Unremarkable, her mother had seemed to think, because most of what she said pertained to her sore feet.

In the past few years—while Rós was away at college, while we built our life together in the U.S.—much of the Keflavík base was converted for civilian use. After all, most of it was family housing and the school. However, one of the condominium buildings, the real reason Rós wants to see the base, has remained abandoned. People were scheduled to move in, but all plans were dropped, she says.

I push my spoon into the skyr and sit back. My body is heavy with the sleep it hasn't had. Rós, though, seems unburdened, as if this eternal light feeds her. Her brown skin glows with it.

"So what's with the condos?" I ask. "Mold? Structural issues?"

She leans forward. "Wrong weather."

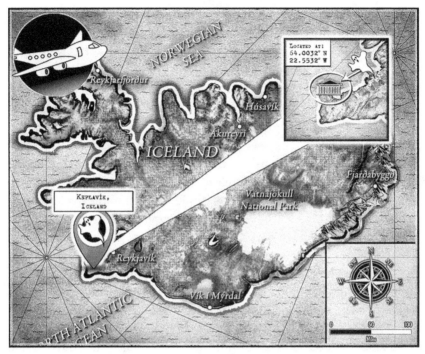

HAUNTED KEFLAVÍK, ICELAND

IT IS AS any other neighborhood. Children play in the grassy fields between the residential buildings. Families leave and return in their cars. Despite the evidence of life, it is quiet. The sun is pale with its light, as if it has reserved its warmer hues for southern latitudes. I feel lulled. I feel unreal. The sky is open.

If here I stare at my feet too much, for once, it's not anxiety. The volcanic rock peeks through patches of grass, a determined reminder of what made this land. Black rock worn to black gravel and, at the coasts, to black sand. I toe a patch of it when we stop walking, grinding my boot into this new earth.

The road winds among red and blue and green rooftops, the sides of each three-story condo the same strange yellow. I follow Rós. She consults no map, just walks determinedly ahead. She will know it when she sees it, she'd said.

Wind pushes, pulls, insistent. It is loud enough in our ears to be a living thing. Rós lets it tug her cardigan while I zip my jacket and pocket my hands. Eventually, she stops in front of one of the condos, and it turns out that I also know *this* is the one. This shadow is different from other summer shadows. This chill feels old, leftover from another time. I look around us. It is noon, and the sun is high. None of the other buildings cast a long shadow, none of them defy physics and light.

Two children pause their play to watch us. At home, I'd think their staring was a result of seeing two Black girls holding hands, any of the usual things. But here, I know it's because of the building—and Rós' proximity to it.

They shout something quick in unison, something I can't parse with my limited vocabulary.

Rós frowns and looks up into the dark windows. "I will tell you if we find any elves," she responds in English.

The children shake their heads just as Rós steps into the shadow—and falls. I hurry to her side only to feel the ground slip from under me. Suddenly, I am breathless and staring up into a dark and angry sky. Snow whips down on the cutting wind, searing the exposed skin of my cheeks.

"Black ice," Rós yells above the howling wind. She's braced herself against the building and holds one hand down to me. I take it instinctively, still disoriented from landing on my back and having my breath knocked out of me.

I look for the children and find them gone. The cars parked at the condos have vanished. I turn back to Rós and find her disappeared from the place she'd stood. I call for her, I turn around and around, heart kicking into a panicked rhythm. I catalogue the snowdrifts, the storm. Rós' advice comes back to me in her own voice. *Small steps on the ice. Keep your center of gravity level with your feet.*

I cross the sidewalk back into the parking lot, but the storm doesn't abate. Where we'd once stood in summer sunshine, there is suddenly none. I walk to the next condo, the next, but there is no end to the storm. Behind me, I've carved a trail through snow drifts, and snow dusts my jeans up to my thighs. I'm already shivering in my inadequate clothes. The gate we entered at the base perimeter has become lost in the white-out.

There is nothing to do but retreat inside. I know what Rós would say about the severity of Icelandic snowstorms, her quoted statistics about exposure and frostbite. She's told me the stories about how seriously people take the storms, about what can happen if you don't. In the path behind me, the whirlwind of snow parts around a figure in a red cardigan, a beacon in the night. I think—I *think*—I see an arm reaching toward me, a mouth opened wide. I move to her; the wind doubles down. I put up a hand to shield my face, and when I can look again, she is gone.

Every condo door is locked. I pick my way back through the snow and ice to where we started, leaning into the wind and fighting for each step. With every other glance, the red of Rós' cardigan flutters wildly ahead of me, like a bird caught in a trap. I cling to the visual, the only guide in the white-out, as I squint against the assault of snow and icy wind. I turn my head away, and the wind stings my cheek so numb it aches. Streetlamps quaver, their light sickly halos of yellow in the deep dark. Ahead, the doors to the strange condo are open, a beacon in the storm. Within them, light shines. I only hope that Rós has gone this way, that we will reunite at this shelter. I pull the stiff door closed. A sharp metal screech pierces the air, and then the howl of the wind is no longer a deafening thing, a fierce creature muzzled to a low growl. A pile of snow has started to form in the foyer, but being out of the wind's reach is a relief.

I lean against a wall, and only then do I realize how much I'm shaking.

"I'm sorry," says Rós, breathless. She sounds as if she's speaking from a great distance through a distorting fog.

I look up, around, but she isn't here, not quite. She ghosts around the edges of my vision, a smear of motion and red.

I am numb in more ways than one. I realize I should breathe. Try to locate my edges. Rós is here, even if in some faded state. I wish we could hold each other. I do not cry although I wish I could. I'm used to one kind of numbness, and that's the one I lean into. It is familiar and therefore a comfort.

Construction supplies and building materials litter the space in front of the stairway. These are heavy things, not the sort of stuff that could be moved without intention. They're scattered as if hastily dropped. I do not want to think of what would make someone drop something so heavy, of what would make someone abandon such expensive tools.

The storm outside continues to rage.

Neither of us asks the obvious question. It feels like it might trap us as much as the storm, as much as whatever strangeness pulled us out of our season and into this one.

At least there is light. It feels too dim for the stairway, casting broken geometric shadows through the rails. This place smells like road salt and ice. To the right, there's a room of what looks like post boxes, all neatly shut. Through the window into the room, I see a bulletin board with faded flyers. I can't read them from here.

The door to the post room swings open easily. Here also the light feels too yellow, too inadequate to beat back the oppressive dark. All the flyers are the same, all in plain black and white. In the corner, there's a too-dark image of someone staring out a window. It's one of those pictures that obviously used to be in color but was printed badly to save money on color ink. In large letters, the flyer asks FEELING DOWN? There's a warning about the winter, the long dark and what it can do to people. At the bottom, there are tear-off numbers for a hotline, the bottoms of the flyers jagged with them. I tear one off, another. I recognize the need that has overtaken me— the need for someone to see and affirm the pain, the loneliness—but this feeling is not mine. I stuff them into my pockets as if that will ease the ache in my chest. I snatch a flyer down and crumple it into my jacket pocket. With every move, there's the rasping susurrations of paper. It grows louder, filling the room like the deafening howl of the wind.

Her hand is light on my arm, the touch a question. The papery rustle dies. I step away from the board and breathe out all the tension it'd heaped on me, like expelling a wound. Rós' face is close but blurred. I try to place one of the slips of paper into her faded hand. It passes through and flutters to the floor. I see tension around her eyes; then she's gone. When I look back to the board, all the paper I'd torn down is replaced, but the copy has changed. Only the hotline number remains.

I check my phone and am surprised to find service bars. I try the number for Rós' Icelandic grandmother, whom we'd planned to stay with later in our trip. After several faint rings, someone picks up. It is not Rós' grandmother. They give their name and tell me that I've reached a mental health crisis line. I look at the screen and find the number I'd dialed is the same as the one on the flyers. I apologize and hang up, try again. I reach the same operator. They do not seem annoyed to hear from me again—either they've forgotten or are just being professional. I apologize again and wander back into the foyer, phone in hand. FEELING DOWN? The flyers have changed again when I glance back. I cannot access the internet. None of my apps will load. All other numbers I try ring and ring without voicemail. FEELING DOWN?

I dial the number on the flyer. It doesn't ring. Immediately, I hear the voice of the operator, the same one, thanking me for calling. They sound so sincere, so kind, that it hurts. I want to believe they can help.

"I think—I think I'm. Trapped. Somehow. I'm on the old base ... " I begin. The operator expresses confusion. "No, this isn't a mental health emergency, but it is an emergency. I can't seem to reach anyone else. Can you connect me to ... " The line goes dead when she transfers me. I realize it's not cold enough to see my breath on the air. There must be heat coming from somewhere—but it's still cold.

I step over the strewn tools and construction materials. Up the stairs, something rattles in the wind. A window must be open somewhere. Its whistle is sharp as if squeezed through a small space.

FEELING DOWN?

I recognize the feeling that lives here, though I didn't expect to find it in summer. It lives at the end and beginning of every year, like a bookend to each segment of my life.

I call the hotline number again. "I feel—trapped," I say after the operator thanks me for calling.

"It can feel like that, can't it?" they say. They encourage me to say more. I dig through my memory of previous winters and think of the way my mood predictably darkens with the season. This is what I give. The operator soothes. They name resources and give advice. They say, "The way out is forward."

"What?" I say, even though I heard them fine. I start toward the stairs.

"The way out is forward," they repeat.

"Thank you."

The rail is icy when I lay my hand on it, and so I pocket my hands again. I take the stairs up.

At each landing, the hall splits off to the left and right. Two apartments comprise each side. The walls are heavy concrete blocks painted white. These buildings have the character of something built to withstand and endure, and that is what they offer. There is no softness or art. Nothing to distract one from the way that winter closes in and creeps into the mind.

The doors to the right are bolted shut. To the left, the sustained howl of the wind becomes a sharp whistle. I try the first door and find it locked. The door at the end of the hall, however, rattles in its frame. Cold pushes from under it and settles around my ankles. I find the door unlocked, brace my shoulder against it, and push against the wind. As soon as I'm inside, the wind catches the door and slams it shut behind me, a sharp crack splitting time into before and after.

The hall is dark. To the left, there's the void of a doorway, and at the end, the expanse of a larger room. I venture toward it, peeking into the smaller doorway as I pass. Within, the white outline of a refrigerator is broken up by shadow and the sickly yellow light thrown by the streetlamp, the familiar shapes of its edges smudged soft by the shadow and turned sharp by the light. The large space at the end of the hall turns out to be a living room, although sparsely furnished with what looks to be stiff waiting room chairs. Icy air whips in through the open windows, but I'm drawn to circle the chairs, feeling toward the heavy impression inhabiting one of them. I have the urge to reach out and massage nonexistent shoulders, to lean over the person-shaped emptiness and whisper into a shadow ear. The air around me shrieks with wind. I grip the arm of a chair, squeeze the upholstery, and settle myself into the heavy impression on its seat.

Or: it settles into me.

I am a list of undone things, the ache of too much restless rest, an anxious craving for foods I don't want. I breathe it in and try not to drown. I bring a memory of the eternal sun and the embrace of a loved one. I bring the last undisturbed sleep I had and a memory of sunrise.

The windows behind me snap shut. I open my eyes, not realizing I'd closed them. A boxy television against the far wall flickers on, shining gray light through the room. An afterimage of Rós briefly smears the space beside me.

On the screen, a woman stares out the window from within a dark room. The voiceover asks about sudden changes in mood or behavior in oneself or loved ones. There's a list of symptoms. The PSA ends by flashing a number across the screen, the same one that fills my pockets. The announcement begins to loop before cutting out into static.

The rest of the apartment is filled with similar placeholder furniture—unremarkable, uncomfortable, and sparse. Furniture that has been used by many and loved by none.

On the windowsill of a child's bedroom, I find a smooth, palm-sized lava rock. I pick it up, turn it over once, twice. I hold it up to the lamplight from the window, and Rós' ghostly hand materializes to point out a smear of paint on one side. A child has tried to paint a flower. Someone has found joy in this landscape. I hold to it, turn it over in my hand like a worry stone.

I climb the stairs to each floor and find the doors where the wind rushes in, the places where emotional impressions have settled deep into a space—the sunken center of a mattress, in front of a bathroom mirror, at a window overlooking a frozen playground. I inhabit each and give to them and try not to let my own feelings overtake me. I squeeze the stone in my hand. I remember Rós—to remember love and to give love. I have to believe that I'll find her again.

The way out is through.

On the third and final floor, the wind is loudest. The lights in the hall have gone out. From the landing, the windows into the condo's common room are black mirrors. I don't think of myself as a superstitious person, but I am reluctant to look into them. I am struck with the fear that I might see the personifications of the impressions I've encountered—unfamiliar ghostly faces blurred by time. I try to walk past, but my attention is drawn. No, the impressions are soothed. They are no longer here. When I look, there is only the smudged reflection of my own face. I step toward it as if that might resolve the reflection into something familiar. Instead, Rós appears beside me, clear for the first time since we fell into winter. I don't turn, knowing that if I do, she will be gone. It seems that she sees me as well, and we make eye contact in the glass. She points down one of the halls and disappears.

There's no need to check all the doors on this floor. The wind and the remaining presence are enough of a signal. In this last apartment, the outside lamplight doesn't shine in. I find the open window in the bedroom.

The room is empty but for a plain bed frame and a bare mattress. Someone slept too long here in the dark. Their idle thoughts and nightmares have pooled at its center like a stain. I crawl into the space, and it immediately pulls me under, starving for comfort and companionship. They have gone so long unseen and unheard that they do not know what to ask. They have lost how to name the thing consuming them.

I roll over (when did I lay down?) and it is an effort with a body so weighted. Rós is at the bedside with tea. She tries to smile at me and sets it on the coaster. She gives me a warm blanket fresh from the dryer and takes the old one away. The emptiness presses tears into my eyes. I could cry for them.

I wake up (when did I fall asleep?) and Rós is making soft clattering noises in the kitchen. I picture her taking down plates from the cupboard. The house smells faintly sweet. She appears in the doorway with a plate of breakfast.

I pull on an oversized shirt. The light in the room is different. Late evening sunset limns the edges of the curtains. I realize I'm back in our bedroom at home. My skin smells of lavender. Rós has coaxed the tension out of my shoulders. I turn to thank her and find her gone. I begin to doubt she was ever here. But there is her impression in the sheets. I go looking for her, but the apartment is wrong. Our rooms are not here, not laid out like this. I trail my hand along the wall of the hall, and it turns cool and stony under my fingertips. I call out for Rós. The furniture in the living room is not the eclectic antiques Rós picked out. They are plain and worn. Dull navy in the evening light. All wrong colors. I throw open the curtains, and it is abruptly night. Sickly yellow light falls across the floor.

I am in bed (when did I crawl back into bed?), and I can't move. I curl my fingers against the bare mattress and find the stone still in my grasp. There are no more fresh blankets or steaming tea. I am alone in an empty room, and I have lost time. The storm still surges.

"You have to let me go," I say to the emptiness. "I've shown the others peace, and they let me go."

It presses down, insistent. My chest feels full of water. I understand.

By the end of winter, crying feels impossible. Sometimes it's not sadness but numbness that overwhelms.

I let the water surge, tighten my throat, press behind my eyes. These are another person's tears, but I welcome them as if they are my own. The pressure abates, and I am able to move just as full-body sobs have me curling in on myself. I'm lost in it, and through the loss I find my own fresh fear that there is no end to this, that I will exist as this grayer, weaker version of myself forever. That I will not escape winter and that no one would weather it with me.

"Isa?"

She is a specter, but she is here. Rós looks as shocked to see me as I am to see her. She reaches out to me, but our realities are desynchronized, and our hands pass through each other.

"Rós," I say, just as she opens her mouth and is gone.

I am alone again, fully alone. The pressure has been soothed and is departed. My face is puffy, and the chill raises new goosebumps on my skin, but I am lighter. I can take a full breath.

The building is settled. I emerge from the final apartment to find the world on the other side of the threshold quieter, but not only for the lack of wind-rattled doors. Now, it is truly quiet, the passing of a storm.

I return to the common room, its windows still wide and dark but silvery with moonlight. It contains the same stiff office furniture as the rest of the building, but there's a shimmer of color that draws me in. I step around the dark masses of furniture and to the window.

Ribbons of teal and emerald light thread through the dissipating storm clouds. The beast in the wind has retreated. The sky is opening. Perhaps, perhaps this is the other side. On the ground below, I spot a flutter of red.

I tear down the steps. Some are slick with melted snow, but I grip the rail and keep running, each step a frantic squeak. Through the glass-paneled doors, I see Rós. She stands with her back to me, cardigan drawn tight around her as she looks up at the colored sky. I pull the door open, and the screech of its hinges draws her attention to me. I've forgotten about the ice, and so has she. We are falling into each other's arms—and into sunlight.

We land hard on the pavement, but we will check for bruises later. For now, we speak over each other, hands finding one another again and again. Gripping a shoulder, cupping a face, threading fingers through hair. The sun shines down. We're back in our season.

Rós smiles, smoothing a hand down my side when she pauses and pats at my pocket. She withdraws the painted lava rock, and her expression falls at the sight of it. Her gaze flicks back to me.

"It was real," I say.

She looks back to the building. Its shadow has retreated to something natural. "I don't want to think that it was."

We stand. I think she might throw the rock, but for now it remains clenched tight in her hand. I look back at the condo. Rós doesn't. She's too focused on me.

"Will you be okay? Should we go home? Should I—" She gestures vaguely, drops her hands to her sides.

The sun hasn't moved in the sky. The children—still staring—stand where they last did, but I feel like I have moved through so much time. I shiver the early winter away.

DID YOU KNOW?

TAMARA JERÉE is a graduate of the Odyssey Writing Workshop. Their short stories appear in *FIYAH Magazine*, *Strange Horizons*, and *Anathema Magazine*. Their poetry was nominated for the inaugural Ignyte Award. You can find them on Twitter @TamaraJeree or visit their website tamarajeree.com.

THE CARETAKER'S HUT

BY KEVIN J. KENNEDY

The caretaker's hut at Burnfoot Park

IT had been a long time since there was a caretaker in Burnfoot Park. It was hard to tell though. The park was immaculate. Beautiful flowers, never a piece of trash to be found on the grounds, and no spray paint on any of the small buildings there.

The previous caretaker had been found dead in his hut. Murdered. Foul play was suspected, but it was tough to pin anything on the local youth gangs. Airdrie, in central Scotland, had become a no-go area. Luckily, the gangs had all started to disappear, one by one. After the caretaker's death the park became quieter, more tranquil.

The hut still stood, always locked, and no one was ever seen going in or out, but if you asked the locals, they would tell you they still heard the old caretaker whistling at night as he done his rounds.

KEVIN J. KENNEDY is an author, an editor, and runs KJK Publishing, the company behind anthology collections such as *100 Word Horrors* and *The Horror Collection*.

* FILE UNDER: *Haunted Caretaker's Hut*

END OF THE ROAD

BY RAY CLULEY

THERE'S a multi-story carpark in Swansea, Wales, that suffers numerous hauntings. Manifestations vary, but the most common include the sound of an engine idling when no vehicles are present, and the appearance of a figure seen to leap from the highest level only to disappear upon striking the ground. The carpark was a popular spot for those looking to end their lives and was closed in the late 1990s, although for many years after it remained a suicide hotspot.

Beware falling objects at site of the old Swansea Carpark

It was demolished in 2012, and the area awaits redevelopment, although the sound of a running engine can still be heard on quiet nights, and figures still plummet from heights no longer available to them, seeking deaths they cannot claim again.

RAY CLULEY is an award-winning writer based in the UK with stories published (and republished) in a variety of venues. You can find out more at: probablymonsters.wordpress.com.

* FILE UNDER: *Haunted Carpark*

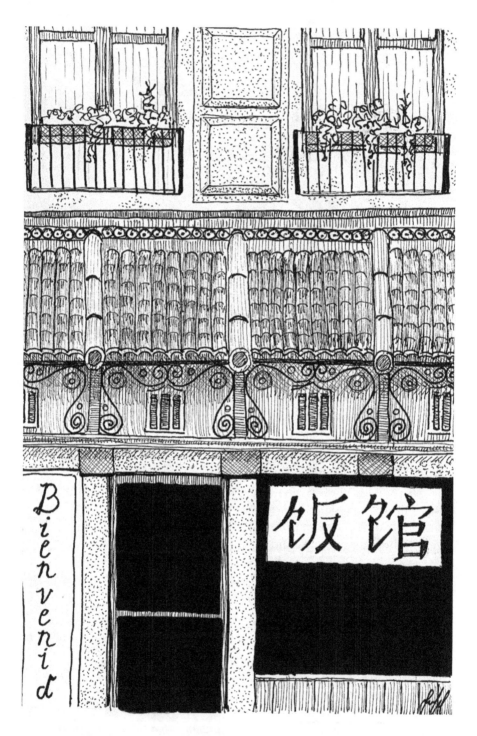

My mission right now is to save my family's restaurant . . .

QUE VAGI BÉ

STRUCTURE TYPE: RESTAURANT
LOCATION: BARCELONA, SPAIN
LAT./ LONG: 41.3978° N, 2.1723° E
BUILT: CIRCA 2002
GROUND ELEVATION: 128 FT. (39 M.)
WRITTEN BY: S. QIOUYI LU

TRAVEL GUIDE NOTES

TRAVELLING SOUTHWARD TO Europe's Iberian Peninsula, we arrive at this next story, an ingenious confluence of three cultures, exploring relationships, history, and languages of a Chinese-American restaurateur living in Barcelona, Spain. Don't be fooled by the humor and pop-references; there are profound themes here of companionship, national independence, and personal acceptance.

And so much more.

With a background in linguistics and translation, S. Qiouyi Lu plays well with the nuances of written language and has built a noteworthy Curriculum Vitae of academia, leadership, and published-genre fiction stories in markets such as *Tor.com*, *Black Static*, and *Clarkesworld*. Know that regardless of heritage or locality, two common ideals run through every society: The search for truth and the search for good eats. S. speaks herein to both.

As is pleasantly said in Catalan (or *catalan*, depending on your convention), "Que vagi bé."

—Charlatan Bardot

PER GIGAMESH

HERE'S THE THING ABOUT LIVING IN BARCELONA: It's an amazing city with culture running deep in its marrow. There's a fire that always burns in its people. Barcelonians will not hesitate to express their opinions and protest for their rights.

Loudly.

So, you can imagine that the well-being of a single Chinese restaurant tucked into a side alley off Pg. de Sant Joan isn't a priority for your average Barcelonian. Fair. After all, the latest round of rallies for Catalonian independence has lasted for months. People have more pressing concerns right now. One restaurant goes under? No big deal. A new one can spring right up in its place. But an entire region, an entire people? Destroyable, but hardly ever restored.

As for me, I'm just the grown-ass kid of the restauranteurs in question. Michael Ming. Yeah, no "exotic" Chinese name—even my middle name is just my mom's surname, in the Spanish tradition. So, my full name is Michael Chang Ming. Predictably, I get jokes about being Ming the Merciless or Señor Chang from the show *Community*, complete with terribly racist impersonations of both characters.

Eh. Whatever. Even if others think it's futile or that I'm a joke, my mission right now is to save my family's restaurant. My parents travel back to China frequently and sometimes, in my opinion, frivolously. They go under the pretense of making business deals, but very few of the projects pan out. In fact, they usually lose money on trips, and lately they've been turning them into vacations. I'm not interested in traveling to China with them—I hate flying, first of all, and we can't take a train over, which would be my ideal method of travel—so I'm left managing the restaurant on my own.

Well, it's not like I've never been left home alone before. In fact, my parents have been leaving me home alone since I was ten, and I've been, in some capacity, in charge of the restaurant since I was fourteen. It's our only real income. We've been treading water for a while, and now we're sinking. Despite my parents' comments on changing careers, I'm still stubbornly clinging to the restaurant. Call it pride or call it familiarity, I'm not sure. I wouldn't call running a restaurant my purpose in life, but, well, it's currently my main preoccupation, at least.

My parents have already gotten loans to put into equipment, advertising, and remodeling, even as our menu and recipes remain the

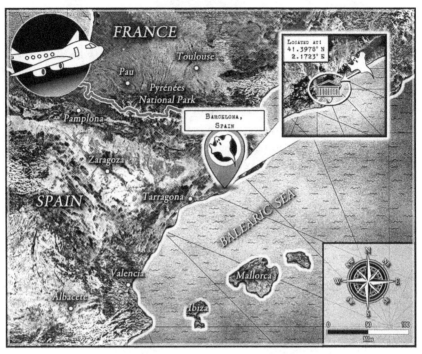

HAUNTED BARCELONA, SPAIN

same—I wrap a lot of the dumplings myself, and I put in the extra hours when we're short-staffed, especially when Katherine, head of the front of the house, isn't available. I always make sure to pay our workers first, but that leaves me with a very paltry income after expenses are deducted.

I've tried hustling for cash with side jobs. I work at the restaurant in the evenings and leave Katherine in charge during the day when I go to work at the body shop. I managed to find an application for my engineering degree as a motorcycle mechanic, which is more in line with what I'd actually like to do as a career, although a mechanic position doesn't quite feel like my calling, either. But working days and nights, with the occasional rideshare or delivery income, is way too exhausting for me to do long-term. I haven't gotten any approvals for my own loan requests, either.

So, I know it might sound wild to some folks, but tonight, while I'm home alone again in the apartment over our storefront, I'm holding a séance. Or, "communing with the elders," in more Chinese terms. I mean, my people have survived wars and famines, again and again. My ancestors are badass, especially Auntie Qian, who I'm hoping to speak to today. She really had her shit together. She made it in the United States even while the Chinese Exclusion Act was in place. I'm sure she'd have some great business advice.

Unfortunately, it's difficult to look up how to properly summon a spirit. Sure, there are books about it—I read them in the aisles of Librería Gigamesh, hoping to absorb information before anyone could ask me why or shoo me away for treating the bookstore like a library. But even though there are lots of people who claim to have a reliable method for contacting the dead, there's little to no verifiable evidence that summoning a spirit is actually *possible*.

I'm in uncharted territory. I keep my mind open as I kneel before the summoning circle I've cobbled together. It's more of an oval, really: a shaky sea salt line with a few scented candles (all we have at home), some oranges, and a few fresh persimmons. There's also a copy of *Kung Fu Hustle*, the most powerful representation of Big Auntie Energy I can think of. Oh, and I tossed in a pack of Djarum Black clove cigarettes for good measure.

All right. Lighting the candles now, one by one. Jasmine, cedar, juniper, vanilla. A strange but weirdly familiar mix of smells. I glance around and remind myself that it doesn't matter if I look crazy doing this, as there's no one around to witness me.

For now.

"Uh ..."

The juniper candle flickers.

"I'm not really sure what I need to say here, but ... "

An idea strikes me. I give the pack of cigarettes a good couple of smacks, then take one out. The sweet scent of cloves layers over the already rich smellscape. When I light the cigarette by the flame of the cedar-scented candle, the smoke adds the last note to complete the perfume of the scene.

I sit back and wait, the cigarette between my fingers. I'm tempted to take a drag, but I don't smoke. Instead, I take deep breaths. One, then another. One more, in, out; in ...

"Oh, shit."

An ember has ashed off the end of the cigarette and burned a hole in my sweats. Cursing, I look around the room and don't see anything that can be used as an ashtray. Sighing, I extinguish the cigarette by dunking it into the pool of wax around the wick of the vanilla candle.

OOH. NOW *THAT'S* A FLAVOR I HAVEN'T TRIED.

"Què collons?" I say. Bewildered, I stand up and spin around, looking for anyone who could have said something. The fan hums innocently as it circulates air through my bedroom.

I'm still alone.

IT'S NOT THAT HARD TO UNDERSTAND, IS IT? CLOVE PLUS VANILLA EQUALS DELICIOUS.

"That's not what I'm objecting to!" My voice comes out in a hiss. Even if no one hears, I still feel awkward speaking aloud with what appears to be a voice in my head. I pinch the bridge of my nose à la *South Park*'s Stan Marsh and squeeze my eyes shut.

"Okay, first of all, am I even speaking to Auntie Qian?"

WHO?

"Ai, Déu meu," I say. With a long exhale, I stop pinching my bridge and reluctantly open my eyes.

"Then who am I speaking to?"

WHOM.

"Huh?"

WHOMST, IF YOU'D LIKE TO HYPERCORRECT.

"Whomst the fuck?"

My words linger in the air like a slow drop of molasses. The room has gone dark and quiet save for the crackling, dancing flames of the candles. Despite the tranquility, I'm uneasy. I've always been sensitive to people's energies—side effect of having to communicate with adults while being patronized for my age—but never have I been in this position, holding up a lightning rod for a spirit to strike and reveal the full extent of my emotions and doubts.

THAT'S MORE LIKE IT.

A soft breeze sighs through the room, making the candles flicker.

I've already made sure every door and window is locked.

My room is never drafty.

EM DIC ANDRÉS MONTOYA DE LA CRUZ Y LA ESTRELLA, BUT YOU CAN CALL ME "ANDREU."

"All right ... Andreu," I say, as if I'm a cow chewing cud who's been asked to spit it out.

I TU?

"Just call me Mike."

NOPE. DOESN'T WORK LIKE THAT. YOU SUMMONED ME; IT'S BASIC COURTESY TO TELL ME YOUR ENTIRE NAME.

I'm beginning to regret summoning Andreu. But, well, no one's made a *Debrett's* for séances. Guess it's only fair.

"Michael Chang Ming. 江明科, if you can speak Chinese at all."

江明科?

"Holy shit. Your pronunciation is really good."

THAT'S WHAT HAPPENS WHEN YOU EAT YOUR WORDS SO MUCH THAT YOU CAN PUT OTHERS' ONTO YOUR TONGUE.

I'm pondering Andreu's words so hard that I nearly miss the sound of the steamer pot boiling dry in the kitchen. I curse under my breath.

"Hold on. I gotta get this."

It strikes me as I'm jogging over to the kitchen that I don't actually know what Andreu looks like, or how I'd confirm whether he's still in the room or if he's following me. I guess those are secondary concerns when the pot's already gone dry and the candles are still lit in the other room.

Major fire hazards.

I take the top off the bamboo steamer. The 小籠包 look cooked through, their wrappers glistening with steam. I turn off the heat, relieved. I hate scorching the steamer.

WHAT ARE THOSE?

I sigh, this time with resignation. Soup dumplings are the most popular dish on our menu. As waiter, cashier, and maître d'hôtel, I have to explain this shit all the time to customers, so much so that I've picked up not just castellano, but also enough català to explain the buns to the Barcelonians in their mother tongue, too.

Well, I guess I can explain one more time as confirmation that there *is* a spirit here to explain to.

"They're Shanghai-style soup dumplings. Back in the old country, we'd call them pissing buns because of how the meat juice squirts into your mouth when you bite down. But, well, that doesn't translate as well here. So we call them soup dumplings, even if they're more properly known as 小籠包."

QUINA MERDA. REALLY WISH I HAD A BODY TO EXPERIENCE FOOD AGAIN.

I'm not sure what to say to that. I shrug.

"That's rough, buddy."

ACTUALLY . . .

I'm going through the motions of plating the buns and making dipping sauce. I don't have much of an appetite, but my muscle memory is a comforting lifeline to normalcy that I find myself desperately clinging to, now that I'm accepting that yes, there is indeed a spirit here. I set the plate on the dining table and look at it dubiously. The buns waft steam, as if tempting me to eat them, like all those cartoons of *Tom & Jerry* being whisked off their feet by the aroma of hot food.

As I'm debating whether I'm hungry enough to eat, a cold wind blasts through the dining room, rattling the china cabinet enough to alarm me. My skin breaks out in goosebumps. Steam stops wafting up from the buns, which have suddenly gone cold.

"Wh..."

With dread, I look down at the soup dumplings. There's no confirmation of what's happened—the dumplings remain as still as they were before. Yet I know even before Andreu says anything that he's possessed the dumplings, creating a vessel for his ghostly body out of the food.

WOW. SO THIS IS WHAT IT FEELS LIKE TO BE A LITTLE DUMP.

"Oh my God," I say, squeezing my eyes shut at the pun. I'd give Andreu shit for it, but, well, I'm the one who said they're called "pissing buns" in the first place. I can't be mad about it.

SO...

I look down at the dumplings. The worst part is that there're no googly eyes, no food moving and emoting like in Pixar movies. Just a frigid plate with buns that now look greasy instead of glitteringly delicious.

Amazing how quickly my growing hunger retreats.

HEY. MIKE. DIDN'T YOU WANT SOMEONE TO HELP OUT WITH YOUR RESTAURANT? I COULD DO THAT. BUT WE GOTTA MAKE A UNION FIRST.

"Uh... I don't think I can marry or be a business partner with a ghost."

SIGH... 江明科, YOU ARE FAR TOO LITERAL.

The proper use of my full Chinese name activates my memory centers of deep parental disappointment. The most powerful authority: one that can drag you on a guilt trip. Frozen in place, I hear Andreu's next words clearly.

EAT ME.

"What?"

YOU HEARD ME.

"Really? Are you kidding me?"

YOU'VE NEVER WATCHED *ALICE IN WONDERLAND*? *SHE* FOLLOWED DIRECTIONS. SHE ATE IT *ALL*.

"Déu meu," I mutter.

EVER CONSIDERED THAT MAYBE YOU'RE NOT THE CHESHIRE CAT OR THE CATERPILLAR, BUT ALICE?

"Uh... no?"

LISTEN, IT'S NOT A GENDER THING, TRUST ME. YOU'VE JUST GOT ALICE IN YOUR BLOOD.

"Did you... did you just reference Astrovamps?"

WHEN YOU'RE A SPIRIT, YOU TEND TO FIND KINDRED SPIRITS. MINE HAPPEN TO BE THE ONES WHO YELL VERY LOUDLY AND BEAUTIFULLY. LIKE... ALL YOU REALLY GOTTA DO IS PLAY "IMMIGRANT SONG" AND I'LL HAUNT YOUR RADIO.

"Wh—"

JUST. EAT. ME.

"I don't . . . isn't that, like . . . cannibalism, or something?"

I CAN'T BELIEVE YOU LIVE DOWN THE STREET FROM LA SAGRADA FAMÍLIA AND YOU'RE ASKING IF EATING THE BODY OF A SOUP DUMP WILL TRANSMUTATE IT INTO HUMAN FLESH. IT'S STILL PORK.

"Okay, okay, *fine.*"

I don't bother to get chopsticks to eat the dumplings properly. I pick one up, baffled by how it warms just slightly between my fingers. I pop the whole thing into my mouth and bite down.

The juice, in defiance of thermodynamic laws, bursts so hot in my mouth that it scalds my tongue.

"Motherfucker," I say.

TOLD YOU, I'M ANDRÉS MONTOYA DE LA CRUZ Y LA ESTRELLA, NOT OEDIPUS REX.

"I'm—"

YOU HAVE TO EAT ONE MORE. THIS MUST BE WITNESSED IN DUPLICATE.

I roll my eyes. Andreu must've been some kind of lawyer with all his talk of contracts and witnessing. I pick up another bun. But, rather than warming in my fingers, this time, the dumpling gets colder and colder, more and more swiftly, until I could swear when I bite down that my teeth are cutting through a barely thawed core and aspic instead of soup.

Ugh. Worst equivalent exchange ever. With difficulty, I swallow the cold, greasy lump.

"Happy now?"

VERY. NOW, LET'S GET TO WORK.

IT'S BEEN THREE MONTHS since Andreu started haunting the Soup & Dumpling. Turns out there's so much great food in Barcelona that what we needed the most was an *attraction*, not superficial changes to the décor or any changes to the menu at all. Our previous storefront was a little too plain and hole-in-the-wall to grab people's attention off Pg. de Sant Joan.

My parents immigrated to Barcelona from Los Angeles. They've taken me back to the States a few times. Turns out, while Barcelona has some incredible donuts, they don't have any Krispy Kremes with their badass donut conveyer belts.

It was Andreu's idea to make a dumpling machine, but I'm the one who was able to visualize and create it. My experience as a mechanic definitely helped with that. My parents were hesitant about it at first—they saw having a machine working for us as mass-producing soup dumplings and giving up their handmade charm—but, if anything, having a steam-powered, well, *steamer* for the dumpling gets so many oohs and ahhs that we're barely able to keep up with the actual prep of wrapping the filling. We sell out often, sometimes before noon. The machine is such a hit that we're even listed in *Atlas Obscura* now.

Andreu ended up sticking around. I guess the pork buns still transmuted into *something* that gives him the spiritual roots to exist around me, rather than coming and going whenever he's lucky enough to catch someone doing a séance. Which, he told me, doesn't happen often at all— there had only been two in the building previously, but no one had been willing to strike a deal with him before he finally crossed paths with me.

In the three months since the séance, Andreu and I have learned a lot about each other. I never asked Andreu how he died, and he never offers an explanation. All he said was that it happened inside the very apartment I'm now living in. But he did tell me that he passed in 1888, right before the Esposició Universal, and the construction of both the Arc del Triomf and Ciutadella Park. Both of those spots are nearby and are major attractions for tourists.

"Have you ever been?" I asked him one day.

NO. GHOSTS CAN ONLY HAUNT THE PLACES WHERE THEY DIED. SO I HAVEN'T BEEN ABLE TO LEAVE THE APARTMENT SINCE, WELL, 1888. BUT I'VE HEARD ALL ABOUT WHAT'S GOING ON OUTSIDE. WHATEVER BUSINESS IS DOWNSTAIRS—WHETHER IT'S A RESTAURANT LIKE YOURS, A GIFT SHOP, A SALON—PEOPLE ALWAYS END UP CHATTERING ABOUT CURRENT EVENTS. SO I KNOW WHAT'S HAPPENING, EVEN IF I HAVEN'T BEEN ABLE TO SEE IT WITH MY OWN EYES.

I offered to take him around and show him the spirit of the Esposició Universal, which, he ended up telling me, he'd been very excited to see, and disappointed that he couldn't. So I took my time wandering around all the sites, until we got to the statue of Christopher Columbus.

SPIT ON IT.

"What? Why?"

COLUMBUS IS A COLONIZER. HE DOESN'T DESERVE OUR RESPECT.

I did as he said. Over those three months, we'd also gotten to know a bit of each other's politics. Kinda hard to stay out of politics when you're in Catalunya, after all. I've finally found someone I can kvetch with about being neglected and having to grow up quickly for my family to pursue the "American Dream." My parents kept that fallacy alive, despite their move to

Spain, where things work very differently. My parents would still rather attempt assimilation again, chasing after business trends that they think will be in demand with Western capitalism and the mainstream, than try an entirely new way of life.

Me, I've committed myself to doing what I do well. Fuck the status quo.

Andreu, meanwhile, was never a lawyer. But, when he passed, he'd been going to university, where he found himself critical of Spanish hegemony and of colonization, though many of his peers didn't think either mattered. He's explained to me how colonization has fucked the world over again and again, and how, in the hundred-some years since his death, he's only seen it all get worse. To the point where he's dragged me to go out and protest as part of the Catalonian independence rallies. Metaphorically dragged me, I mean; he can't actually control my body at all, but he's very convincing and has gotten me to do a lot of things I was previously too anxious about to try, like going to all these spots in the city in the first place.

Today, we're going to see the Sagrada Família, which we've finally gotten tickets to. The whole walk over, Andreu goes on about how it's absurd to have tickets to enter a place of worship to begin with. Even though I've lived in Barcelona all thirty years of my life, I've never seen the inside of the Sagrada Família until now, after we've made enough of an initial profit off the machine—which, unsurprisingly, we named the Andreu 3000—for me to afford tickets. Then, he goes on a lengthy diatribe about Catalonian independence, culture, and identity, expounding on how Spanish influence encroaches on and suppresses the culture.

I MEAN, LOOK AT MY NAME! I'M CATALONIAN; I SHOULD HAVE A CATALONIAN NAME, LIKE ANDREU. BUT I'M *ANDRÉS MONTOYA DE LA CRUZ Y LA ESTRELLA*, FOR CHRIST'S SAKE. EVEN MY NAME HAS TO BE SPANISH? COME ON.

I don't call many things sacred. But, just standing there in the cathedral, under the ornate, surrealist vaulted ceilings, the eldritch organic shapes, the spirit of Déu suffusing the air, entering my lungs as I take a seat in a pew and bow my head—I may not be religious, and Andreu left his religion young, but we both identify this as sacred. And, even if the actual food has already passed through my body, Andreu did end up transmuting: his voice remains in my heart, where he's transformed into a snarky and warm presence who provides fantastic insight on everything I experience.

Andreu's family has been in Catalunya for as long as there's been a Catalunya to be had. My cultural touchstones, meanwhile, aren't the Spanish ones, but the estadounidense pop culture that permeates the world. So, even without Catholicism, we still reach for the same cultural touchstones that allow us to explain ourselves to each other in a familiar, sacred language of our own.

The demonstrations for Catalonian independence are still going on. We've had so many people drop by the restaurant because they were around for the protests. Thinking that my Chinese face won't understand English, castellano, or català, they bitch about politics over the food I serve, speaking in the most common language of them all: Emotion. Passion. Ethics.

Truth.

You know, I never wanted to be in the spotlight, anyway. Someone's got to keep the machines running and the food hot. It's both a blessing and a curse to have the complete stranger of a soul named Andreu Montoya de la Cruz y la Estrella sharing my body with me. A curse because he will not stop making terrible puns based on our shared knowledge of estadounidense geekery; a blessing because I will never be alone, will never experience anything alone ever again.

I never told Andreu about the neglect I've suffered, but I know he can sense the sheer size of the void in my heart created through absence. Moreover, he's not interested in molding himself to fit that shape. It's merely a nook that he can fit in, safely, so he is never forgotten again.

We are witnessed in duplicate, always. And whether someone says "independence," "independencia," or "independència," I know that food is an integral part of the struggle. It's one of the first things my ancestors would lay waste to in a war to weaken their enemies, after all.

Someone has to feed the revolutionaries. And we Chinese? Will always feed you, every time. Perhaps with a scowl, perhaps with a smile. But no matter my exterior, no matter what anyone else sees, no matter the outcome of these protests, I will always hear Andreu's voice in my heart egging me on:

Let's get to work.

Did You Know?

S. QIOUYI LU writes, translates, and edits between two coasts of the Pacific. Eir work has appeared in several award-winning venues. E edits the magazine *Arsenika* and runs *microverses*, a hub for tiny narratives. You can find out more about S. at eir website s.qiouyi.lu or on Twitter @sqiouyilu.

SOAKING IN ROMAN REJUVENATION
BY Setsu Uzumé

TWO hours south of Belgrade is the idyllic village of Vrnjci, famous for its mineral baths, which maintain a precise temperature of 37 °C. Despite its fame, economic growth has been glacial. While Hungarian, Russian, American, and other hotel chains sought to capitalize on hyperinflation through the 1990s, summer construction projects always ground to a halt, citing damage associated with frost. Worse, workers would be found dead in the woods, sometimes miles from the site. Maps of the deaths, as far back as Baron Herder's 1836 restoration project, revealed a pattern: Eight workers are always found, frozen, at equidistant cardinal and intercardinal points, with Vrnjci's hot spring at the center. The last hotel investor, a Turkish firm, pulled out in 2005; payment was disbursed to all but eight workers, who never showed up to collect their paychecks.

The most recent reports on Vrnjci offer the least likely explanation, that the posture of the frozen construction workers match that of second century Roman remains discovered at the site, all curled into themselves, hands clutching their hearts. Forensic archaeologists noted clavicle and pelvic breaks. All died freezing, gasping, clutching at their core as water wormed into them, swallowed them, and—slow as roots—spitted them on the pipes.

This is, of course, nonsense. If you find yourself soaking at a spa in Vrnjci, and suddenly feel faint, chilly, or drained—relax. The water's fine.

Setsu's work has two settings: *Cast of Wonders* and *Grimdark Magazine*.

* FILE UNDER: *Haunted Hot Spring*

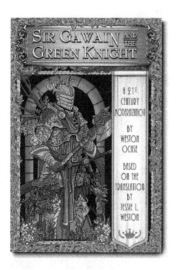

FASTEN YOUR

SAFETY BELTS...

NEXT STOP:

ASIA

HAUNTED ASIA

KAZAKHSTAN

BEKAA VALLEY, LEBANON

KABUL, AFGHANISTAN

NORTHWEST

TOKYO, JAPAN

LHASA (TIBET), CHINA

NAKHON SAWAN, THAILAND

MANILA, PHILIPPINES

BANGALORE (KARNATAKA), INDIA

SINGAPORE

SOUTHEAST

MALANG (EAST JAVA), INDONESIA

0 100 200 300 400 500
Miles

ASIA

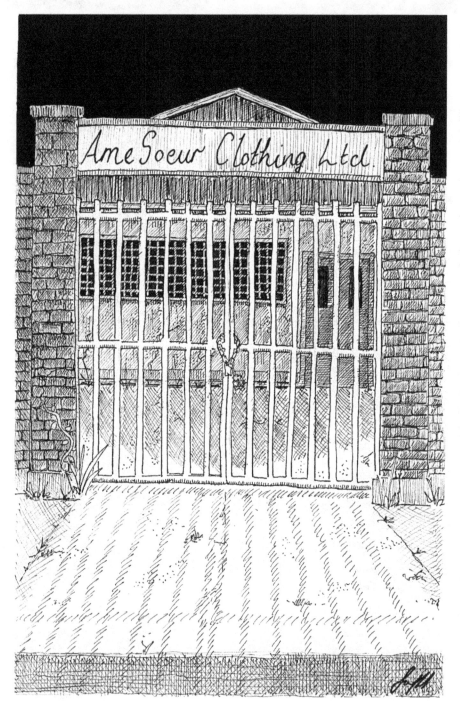

For years, I'd heard about the noises that
came out of the abandoned property . . .

SOUL SISTERS

STRUCTURE TYPE: CLOTHING FACTORY
LOCATION: MANILA, PHILIPPINES
LAT./ LONG: 14.4389° N, 121.0242° E
BUILT: CIRCA 1987
GROUND ELEVATION: 115 FT. (35 M.)
WRITTEN BY: MICHELLE TANG

TRAVEL GUIDE NOTES

DEATH AND GRIEF may cause us to do strange things, to act irrationally or disobey rules we've previously observed. So it is for Rosie, mourning the death of her newborn child, as she travels back to a family-run clothing factory, closed since her girlhood. What lies inside may haunt still, but there's a certain healing that might also be found when facing the ghosts of our past.

This is a story I selected from the open submission call, and the more times I read it, the more I enjoy it. Philippines-native Michelle Tang writes with a heartfelt sincerity in exploring the relationship of family, friends, and tragedy. She told me that the setting of this story comes from her own childhood, so perhaps that is why it feels so resonant. And perhaps it matters not when the bond of loved ones is concerned, and the difference between life and afterlife is negligible for "Soul Sisters."

—Charlatan Bardot

THE AME-SOEUR CLOTHING FACTORY ON 437
Buencamino Road was well-known to the locals, who gave it a
wide berth. For years, I'd heard about the noises that came out of
the abandoned property, had begged to return, but my father always
forbade me.

Now, in the dead of night on a week my family was distracted by the
mourning I should have been part of, I'd stolen away.

I drove slowly for some time, trying to fit my memories of the
neighborhood to the sights outside my car windows, but everything had
grown and changed in a decade. Then dull metal numbers rusting on a
crumbling brick column caught my eye—I'd arrived. One of the keys I'd
stolen unlocked the massive gate door, and I got out to swing it wide open
so I could drive my Camry inside.

I stared at the clothing factory everyone had whispered about for years.
The squat, two-room structure with a single long window looked too small to
fit the four industrial sewing machines and women it had contained, too small
for me to have played happily beneath legs and around packed boxes.
Desiccated weeds grew around the cement building; they stuck out in the
space between floor and wall like reaching arms. The white adobe walls had
grayed in the last fifteen years: they were marred with cracks, and weathered like
my mother's headstone I dutifully visited with my father. My father's office was
attached to the building, an office he still frequented several times a year to store
important paperwork, and I knew that he also sent servants over once in a
while to maintain the grounds. As I shut the gate door behind my car, my eyes
scanned for movement, but nobody stayed on the property overnight.

Once, the factory door had been painted as white as the walls, so close
in color a visitor might not notice the door at all. Now it was rusted red and
pocked with age. The second key in the ring resisted turning in the lock, and
I wondered if there'd been another one I should have stolen from my
father's desk. I twisted the key hard with both hands. The tumbler turned,
grudging and slow.

A glimmer of doubt poked through the grief inside me, but I'd come
this far, and pulled the door open anyway. Its hinges shrieked loud in the
quiet night and set some of the dogs on the street to barking. I held my
breath and stepped inside the dark factory.

I gripped the flashlight I usually kept in the car, and under its weak
beam, I found the light switch I once could barely reach. For a moment,
nothing happened, and I thought of my father's office, which must still have
electricity. My breath came quicker in this place of shadows and silence—

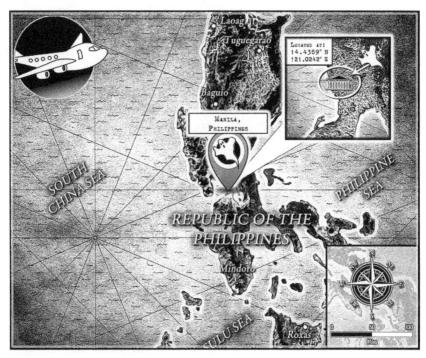

HAUNTED MANILA, PHILIPPINES

for a strange moment I expected to see a cloud escape from my nostrils as I exhaled, as though I were someplace cold, instead of Manila in the middle of the dry season.

The fluorescent lightbulbs suspended overhead within metal cages flickered for a few seconds before they began to buzz like the mosquitoes outside. I'd expected the factory to be empty. Cleaned out and hollow, like I was. But the sewing machines remained, curved metal beasts that screwed onto individual tables, which were themselves bolted onto the ancient linoleum floor. The sole window was covered, obstructed by the large air conditioning unit I'd convinced my father to buy for the factory women. After so many years, I'd forgotten about the air-con, the blunt, heavy appliance that three of the women couldn't lift on their own. They had tried, giggling, even Ate Mina cracking a rare smile as the dark brown cube wobbled between them. It took Celeste, whose shoulders were as wide as my father's and her forearms even thicker, to cram it into the open window. With the air-con in place, the room had seemed darker, but the fluorescent lights had always been bright enough.

I made my way past the dust-covered machines, silent and brooding things, bent over like Rodin's *Thinker*, and came to Sienna's station. A cramp overtook me then, the present intruding on the past, and I slumped onto her high wooden stool. I pressed my hands on my stomach and took deep breaths, stared past my swollen legs, at the old flip-flops I had worn in the hospital. Sienna used to perch on this seat like a graceful heron—one foot hooked onto the rung, and the other stretched long and straight to reach the machine pedal. I'd squatted beneath the table as her slender brown foot pressed and released the pedal, waited for the vibrating rumble of her machine in response, and pretended she was driving us to one of the places in her stories.

The pain in my abdomen eased. I released the memory as my fingers slid inside the small, empty gap between table and machine where I used to leave Sienna messages. The gesture was an old habit from my childhood, but it brought me a moment of comfort. I'd handwritten the notes carefully in broken English I learned in school.

"I am here," meant that I was waiting outside for her to come out and play; "I watch Sienna," told her I was peeking at her from a hidden location that she had to discover; "I love you." As an adult, my cheeks burned to think of how I must have annoyed the poor girl, only a handful of years older than I was, how tiresome she must have found me when she had sewing to do. And yet she'd never shown me anything but warm patience, a feeling I mistook for her love. In a childhood without a mother, I had found another to take her place, whether Sienna wanted to or not.

The air was almost as I'd remembered: thicker than the air outside, and smelling of clean linen with a sour note of iron. Only the paint smell had faded. I wandered to the narrow doorway which led to the tiny second room, where they'd done the silk-screening. The long table still filled the space; they'd cleaned out the material and boxes in the sewing room, but had left the merchandise in here untouched. A mound of blank tee-shirts still waited to be silk-screened at one end of the table. Near the door, individually packaged shirts were piled for delivery. The tags sewn inside the shirts had "Ame-Soeur Clothing, Ltd." sewn in black thread on it, a name my mother had chosen when she'd first started the company with my father. My father always told me that they were soulmates, that she'd thought the French translation sounded classy and sweet. Boxes and paint cans were stacked deep and shoulder-high around all four walls, blocking the other doorway outside. I'd grown up watching the women pour vivid colors, one at a time, into different silkscreen frames. The squeegee blade transformed the dollop of paint into an even, smooth sheet. When the box was lifted, the plain shirt had been tattooed with bright designs, like magic.

Suddenly a rattle of heavy machinery thundered from the next room.

I jerked and whirled around, but the sound had already stopped. I'd closed the gate once I parked. Who else would come to this desolate place, at this time of night? I strained my ears while I positioned my keys between my closed, sweaty fingers, in case I needed a weapon. I edged toward the doorway, as close to the wall as the paint cans and boxes allowed. The noise rumbled again, louder and longer. So loud the floor beneath my flip-flops shook. The sewing machines, all of them, by the sounds of it, were running.

There must be an easy explanation for this. Maybe there'd been an electrical surge when I turned on the lights that set their engines humming. My shoulders were hunched so close to my ears that they ached. Staccato mechanical sounds filled the air next, like four clacking typewriters. The machines were not just idling from some surge; the sewing needles, long and sharp, were stabbing downward, hungry for cloth to pierce. Only pressure on their foot pedals could control them.

I clenched my eyes shut. Sweat trickled down my temples into the clothing I'd worn for days. My father had always dismissed the rumors of the factory being haunted as old wives' tales. *And yet he never let me come back.* I huddled in the dark of the silk-screen room, unable to see who was working the machines.

Faint voices spoke. They grew louder as I listened, until I could make out the words. Another cramp took hold of me, but I was no longer sure if the pain was from my recent loss or my memories. I knew those voices. Their faces came back to me, faces I had known since I was a toddler: Mina's, stern and drawn; Celeste's, round and pretty; Rochelle, pale and heavy-browed. A soft voice sang, audible over the jokes and huffs of laughter, even over the engine thrums of the sewing machines. It was a voice I used to fall asleep to as a child, curled against a thin, warm body. It sang the same song I used to sing as I rubbed my recently-swollen belly.

For a moment, I wondered if my father had lied to me, if the women had survived and continued to sew in this space. I shook my head. My father would never do that to me. I myself had seen the emptiness of the room. I made the sign of the cross and mouthed a short prayer. Why, then, would the spirits of these women remain, so long after the accident? What had happened here? Why had I fled the cloying support of my home to come here tonight?

The worst had already happened to me. Nothing from this world or the next could inflict more pain than I already carried. Still, I steeled myself before I stepped from the shadows of the silk-screen room into the doorway. The machines and voices stopped, the needles slowing in their vertical paths until they stilled. The air was rife with unsaid words and invisible movements. I shuffled toward the middle of the room. I closed my eyes, my heart hammering, and pictured the women again. Ates Mina, Celeste, Rochelle. Ate Sienna. They sat at each of their stations, laughing and teasing each other, as their feet tapped the pedals, as swathes of material passed through their fingers.

A chill breeze whooshed over my sweat-dampened skin, and I spun to look behind me. The air-con, fifteen years old and yet barely used, was running. I shivered and went to turn it off, but the knob was already turned to zero. My fingers traced the cord along its length, gritty with dust, until I came to the end—the end, which came freely to my hand, unplugged.

The room filled with a foul stench, and my head swam. I leaned on the sewing tables as I rushed to the door, desperate for fresh air. I pushed against the door—it didn't budge. I heaved a shoulder against the rough metal as toxic fumes filled my lungs. Memories flashed behind my heavy eyelids. Me, playing alone outside my father's office, waiting for Sienna to find my note. The afternoon sun scorched my shoulders and the top of my head. My father yelled at me to move away from the delivery truck, which backed up in its own diesel exhaust to pick up the boxes of clothing for distribution. The driver had been a stranger. He parked the truck in front of the factory door and jumped down to speak to my father in his office.

I'd waited for the new man to come out, to tell him he didn't park in the right spot. He had taken so long, bombarding my father with questions. The rubber of my shoes stuck on the burning pavement, and the turon I'd brought for the seamstresses were wilting in the heat. My awareness that something was wrong arrived too slow. The sewing machines had fallen silent, replaced by the steady chugging from the truck engine. The metal door of the factory was ajar, pressed against the back of delivery truck. One woman screamed, or perhaps no one had.

"Daddy!" I'd shouted. "Help!"

I'd run to the crack in the door. The room was full of thick, filthy exhaust. Ates Celeste and Rochelle had pushed against the door, trying to get free, or to breathe in some clean air, perhaps. They'd collapsed on the floor. I'd squeezed my young body inside, the metal edges of both door and doorway scraping painfully across my torso. The cloudy air was so foul, I could barely stand. Inside, I'd crawled toward the window.

Sienna and Mina lay beneath the new air-con I'd convinced my father to buy them. It was jammed tight in the window sill, too heavy and too high to move. The women weren't breathing.

The air cleared, and I took in gasping breaths. I blinked my eyes open to see the cleaned-out factory once more. The memory was over a decade old, but my realization brought me to my knees. I was wrong in thinking I couldn't feel worse. Not just my daughter's life I'd failed, but four more. I curled into a fetal position, like the last sonogram I'd seen of my daughter. I pounded the grimy floor with my fists and screamed until I choked on tears and dirt. The sewing machines began to roar again—the floors shook beneath me, oddly soothing. The needles clacked sharp and irregular on the receiving plates. The fit passed, and I took in a hitching breath.

"I'm so sorry," I said, over the rumble and clicks of the machines. "I didn't realize until now. It wasn't an accident, it was my fault. If I hadn't made my father buy the air-con, if I had told the truck driver to move right away . . . I deserved to lose Sienna. That's what I named my daughter. Sienna."

The rest of my words tangled up with the tears in my throat. Guilt and grief carved my insides out, created a hole so cavernous that I was made of nothing more than skin and regret. I collapsed on the tile, blinked bleary eyes at the fluorescent lights, which blurred and stretched like bright ghosts above me.

Let me stay here, please, until my life is gone too. My abdomen cramped again, and I closed my eyes, let the vibrating ground beneath my shoulder blades lull me to sleep, and the clacking needles were like a lullaby.

Their voices woke me, but I kept my eyes shut. Whatever magic worked to bring these women back made them disappear when I looked for them, so I pretended to sleep. My heart filled to hear their voices, warm with concern for me.

"Oh, bata," Ate Mina's voice said. "Always so dramatic."

"Hush, Mina," I imagined Ate Celeste's wide hands over her thick hips. "She's just lost her child."

"Why did she come back here, after so many years?"

"She has no mother. She runs to the last place she had one."

"Kawawa naman." Pity filled their voices. Pity and pain, but no anger.

Something brushed the hair away from my face. Sienna's voice, and I could not mistake the love it carried. "Rest now, Rosie. You sleep, and when you wake up, you will feel better."

I slept while their voices chattered around me, as I used to when I was a young girl, lying on heaps of unsewn material.

I awoke to a silent room, only the unplugged air-con still humming. The grime on the window was too thick to see, but I knew the sun had risen by the sunlight that shone in from beneath the metal door. Amid the dirt smeared into mud by my tears, there lay a small note, written in a childish script. I pushed my aching body upright and picked up the slip of paper.

I am here. I traced my finger over the pink roses on the stationary I once cherished, the familiar block letters that filled my old diaries at home. It was one of the notes I'd written for Ate Sienna, many years ago.

Near her station, another piece of paper fluttered on the ground, like butterfly wings, in the breeze of the air-con. I forced my legs to take my weight, stooped like an old woman to pick up the note. *I love you.*

Sienna's machine rumbled at me. My knees shook as I slid onto her stool. Tucked beneath the space that was empty last night, she'd left a last note. *I watch Sienna.*

Something released inside me. The pain and guilt would always be there, but perhaps it would fade after tonight. I pushed open the metal door of the Ame-Soeur Clothing factory, which squeaked but opened easily, and strode out into the bright day. My family was surely worried sick about me. I thought about family then, about how four friends might become soul-sisters, with bonds that grew stronger throughout their lives—and remained strong through death.

Before I started the car, I lowered my window and listened to the noises coming from the abandoned building: women laughed and cooed, and a familiar voice sang a lullaby I knew all too well. From inside the clothing factory, a baby burbled.

Did You Know?

MICHELLE TANG writes speculative fiction in Canada, where she lives with her partner and two children. Her short stories have been published in several anthologies, including *Terrifying Ghosts* (forthcoming), *Night Terrors Vol. 2*, and *Once Upon an Enchanted Forest*. Michelle's mother owned a tiny clothing factory in Manila, which inspired the setting for this story. When she isn't writing, Michelle enjoys video games, horror movies, and taking naps.

AL MUTAQADIMAH (THE BEGINNING)

BY SARA SAAB

FALLEN crab apples blanket the terrace, but there's not a tree in sight. Walkway parched and bonelike. A stroll around the perimeter reveals no entrance. Saffron cobs of poison arum stab out from the earth beneath the skirting boards, as though the structure were a source of moisture. No doors— but there is a solitary window. Between its filigreed bars and behind its immaculate glass, a bowled sink, mossy as a terrarium. Beyond, the only visible furniture in a cavernous interior: an intensely spotlit

The beginning of the end

gramophone soundlessly spinning a Fairuz record. Above this window, the hand-painted sign is in Arabic, and still clings on. *The beginning of the end*, it says. *Ya leil, oh woe, oh woe.*

SARA SAAB was born in Beirut, Lebanon, and now lives in North London. Her fiction has appeared in *Clarkesworld*, *Shimmer*, *The White Review*, and elsewhere.

* FILE UNDER: *Haunted Entryless Room*

. . . all of that was daylight logic, and the RSJ Katrijn,
like all dead places, only obeyed the rules of night.

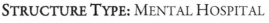
FOOLS RUSH IN

FEATURE ENTRY 7

STRUCTURE TYPE: MENTAL HOSPITAL
LOCATION: MALANG (EAST JAVA), INDONESIA
LAT./ LONG: 7.9475° S, 112.5983° E
BUILT: CIRCA 1864
GROUND ELEVATION: 1,677 FT. (511 M.)
WRITTEN BY: NADIA BULKIN

TRAVEL GUIDE NOTES

IN AN ANTHOLOGY of haunted buildings, a Mental Hospital (read: *Insane Asylum*) seems the archetypical go-to structure for tales of insanity, torture, and other gruesome horror, yet author Nadia Bulkin is not one to rely upon such tropes.

A mental hospital is a place of anguish, certainly, but also of potential healing. A broad, swinging balance between trauma and hope and all the unexpected peculiarities that lay in between. A place where things imagined have greater footing to breach reality, more so than any other site. There is much to explore, not only within the structure, but within the mind.

So indeed the haunting is here, but so too is setting and history. So too are the characters, ghost hunters facing guilt and certain amends. So too is Nadia's resonant writing, as eloquent, melancholy, and—most of all—relatable. Who among us would not dread publicly to face a past shame? In Indonesia, ghosts of all sorts may abound, especially those found when "Fools Rush In."

—**Charlatan Bardot**

T HE TAXI PULLED UP OUTSIDE THE GRAFFITI-COVERED
walls of RSJ Katrijn's main administrative building sooner than Leo
would have liked. Despite being Dutch, the RSJ Katrijn had that
bastardized "Indies" look—the enormous pyramidal roof that sat like an
oversized farmer's hat over two tall shadowy stories, the thousands of
sunbaked terracotta shingles piled on top of white European columns, the
enormous windows with plantation-style shutters. As if it had dreamt of
being a royal pavilion instead of a mental hospital, back when it was alive.

It occurred to Leo that those person-sized windows made the hospital
look like one of those giant mountain-dwelling moths. He'd only seen them
in high school science textbooks and on field trips to the National Museum,
so he didn't know anything about these moths except that they disguised
their paper-thin fragility with bright yellow eye-spots, the better to look like
the wide-awake face of a carnivorous bird.

Past the front gate, a paved driveway led up off the road straight to the
front doors of the hospital to allow for more convenient drop-off and pick-
up of patients, had there still been patients. The three other surviving
alumni of the Haunted Hospital episode of *The World Beyond* stood
waiting by the doors, almost like dutiful nurses. The gate was only semi-
functional—mostly decorative, if Leo remembered correctly—but the taxi
driver clearly did not want to get any closer to the beast, and simply grunted
the fare.

He couldn't blame the man. The RSJ Katrijn, which had stood empty
since the 1950s, was like one of those infected rotting animals that even the
vultures wouldn't touch. There had been a brief attempt at "reclaiming" the
building after chasing the Dutch out, as a mental hospital or whatever else
would take, but nothing stuck. No one wanted to be there—not doctors nor
bureaucrats nor construction workers. Bad vibes. Cursed. He suspected that
these vibes only got worse as it decayed, as more and more of its paint finish
and roof tiles slipped off like skin.

As he thumbed through his wallet and handed over the cash, Leo felt a
deep desire to tell the taxi driver why he was there—the sad story about
Rizal's motorcycle accident, the shame he had carried since that disastrous
episode of *The World Beyond* in which he had spoken the terrible lie for the
first time—but the old man just counted his money in silence and waited
for him to get out. As if he already knew.

In Leo's most anxious nightmares, everyone in the world already
knew—his parents, his friends, the guy he bought bakso from, every woman
he might possibly be interested in, every single person he met on every single

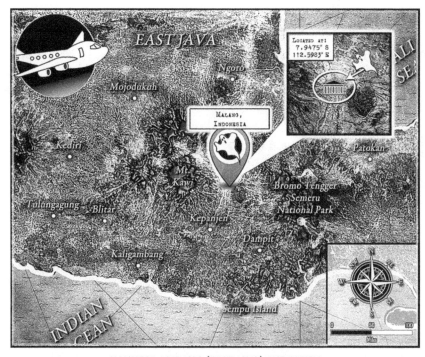

Located at:
7.9475° S
112.5983° E

MALANG,
INDONESIA

HAUNTED MALANG (EAST JAVA), INDONESIA

production set. When he was awake, he sometimes tried to trick himself into believing that if he just told the truth about what happened that night, the only thing that would follow would be a wash of relief. Everyone would understand. No one would be angry. But his dreams confirmed that this was delusion. Because in sleep-world, everyone always reacted with a disgust that felt not only real, but deserved.

THE OTHERS HAILED him through the gate with stiff puppet arms. He tucked his head down while squeezing through an opening in the gate. When they were filming *The World Beyond* last year, it was at this very boundary crossing that he'd first started feeling sick. But, Leo told himself, surely his tolerance for frightening situations had improved since then. Since appearing on *The World Beyond,* fearlessness had become part of his persona. He competed on daredevil reality shows, interviewed supposed murderers, was in an energy drink commercial where he faked jumping out of an airplane. He was Fearless Leo now. He could go inside.

The last time he walked up this driveway, a production crew had been waiting for him at the other end. Lights, cameras, cigarette butts. There was their guide, a supposed groundskeeper who walked them through the empty halls and pointed out rooms and stairwells where ghosts had been spotted. Leo was pretty sure that guy turned out to be an actor—he'd seen him since, in a toothpaste commercial. All this fakery should have made him feel calmer about having faked the completion of his assigned dare—but in the dark, it didn't.

This time, there were only these three of his former castmates. Yudhi, who had to try to summon the ghost of the hospital administrator with a Ouija board. Poppy, who had to sit in the infirmary for six hours. Those two had apparently started dating, as well as gotten nicer clothes and slicker haircuts. Then there was the other girl—Astrid—who'd quit in the middle of her attempt to channel the spirit of a Dutch soldier who'd been quartered at the hospital during World War II. She had not received any share of the prize money and, accordingly, had clearly not updated her "night market grunge" wardrobe.

"It's been a while," Leo said. "So, what's going on?"

The three of them looked at each other, exchanging one too many glances for Leo's comfort. The invitation for a reunion had come from Yudhi, but Leo had the distinct impression now that the other three had planned it without him. He tried to shake off his whispering suspicions. He hadn't exactly made an effort to stay in touch. Eventually, Yudhi answered: "Poppy's sick."

Leo glanced at slight, demure Poppy, dressed in delicate white cotton that made him think, instantly, of a burial shroud. The sort of burial shroud that would have been used when carting away dead patients in the middle of the night. There was a morgue on the premises, wasn't there? Yes, in one of the tiny bungalows set behind the main hospital building—where the servant quarters would be, if an extremely stupid rich family decided to turn this place into a mansion. He remembered because Rizal had to do his dare in there: sit in the morgue alone in radio silence for thirty minutes. "Sick with what?"

"They're not sure," Poppy said, quietly. "Something about my lungs."

"See, with what happened to Rizal . . . and now Poppy . . . " Yudhi squeezed the girl's arm. "We felt like we needed to ask for closure from this place. Forgiveness, you know. Since we got paid to do a stupid reality TV show here without paying it proper respect." Astrid cleared her throat pointedly. "Okay, not all of us. But we all took part in using the hospital for entertainment."

Leo wanted to protest that filming *The World Beyond* had not been very *entertaining* for any of them—he couldn't sleep without drugs for six months afterward—and that it wasn't on them to beg forgiveness from dead Dutch psych doctors. Why should *they* apologize for disturbing ghosts who shouldn't have been here in the first place? Why should *they* apologize for bastardizing a colonial building that had been built on *their* land, without *their* consent?

But just thinking this way made him queasy. Don't tempt fate, as his mother would say. As if by telling his younger siblings some bullshit story about a ghost in a grocery store, he would actually *make* the store haunted. It didn't make sense in the daylight, and certainly not to visiting Australians who wanted to hear ghost stories. But the spirit world didn't operate by the rules of daylight. That was his mother's whole point.

"Good idea," he said, and Yudhi nodded curtly before shoving open the front door.

INSIDE, THE WALLS of the hospital were still covered in graffiti, the floor now caked in even more dirt. The damp smell of mildew and undead weeds was even stronger than before. But what had felt a bit like a spooky film set last time—he suspected the red *DEVIL* tag that they spent a lot of time filming might have been made by one of the crew—now bore a still, suffocating weight.

"Smells horrible," Leo mumbled, before a wooden groan and a drop into darkness nearly lifted him clean out of his body. Flashlights came on, and out of the corner of his eye he saw Astrid moving away from the now-closed front door, sending him a long, shadowed stare. *Come on, Leo*, he thought to himself. *Toughen up.*

They arranged themselves in a square in the center of what had been, many decades ago, the hospital's lobby—now marked by little more than holes in the floor where the registration desk had once stood. Yudhi took a piece of paper out of his jacket pocket, then cleared his throat and began to read.

Leo would have expected a ritual of closure to invoke words like "peace" and "acceptance" and "gratitude." Yudhi's ritual was filled with words like "ask" and "speak" and "awaken." A breeze whistled through the barely-open windows, as if answering an invitation. Leo started getting twitchy, which seemed like the opposite of what this ritual was supposed to accomplish.

"You sure that's the right ritual?" The three of them stared at him indignantly. "It just doesn't sound very ... you know ... final."

"It's the right ritual," Yudhi said.

After Yudhi finished reading, they listened to the RSJ Katrijn for a response. Somewhere in the building—down the hallway, on the second floor?—there was a loud bang. Like a door closing? Like a beam falling? Or maybe the hospital's jaw snapping open. What if this place came tumbling down right onto their heads? No one cared to keep these old colonial buildings from succumbing to the decay that they were due.

"So that's it?" Leo said, anxious to be out of the building. "Because I've got to catch a flight, I have an audition on Monday . . . "

"Oh, shut up about your stupid auditions, Leo," Astrid snapped. "You're a good actor, I bet you can just walk on set and get the part."

Her irritation was so palpable, and so sudden, that it rocked him back on his heels. He tried to be flippant about it—"calm down, Astrid"—but that was only sandpaper he was using to file down the anxiety in his heart. It scared him even more to see that neither Yudhi nor Poppy appeared surprised by Astrid's outburst. Poppy sympathetically rubbed Astrid's arm, and Yudhi raised his index finger to warn Leo, "Don't play dumb," followed by the words he had hoped never to hear from any of his former castmates: "We know that you didn't actually do your dare."

Leo's ears plugged as the air pressure suddenly shifted, as if he'd been transported to a great height and was now on the brink of falling. The other three all started shouting at once, creating a cacophony of anger that went rippling down the empty hallways of the RSJ Katrijn like a tidal wave. "Producer told us . . . " "You cursed us . . . " "So selfish . . . " "Why didn't you just quit?"

Why hadn't he just quit? It was partly about the money. After Astrid quit, his share of the prize went up by twenty-five million rupiah. But it was mostly because he could not fathom admitting on camera, on television, for the entire world to see, that this place and all its goddamned Dutch ghosts still had that much power over a local kid who had more right to this land— it was literally in the national anthem, *the land where I shed my blood*—than all those ghosts combined.

"Now look what's happening!" Yudhi was yelling like a cleric. "Rizal gets smashed up in traffic! Poppy's never been sick a day in her life before this!" He looked at his beloved with that bulldozer determination, the look of a man who had already made up his mind. Poppy averted her gaze in polite sadness. "And it's all your fault, Leo! It's all because of you!"

NOW LEO UNDERSTOOD why they looked so sick—all of them, not just Poppy. They all thought they were going to *(die)*. He clapped his hand over his mouth as soon as the thought occurred to him, trying to keep it inside his head and out of the hospital's reach—a pointless exercise, since he was already inside the RSJ Katrijn. He was breathing the hospital. The hospital was breathing him.

"You need to go do the dare again," Yudhi was saying. "For real this time."

His brain wanted to say no. His brain wanted to say: I didn't create a curse and the hospital isn't haunted and I'm not going to go up to a rickety second floor and shut myself in a room for half an hour just because you see a connection that isn't there. Even though all of that was daylight logic, and the RSJ Katrijn, like all dead places, only obeyed the rules of night.

Instead, he said: "Okay. Okay. I'll do it."

They argued about whether he needed to wear a camera. Astrid worried that they needed to *exactly* replicate the conditions of the original dare; Yudhi said there was no point. But they agreed that he couldn't take his phone. "How will I know when it's been thirty minutes?" he asked, and Yudhi lent him his watch, because it had a stopwatch on it. Nice of him.

"So you'll know exactly when you can run back downstairs," Yudhi said, in a tone of voice that was not-so-nice.

They repeatedly and painstakingly reminded him of the dare's specifics. "Take it seriously," they begged, "say it like you mean it." No doubt they were afraid that he would screw it up again, but if they only knew how many times he had kneaded over these instructions in the months that had passed since they were last at the hospital. He sometimes woke at 5 a.m., yelling "Using your phone is not allowed!" at what he thought were his fellow contestants crowding the bedroom doorway, though they only ever turned out to be shadows.

Astrid gave him her flashlight. Then he went down the main hallway and up the stairs to his left. He had not needed to ask for directions; his legs carried him through the hospital's innards as if entranced, as if they had been waiting for months to return him to the room in question. He wondered if he was going back into an abandoned mental patients' ward because he was actually insane, and because his body knew—on a subconscious level—that he really did need help.

He went halfway down the upstairs hallway until he reached one of the few rooms that still had a door. It still had a door, the groundskeeper had explained, because even the vandals knew they had to keep the room's unspecified "evil" inside. He gave the door a gentle, creaky push, and slipped inside without lifting his flashlight to look where he was going. He closed the door behind him without letting himself think about it. The last time he tried to do this dare, he hadn't closed it. That was how he'd failed. Well, that and running out of the room ten minutes early.

He squatted in the dark until he found the floor, then sat, then lay down. He shifted onto his back, holding his muscles so tightly that he would surely pay for it tomorrow, and then said out loud, "Please, doctor, help me." He repeated it twice, as the dare instructed. Then he set Yudhi's stopwatch to thirty minutes, and aimed Astrid's flashlight toward the ceiling. Here was his chance to be the Fearless Leo he was always claiming to be.

Memories of his aborted attempt to complete this dare snuck into his head unbidden—the black shadows he had seen creep across the ceiling, the disembodied voices he'd heard humming like mosquitoes around his head, the electric certainty that if he didn't get out right that *instant* he would vomit and then who knows, maybe die?—and he ferociously batted them away.

Time ticked by.

He wondered if the ghosts of the hospital staff would even recognize this country anymore. But then who was to say they'd recognize Amsterdam? He knew friends who'd gone to visit, posing with fake-looking tulips, making funny faces in front of big dark museums, giggling at the windows of the red-light district. Maybe that was why these old colonist ghosts stayed in places like the RSJ Katrijn. Dripping, decrepit places where they could make believe they were still sitting in the gilded thrones of their own empire.

Yudhi's stopwatch went off.

Nothing had appeared. No figure—Dutch or otherwise—no orb, no mysteriously moving object. The room was quiet save for his breathing. So that was it? Instantly, feeling returned to parts of his body that had spent the last half-hour in a sort of stasis—his heart started pounding, his lungs started inflating. He was alive. They were dead and gone, and he was alive.

He scrambled to his feet, pulled the door open without too much of a fuss, and started hurrying—joyously—back to the stairs, chuckling this time at the graffiti the flashlight caught on the walls. This was going to be a hilarious story to tell his future children, to teach them not to let the fear of the past consume their present, to walk bravely into the future.

And then his foot didn't hit a step where it should have. What had seemed at first to be an orderly descent turned with alarming suddenness into chaos—the flashlight went flying, his kneecaps thumped against sharp ceramic edges, his hands slapped against an ever-sliding wall, and he managed to think to himself "not the head" but not quite fast enough to shield his skull.

THE OTHERS HEARD a crash, muffled by distance and concrete, and then found Leo's crumpled body at the bottom of the same stairs he'd gone up thirty-five minutes prior. Yudhi's flashlight lit up the twisted face first; he swore and turned the beam away.

"Do you think he did the dare?" Poppy asked. "I mean, before he died."

Astrid gave her a sharp glare. "He was coming downstairs, wasn't he?"

"He could have backed out again," Yudhi said. "We don't know."

Astrid shook her head. She reached down for the flashlight that had rolled to a stop next to poor, dead, foolish Leo and gave it a whack to turn it back on. The idiot should have just followed her lead while they were filming and quit when he got scared. The dares they had to do on *The World Beyond* were risky beyond reason—maybe not physically, but psychically. No one would have blamed him. "No," she said, "I think he did it."

"So we're safe?" Yudhi gently put his hand on Poppy's back, as if he was one of her baffled doctors listening with a stethoscope. "We're okay?"

Poppy put her hand to her sternum and took a big, raggedy breath. "I do feel better. I think."

"Alhamdulillah," said Yudhi, and knelt down to take his watch back.

They made their way out of the hospital and back to the car, taking their time now that the building felt less menacing. They could hear the sounds of the living again—engines sputtering, horns squawking, even the sunset call to prayer. The hospital had been defanged. They were free.

Poppy was tired, and needed to stretch out in the backseat. Meanwhile Astrid had to hop back out of the car to push open the front gate, and as she did so, she took what she hoped would be her last look at the RSJ Katrijn. Its enormous windows, she realized, look like the eye-spots of a giant moth.

"We should tell somebody," Astrid said, when she got back in the car. "Like his family."

"We will, we will," Yudhi said.

From the backseat, Poppy coughed.

Did You Know?

NADIA BULKIN is the author of the short story collection *She Said Destroy* (Word Horde, 2017). She has been nominated for the Shirley Jackson Award five times. She grew up in Jakarta, Indonesia with her Javanese father and American mother, before relocating to Lincoln, Nebraska. She has two political science degrees and lives in Washington, D.C.

CAFÉ TANUKI

BY UMIYURI KATSUYAMA
TRANSLATED BY TOSHIYA KAMEI

ONE evening, a Tokyoite passed an out-of-business café he'd once frequented. Unexpectedly, it seemed reopened. Lured by the lights seeping from inside, he stepped in. A peculiar smell stung his nose. He gave his order to an unfamiliar waiter and took a seat. When he sipped from his cup, it was mud. Startled, he left a 1,000-yen banknote and left.

A few days later, he bumped into the former proprietor of the café in a bookstore. He recounted the incident to him.

Café Tanuki: open, even while closed

"Not again," the proprietor said and cursed under his breath. "Must be a tanuki," he added, handing his former customer 1,000 yen.

UMIYURI KATSUYAMA is a multiple-award-winning writer of fantasy and horror, often based on Asian folklore motifs. Her most recent novel, *Chuushi, ayashii nabe to tabi wo suru*, was published in 2018.

* FILE UNDER: *Haunted Café*

THE HIDDEN TEMPLE OF NAKHON SAWAN

BY RENA MASON

The appropriately-named "vile temple"

THE secret sect of Thai monks who'd buried and guarded it called it Wat Chặw Rāy, because it was a most vile temple.

Arthit prayed on his watch, and his voice crescendoed as he approached. At the end of the *ubosot*, on a black altar, sat the life-sized blasphemy carved from a substance so dark, staring at it caused madness. Priceless red rubies floated in the effigy's orbits. Arthit dared nothing more than a glance at the gems. The last guard to gaze upon them gouged his eyes out and swallowed them whole. Glimpsing nothing disturbed, he raised his saffron robe to break his look and hurried away.

A low rumble and the soft grinding of stone sounded behind him.

RENA MASON is an American author of Thai-Chinese descent, and the Bram Stoker Award® winner of *The Evolutionist*, and "The Devil's Throat" as well as a 2014 Stage 32/The Blood List Search for New Blood Quarter-Finalist. Her horror fiction often mashes genres. For more information, visit her website or follow her at: www.RenaMason.Ink; Twitter: @RenaMason88; Facebook: www.facebook.com/rena.mason.

* FILE UNDER: *Haunted Temple*

. . . in there it's a shared experience where they
saw and lived many different deaths.

BLOOD MEMORIES

FEATURE
ENTRY 8

STRUCTURE TYPE: TANK MONUMENT
LOCATION: KABUL, AFGHANISTAN
LAT./ LONG: 34.5452° N, 69.2000° E
BUILT: CIRCA 1980
GROUND ELEVATION: 5,886 FT. (1,794 M.)
WRITTEN BY: WESTON OCHSE

TRAVEL GUIDE NOTES

ONE OF THE most ethnically-diverse nations on the planet, Afghanistan is also one of the most war-torn (currently leading that bleak list) due to geographic position, religious differences, political strife, and a litany of other claims and cultural-economic factors. So is it any surprise that its land should be filled with hauntings? It's nickname, after all, *is* "The Graveyard of Empires."

Multiple award-winning author Weston Ochse draws on his own military experience in this next story, exploring the relic of—and what lays within—an abandoned tank-turned-monument to military perpetuation; for eyes that have seen too much are not reserved only for man.

Besides writing, Wes also happens to be a career soldier, and has lived and served several years in Afghanistan while in the U.S. Army fighting Taliban insurgents. Several of his best-selling novels revolve around military clashes and character studies in this region, contrasting the beauty of the country against warfare's obliteration.

He, and the inhabitants of this nation, and the buildings, and the land, and the shadowy things that reside amongst them all, each, surely, have their own "Blood Memories."

—Charlatan Bardot

FEW CITIES HAVE HAD AS HOARY A HISTORY AS KABUL, Afghanistan. From 709 BCE to the present, five countries have tried seven times to take the city, leaving behind the skeletal remains of their efforts. From siege engines to Enfield rifles to shattered airplanes to the most iconic mechanism of warfare, the desert sands have reclaimed the tank. Dead tanks surround the city, many of their rusted barrels still pointing at long forgotten targets in the neighborhoods of *Shash Darak*, *Wazir Akbar Khan*, *Sherpur*, and *Qala-e-Naj*. Brought to full stop not by other tanks or superior firepower, but Mujahedeen, supplied with rockets by a then-bully America.

It is to one of these that we go, where a young army specialist new to Afghanistan is trying to forget his fear. He and a woman are scrambling over an old T72 tank. Afghani taggers have painted the outside of the steel beast in various colors, creating a kaleidoscope of rust and lost dreams. The tracks have long since been dismantled, leaving spoked wheels to grip nothing but the polluted air of the capital of Afghanistan. The driver's hatch has been welded shut, but the top hatch still functions.

Around them is the hustle of Kabul. The sounds and stench of a capital city. Corollas and pickups roar back and forth along a nearby road. Women wearing blue-length burkas walk beside men in mostly traditional garb— long linen shirts and long pants ending at well-worn and workman-like sandals. Locals idle on the other side of the road watching the scene, cars flitting past, their hands inside their clothes.

Staff Sergeant Kelly stands atop the tank and stares into the shadows within and shudders. She can almost hear the screams, voices of the damned, as they shout and command to be let free, instead burned in a conflagration, unable to get out because of the machine gun fire trained on them. She's been in there before. She took the dare. She knows the ghosts remain and want to feed on the fear of others as they'd fed on hers. But the exchange was in her favor. No longer does she fear. No longer does the idea of a roadside bomb send her shivering into silence.

"Do you believe that this once rolled by the Red Square in a parade?" she asks her new subordinate, Specialist Sergio Montalvo.

"Like all of us. We parade real good. It's war that eats us up." He peers inside. "Are you sure this is a thing?"

"If you mean, spend the night and you'll no longer be scared, of course it's a thing. Everyone in the platoon has done it." She punches him in the shoulder. "You're not going to back down, are you?"

He glances back longingly at their armored SUV, then once again inside the old tank.

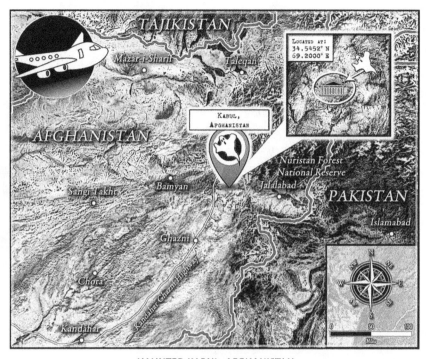

HAUNTED KABUL, AFGHANISTAN

"All I have to do is spend the night and my butt won't clench when we drive Massoud Circle, is that it?" He shakes his head. "Sounds pretty far-fetched."

"It's one hundred percent true. I didn't believe it either, but you've seen me. Do I act scared?"

He eyes her. He's seen her in action, running to the gate when they were under attack, rather than cowering in place like the rest of the knuckleheads. She knows he wants to be like her, but he's too macho to admit it. He can't let a mere girl be braver than he is.

His shoulders sag in defeat. "Fine. You pulling guard duty?"

"Yes, Monty. I'll be in the SUV to make sure the Taliban doesn't come and steal you."

He laughs self-consciously, then begins to climb inside.

She hands him a small mag flashlight, two bottles of water, and a bag of MREs. "Please don't piss in the tank. Use these," she says, gesturing to the water bottles.

He nods, takes one last look at the sky, then descends.

She lowers the heavy armored top of the hatch and latches it.

He could be banging on the hatch even now and she wouldn't hear it. She checks her watch. Almost seven at night. He has ten hours before sunrise. She'll use them to catch up on *Game of Thrones* on her laptop. She slides behind the wheel of the SUV, locks the doors, places her pistol on the passenger seat, and spends the next five hours watching Sansa being treated like shit and the Mother of Dragons gathering her army.

She eventually falls asleep.

At the crack of dawn, she gets out, relieves herself behind the SUV, then climbs atop the tank. She unlatches the hatch and lifts it with a grunt. "Up and at 'em, Monty. Time to go."

She hears nothing.

"No games. I want to get back for breakfast. I'm starved."

Still nothing.

She leans all the way inside. She sees that both of the water bottles have been drained of water and filled with urine. He'd eaten some of his MRE. But as for Monty, he is nowhere in sight.

"Shit. Shit. Shit. Shit. Shit."

How is she going to explain this to SFC Morrel? He's going to have her ass.

She checks again, this time climbing all the way inside.

No sign.

She has to come to terms. He's gone.

By the time she gets on her radio and calls in, the sun is up and the sounds of the city cause a constant hum in the background. Another SUV pulls up and SFC Morrel gets out of the passenger seat, full body armor, pistol in a holster on his chest.

Sgt. Doughtery climbs out from behind the wheel, similarly dressed.

They both saunter up to her, glancing at the tank as they come.

"Where is he?" Morrell asks.

"I told you. He's gone."

He offers a doubtful smile.

Doughtery rolls her eyes.

"Right. The joke's over, okay?"

SSG Kelly shifts her feet. "No joke. He's gone."

"What happened?" Morrell asks.

"Same as we always do. We bring the FNG here, lock him in, then pull him out the next morning."

"Did you leave him or fall asleep?" Morrell asks.

"I didn't go nowhere. And sure, I fell asleep. But the latch was as I left it. No one touched it."

Morrell stares at the tank for a long time, then kicks at the dirt. "Then we have a problem."

"What's going on, Sergeant?" Kelly asks.

"This happened once before," he says.

"You mean, someone going missing inside the tank?"

He nods.

SFC Morrell had been here going on two years, pulling back-to-back tours. He'd been the one to introduce the tank and its test to the rest of them, but he'd never once mentioned they could disappear.

She stares incredulously at him. "You knew this could happen and you didn't say anything?"

"I thought it was a one-off," he says. "I never thought it would happen again."

"Who'd it happen to?"

"Private Witner."

She remembers the name, but not the person. "I thought he was blown up by an IED."

"That's what we told his family so they could get closure and restitution. The truth is we never knew what happened to him." He shakes his head. "It was the right thing to do even if it was for the wrong reason. I don't want to have to do it again."

"How can we not?" she asks.

"Witner happened back when there were IEDs going off all the time. There hasn't been one in months and if we claim one, there's certainly going to be an investigation. Plus, I've been wondering if he's really gone."

"What does that mean?"

"Some of the others who've heard the screams say that Witner's voice is included. He's in there, but . . . not," he says, gesturing to the tank.

She's heard the screams as well. It was part of the process. You couldn't tell people the tank is haunted. They have to experience it for themselves. And everyone did. Most didn't want to talk about it, but in there it's a shared experience where they saw and lived many different deaths.

"Then I need to go in," she says. "If there's even a chance, I need to try and bring him back."

An hour later, she's inside the tank, the latch closed above her, an MRE and two bottles of water by her side. She has her phone, but in Afghanistan, she's only used it for taking pictures, listening to music, or using the flashlight app. She does this now, illuminating the darkness with a rectangle of bright light, revealing the inside of the tank. She's been in only once and vowed to never return. She sees many of the same claw marks on the inside, some her own, more since she'd been there. The dials and gauges had long since been broken or removed as souvenirs. Nothing works inside of the metal hulk except for the single hatch above her, now latched and impossible to open from the inside.

The reoccurring idea that something might happen outside to SFC Morrell and Sgt. Doughtery, and no would know she was there keeps rattling around her brain. Between the micro-moments of panic, she tries to center herself, listening to the silence, willing the sounds of a far past battle to surround her. She continues to listen as her eyes grow heavy and then she sleeps.

She wakes to the sound of a gunshot.

She immediately looks to the hatch, but there's nothing there.

The walls of the tank are too thick to be penetrated by anything less than a STABO round.

Another shot, this one behind her.

She turns awkwardly but sees nothing.

She grins.

The tank is playing with her.

"Bring it," she says.

Suddenly, the rattle of fire opens into a conflagration, gunshots as frequent as bees bursting from an angry hive. But there is no blood. There is no pain. Because this isn't her battle. She is just there as a witness. Her hands go to the metal, caressing the machine blindly. She feels the deformations from the explosion, along with the rivets and seams from the factory. The tank is not meant to last this long. It has outlived all occupants.

But it's still here and somehow alive. It's more than a witness, it's a mirror, a gateway. Is that what happened to Monty and Witner? Did they somehow move from listening to becoming part of it? She knows if there's ever a chance to find out she will need to discover the verities.

She feels warmth on the metal.

Then heat so hot her fingers begin to blister.

She shrieks, wrenching her hands away from the inside walls of the tank. She drops her phone and the screen shatters. With shaking hands, she opens a bottle and pours water on the wounds. Where the water goes the wounds disappear and, with them, the pain.

She stares in wonder at her hands, free of blisters or damage.

Had she truly been hurt?

Or did the water dispel it somehow?

An idea comes to her and she pours the rest of the water on the inside metal of the tank. Where it touches, the metal sizzles and the sounds of battle increase. When the steam clears, there's a porthole large enough for her to shove her head through, which she does, but jerks it back as a horse thunders past. She blinks fiercely, trying to make the visions disappear, but they don't. The porthole still remains.

She removes the cap from the other bottle and pours half over the metal beside the porthole. The metal sizzles then disappears. She is able to squeeze through, even in her body armor. She labors to stand and catch her bearings.

A scream comes from her right.

A man on horse bears down on her.

She searches for something and spies a length of metal on the ground. Snatching it up, she braces it against the spoke of the tank and catches the horse in mid stride, impaling it. The beast screeches. The man flies from his mount and lands on the dust behind her. She rushes over, pulls her knife from her back, and stabs him through the neck, one, two, three times before she can even think about it.

Then she falls to the ground, managing to sit.

"What. The. Actual. Fuck," she says to the universe.

Bile rises inside her as she wipes the knife on the ground to clean it.

She stares at the man. Clearly a Muj, but a Mujahedeen from the old times. Instead of a rifle, he carries a sword and some sort of short spear.

She jerks her head up as machine gun fire erupts to her left. Two men run toward her. She needs a weapon. She goes to reach inside the tank, but the hole she'd used to transit into this crazy world is gone. She stands and backs up against the metal beast.

Bloody foam froths at the horse's mouth as its breaths become weaker and weaker.

"Kelly? Is that you?"

One of the running men is Monty.

The other also wears ACUs, but no battle rattle. He must be Witner. He has red hair and is as slim as she is.

They rush to her position.

Monty carries an AK-47.

Witner carries a long rifle that looks as if it were made last century. An Enfield?

"Kelly, this is—"

"Witner. Yes, I heard. Morrell told me."

Witner gives her a baleful look. "He's the one who put me in here."

"Well, we need to get back out. Any ideas?" she asks.

They both shake their head.

"Think we'd still be here if we had any good ones?" Witner says.

A clang sounds next to them as a round splats against the tank armor.

"Son of a—" Witner gets down on one knee, using the tank fender for support of the long gun. He sights in, then fires, the sounds deafening by comparison to a modern rifle. "Got him."

Monty grins wickedly. "This place is deadly fun."

"What is the place?" she asks.

"It's like *The Neverending Story* meets *Westworld*," Monty says a little too gleefully. "You can't die. If you get shot, you wake back up like it never happened."

She shakes her head. "*Neverending Story*? Is that the one with the giant flying dog?"

"That's Falkor," says Witner. "He's really a luckdragon."

"You guys aren't making any sense."

Witner spreads his fingers and points, arcing his hand around. "Everything exists about as far as the eye can see. This tank is at the center of it. And out there—nothing."

"Nothing as in you just fall off the edge?" she asks.

"Nothing as in it all turns gray and you can walk forever but never get anywhere."

The sound of metallic squeaking interrupted them.

"Tank tracks," Monty says.

"Here come the Russians," Witner says.

"Russians?" She whirls toward the sound and sees a line of tanks. "Who invited them?"

Monty and Witner began running. "Follow us."

"I thought you said we can't die."

"We can't," Monty says. "But that doesn't mean it doesn't hurt, though."

She follows them into a building. Or what's left of it. The place is like a Hollywood mockup. There is nothing inside nor even back or side walls. No furniture. Emptiness. "What gives?" she asks.

"Nothing exists except what the tank can see," Witner says.

"The tank? Seeing?"

"I think so," Monty says. "Witner's been here quite a while. He thinks we're living in the memory of the tank. Everything it saw, heard, and felt."

"Memory of a tank?" She scoffs. "That's impossible."

"This is all impossible, Sergeant," Witner says. "Look around you. What part of this looks possible to you?"

She looks at the gray nothing, then the featureless backside of the wall.

"Are there others?"

"Some Russians who keep to themselves playing a never-ending card game live on the other side of the tank. We killed each other until it got boring. Now, we just wave if we see them."

"What do you eat or drink here?" she asks.

"Nothing. If you get too hungry or thirsty, just kill yourself. You'll wake up refreshed."

"Miserable hell," she says. "I can't stay here."

"Best of luck finding a way out." Witner grins.

"We could get out the way we got in," she says, holding up the half bottle of water.

Witner shakes his head.

"Why are you shaking your head?" she asks. "Have you even tried?"

"What we're seeing is some sort of memory loop. It goes on for a time, then replays. I think it goes all the way back to 1980 during the Russian invasion of Afghanistan. Everything just resets like a homicidal groundhog day."

"So we're in a forty-year loop?"

"Seems that way."

"When do the Americans arrive?"

He peers out the side of the wall. "Should be soon. Things tend to speed up from here."

"If you see everything the tank has seen, then you see us, you see yourself get in the tank," she says.

He shakes his head. "For some reason I only see violence."

"Maybe as a weapon of war, it doesn't understand anything else," Monty says.

She knocks her forehead with a hand mired with dried blood drops. "There has to be a way." Then she snaps her fingers. "The Russians."

"What about them?"

"That was their tank. They were inside it. That's how they got here. Only people who have been inside it get here. That's why there aren't hundreds or thousands here."

"I still don't understand how this works," Monty said.

"Listen, you can't get in from outside. You have to get in to get out. It's like *Through the Looking-Glass*."

Monty grins.

"What?" she asks, thrusting out a leg, hands on hips. "Don't you know *Alice in Wonderland*?"

He holds up his hands. "No. It's not that. It's that we've trained for so many scenarios and in multiple environments in the Army and we've broken down to the point where our best ideas are coming from a so-so Bill Murray movie, a kid's movie that has a flying luck dragon, and a book about a magical mirror that lets you see things differently. I can't wait to write the After Action Report for this one."

"And I can't wait to read it," she cries. "Come on, let's go."

She rounds the corner, takes three steps, and gets four rounds in her chest. They were right about the pain. Fucking hell. Then it all goes black.

THE SOUND OF a horse charging. She turns. A sword sweeps down and removes her head.

Die

Rinse

Repeat

THE SOUND OF a horse charging. She turns. A sword sweeps down and she ducks.

Machine gun fire comes from her left as Monty runs to her. Rounds rip through the Muj who was about to behead her. He falls onto the tank and rolls off. The horse continues its gallop, then off into the gray.

She pulls herself up from her crouch. "How many times did I die?"

"Twenty-seven," Monty says. "That Muj really had your number."

"I died twenty-seven fucking times?" she feels her chest and arms but there are no wounds.

"Imagine the number of medals you'd have. What is that, the Purple Heart with twenty-six oak leaf clusters? You wouldn't be able to stand straight."

She slugs him in the shoulder. "Stop worrying about medals and worry about how to get out of here."

Witner meets them behind the same wall they called home before.

"Welcome back, Sarge."

She nods. "How long between deaths?"

"Seems like a day but could be several hours. Time passes here differently, I think."

"Fine then. Come one. Let's go meet the Russians."

She takes off, this time more carefully. She's flanked by the two soldiers, who occasionally fire at targets. But they move quickly and cover a lot of ground. A café is on a corner far behind the tank. They make it there without trouble and tumble inside like they're all sharing the same assholes and elbows.

Three Russians in stained white tank tops, army pants, and boots sit around a table playing cards. Each of them has various burns about their necks and arms.

"Which one of you is in charge?" she asks.

"Nyet," an older man says, waving her away with the back of a hand. His face looks like it's befriended the back of a frying pan one too many times.

The other two men are younger, but each looks as if they've seen too much of the wrong side of the world. One has shrapnel wounds on the left side of his face, giving him a permanent sneer. The other is a baby face with dead eyes.

They're playing cards, and the front wall is covered with thousands of numbers. She looks closer and sees that they've been playing a forever game of Gin Rummy.

"Do any of you speak English?" she asks.

"No," says Baby Face in a heavy accent. "Now, go away."

She crosses her arms. "I have an idea to get us all out."

"No," the man repeated. "We have tried everything."

"Have you? she asks.

The older man growls in Russian, words like gravel falling on asphalt.

They converse for a moment, then Baby Face looks at her. "He says to go away. We have a game to play. But if you want to stay, then we can play with you."

Anger flares and she pulls out a pistol and shoots the old man in the head.

The other two leap back, knocking over the table and a gunfight ensues.

Witner and Monty die, as do the two Russians.

She took three rounds in her body armor. She sighs. Being the only one alive, she puts the pistol to her head and fires.

THIS TIME SHE only dies three times from the Muj, but is shot along with Monty trying to cross the area to the café.

AFTER SIX MORE deaths they make the café again. She stalks through the door and places a gun to the older man's head.

"Is this how you want to play it?"

He sneers at her and shoots her in the stomach.

She blows a hole in his head.

NO DEATHS.

They make it across the space.

She calls out from the other side of the wall, even as Mujahadeen on horses surround the tank and beat at it with their spears.

"We can do this forever or you can listen to my idea," she calls.

More gravel on asphalt from the old man, then Baby Face says, "What's your idea?"

She shares Witner's thoughts about the tank and how they are living inside its memories, from whence it died to the modern present. She also says that the spirit of the tank cannot pass on until it has been rejoined by the Russians. They must return to the tank. They must rejoin with it.

"But what about you?" Baby Face asks.

"We have to come as well. We are part of it also. We've shared its memories of death and dying."

"There was a fire. We barely escaped it," he says. "If we return we will probably die."

"Do you really want to live the way you have been? Playing Gin and dying over and over and over?" she holds her breath, knowing that this is her final chance without having to shoot them again, and death is becoming so tiresome.

They argue for some time. Finally Baby Face is standing beside her in the doorway. He offers her a smile and lowers his head.

"We say you are right. But we don't think it will work."

"If it does, we all might die," she says.

"Сли боишься волков, не ходи в лес," he says, the words sounding like *Yesli boish'sya volkov, ne khodi v les.*

"I'm sorry. I don't speak Russian."

"Of course not. It means *'if you're scared of wolves, don't go in the woods.'*"

She nods. "Nothing ventured, nothing gained."

"Dah! Same thing. When do we do it?"

"I think the reset happens when the Mujahedeen are still present."

Ten, twenty, fifty, a thousand minutes later, the memory resets. The tank is ablaze and surrounded by Mujahedeen with archaic weapons, circling the dying metal beast on horses. One carries a Stinger Missile Firing tube, dangling from his saddle.

Three Americans and three Russians race across the space, firing their weapons in unison, a fusillade of automatic fire catching the Mujahedeen by surprise. Many of them fall. Several race away.

The memory flashes forward and the tank is no longer ablaze. A single Muj races toward them. Kelly recognizes him—her nemesis. She pulls her pistol, spreads her legs, takes aim, and fires, knocking him backward. She steps aside and the horse continues on, carrying its dead rider with it.

The Russians scamper up the side of the tank and slip into the hatch. Witner is next. She gestures for Monty to join them, but he hesitates.

"I want to stay, Sergeant."

"What are you talking about?"

"I love it here. This is the most fun I've ever had."

"Don't be a fool."

"I have no responsibilities here. I can't die. I can't be harmed. I can kill anyone."

"I get you, killer, but you have to join us. It's all or no one."

"Please, Sarge."

She shakes her head, hearing in the distance the squeaking tracks of more tanks.

He starts to raise a weapon on her.

She gives him a torrid look.

He lowers it, tosses the gun away, and climbs inside.

When she climbs in, he says, "Sorry, Sarge."

"Forget about it."

To call the interior cramped would be an understatement. Witner is wedged in the space behind the driver, Baby Face. Monty sits by the man with the shrapnel in his face who is the gunner. The old Russian pulls the hatch shut, then sits on his tank command platform. He speaks to her.

Baby Face says, "He asks, what now?"

"Now that you are back inside, it should reset properly."

She sits, staring at the metal floor of the tank, aware of the men around her, the rankness, the stifling air, shared breaths, almost making it hard to breathe. The time seems interminable. She has no idea if she's even half right, but she has to try something. While Monty loves the gamesmanship of a world where death is not a reality, it also takes the excitement of life away. Life can't be a certainty. If it is, then why live it? Life needs to be messy. It needs to be undetermined. It needs to be able to break down so one can fix it up. It isn't that she needs the game of life to be on difficult mode, but she does need it to be challenging. All of her life, she's worked to become who she is and earned everything she achieved. She'll be damned if she'll throw it all away.

With a jerk and the roar of the tank engine, the memory resets.

Baby Face shouts from the driver's seat, sitting low and spying through a thin line of prismed glass.

Scarface cheers.

The old man growls, stands and opens the hatch.

He commands, and the turret rotates. The sound of his machine gun and hot brass falling into the compartment makes the Americans cover their ears and try to dodge the super-heated metal.

Scarface opens the firing tube and rams in a 125mm shell. He shoves the door closed and locks it. Two seconds later the tank bucks as the round fires, screaming out of the tube toward an unknown target.

Then the commander closes the hatch and shouts something tinged in fear and anger.

The driver yanks the tank into a ninety-degree turn and then a series of explosions strikes outside. The tank halts with a spine-breaking jerk. The driver shouts something. The commander opens the hatch a few inches and two Molotov cocktails surge through the gap. They strike the inside of the tank, spraying gasoline and gel over the occupants.

Everybody screams as heat and fire light the air.

The gunner pulls out a fire extinguisher and madly sprays.

Gunshots come from outside, but those inside are still screaming.

The fire sizzles across their bodies and the heat boils them from the outside in.

Except it doesn't.

Nothing happens to them that didn't happen before.

The fire was not theirs. It was the Russians. It was part of their memory.

As they each realize this, they cease their screams until all that remains is silence, the smell of death, and the sounds of battle from outside.

Each of the Russians remain in the place they'd been, bodies burned, limbs shriveled, skin melted to the tank metal.

The stench is horrendous. Still, the Americans stay inside the tank in an attempt to allow the memory to reset, but inside there seems to be no passage of time and no ability to see change. Finally, they lose patience. They exit one by one, eager grins on their faces.

But this is not their Kabul.

Around them are more T72 tanks and with them, more Russians, now heaping the bodies of dead Mujahedeens into piles.

The Americans stand shocked.

One Russian sees them and shouts.

Witner takes off running.

A soldier raises a rifle and stiches his back with rounds.

Witner falls dead—for real this time, it seems.

Two Russian soldiers approach Monty and Kelly. They gesture for them to get on their knees.

They do.

Monty begins to cry.

Kelly makes a determined face.

They will not break her.

She will survive.

"*Yesli boish'sya volkov, ne khodi v les,*" she says.

Looking around, she now knows where she is.

Welcome to Kabul—1980.

She also knows one more thing.

Life is still as interesting as it used to be.

DID YOU KNOW?

WESTON OCHSE is the author of more than thirty books, including *Pets During Wartime*, *Bone Chase*, and *SEAL Team 666*. He's the recipient of the Bram Stoker Award as well as four New Mexico-Arizona Book Awards. He's been to Kabul more times than he's cared to and has visited the haunted tanks that sit in vigil along the ridges of the old city, but never has he climbed into one, nor will he ever. Visit him online at westonochse.com.

A SERIES OF OCCURRENCES AT LHASA HOTEL

BY HAN SONG

(Author's True Experience)

THERE used to be a hotel on Dosengue Road in Lhasa called the Youth Apartment. Years ago, a group of us checked in. On the first day, my friend Zhang Yi's hip broke without any reason, and he could not move. Then Li Jiang fell severely ill and was hospitalized. Feng Changyong and I were in the guest room one night in our beds, and we saw a white figure appear, floating from the window to the front door. We were too frightened to move!

The next morning, I found the door was standing half-open although I had locked it from the inside. We spoke to a local official, Liu Wei, about it, and he told us a woman had been hanged in that room not long before. She'd been the second wife of a newspaper reporter.

The reporter's first wife had been chopped to pieces by him. Liu Wei had kept the chopping board for a long time.

The hotel was later changed into a market.

HAN SONG is a Chinese science fiction writer and a journalist at the Xinhua News Agency. Considered one of the three most important voices in contemporary Chinese science fiction, he's published eighteen fiction and non-fiction books, eight collections of short fiction stories, and is a multiple recipient of the Chinese Galaxy Award (China's highest profile sci-fi prize), as well as the Chinese Nebula Award and Asian-Pacific Sci-fi Gravity Award.

* FILE UNDER: *Haunted Hotel*

It was the liminal space I sought . . .

WHERE DO BROKEN DREAMS GO?

FEATURE ENTRY 9

STRUCTURE TYPE: HIGH-RISE APARTMENT BUILDING

LOCATION: KALACHI, KAZAKHSTAN

LAT./ LONG: 52.2455° N, 66.5387° E

BUILT: CIRCA 1974

GROUND ELEVATION: 676 FT. (206 M.)

WRITTEN BY: ANDREW HOOK

TRAVEL GUIDE NOTES

THIS IS ANOTHER story selected through the open submission window, and it aligns perfectly to the themes and aims of this anthology. It's beautifully written, thoughtful, and haunting on multiple levels, not least of which is that what follows is based on a strange-but-true news account of the village of Kalachi (nicknamed "Village of the Damned") in central Asia's Kazakhstan; between 2013–2015 its residents were affected by a mysterious sleeping sickness causing days-long slumber and bizarre hallucinations. Blamed on various causes such as mass psychosis, radiation, poisoning from counterfeit vodka, or even extra-terrestrial activity, the village was eventually evacuated and its residents relocated. The sleeping effect still remains however, and tourists and journalists continue to visit this "ghost" town, experiencing all manner of unsettling reactions.

Following is but one photographer's experience in Kalachi and the wonder of what is real or not while begging the question, "Where Do Broken Dreams Go?"

—Charlatan Bardot

SERGEI ALMOST TOOK MY HAND.
"In here."
I entered the doorway. Broken glass replaced the sound of ice as it scrunched into my boot tread. The respite from the cold streets was welcome. Within a short distance it was too dark to see much at all. Sergei nudged me. Warily I stopped blinking, and noticed the flashlight that he held.

"Take this," he said. "I have my phone."

It was solid rubber. I depressed the switch and a swathe of light shone across the open hallway. The building was breezeblock pretty. Ceiling tiles littered the floor. Wires no longer connected to the main supply hung down like plastic ivy. None of the windows were intact. In the corners where damp gathered, frost-bitten plants extended green fingers as cautiously as children daring each other to test an electric fence. My beam was joined by the pale light from Sergei's phone. I could just discern the drab colors of his military clothing. Not that his uniform held meaning. Here the men were either dressed in fatigues or business suits. The real Kazakhstan was miles away.

He beckoned with the light. On the opposite wall our shadows sparked to life. I turned my head and saw Timofei had followed us inside. If I distrusted Sergei, then I was fearful of Timofei. When he smiled, his teeth resembled rows of broken terraced houses.

Sergei spoke in Kazakh, which was even more alien than my rudimentary understanding of Russian. My pre-trip research had proved inadequate, I could remember it as an agglutinative language employing vocal harmony but nothing more. That didn't translate the bark which stopped Timofei in his tracks and made him back out of the doorway.

"I told him," Sergei said, "to keep watch."

I squeezed the flashlight for reassurance. The words *Why are we here?* paused in my throat. Then—like Timofei—they also backed down. I knew why we were here. What I wasn't sure about was if I wanted to be.

"I go first."

Sergei crossed the expanse. The tiles broke like communion wafers under his feet. When I followed it felt as though I were walking across an ice floe, or the disconnected flooring in a House of Fun. He stopped before a stairway. I could tell he considered looking back, shining his light in my face for dramatic intent. Perhaps he wanted to see how my curls, peeking out from around my parka like an emergent sunflower, might look in the half-light. But he decided against it and lifted one boot onto the first step and then the other. Slowly, we ascended.

HAUNTED KALACHI, KAZAKHSTAN

I knew he was armed, that he kept his weapon tethered to his belt. With each step the barrel jerked a little in my direction. Graffiti decorated the stairwell where it had been absent below. I wondered if these were warnings. Probably not. There was enough to be freaky about without adding my imagination. Yet was it simply the isolation which bothered me? Or the country, the culture? I should have been used to it.

We reached the second floor. There were eight in total. I'd counted them from outside, although it was clear the upper levels had no flooring. "Bombs?" I'd asked. My cheeks inflated and deflated with a guttural sound as I gestured. Sergei shook his head.

Nature, I thought he said.

The second floor was as wrecked as the first. Dividing walls undivided with only a few pillars keeping the structure together. What were once individual rooms, functional apartments, were now no more than shells. I searched for photo opportunities: a discarded teddy bear or the arm of a doll, perhaps a child's coat, or an abandoned piece of technology. But there was nothing. I slipped the camera off my shoulder all the same. The light was a little better up here, closer to the sun. I was about to unclip the lens cap when Sergei crouched, knelt, then fell to the floor.

What else was there to do but to follow?

MY DREAMS WERE gracious. I saw antelope and willow trees. Familiar figures spoke to me in guises I didn't recognize. A lover or past lover or soon-to-be lover took my hand in his. Our palms were smooth, the backs hairy. I plucked those hairs and placed them into an iron suitcase. Just as it was getting interesting, I woke.

Timofei stood in the corner of the room. I smelt a thick stench of urine, and as I saw him turn I caught sight of him zipping up his trousers. I closed my eyes. The vestiges of the dream remained, ethereal tendrils. If I let myself go I would be pulled back into the arms of my lover, I would continue the dream as though it had been paused like live television. But now that I was aware of Timofei, I couldn't allow myself to sleep.

He saw me open my eyes. Watched as I rose unsteadily. Sergei remained on the floor. I coughed. I realized the light in the room had changed. The hum of a generator pricked my consciousness and then I realized Timofei had installed two arc lights in the open space. I no longer held the flashlight, and when I looked to the floor I saw it was switched off. At the windows, darkness pooled.

"How long have I slept?"

Timofei grunted, gestured to his watch. I shook sleep from my head and pulled my mobile from my pocket. We'd entered the building around ten in the morning. It was now close to midnight.

Timofei crossed the space and passed me. He bent by Sergei and gave him a nudge. I had a feeling it wasn't the first time. In intense light I saw Sergei's eyes moving beneath the lids. Not a simple matter of REM but an effort to open them. Still, he went on sleeping. Timofei kicked him in the gut. A friendly kick that you might give to a mate after a party when they'd zonked out on your floor. Harder than that you would give a colleague. Nothing much seemed to happen. Timofei's English was non-existent and he pretended not to know Russian. Sergei had hinted at something in his past. So we sat for a couple of hours and I ate the pale ham sandwich Timofei handed me. I took comfort that I was almost androgynous in my parka and combat fatigues.

Sergei woke like a newborn kitten, blind and pawing for its mother. He was clawing to return into dream, and I wondered if I had looked the same. Suddenly I felt ashamed, embarrassed to have slept under what must have been Timofei's gaze. I realized he could have touched me.

Timofei shook Sergei by the shoulder. After some time he sat. He ate bread and sausage. Only after a good twenty minutes had passed did he look me in the eye and say, "Did you get your pictures?"

WE RELOCATED TO a bar in the next town. Timofei lined up alcohol like bowling pins. If there were legal opening hours then the bartender didn't care. I took one shot, then two. It was warm in the bar and I'd slipped out of my parka and was aware my golden tresses reflected in the optics. I had a feeling of displacement. As though when I slept everything around me was replaced with something else, something identical yet not the same. These were observations I couldn't share with the two men. Instead Sergei told me what I already knew.

"It started four years ago. The villagers in Kalachi began sleeping for several days. They couldn't be woken. It was sudden, unexplained. They suggested it was due to the nearby uranium mine, but the radiation levels here are normal. Those affected complained of memory loss, hallucinations. The population was small, under six hundred. When the heads of neighboring districts offered new housing and jobs, over half the residents took it."

"And the other half?"

"They decided to stay. Until the first half left. And then they realized they needed them to survive."

"How long has it been deserted?"

"Two years."

"And when did you find the epicenter?"

Sergei looked to Timofei, as though he might proffer the right word in translation. Then he turned back to me. "Again?"

"When did you find the building? The one we were just in."

"We were contracted to take the buildings down. You saw we didn't make much progress. One morning I woke with all my men asleep in a circle. It spooked them. They wouldn't go back."

"And the government has been happy to leave it like that?"

Sergei shrugged. "We are not a rich country, but we have many open spaces. We don't need to maintain areas where no one wishes to live."

He rubbed the day's stubble with the back of his hand, as though satisfying an itch. Then he downed one of the shots and glanced at Timofei. I assumed something passed between them though I didn't see it.

I excused myself and headed for the toilet, taking my camera with me. It wasn't a matter of trust and I knew they wouldn't be offended. Everyone here carried their belongings with them. They were a form of identification.

The toilet door was metal. A cold bolt kept it closed. I paused, then sat. I pulled my camera from the bag, flicked through the images. I'd taken nothing when I slept.

I remembered being younger, probably early teens. I had begun to sleep naked. My bedroom window was open. It was summer and a cool breeze invaded my room like autumn. I had dreamt, woken, slept and dreamt again. This happened four or five times. Yet the dream was continuous. Or so I'd thought. On waking for the last time, with the sun's rays settling hairs on my skin, I'd realized I couldn't be sure that the dream had been linear and unbroken. I might simply have dreamt that I'd awoken.

Where do broken dreams go? Those unfinished masterpieces.

I returned to the bar. Timofei and Sergei were laughing. There was a slight aberration in the humor when they saw me, or I might have imagined that. "Come," Sergei said, "let's go to bed."

I WASN'T TIRED. My eyes considered the circumstances of my hotel room. Wooden furniture was bolted to the floor. The ensuite toilet had no door. When I washed my face the water was gritty as though sieved through plaster. The mirror over the dressing table was rusted around the edges, almost in a decorative pattern. I had stayed in worse rooms.

Sergei had lingered outside my door when he said goodnight. It had been after 4 a.m. Timofei stood at the end of the corridor, a key in his hand. They were sharing a room. I thought Sergei might touch me again, just as I'd thought when we entered that building. But his fingers stayed a respectful distance. Then, without a word, he walked away.

Doctors hadn't discovered the cause of the illness. If it *was* an illness. Some had suggested mass psychosis. I was drawn to the village through a network of obscure internet theories, most of them fanciful. It seemed anything could be blamed on the government—aliens, espionage, terrorism—when in fact the truth was usually stranger. Even my normally rational mind had wondered whether the village had somehow been a portal between the real world and the dream world. Even I, who believed such things didn't exist, had a hankering for them.

I lay back on the bed, the woolen coverlet with its knots and spirals patterning my naked back. Heating in the room was cranked to the max, but there was no internal thermostat. The curtains were closed, but ripped in places. It wouldn't take long for the sun to rise and then it would be impossible to relax.

My body was ageing. I considered different dreams: those linked to hopes and desires, or day time reveries where the world wasn't as hopeless as I knew it to be. I had seen things: horrors with my eyes captured by my lens. After fourteen years I was ready for an out in that career. I was ready for some love in the world.

I knew I wouldn't find it here.

Disturbed, I leaned over the side of the bed and pulled my camera onto my chest. Again I accessed the images. The shots I had taken from the plane of clouds that make the world appear upside down; the austere airport, views from the taxi of half-finished buildings nestled against modern structures against half-demolished buildings. Everything ramshackle yet everything in place. The search for a guide and the procession of males which led me to Sergei. The minibus that broke down twice on the road to Kalachi. My viewfinder was filled with stereotypes that I might have created in a daydream without setting foot on Kazakhstan soil. I had a sudden realization that I was lying to this country. That what I would take back wouldn't be the truth, but only what I expected to see.

Then came the new photos. Distorted and impossible. The camera fell from my body. I paid little regard since I had fallen asleep.

But with my eyes open I heard hooves in the hallway.

A FEW YEARS later I found myself again in Kalachi. The journey was unexpected. When you've visited the arse-end of the world you don't expect a reason to go back. I had never sold those photographs. Anyone could see they had been Photoshopped—but of course, they hadn't. The strange extremities, the aberrations, the dislocations: even I didn't completely believe them. I'd decided to convince myself there was a technical malfunction, despite no mechanical evidence to support it. I decided to stop taking photographs for a while. To find new outlets for creativity, for work. But even when a wildebeest knows of the crocodile in the river, it still has to stop and drink. I was the wildebeest now.

The Kazakhstan government had turned around on the uranium question, like an ice-skater cutting itself a circle. They advised the sleeping sickness was due to heightened levels of carbon monoxide and hydrocarbons in the air. That it wasn't some form of mass psychosis or other illness. When I heard the news I was in Goa, taking a sabbatical. I considered sending those experts my photographs with my address scrawled on the back. Postcards from the edge.

Kalachi was as much as the same as I wanted to forget it. Wide streets, concrete buildings. The only difference was the lack of Sergei and Timofei, although no doubt there were other Sergeis, other Timofeis. The hotel in which I stayed in the nearest inhabited town remained intact. I was informed that a coach party had just left. The manager assumed I had missed my connection. The area now catered for a particular sort of tourism. People came to Kalachi to fall unconscious. To dream the impossible dream.

I hadn't been fooled by uranium. It was the liminal space I sought. The interstice between something happening and something not.

When I asked if I could hire a car the manager directed me to a local and a motorcycle. Her name was Aruzhan. Hugging her as we travelled, her blonde hair wrapped itself around my face as the wind slowly tugged loose strands from her helmet. She was an expert at avoiding potholes that might take out a bus. I liked her immensely. There wasn't the frisson I had with Sergei and Timofei. No ulterior motives.

"Do you believe in the uranium story?" I asked.

"The children here, they saw winged horses, snakes in their beds, and worms eating their hands."

"And you?"

"I came after. To make money out of those who wanted to see such things."

There were no more residents in Kalachi. It took us a while to find what Sergei had defined as the epicenter. The building was eight stories no more. What remained was a pile of rubble set off to one side with an intention of reclamation. The foundations of the building remained in the earth, delineating a floor plan not unlike the remains of a Roman fort. Barely peeking out of the ground amidst abundant overgrowth. Sizeable trip hazards.

Aruzhan claimed to be immune to the area, yet when I turned to ask her a question I found her slouched against the motorcycle. Her right hand bunched inside her helmet like a thermoplastic fist.

I invited myself over the threshold. I sought closure, found enclosure. I wanted to smell the meat in a pale ham sandwich, wanted the movement of Sergei's eyes under his lids undulating like a working fairground ride shrouded in tarp, I wanted to see Timofei's feet in those ridiculous hooves as he kicked down the hallway, I wanted to see the inside of my own stomach again. Through my skin. I wanted to awake abruptly, grab a shard of dream, and cut myself with it. I wanted confirmation it was real.

"Hey!" I shouted to Aruzhan, just before I fell.

A haunted building haunts. The haunted becomes the haunter.

Upon waking, I catch her deleting images from my camera.

DID YOU KNOW?

ANDREW HOOK is a much-published writer whose most recent publications are *O For Obscurity, Or, The Story Of N*, a quasi-biography of The Mysterious N Senada written in collaboration with the legendary avant-garde collective known as The Residents, and *Frequencies of Existence*, his seventh short story collection (NewCon Press). He lives and works in Norwich, UK, and can be found at www.andrew-hook.com amongst other places.

TAMARIND CANDY

BY K. HARI KUMAR

I LIVED in Bangalore while in first grade. Every afternoon, my school bus dropped me at the stop, and from there it was a fifteen minutes' walk home with an older friend. One day, the friend didn't show up in school. So, after getting off the bus I walked home by myself.

I lost my way and soon stood in front of a large rusted iron gate enclosing a compound with high walls. I spotted a pale woman with a thick vertical stroke of vermillion on her forehead. She approached me and offered a tamarind candy. When I looked into her eyes, my limbs froze, the smell of burning flesh filled my lungs, and I witnessed a gruesome act of violence on a child of my age before passing out on the road.

I woke in my bed. It was revealed to me later that that compound was a *smashānam*† where a woman and her son were sacrificed by her evil husband fifty years ago.

K. HARI KUMAR is one of India's top horror writers whose stories have been adapted to screen in multiple Indian languages. His bestselling book *India's Most Haunted* is the largest collection (in India) of horror stories written by a solo author in a single edition.

* FILE UNDER: *Haunted Smashānam*

---

† A Hindu crematory ground, where dead bodies are brought to be burnt on a pyre, usually located on the outskirts of a town.

ONE DAY AT RECESS IN THE CONVENT OF THE BLESSED MOTHER ON VICTORIA STREET

BY CHRISTINA SNG

I TURNED my head, and my classmates were gone.

Why did we have to play hide-and-seek in this old dilapidated churchyard?

I shivered as I stepped into the moss-covered mausoleum, scanning the tombstones. A muddy school shoe peeked out from behind the nearest one.

Blessed Mother Cemetery, behind the school chapel

"I found you!" I called, but the foot didn't move. I cautiously approached but saw no one there, only the shoe.

As I picked it up, the tombstone's inscription caught my eye: "HERE LIES CHRISTINA SNG WHO WAS TOO CURIOUS FOR HER OWN GOOD. BORN 1972. DIED 1884."

I gasped in terror and dissipated into dust.

CHRISTINA SNG is the author of several volumes of poetry, including *A Collection of Nightmares*, winner of the Bram Stoker Award. She writes and paints in Singapore, where she lives with her children and a menagerie of curious pets.

* FILE UNDER: *Haunted Mausoleum*

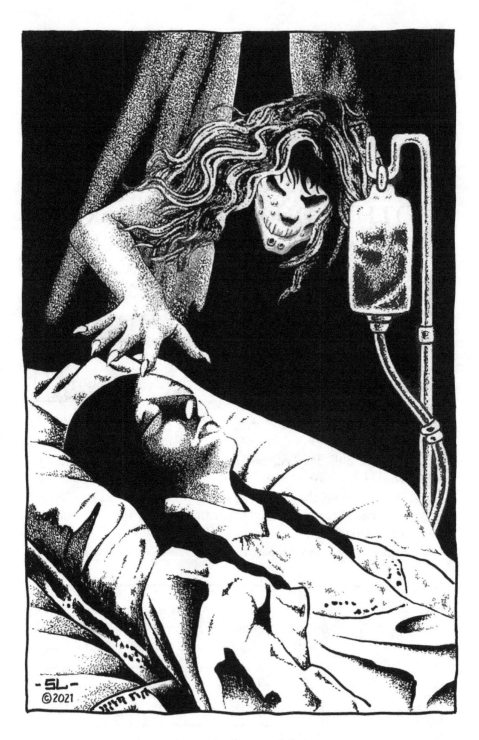

She woke and glimpsed fingers . . .

ABOVE AIMI

STRUCTURE TYPE: HOSPITAL
LOCATION: MUKŌMACHI, JAPAN
LAT./ LONG: 35.6462° N, 138.6136° E
BUILT: CIRCA 1945
ELEVATION: 850 FT. (259 M.)
WRITTEN BY: THERSA MATSUURA

TRAVEL GUIDE NOTES

HOSPITALS BY THEIR very nature are one of the most horror-inducing building types to be imagined, just one step down (a very small step) from morgues, funeral homes, and other architecture purposed for death. On the one hand, hospitals are for healing—a very benevolent notion—but for most people, it's also, ultimately, the last stop before the great and final darkness, a stop often unplanned for and filled with pain, terror, confusion, and woe. And sometimes worse.

Writing from the eastern coast of Japan, Thersa Matsuura advances the superstition of medical ward-ghosts and malevolent dread with her take on this visit to Mukōmachi's emergency center. Thersa told me that although the hospital itself is fictional, much of the setting, imagery, and events are based on personal experience and observation from other, similar hospitals, which, for me, now evokes a new form of nightmare.

In the following tale, Aimi Koike is an ordinary young woman, more or less healthy, but taken by a sudden affliction that sends her to the hospital and onto a greater journey of dissolution . . . for what is it exactly that creeps and clicks in the ceiling holes above her bed, and "Above Aimi"?

—Charlatan Bardot

I T WAS AFTER MIDNIGHT, POURING RAIN. AIMI, IN HER
pajamas, stumbled across the near-empty parking lot toward the ER
entrance. It glowed tears of red and yellow through her rain-streaked
glasses. Maybe they could save her.

Fifteen minutes earlier, she'd been sitting on the tatami-mat floor of her
new, still furniture-less apartment, catching up on the latest *Golden Kamuey*
episode and thinking how good it felt to start over. Sipping a tall can of
Sapporo Super Dry and nibbling a piece of cold pizza, thoroughly enjoying
this new sense of freedom until a sudden pain lanced her chest.

She'd recognized it immediately, the monster that had taken her father
when she was eight and his father before him. Because she'd known she
might only have minutes to live, Aimi didn't want to risk an ambulance that
might not arrive in time. She'd decided to try and make it to the small
hospital two blocks from her apartment by herself. It may be old and rundown, but at least it was close. And it was a hospital.

Waterlogged slippers sloshed comically with each step. If she wasn't so
close to death, she might have laughed. Her whole life played out this way,
just when she thought things were going well, the bottom fell out.

She'd moved to the small town of Mukōmachi only two weeks ago. Tokyo
was eating her alive, a dead end job, a toxic boyfriend, and a funk that threatened
to turn into a full-blown depression if she didn't do something fast.

Had this happened there, at least she'd have had a friend nearby or a
sympathetic neighbor to drive her, pat her hand, and tell her everything
would be okay. But here she had to save herself.

The automatic doors swished open and Aimi, drenched, clutching her
chest, staggered in. A combination of relief that she'd made it coupled with
the sudden ironic memory of her mother's insistent advice three months
prior, encouraging her to leave the big city, relocate to a more rural area,
made Aimi cackle wildly. The night staff turned.

Another blast of pain, and she collapsed on the floor. The night
watchman rushed over to help her. She puked on his shoes.

SO IT WASN'T a heart attack after all. Gallstones. How embarrassing was
that?

It was early, pre-dawn. Aimi lie flat on her back on a thin-matressed bed
regretting all her life choices. She was also trying to shake a strange sleep, the
kind that was vivid and nightmarish, but on waking remains out of reach,
like monsters still lurking around the corner, ready to pounce. She couldn't

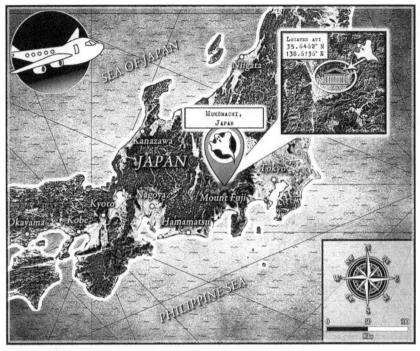

Located at:
35.6462° N
138.6136° E

SEA OF JAPAN

Niigata

MUKŌMACHI,
JAPAN

Kanazawa

JAPAN

Tokyo

Nagoya

Mount Fuji

Kyoto

Okayama   Kobe

Hamamatsu

PHILIPPINE SEA

HAUNTED MUKŌMACHI, JAPAN

remember a single detail and had a hunch she probably didn't want to anyway.

And she hadn't been the only one with troubled sleep. A curtain hanging from a U-shaped rail in the ceiling blocked her view of the rest of the room, but she knew there were other patients there, hidden behind their own curtains; at least one of them had been having an animated argument in her sleep for the past hour.

Aimi stared up at the dark ceiling that began to reveal itself little by little with early morning sunlight. Dozens of large brown water stains could now be seen. And, worse, a missing tile directly overhead. How does that happen? How does that not get fixed?

In hindsight, maybe she should have taken that ambulance to the bigger hospital downtown after all. From what she could see, this place was even older than she had imagined. But the doctor last night had seemed confident and had explained in detail what all the scans, tests, and images meant.

Aimi touched her sternum with her thumb. Her pain a dull thud thanks to the IV and whatever magic liquid that plastic bag contained. But her back was starting to get stiff. She sat up, searching for the remote to put the bed into a sitting position. All she found was a yellowing nurse call button.

"It's not automatic."

The voice startled her. She hadn't heard anyone come into the room, much less pull open the curtain, and peek in.

"Excuse me?" Aimi asked.

A nurse was already on her knees at the foot of the bed, smiling and turning a hand crank. "What angle would you like?"

"Um," Aimi answered as the bed at her back slowly clicked up by degrees.

"How's that? Good for meals, reading, and enjoying conversations with visitors."

The nurse was the same as her, in her mid-twenties, Aimi guessed. She had a pleasant heart-shaped face with big, almost hazel eyes. They looked even larger due to two long, careful strokes of black eyeliner drawn across each lid, narrowing into upturned points at the corners. It gave the woman a feline-like appearance. She was quite pretty except for her hair. Long, shiny black with bangs, but something was off about it. Maybe it was the straightness of those bangs—like they'd been cut only minutes before.

"That's perfect," Aimi said. "Thank you."

"How did you sleep last night?" the nurse asked, running a finger down the charts. "You were in quite a state, I hear."

"I'm feeling much better, thank you."

"Did Suzuki-san keep you up?" The pretty cat-like nurse slid the curtains open, revealing the entire room.

Four beds. Only two were occupied though, hers and the one directly across. There, an elderly woman was propped up at the same angle, a series of tubes and wires connecting her to an array of machines that whirred and beeped hypnotically. That must be Suzuki-san.

The woman looked to be asleep and, while not talking at the moment, still seemed to be having that unpleasant dream. Her brow was knitted and her mouth chewed vigorously at some invisible, perhaps sour, taste.

"No," Aimi replied.

"You must be a deep sleeper then. That's good." The nurse handed Aimi a thermometer for under her arm. "It's always difficult to put other patients in here." She leaned forward and whispered, "The rumor is Suzuki-san isn't a very good roommate."

"Really?"

"I'm joking." The nurse laughed, took the thermometer, and scribbled the numbers on the clipboard. "She's just quite the sleep-talker."

"There was some of that this morning." This time Aimi laughed.

"These days she's no trouble at all." Pretty Cat said. "She used to be a firecracker when she first came though."

"She's been here awhile?"

"Yes, about six or seven months." Pretty Cat slipped a blood pressure cuff on Aimi's arm. "She liked to wander. She'd disappear and we'd have to go look for her. An hour later we'd get a call from the pediatrics floor. She was down there folding origami with the children." She squeezed the bulb, tightening the cuff.

"She doesn't look to be doing so good now."

The blood pressure pump hissed as it deflated. The nurse wrote down more numbers then removed the cuff. She made a serious face and pointed to her temple.

"That took her ability to walk, four months ago. And since becoming bedridden she seems to have a touch of dementia now, too."

"That's so sad."

"Yes, it is. But she's loved by everyone here," the nurse said, putting the blood pressure gear back on the cart. "Especially the children down on Pediatrics."

Aimi laughed, but felt bad for doing so.

"Looks like your laparoscopy is scheduled for tomorrow morning." Pretty Cat tapped the chart. "Seven a.m."

"That's what I hear."

"There's nothing to be nervous about." The nurse pulled a syringe from one of the pockets at her hip, inserted it into the port on the IV bag, and pushed. "It's a very routine procedure," she said and rotated the bag several times before returning it to its hook and starting the drip again.

Aimi rubbed the faded piping that ran around the cuff of her mint-colored hospital pajamas. The cloth was soft, very close to threadbare. How many patients had worn them before her? She smiled and thought maybe she should get a second opinion.

PRO, AIMI THOUGHT. *The grilled salmon and miso soup breakfast was amazing.*

She pushed her IV stand back and forth down the dingy sand-colored hall, debating whether or not to march straight to the nurse's station and sign herself out. Was this gut feeling a warning or a normal reaction to the relative shock of being hospitalized so suddenly and needing emergency surgery?

Kiyoko, her best friend who she'd left back in Shinjuku, had suggested listing the positives and negatives of all hefty decisions, like quitting her job and fleeing to a quaint little town at the foot of Mount Fuji. Considering her current state of affairs, Aimi wondered if that had indeed been good advice. But right now it was all she had.

She passed three old men strolling around the green tea vending machine. They rubbed their crooked limbs, complaining about their wives, and bragging about grandchildren who could not possibly be so remarkable. Her IV stand's squeaking and clicking wheels caught and jerked hard to the side nearly pulling her off her feet.

A negative right there, Aimi thought. Sure the machines were high tech and the doctors and nurses seemed competent, but everything else, the beds, the IV stands, the walls, floors, and that too-low, gross ceiling were another matter.

"You okay?"

All three men were at her side offering help. One quickly dropped to his knees to examine the offending wheel. She couldn't argue with the fact the people here were nice. None of the chilliness of the city. A pro.

"Thank you." She waited for them to finish tinkering with the stand, reprimanding the floor, then thanked them again with a bow, before continuing on her way. She hadn't taken two steps before a smell hit her.

Con. Everywhere in varying degrees the smell of bleach tinged with cheap lemon cleaner tried to mask a more overpowering reek. Aimi identified it as piss and shit, and a more dreadful rot that she imagined exuded from the bowels of the building itself. How old was this place anyway?

"Here you are!" Pretty Cat came running up behind her. "It's time for lunch. You must be starving."

It couldn't be noon already? She'd left for her walk after breakfast a little after 8:00. Aimi pulled her phone from the pocket in her pajamas. It was now 12:11.

A LUNCH OF udon noodles and two phone calls later, Aimi was back to pacing the floor once more, from the big window that looked down on an impressively gray parking lot on one end, to the elevators that—every time she reached them—*binged* open to reveal an empty car, then closed again on the other.

She began to understand why the six-month-younger version of Suzuki-san had taken to roaming around. Maybe it was boredom, maybe it was a cocktail of anxiety, claustrophobia, and the general fear of being hospitalized, or maybe it was the itchy feeling, like thousands of microscopic bugs crawling under her skin. Whatever it was, Aimi couldn't shake the feeling she needed to keep moving in here.

She wasn't the only one either. If they weren't bedridden, asleep, or unconscious, most of the other patients meandered around, caught in their own absurd loops and obsessive thoughts.

Her mother—who had never fully recovered from the horror of losing her husband so suddenly and at such a young age—was adamant on the last phone call that Aimi listen to the doctor, have the surgery, and get back to settling into a more laid-back and happier life. But Aimi wasn't sure until she talked with Kiyoko, who not only shared her mother's sentiment, but also scolded her for acting like a baby.

Strolling the floor, still strolling now, this at least felt good. It gave her purpose, and it made sense to even out the warped floors and angled walls. She bet that was why the other patients all did it. There was a sense of connection she shared with them, an understanding.

But then there were times she felt compelled to stop, like when she admired that blank space on the wall, the outline of a picture that had been taken down still visible. It was then that the crawling under her skin rose to the surface and the bugs tried to escape.

What kind of picture had it been? Why did they take it down? Why did it want her to stop here every time she passed?

Aimi scratched at her forearm, her neck, her cheek. Maybe it was an allergic reaction to the medicine. She'd have to remember to ask.

"Quiet!" Those incessant wheels kept clicking even though the IV stand was stopped by her side.

Then it hit her. It wasn't the wheels that had been making the noise all this time. She looked up. *Click click click . . .*

Rats!

SOME SOUND LOGIC, a few tears, and two nurses on a stepladder later, and the hole above her bed was covered with an opaque tarp secured by duct tape. The promise was that they'd call to get the tile replaced Monday, and, also, the hospital didn't have a rat problem.

Aimi lie in bed, covers pulled to her neck, exhausted. She glanced at her phone. 3 p.m. She buried the device under her pillow. All those messages from her mother and concerned friends were too much racket. She needed to rest. Maybe a nap.

From the room next door came an undulating, guttural moan that she realized she'd already grown used to. The nurses, too, evidently, because they never seemed to offer the poor sufferer any help. Aimi sighed, thinking it almost sounded like the hospital itself was crying out, in constant pain.

Maybe it was.

Aimi fell asleep to the soothing hum and hiss and *bloop-bloop* of Suzuki-san's fancy machines trying to keep time with her erratic snoring and the clicking of hot water pipes in the ceiling.

SHE GASPED AWAKE inside a dream, a camera eye pointed down at a huddle of broken people gathered around her bed. Her sleeping body blinded, she couldn't see their faces. She could feel, though, lying there, sheet pulled to her neck, the weight of one hand resting on her stomach. Even the poisonous presence of the pebble-filled organ throbbing low underneath her ribcage, remnants of the gallstone attack she'd had . . . when? Yesterday. Or was it longer? The day before that? How long had she been here?

The figures were muttering. Incoherent. She saw the tops of their greasy heads looking down at her sleeping form. They were discussing something. Her above-self watched as one of them leaned closer. Then came the touch of a single wormy finger tucking a strand of hair behind her ear. She felt it in both bodies. Shards of ice raced through her as she tried to scream down at herself to wake up.

"Who's here?" Suzuki-san's voice was suddenly lucid from behind her curtain.

They all turned at once in the elderly woman's direction. Then, after exchanging looks or some ghostly telepathy, one by one, insect-like, they scuttled up the dirty wall, coming her way. Aimi's above-body jolted, and when it did she fell.

She woke up.

SHE BOLTED UPRIGHT making Pretty Cat jump and nearly drop the IV bag from her hands.

"What time is it?" Aimi asked.

"Almost time to go back to sleep," Pretty Cat said, pointing to the window with the empty syringe before slipping it back into her pocket. The setting sun painted the glass pink and orange. "I'm afraid no dinner tonight."

"What day is it? How long have I been here?"

"Tomorrow is your surgery," the nurse said as she re-hooked the plastic bag to the IV stand. "Did you forget?"

That didn't answer her question. Aimi looked up. The tarp was gone. "What happened to it?"

"Oh, that, there were some bad pipes years ago. They really do need to get the whole thing redone."

"No, they covered it up. The other nurses," Aimi said. She suddenly felt trapped, panic rising in her chest.

"What other nurses?" Those razor-straight bangs. Aimi suddenly had the vision of the nurse in front of a mirror with a pair of ridiculously long scissors, clipping.

"Some air?" Pretty Cat swept back the curtain to reveal Suzuki-san sitting bolt upright in her bed, staring right at Aimi.

"She's moving," the old woman said suddenly, more lucid than Aimi had yet heard her.

MIND CLEAR AS a freshly rung temple bell. The vibrations thrumming to her toes. Slippers stashed away, bare feet slippery and gliding across the icy cold floor that receded as she breathed out, rose when she breathed in. The ceiling, too, played the game. Its pulling away, pushing down. Pulling away, pushing down. She giggled at the sensation of being stretched and shrunk as the building breathed. Music played inside the walls, inside her head. She danced and spun. Her partners, just out of reach, she could hear them, the clicking heels of ghosts hidden away in the velvety shadows that gathered and crowded in close to watch. She twirled into another shadow and they scattered—

"WHAT ARE YOU doing here?" came a surprised whisper from behind. "You should be in bed."

Don't move. Don't let them catch you. Don't let them put you back in the room, Aimi thought.

"Hello?"

A touch on her elbow. Aimi composed herself, smiled, and turned gracefully to face the woman with the flashlight who leapt back when she saw Aimi.

"Where's your IV!?" The night nurse gasped.

A sharp tang of her fear filled Aimi's mouth and ran down her throat.

"What did you do?" The flashlight beam bounced from her arm, down the front of her pajamas, moved along the floor, that slippery circle she'd been dancing, and then returned back to Aimi's smiling face.

"Dancing, of course."

TETHERED BY THE other arm now, another venomous drip.

"Are you comfortable?" The night nurse tightened the second Velcro strap to her wrist. "It's only for a little bit." She looked at her watch. "Five hours. The morning nurse will be in at six to wake you and get you ready for surgery."

"Mm." Aimi could still hear the music, far away now.

"I'm sorry about this. Here." The nurse placed the call button in her hand. "If you need anything just push this. I'll come running."

Aimi had the nurse leave the bed cranked up to a 25-degree angle. It was more comfortable. She also asked her to leave the curtain open. The enclosed space, the sense of being watched from above, being tied down, it all nudged her to the edge of a full-blown panic attack.

The nurse left and Aimi lie there in her thin blue LED nightlight and tried to catch what Suzuki-san and her night demon argued about. It was hard to hear over the humming, ticking, hissing machines. Aimi's last thought before she fell asleep was Suzuki-san was very good at speaking two distinct voices.

SHE WOKE TO a noise in the room. Rustling, something wet, choking? Aimi blinked her eyes, her body dull from whatever they'd shot into her IV. Still dark out. How long had she been asleep? What had woken her? She glanced around the room until she saw it and froze.

Suzuki-san's curtain had been pulled open, and there in the blue ethereal glow a figure straddled the old woman's chest, her knees pinning down Suzuki-san's arms. The stranger faced away from Aimi. Threadbare pajamas stretched tight across her back, ribs clearly visible.

A patient? But Aimi had made the rounds so many times, been in and out of all the rooms. She had never met this woman with long tangled and knotted white hair falling all the way down her back.

Was she choking Suzuki-san? Aimi's heart pounding, she tried to push the nurse call button only to find it was not in her hand, her tied hand. She couldn't move her arms. But she had to stop whatever was occurring.

"Don't." Aimi's voice sounded throttled in her throat.

The figure inhaled sharply and stopped. Aimi pulled at the restraints, twisted her wrists, kicking her legs.

"Help!" Louder this time.

The thing pushed herself up, her back broadening. Slowly she twisted around to look at Aimi. A horrible face sagged as if in the early stages of decay, but her eyes were clear and glassy and filled with hate. An overpowering sense of dread filled Aimi. She felt she would burst out in tears, watching the hag withdraw her hand from inside Suzuki-san's mouth.

"Someone, anyone, help!" Aimi shouted.

The hag's attention was now on her, staring, giving an unsettling grin. Aimi sensed an enormous coiled power and thought the hag might spring on her at any instant. Instead the hag hissed, stepped off the side of the bed, and dropped to all fours. Suzuki-san coughed and wheezed. Her machines never changing their monotonous song. They'd betrayed her. How many times had they betrayed her?

The hag crept across the floor toward Aimi, the room growing colder as she slowly approached. Aimi fought her restraints, rattling the metal of the bed, crying out over the squealing bedsprings. Footsteps ran down the hall.

"Is everything okay?" A flashlight blinded Aimi for an instant. Then nothing.

IN AN UNDERWATER blur someone with a lilting, cooing voice spoke.

"Ready?"

Moving down the hall. *Bing.* The elevator doors opened. Was anyone inside this time? *Bing.* Now she was gliding right underneath that wretched ceiling. Maybe she could touch it. The next room was bigger, bright, glinting metal and white, warm voices muffled under masks. A half dozen people busy and serious gathered around.

"Ready?" The doctor's voice calmed her. Everything else pulled away. "Count back from one hundred for me?"

"One hundred, ninety-nine . . . "

TAP TAP TAP. A cool hand lightly hitting her cheek.

"Tell me your name."

Tap tap.

"Where are you?"

"Aimi," her voice painful in her throat. "Hospital."

"Good."

THE ORCHESTRA OF Suzuki-san's machines and that vague sense of unease alerted Aimi that she was back in her room. Waking was a fight. The queasy sick of anesthesia kept plunging her back into dark until eventually she found herself in sleep paralysis, something that hadn't happened since university.

Her mind awake, alert. Her body frozen. She felt the tubes growing out of her, the ache of surgery and of having been lying down for so long. She attempted to turn in her dream body, to relieve some of the pressure on her lower back when she separated and was now that seeing eye from above, looking down on her sleeping form. At least she was alone this time, no strange creatures like that dream she'd had . . . when? Days ago? Weeks ago?

It almost felt like she crouched inside the ceiling, looking down through that broken panel. The thought ran through her head, had it always been her staring down this whole time? Was she trying to warn herself?

Suddenly a movement caught her attention, the hyperaware above-Aimi. She realized that no matter how real if felt, this had to be a dream, too. Why? Because the movement came from Suzuki-san who was no longer lying prone in her bed arguing with the hag as before. Suzuki-san was up and tottering about. A little off-balance, but light-spirited, almost dancing. Impossible. Pretty Cat had told Aimi that very first day that the old woman had been bedridden for four months. There would be no way she could get up and move around. Much less dance.

As soon as Aimi had this thought, the old woman seemed to notice. She stopped and shuffled over. She held Aimi's hand. Her skin dry and rough. It felt so real.

A clicking noise behind her tore above-Aimi's attention from the scene below, and the realization came that she wasn't alone.

She gripped the edges of the tile and heard it crack. The popping sound and the feeling of dust sprinkling her skin brought her back into her sleeping body. She woke, opening her eyes and feeling as if something heavy rolled on top of her.

There was no Suzuki-san by her side, but she glimpsed fingers releasing the edge of the ceiling tile above and retreating back into the bowels of hospital.

Suzuki-san's voice echoed in her ear.

Thank you.

THE NEXT MORNING—or the morning after that, she didn't know— it was silence that woke her. No machines, no snores, no frantic voice yelling. But a presence in the room, a shadow standing behind her closed curtain.

"Who's there?"

The figure moved away. Something was off, a sense of panic rising in her chest. She had to get out of here. Aimi reached for the nurse call button, but felt something else already in her hand.

She opened her fist slowly. There in her palm was a tooth, yellow and brown with age, a bloody root where it had recently been pulled out.

Aimi screamed.

IT TOOK A long time to calm her down.

Pretty Cat searched everywhere but couldn't find the tooth. "Maybe it was only a dream," she said, hazel cat eyes unblinking. Then, as an afterthought, "Oh, Suzuki-san passed away in the night."

"ALMOST TIME FOR lights out." Pretty Cat jotted down the numbers and dropped the thermometer into one of the deep white pockets at her hip. "Normal," she said, replacing the chart. "Very good."

A lie. No fever? Impossible. The nerves under Aimi's skin scraped and burned worse than ever, like a thousand match heads being struck at once. Everything ached. Her body screamed to move, to flee. How long had she lain here?

"That's good," Aimi said.

"Are you sleeping well finally?"

Pretty Cat thumbed over her shoulder at the empty bed, new sheets stretched tight across the mattress, tiny pillow fluffed into a tiny ball. The out-of-place, futuristic machines lined up, sleeping. For the moment at least.

Aimi, feeling the weight of a stare, turned her head to the empty bed next to Suzuki-san's. Only it wasn't empty. She startled—could the nurse not see her? Hunched over, sitting with her legs up, ropey, dark arms wrapped around her knees? Her chin tucked, she looked out of the tops of glassy, sunken eyes, her skin the color of bruises. A crown of thinning white hair tied into fierce knots hung down her shoulders.

"You okay?" the nurse asked. "If you want, I can give you something." Her hand went to her other pocket where she kept the ever-present syringe.

"No, I'm good." Aimi cut her off.

That's what they wanted, for her to fall into one of those tar-like sleeps. That would make it easier for them, wouldn't it?

Down the hall someone cried out, the crash and shatter of something being thrown against a wall. Several inmates from other rooms howled their support. The whole floor was losing its mind. Of course they were. They knew she—the hag—was loose, and they didn't know where she was going next.

"If everything is okay then I'll see you tomorrow." Pretty Cat turned to leave.

"Goodnight." At the door the nurse gave a little bow before clicking off the overhead lights for the night and disappearing down the hall.

That half second of darkness before her eyes adjusted to the bluish tint radiating off the bed nightlights and when she looked again, the hag was gone. Panic squeezed her throat, drummed her chest. The hag was already moving. Aimi looked around the room. She had to get to work fast.

First, remove the controlling brain fog.

Aimi touched the tape that secured the IV line growing from the crook of her arm. The sight of blood made her nauseous. But she was desperate. She had to get free. She pulled it out from her vein, and salty liquid squirted onto the floor. There. The drip-drip poison line removed, she felt more clearheaded already. Proof of what they were doing.

Next.

There were two more tethers to break. Aimi closed her eyes, gritted her teeth and concentrated on removing both the drain tube in her stomach and the catheter taped to her thigh. She flung the mess to the floor. Almost free.

She scanned the room again. The hag was near. A presence like a feral, almost-imperceptible growl filled the air. And the smell of rot. There were too many shadows; she could be anywhere, waiting to leap, latch on, consume her as she had poor Suzuki-san.

A sound made Aimi look up. From the black maw that opened into the hospital itself came a damp loamy chill, the breathing, and the now-familiar *click click click* that had followed her.

Aimi laughed. With her clear head she knew the sound for what it was: *Bones,* she thought. Fingernails and bones.

The hole is where they all went to hide. The bugs under their skin burrowing so deep into their bones. They had to creep, had to keep moving to keep the tilts and angles tamped down. But sometimes they'd stop to watch. But they grew nervous and clicked until they crept again.

Aimi's body ached in deep places, missing organs, pulled wires, broken gears, shattered parts. What else had they taken? But despite that, she felt stronger than she had in days, weeks. She still didn't know how long she'd been here.

No longer bound, Aimi eased herself to her feet, legs weak from so many days of poisoning and disuse, and stood on the old hospital bed. She found her balance just as movement caught her eye. At the end of her bed, the hag's long yellowed fingers gripped the rail, darkly-lined face and greasy moving hair. She had too many teeth.

Aimi reached up, stretched. *Please, please . . .*

Click click click.

The mattress moved, the hag now on the bed, one hand reaching to wrap around her ankle.

"No," Aimi whimpered. For once she wished her luck would change, for once escape her rotten fate.

Just when the expected the hag's claws to yank her from her feet, something latched onto her forearms. From above, in the vast black belly of the building, skeletal arms reached down, *click click click.* Bones and nails. Shadow faces of the long dead, snapping mouths. They would save her. Aimi felt herself lifted away from the hag.

She cackled with joy.

Freedom.

DID YOU KNOW?

THERSA MATSUURA is an American author who has lived half her life in rural Japan. Being fluent in Japanese allows her to explore lesser-known parts of the culture, obscure folktales, strange superstitions, and curious myths. She uses this research to inspire her own stories.

Thersa is the author of two short story collections: *A Robe of Feathers and Other Stories* (Counterpoint LLC, 2009) and *The Carp-Faced Boy and Other Tales* (Independent Legions Press, 2017). The latter was a finalist for a Bram Stoker Award (2017). Throughout the years, she's also had stories and articles published in various magazines, journals, anthologies, and serialized in newspapers.

Thersa is a graduate of Clarion West (2015) and a recipient of Horror Writers Association's Mary Wollstonecraft Shelley Scholarship (2015). When not writing, she works on her two bimonthly podcasts, Uncanny Japan and Soothing Stories Podcast.

You can find her at www.thersamatsuura.com.

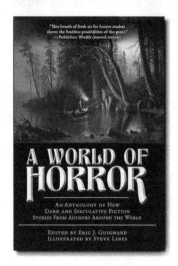

FASTEN YOUR

SAFETY BELTS . . .

NEXT STOP:

AUSTRALIA and

GREATER OCEANIA

HAUNTED OCEANIA

Teti'aroa,
French Polynesia

Wittenoom,
Australia

Brisbane,
Australia

Port Macquarie,

Kiama,
Australia

Foster,
Australia

Waihi,
New Zeal

Dunedin,
New Zealand

0 100 200 300 400 500
Miles

AUSTRALIA AND GREATER OCEANIA

I've been to that aquarium, abandoned as it is and no longer fit for purpose. I've walked through its ruins...

TIDEMARKS

FEATURE ENTRY 11

STRUCTURE TYPE: AQUARIUM
LOCATION: DUNEDIN, NEW ZEALAND
LAT./ LONG.: 45.7734° S, 170.7284° E
BUILT: CIRCA 1966
GROUND ELEVATION: 23 FT. (7 M.)
WRITTEN BY: OCTAVIA CADE

TRAVEL GUIDE NOTES

NEW ZEALAND IS considered one of the world's great "hot spots" for rich biodiversity, but has been facing increasing dangers of species extinction recently, both in vegetative and in animal life, due to climate change, habitat loss, and other harmful environmental factors. On the front lines of this concern is scientist and author Octavia Cade, PhD, who writes frequently on the topics of ecological and biodiversity loss. As she tells me, this following story is, in fact, inspired by graduate school research studies at a marine laboratory, set next to colonies of migratory birds and sea life.

Haunting and elegant, this inclusion may be seen as a love letter to the lost, or it can be a found-journal fragment; it can be the divergence of choices made, and their lasting impact, or it can be whatever else you choose—such is its intrigue. As for me, I elect to read this as a poetic contemplation on what it means to confront the phantoms in our life. Friends, strangers, even birds—should one look hard enough, they all may be found of the periphery of "Tidemarks."

—**Charlatan Bardot**

I NEVER EXPECTED TO SEE THEM.
  The arrogance of it, the pride—as if seeing or not seeing made any sort of difference. But I had a reason, so I thought, and that made me better than the people who came through here with lamplights and laughter, expecting the echoes of creatures long gone, mistaking phosphorescence for phantoms. Not that there was much of that, even, but in the middle of the night, with atmosphere and poor light . . . people see what they want to. And I wanted to see the dead so badly.

I could see them easily in daylight. They're all there, on the upper floors of the Otago Museum, dead birds behind glass with hard little eyes, figures fluffed out with stuffing, and the feathers smoothed down so that the colors blended into one another, softly. Artifacts of extinction.

"You know you can see them for real," Lucy says. "Out at the old aquarium in Pilots Beach, where the nesting grounds used to be." It's a story I've heard as well—one of those things that gets passed down and down through the marine science department, a faculty folk tale. That late at night, when the ocean's very still and the tide is at its highest point, the penguins come back.

They've been gone for decades. When fish stocks collapsed, the sea birds went with them. The penguins, the albatross at Taiaroa . . . some of the gulls managed to hang on, but then they've always been scavengers.

Lucy's determined that the stories are true. I don't believe it. Wishful thinking, and why would penguins come to an aquarium they never lived at? I've been to that aquarium, abandoned as it is and no longer fit for purpose. I've walked through its ruins. The tanks are empty, the glass broken. Stones in the tanks to account for the shattering. I can't say that I threw any myself—there wasn't exactly a lot of glass left to shatter, less lingering respect than lack of opportunity—but I felt the temptation. The place was a wreck. Just an echoing emptiness, and the outside tanks, more like swimming pools, had standing puddles in the bottom, scummed over and full of sandflies. The whole place in shades of gray and rose, the tidemarks pink and rising.

"Come on," Lucy says. "Call yourself a scientist. Think of it as an experiment."

"In gullibility?" I ask her, and it's a flippant response. Lucy considers it anyway.

"In hope, perhaps," she says. "I hear it comes with feathers."

Better feathers than red tides, I suppose.

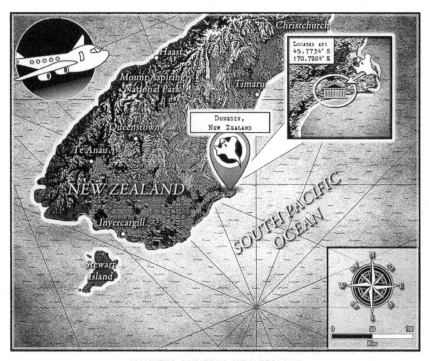

HAUNTED DUNEDIN, NEW ZEALAND

TRUTH WAS I'D heard the legend before I even got to the university. Knew it to be true, as well. I'd seen them when I was a kid: those ghostly shapes, come out of water and waddling. Not what you'd expect of ghosts, nothing elegant about them. No trailing mists, no delicate movement. Just bodies ill-shaped for land, awkward in their stride but limned, just a little, in light that didn't come from stars, and didn't come from plankton, either. I'd say that's when I knew I'd end up in conservation, but that would be a lie. I didn't know until I joined the marine science department and heard the stories about the ghosts, and who could see them.

"No one but scientists," says Lucy. "No one but biologists. That's us." But biology wasn't enough—it was love that brought sight with it. The determination to love something that was gone, to look at lack and choose to love it anyway. You don't have to be a scientist for that. But when love seeps through into *devotion*, when it becomes such a focus for life that the wish to preserve comes above everything else . . .

It's obsession that leads to ghosts. Obsession and nothing else.

Lucy's halfway there already. No one wants to spend time at the old aquarium. Not even kids, who were probably the ones who broke those empty tanks in the first place. The whole building's just high up enough on the headland that the rising tides haven't swallowed it up, but the algal blooms that come with warming waters slop up against those outside pools, paint them red with toxicity and deoxygenated waters. Under moonlight the red tides are black, but under all light they are sticky and soft and carry the scent of rot. It seems almost cruel to watch for ghosts when they have to surface into that, into what climate and run-off have made of the waters that were once their home.

Whatever wonder there is in watching the dead rise out of the sea at the foundations of the aquarium, there is little wonder in seeing them suffocate there, as if reborn into oil slicks. Albatross, falling with those wide, white wings into an ocean the color of blood and never rising again, penguins searching along shorelines for fish until their little starved bodies wash up, stained with red and dissolving in sand, as if they were never there at all.

"There's nothing there to see." That's what I tell Lucy. She doesn't believe me. The ghosts are calling her, she says, but an invitation is something which can be refused.

She wants to see absence for herself. I can't say that I let her, because it's not my place to grant permission, she's a grown woman, and she can make her own decision. Mine is that I don't have to go with her.

(LUCY GOES, AND she doesn't come back. She cut her throat on a shattered piece of aquarium glass, and this is added to the folk tale, between lectures and around water coolers: that the ghosts came for her, and now she haunts there too.)

(Lucy goes and comes back. There's a new streak of gray in her hair, and she dyes it red, bright red, and then one day she can't stand looking at herself in the mirror and shaves it all off. "There was nothing there worth seeing," she says.)

(Lucy goes and comes back and everything is fine. "I guess it's just a silly story," she says, and there's disappointment in her face, and I don't tell her that this is the best that can be hoped for, that she got off lucky, and that there are still the museum birds, behind unbroken glass and perfect.)

That is what ghosts do. They open up possibilities, they bring you face to face with things you don't *want* to face, and there's no guarantee of how you'll react when you see them.

"What would you do if you saw a ghost?" Lucy asks me, before she went out to try and find ghosts of her own. As if there were so many possibilities open for me, as if I hadn't narrowed them down and down until there was only one left.

Turn away. That's what I did. "It's just a silly story," I said. "Nothing there worth seeing." I went out to see ghosts, and I didn't come back. There could have been gray, but I've always dyed my hair so who could tell, really.

WHAT *WOULD* I do if I saw a ghost?

It's a question that's been answered already. I lied about it. That seemed like the best thing to do. I know people say that children are truthful in some fundamental way, more so than adults, but that too is a lie. Children are good at imagination, and at invention, and they recreate the world around them to make it understandable. To make it palatable, I think. That's what I did, anyway. I sneaked out to the aquarium in the middle of the night, because I'd heard that it was haunted and I wanted to see ghosts.

More accurately, I wanted to see birds. If the penguins had been alive I'd have gone during the day, because the shops would have been open then and I could have bought some ice cream and eaten it all up while I waited for them to come out of surf and onto sand. Not a romantic reason, perhaps, but I was not a romantic child. It didn't matter that they were ghosts. It mattered that they were penguins, and if the only way I could see penguins was behind glass in a museum or behind death on the coast, well . . . it was easier to pretend the latter was living than the former.

The aquarium had been a broken, empty place. If I'd had been interested in ghosts for the sake of ghosts it would have seemed a fine place for them. Atmospheric. There was broken glass, of course, pieces of detritus scattered round. The place had looked like a dump, but beneath the emptiness and the absence I could still see the clean lines where the tanks had been, the displays on the walls that had said which tank contained sea urchins and which contained starfish, which held crabs and black coral and cod.

One of the tanks was still intact. There was nothing in it, of course—all the inhabitants taken out, all the water drained away. The only thing left was dust. I'd drawn a happy face in it, and the awkward shape of a penguin which only illustrated why science, and not art, had been even then my preferred choice of career. If it had been a different world, with different waters, there might have been a phosphorescent glow to follow the trace of fingers . . . plankton and bright colors and presence, but those things don't belong in empty buildings and empty tanks, so I'd dismissed the brief small spark as a trick of the light, a reflection from the torch I'd brought with me, and not a ghost at all.

I'd decided all the ghosts were outside, you see. Well, that was how the story went. Penguins and albatross and the red surface of water, algal blooms and old blood. I left the tanks behind and went outside, with the aquarium at my back, and looked to the waters and expected the ghosts to come.

And they did.

It was awful. Unbearable. And more than anything, hopeless.

That's the thing about ghost stories. There's supposed to be a *reason* that the ghost is doing what it's doing. Even a kid like me, who'd never read a whole lot of ghost stories, knew there was supposed to be a reason. Ghosts came so that people could find their bodies. They came to pass on a message. They came to get vengeance on those who had killed them. And once you figured out what they wanted, you could make them go away, and it would be a good thing, helping them pass on.

There was no good thing about the aquarium's dead. They washed up in waves, they came to settle on water and sank there. They thrashed and suffered and died like they'd died the first time, and those of them that made it out of the ocean and onto the dark little sliver of beach, well. They stumbled in the memory and presence of algae, they smothered in tides. And there was no reason for it, because there were too many bodies to find and there was nothing that they could tell us and there was no way to bring them back anyway, or to send them on, if that kind of dead ever had anywhere to go that wasn't display cases in museums and a forgettable sort of guilt. That was extinction, and it was the end, and there was nothing to be done about it.

I'd sneaked out to see ghosts, and I'd seen them, and there was nothing magical about it, nothing transcendent. Nothing frightening either. It was just sad, and sick, and although at the time I hadn't known the word *voyeuristic* I knew what it felt like, and how tawdry it was to watch the remains of what had been lost. I didn't understand it all then, my reaction. I was only a kid. But I'd stopped watching before it was over and gone back into the aquarium and found that empty tank full of glass, with a happy face and a bird drawn on it in dust, and I'd smashed that glass until my hands bled all over it, and then I walked away.

There was never a moment when I decided to lie. No, I hadn't seen any ghosts. No, I didn't believe in that sort of thing. But that is what happens when the world needs recreating into a new and less terrible place.

(I WENT AND came back. There was nothing there, it was boring and cold, and the aquarium was locked and I couldn't get inside. There was nothing on the beach but old beer bottles from people who'd come to see the ghosts and also been disappointed, and I cut my hand on the glass throwing it at rocks until I was bored enough and cold enough to come home, and the blood seeped through all my clothes until I was fair floating in it.)

(I went and came back. There were ghost hunters there and they shared their hot chocolate with me, and they said I had a sympathetic face and the penguins would probably come for me but I can't have been sympathetic enough, and eventually they got tired of waiting and started kissing instead. The water was red and oozing and I scooped some up in the empty mug and tested it with my tongue and it made me sick, so sick, I kept throwing up until I couldn't breathe.)

(I went and I never came back. I thought there were ghosts and ghosts and ghosts, and I went down to the edge of water so I could see them, and I slipped on the algae and the red tide took me out, and I never saw any ghosts and didn't become one neither.)

"I bet you never went ghost hunting in your life," says Lucy.

That's just what she knows.

"No," I say. "I never did."

THERE ARE SO many reasons to go back. So many possibilities. Drowning and exsanguinations and absence, the red tide. I could say I went to lay a wreath. I could say it was an act of mourning for a colleague who came to grieve there, or for a kid who sneaked out in the night.

I think in the end I just want proof that I'd convinced myself after all. Lucy has left pieces of herself around the lab, reminders of the person she used to be. My throat closes up when I look at them. I'd like to put her—the person she used to be—to rest. She doesn't look the same (in the funeral home) (at the hairdresser's) (staring into museum glass).

I went in daylight, because if you don't expect to see ghosts, then daylight is when you expect them not to appear the most, and they didn't. There was nothing outside the aquarium where the rising tide came to lap at old walls. Nothing but beer bottles and empty wrappers, and drag marks, as if a body had been pulled out of ocean. Nothing but the tide, the red, red, empty tide.

Inside, the aquarium was still empty, still conspicuously broken. I'd like to say the brown smear on one old and broken tank was the blood I left there when I saw ghosts in childhood and decided not to see them, but it could have been left by an angry child who broke glass with stones instead, because she saw nothing when she had expected, when she had *wanted*, to see different. That, perhaps, is a better story. It's less difficult, and less sad.

In another world that child, grown up and still loving, would have brought a mug of sea water and emptied it into a bloodied tank. It would have been her version of remembrance, and when she dragged her fingers through water the tank would have appeared, briefly, as whole thing and phosphorescent. There would have been starfish inside, and sea fish and devotion, a haunting that hurt a little less.

"Did you see anything?" Lucy asks, or a version of her, anyway.

She wishes so badly that I could.

DID YOU KNOW?

OCTAVIA CADE is a New Zealand writer. She has a PhD in science communication from the University of Otago, in Dunedin, and fondly remembers the penguins and albatross that live on the coast of that city. She's sold close to 60 stories, to markets including *Clarkesworld*, *Asimov's*, and *Strange Horizons*, and her most recent book, *The Impossible Resurrection of Grief*, from Stelliform Press, looks at ecological grief in the wake of biodiversity loss and species extinction. She attended Clarion West 2016, and was the 2020 writer in residence at Massey University. You can find her at ojcade.com, or on Twitter at @OJCade.

INGRAHAM'S BOOKSTORE

BY ALAN BAXTER

The smell of books . . . and more

LEAVING behind the salt smell of the harbor and the sounds of cockatoos playing on the post office clock tower, you enter Ingraham's Bookstore with a sense of anticipation. The building excites imagination with its faux-Gothic façade and amber lighting. Inside, among the perfume of old paper and ink, you walk the narrow spaces to peruse shelves bowed under the weight of many worlds. Leatherbound hardcovers, well-thumbed paperbacks, every kind of guide.

Sometimes, while you explore, the original owner, Mr. Sylvester Ingraham, may loiter just behind your shoulder, whispering recommendations or critiques. He has an opinion on every author, it seems he has read every book. Should you turn to see him, there will be no one there. But you may catch the scent of rotting seaweed and the coppery tang of blood from the inexplicable-yet-fatal wounds with which he was found behind his sales desk that fateful winter morning so long ago.

ALAN BAXTER is a multi-award-winning author of horror, supernatural thrillers, and dark fantasy liberally mixed with crime, mystery, and noir. He's also a martial arts expert, a whisky-soaked swear monkey, and dog lover.

* FILE UNDER: *Haunted Bookstore*

The five lighthouses James Barnet built between 1878 and
1880. Called them the Five Sisters or his *string of pearls* . . .

THE FIVE SISTERS

FEATURE ENTRY 12

STRUCTURE TYPE: LIGHTHOUSE
LOCATION: PORT MACQUARIE (NEW SOUTH WALES), AUSTRALIA
LAT./ LONG: 31.4758° S, 152.9373° E
BUILT: CIRCA 1879
GROUND ELEVATION: 23 FT. (7 M.)
WRITTEN BY: TERRY DOWLING

TRAVEL GUIDE NOTES

I'D LIKE TO start by thanking esteemed author-editor and friend Norman Prentiss for bringing Terry Dowling to my attention. In a sort of Baader-Meinhof-phenomenon moment of comprehension, I realized that I'd been reading Terry's work for years in annual "Best Of" horror genre anthologies (e.g. he had more stories than any other writer selected over the course of the two-decade-long series *Year's Best Fantasy and Horror*), but somehow his name just hadn't coalesced for me in regards to the sum of his work. Now I go back and declare: Goodness! This was the same author who wrote "Nightside Eye" *and* "The Way the Red Clown Hunts You" *and* "Two Steps Along the Road" (IMO, one of the single greatest horror short stories ever written).

For over forty years Terry has been publishing such work, and he's still at it, quietly churning out tale after tale from his hometown of Sydney, Australia. And he's still at it, here—in the newest installment of his Dan Truswell series of stories—inviting us on a winding journey of mystery, dream-"psychosleuthing," otherworldly malfeasance, and a broken line of lighthouses known as "The Five Sisters."

—**Charlatan Bardot**

"**S**USAN DIDN'T JUST DIE IN HER SLEEP. SHE WAS pushed."

Dan had been half listening, still thinking about the file he'd been reading before Peter had come into his small, well-appointed office in the Everton Psychiatric Facility. But then he caught on the final word. "What did you say, Peter?"

"The sleep man was talking about a Susan he knew dying in her sleep and that she was pushed. It really seemed to be bothering him. Then it just came to me that he was right. Whoever she was, she *was* pushed."

"What do you mean 'pushed'?"

"That's it, Doctor Dan. What *does* pushed mean? Why am I so sure?"

Neither of them needed to answer that question. It was how it always worked with Peter Rait—former patient, gifted, well-adjusted schizophrenic-become-hospital handyman, friend, and unofficial aide through long acquaintance, and (there was no escaping Peter's own term for it given his certainties, intuitions, and insights) proven "psychosleuth."

Dan would have made appropriate facial expressions had others been present and that particular term was used, but that would have been part of their agreed-on camouflaging schtick. He never for a moment doubted the younger man's gifts.

"Then who's Susan?"

"No idea. Someone the sleep man knew. But it was *how* he said it, Doctor Dan. So casual. Like he was talking to himself. Didn't care that I heard."

"Then who's the sleep man, Peter?"

"Johnny Barrack over in P3. That guy from Port Macquarie. Keeps going on about sleep and dreams. What they really are. You'll have to ask Johnny."

"I will, Peter."

"Can we do it now? Right now? He's expecting us."

Dan checked his watch, saw that the hospital's lunchtime was well and truly over. "It's bothering you that much?"

"It was *how* he said it, Doctor Dan. That kind of conviction, that intense knowing. You know what I'm like."

Dan studied the face of his tall, lean, former patient, noted the concern in the dark eyes beneath the tousled black hair streaked with gray. "Gotcha." Dan pushed back from his desk. "Let's go see the sleep man."

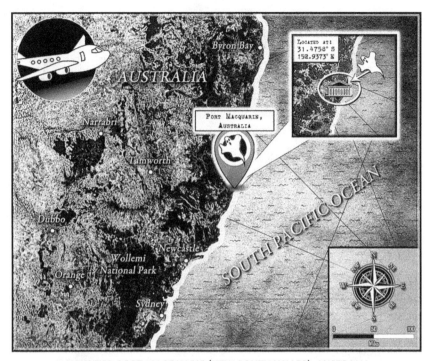

HAUNTED PORT MACQUARIE (NEW SOUTH WALES), AUSTRALIA

WHICH WAS EASY enough. The Prior Wing was not even a minute away from Dan's office, and Johnny Barrack's two-share room was close to the main entrance.

And it was clear that Johnny was glad of the company. He sat on the edge of his bed in day clothes, a large amiable man with a vast smile and small earnest eyes, and when Dan and Peter were settled on the room's two chairs he launched right into it.

"I'm not pushing this, Doctor Truswell. It's my thing. It fascinates me. I keep coming back to it."

"Okay. So Susan was pushed. You wanted me to know that."

"No, Peter did. When I told him, he said that *you* had to know."

"Peter?" Dan looked across to where Peter sat nearest the door.

"I know how it sounds, Doctor Dan, but it has to do with the *muselet*. What Johnny was telling me about the *muselet*." The first time he said the unfamiliar word he pronounced it *muse-a-lay*. The second time it was more like *muse-lay*, Peter almost swallowing the second syllable in the French way so it barely existed.

And, more than ever, it felt like the back and forth of a comedy routine. "Johnny?"

"Doctor Truswell, you'll know a lot of this. But we dream for more than six years of our lives. Do it every night for maybe two hours. Whatever it is, it's a crucial act for the brain, a whole life, whole self-act. Much more than just for the house-keeping catch-up they talk about, you know, defragmenting the personal hard-drive, much more than free-forming play. Even our genitalia are involved. When we dream, males get an erection, women's vulvas become engorged. That sort of whole body act. And we're not meant to remember much about it. Our dreams are *meant* to be forgotten."

"Go on."

"All those stages of sleep, the grand cycle repeating four, five, maybe six times, if we're lucky. The spindles shooting up in Stage 2, the great rolling swells of delta waves in Stage 3, front to back, front to back, the increasing psycho romp through the dream fields. And more and more of such private madness as the cycle repeats, not trivial, not discards and play, regardless of what some experts say. More a vital goal for an elaborate delivery system for the rest of whatever it is we're doing."

"Peter says you're something of the expert here. Do *you* know why we dream, Johnny?"

"That's a good question, Doctor Truswell, but no one does. We ultimately still don't know what *sleep* is for. We note all the sensible physical markers, measure and examine it empirically, note the different chemicals involved, measure the changes to electrical activity in the brain, even how that activity ceases at clinical death, things like that. But even knowing where life comes from, where it goes, what it really does while it's here with all that unknown mental power we possess, again we can only note the markers and offer theories."

"Some very persuasive ones."

"But ultimately inconclusive. Always. The highest lifeform on the planet (we still allow) endangers itself by becoming unconscious for a good *third* of its day. Why we do that has to be tremendously important, absolutely crucial to justify such a bold evolutionary risk."

"You have a theory for why we dream." Dan made sure that it wasn't a question this time. He couldn't afford to encourage this man beyond a certain point.

"The *other* reason for why we dream, yes, I do. Note the 'other' please. Whatever else dreaming is for, we *also* do it so we can each add to a *muselet* we're building for ourselves."

There it was again: *muse-a-lay*, second syllable swallowed so it came over as *muse-lay*.

"Which is what, Johnny?"

Johnny Barrack smiled. "I note the tone, Doctor, but, then again, I *am* in a psych ward, however relaxed and enlightened. A *muselet* is one of those little wire cages clamped tightly around a champagne cork to hold it in the bottle. From the French to muzzle."

"Go on."

"You get the idea. Remove that, and the cork is ejected under pressure."

"And the life leaks away."

"Or can be *stolen* away, Doctor Truswell. But I'll come back to that."

"All right. You're saying part of the reason we dream is to build up a—" He spoke the word for the first time, three syllables made almost two. "—*muselet*?"

"The evidence allows it."

Dan smiled at Johnny's use of *allows*. He *was* being careful. "Like adding to a coral growth night after night."

"That's it. A little bit every time we enter REM sleep, build, build, build."

"For what purpose?" Dan could guess where this was heading, but needed Johnny to say it.

"Doctor, you doubtless know there are points during a healthy, natural sleep cycle where—evidence shows—we actually stare into death, into oblivion, non-existence, for a short time, five, ten, fifteen minutes, rarely longer. The brain, the mind, the self in its myriad complexity can't stand doing it for too long, and we're thrown clear, sent back to repeat the whole cycle again. Why we do it at all remains a mystery."

"And the role of the *muselet*?" Dan managed it again. *Muse-lay*.

"Protects us during those glimpses of death. Keeps us safely tucked in. What was it Nietzsche said? If you stare long into the abyss, the abyss also stares into you? That's how it happens every night. For whatever reason, for brief moments we stare at death and death stares back, all while we're fitting out our dream palace, our last-ditch, anti-death protection station to prevent those glimpses of death becoming more."

"Like what? Killing us? Easing us—*pushing* us—through the portal before we're ready?"

"Doctor Truswell, I'm going slow here. Work with me. At least six years spent dreaming in the average lifespan. This dream matter accumulates over time, acts like a *muselet* to protect the self when it faces those fascinating, devastating moments every night."

"Made of—?"

Johnny didn't let Dan finish. "We can't know. But electro-chemical scribing, I suspect, deep RNA imprinting surely. More like DMT is meant to do?"

Dan worked to grasp the connection. "DMT? Oh, right, got you."

"Dimethyltryptamine." Johnny said it so easily. "The hallucinogen produced in the pineal gland that lets us dream. Washes through the brain during dream sleep. Provides wholly natural hallucinations to counter death-shock too, experts say. Well, Doctor, this could be more. You know Anna Kavan's novel, *Sleep Has His House*? Well, sleep doesn't have a house, but self does. The subconscious works on this protective *muselet* while the self is unconscious in sleep. Works on it every night. The random, wildcard dreams are there too, as entertainment, free play, whatever, but at some point we work on building and maintaining that little cage for ourselves."

Peter Rait chose to play devil's advocate then. "But completely natural, yes? No room for boogeymen. No ghosts or hauntings in any of this, Johnny?"

Johnny Barrack laughed and shrugged. "No, sir. All biochemical. Neurochemical. Peter, when we talked earlier I said how we just don't know what any of this is yet, so why not cast the broadest net? But it's more than just wondering about where the dying self goes and preparing for non-existence. It's about protecting the living self from something that endangers the *muselet* every night. Works against it, wears it away, tips the human into premature death when it fails, I'm sure of it."

Dan offered what Johnny had left unspoken. "Preys on it?"

"Susan was pushed."

And Peter Rait was there on cue. "I'm sure of it too, Doctor Dan. She was."

Dan nodded to show he was considering it, not resisting or opposing. "So who was Susan?"

"Susan Ottile over in Port. Port Macquarie. That's where I'm from." Johnny smiled, his small eyes twinkling. "Originally. Susan was found dead in her bed last Monday morning. Fifty-seven years old. Very fit. No visible cause. Apparently died in her sleep."

"How was she pushed?"

Johnny took a deep breath, then reached out to touch the nearest wall, as if confirming where he was. "Still in the right place. Good. It's what you said, Doctor. Something *preys* on the *muselet*. Reaches out, feeds on it, wears it down. Releases it, if we're unlucky."

"Tips us into death."

"That's it. While we're looking into it."

"But you have no proof."

"No one has *conclusive* proof for any of this yet. The old saw is that sleep is as different from being unconscious as it is from being awake, but we still don't know why we need to *present as unconscious* to rest our brains, why we have to become so vulnerable."

"So, no evidence then."

"I didn't say that. But you'd need to go to Port where Susan died. Speak to Lottie Gill, Susan's friend. They worked together in Susan's hairdressing salon. She found the body and the notes."

"What notes?"

"Let Lottie tell you."

"Johnny, look—"

"Doctor Truswell, you're a sure, sharp, gifted man and a prince of psychiatrists, and Peter here is a fabulous mystery to us all, staff and patients alike, but it's all about what we take to the campfire."

"The campfire?"

"The village campfire. The tribal campfire. If I tell a great story, you'll feed me, invite me back the next night. I won't have to hunt or forage for myself. Well, I've got to leave something for Lottie. She's just lost her closest friend. Needs to be part of it. We made a deal."

While Dan sat considering that, Peter took his chance, no doubt realizing that it was *his* own conviction, not Johnny's, that was guiding Dan now, and that he needed to secure an ongoing role for himself. "Lottie would let us see the place?" The "us" said it all.

"Sure. A nice little flat at the back of the local auto wreckers Susan runs—*ran*—with her brothers, Frank and Joe."

"She worked there?"

"No, she had the hairdressing salon in town. But she started living there after her husband died four years back. She moved in, like I said, started sleeping there, keeping an eye on the place."

"You have Lottie Gill's number?"

"I'll write it down. And listen, you two. Lottie agrees with me about

the *muselet*. Make her tell you about the local lighthouse and the Five
Sisters too."

"Johnny—!"

"Something for the campfire, Doctor Truswell. Ask Lottie."

PORT MACQUARIE WAS nearly three hundred kilometers from rural
Everton, a large picturesque coastal town at the mouth of the Hastings River
that had grown from its penal colony beginnings in the 1800s to one of the
most beautiful beachside communities on the whole New South Wales
coast.

When Dan and Peter pulled up at the Coast Café at 11 a.m. after their
three-hour drive, they found Lottie Gill waiting for them at an outside table
under the awning, a healthy-looking, dark-haired woman in her late forties
wearing jeans, sandals, and the blue floral-print top she had told them to
recognize her by.

After the introductions and expression of condolences, Dan and Peter
joined her for brunch under the awning.

"Something for the campfire, Lottie," Dan said, which made Lottie give
a good hearty laugh.

"Johnny certainly has his way of doing things. But this has really got to
him, Doctor—"

"Dan, please."

"Dan. Susan and he were old friends. The whole family was close, going
back years."

"Lottie, no campfire embellishments now. Give it like a police report, if
you can."

Which she seemed glad to do, telling them how on Monday morning a
week before she had gone to pick up her friend as arranged, and found her
dead in bed. Susan's brothers, Frank and Joe, knew that their sister had a
rostered day off and thought she'd been sleeping in.

"When I couldn't wake her, we called an ambulance and the police."

"They ruled natural causes?"

"They did."

"A fifty-seven year old woman dies. Any medical history?"

"None we knew about."

"Nothing genetic?"

"Parents and grandparents died relatively young, but no family issues
we're aware of."

"So no autopsy?"

"Frank and Joe didn't push for one. The hospital people figured a stroke, an aneurysm, a heart attack, probably sometime between 2 and 4 a.m. They tested for troponin, for poisons, drug overdose, that sort of thing, but that was it. The funeral's been delayed in case, but that should be cleared any time now."

"You went through her things?"

"The boys asked me to."

"She left a will?"

"She did. Nothing much. Her husband died four years ago. Her share in the spare parts business goes to her brothers. Her savings, the house and a block of land at Sawtell, and a few heirlooms go to her daughter, Sally. She works in Sydney and will fly up for the funeral."

Dan nodded, thinking of Johnny Barrack and the calls he must have shared with Susan Ottile.

"Lottie, did Susan have trouble sleeping? Issues she'd raise with Johnny Barrack?"

"Sorry. Guess like the rest of us she worked at having a normal life whenever she could."

"Right. Well, Johnny said she was pushed."

"Yes, okay, but that's Johnny. We've known him since he was a young-un, before, you know, he had to go down to Everton. He was shocked and upset when I gave him the news, but he wanted to know all about it. What the time was, what exactly happened. She was wearing one of those new sleep trackers for him as a favor. You know, looks like a wristwatch, shows sleep duration, the peaks and valleys: light sleep, deep sleep, REM sleep. Johnny wanted to know all that."

"What did it show?"

"What I told Johnny. Just loss of signal. Display interrupted."

Dan felt a thrill go through him imagining the tracker's schematic from the early hours of that Monday, wondering what those devices actually did show under such circumstances: whether a flatline at the critical moment like an ECG reading or just a sudden cessation of signal. A full stop.

"You can show us her flat?"

"Of course. I told Frank and Joe you wanted to see it, which is why I suggested meeting here. It's just a few streets away. But Johnny called them, said you're helping. They're cool about it. And, like I say, Dan, it's not a crime scene."

"Lottie, Johnny also told us about the *muselet* protecting us from something that puts us at risk when we sleep. Did Susan say anything about that?"

"Just that Johnny believed it existed. And that she'd made arrangements, done what her mother and grandmother did, whatever that was."

"She didn't say?"

Peter set down his coffee cup. "The parents and grandparents died relatively young, you said. Like the husband."

"The husband?"

"Died four years ago. Still pretty young too."

The comment clearly troubled Lottie. "Her mother died at 61, I think. The grandmother was 64 or thereabouts. But, hey, like I said, Susan was working at a normal life. Clearly didn't want to say too much. Seemed worried about what too much talk might do. That's why the notes are interesting."

"You've got them?"

"Sure. I'll show them to you when we go 'round to the yard. I made a copy. The police are holding the originals for now."

"Understood. We're also meant to ask about the lighthouse and the Five Sisters."

Lottie nodded. "Right. That was more Susan's territory than Johnny's. Why they got on so well. But let's go 'round to the flat. We can talk there."

BEST PORT SPARES and Autowreckers consisted of a large cinder-block building with a modest and tidy wrecking yard set back behind a chain link fence to one side. Behind a wide front-of-house roller-door and a smaller access door to its left, the large interior extended back, filled with shelves of recycled parts for cars, trucks, and farming equipment, row upon row, stack upon stack, every inch of space filled with things not needed until they were suddenly essential.

Parts dangled from a dozen ceiling rails below mesh-protected skylights, often indeterminate shapes that shifted, turned, and sometimes clanked lightly as they touched in the on-shore breeze that made it through the high ventilation grilles. Despite the nine fluorescent lights along the interior roofing, there were still a lot of shadows, an inevitable gloom that no skylights or fluoro tubes could quite dispel.

Set back beyond the great sweep of shelves and stacks, behind a counter three-quarters of the way in, was a small kitchenette, a curtained shower stall, and a toilet, and—probably a later addition—the small flat Susan had been using.

It was a good-sized room considering, four meters on a side and well-lit by the afternoon light streaming through the large window above the bed. It was sparsely furnished too, with just a pre-fab wardrobe along the wall left of the door, an old-style bed frame, now devoid of its mattress but with folded bedclothes and a very elaborate quilt laid out ready, and a bedside set of drawers adorned with an old-style clock and a decorative Tiffany-style lamp. On the wall to the right of the door, easily visible from the bed, was a framed two-by-two-foot oil painting of a lighthouse, quite likely Tacking Point Light.

"The quilt, the lamp, and that painting there," Lottie began when they were settled in chairs brought in from the workshop, "are the heirlooms I mentioned. Passed down from grandmother to mother. They go to her daughter."

"It's very dramatic," Peter said, clearly taken with the painting. The little tower was shown from below, down on the headland slope, and under a night sky or glowering overcast, caught mid-sweep so light streamed from the lamp room above the gallery.

"It's what first catches my eye whenever I come here. Susan was really interested in local history, all the heritage sites. She was really taken with our lighthouse up on Tacking Point. With all the Five Sisters."

Peter seized on the last comment. "Which are?"

"The five lighthouses James Barnet built between 1878 and 1880. Called them the Five Sisters or his *string of pearls* because the towers and main service buildings are identical. I'll take you up there when we're done here. The towers are all short stocky things, barely eight meters tall because they're up on headlands and didn't need to be taller. You'll find them all along the coast. One at Fingal Head up near the Queensland border, one at Ballina, one here at Tacking Point, one south of us at Crowdy Head, and there was one at Yamba. But the same design. Tacking Point Light up there was fourth of the five built. One of Susan's ancestors had a part in its construction."

Peter was leaning forward, encouraging her. "He worked with this James Barnet?"

"Barnet was the government architect in the late 1800s. Designed that amazing mortuary station down at Railway Square in Sydney, the GPO, lots of lighthouses. But locals carried out the actual construction to his design."

Peter considered that. "So the Five Sisters and the string of pearls aren't necessarily Barnet's names for them?"

"Not sure. Susan could've told you. But one of the locals involved was Andrew Ottile, her ancestor way back. Belonged to that group that was nutty for lighthouses, granted special purposes, all that geomantic, scrying stuff in how they were situated. The Pharos Society."

Dan was frankly astonished to hear words like geomantic and scrying coming from this genial local hairdresser. "You're serious?"

"It was a different world, Dan. Susan would go on about all the buildings Barnet had to get built. Little wonder the work attracted a whole range of types. She'd talk about things her ancestor said, things in his notebooks. Crazy stuff. Either he did the painting or a descendant did when the light became fully automated around 1920."

Dan sat thinking, and was glad when Peter took up the thread again.

"So Andrew Ottile may have named them the Five Sisters."

"He may have. And now I think of it, there are the Three Brothers Mountains right here near Port. Captain Cook named them when he sailed past in 1770, but they'd already been called exactly that by the local Birrpal people thousands of years ago. An amazing coincidence, don't you think? Astonishing really. But maybe that's where the name came from."

While Peter and Lottie talked about namings like the Five Sisters, the Three Brothers, similar landmark namings like the Three Sisters in the Blue Mountains west of Sydney, the Twelve Apostles on the Great Ocean Road in Victoria, Dan found himself studying the gorgeous patchwork quilt folded atop other bedding on the stark frame of the bed, admired the ornate Tiffany lamp with its intricate pink and white leadlight shade and thickened brass stem, finally bringing his attention back to the painting on the wall across from where Susan had slept. He realized that he'd been pondering something, though wasn't sure what. It was Peter asking another question that brought him back to it.

"So no one would know how this tied in?" Peter said. "The Five Sisters? For Susan?"

Lottie shook her head. "All I know is that there was some family involvement in its construction. It may be why Susan lived here, and has— had—this painting in her room. It may have even been painted by that great-great-grandfather. She probably could've told you why here and not at Fingal Head, Yamba, or elsewhere."

"You said there *was* a Barnet lighthouse at Yamba. *Was.* Past tense."

"Right. The original Yamba Light was demolished in 1956 to make way for a reservoir. The new one on Pilot Hill is seventeen meters high, nothing like the original."

Peter leaned forward again, hands laced together. "So the string of pearls was broken. One of the Sisters lost."

"Susan's great-great-grandfather, however far back that goes to 1879, was long dead by then, but he may well have thought of it like that. So might Susan's grandfather, her father too. It must have been a big deal for the Pharos Society."

Peter indicated the painting. "So if the Sisters were identical, *this* could well be the Yamba Light. A substitute, a proxy so the string remained unbroken."

The way Lottie hesitated showed that she hadn't for a moment considered such a possibility. "Well, yes. When you put it like that. They were all the same. It might be the Yamba Light."

"So why is the painting here at Port, Lottie? Why not at Yamba where the lost Sister stood?"

Lottie had the grace to shrug. "I could go crazy wondering about things like that. This is where Susan lived."

Dan nodded, gave a smile of appreciation. "So tell us about the notes?"

"That's the weird part, Dan. They were in an envelope in the second drawer of that bedside table there. But in different hands, using different pens on different types of paper, probably across many years. People had been asked to report on something, and Susan seems to have kept up the tradition. But never any signatures. She knew who they were. The night after she died, there was a new one stuck in the letterbox."

"Which says what?"

Lottie recited from memory. "'The CCTV shows it at 3:48. Two quick pulses, both white. It's on the USB.'"

"You have the USB?"

"No sign of it." She passed over a single handwritten sheet. "But this is all of them. All very brief and, like I say, some quite old."

Dan read the listed comments, which were brief indeed.

Yes, it did. I have no idea when. But it was early. I'm sorry there isn't more. But please tell your Nan.

It probably doesn't matter now, but yes, it did. 3:08 a.m.

3:32. Two pulses. White then pink. Just the two. Hope it helps.

4:08. Yes. But please don't ask again. I do shift work.

The CCTV shows it at 3:48. Two quick pulses, both white. It's on the USB.

Dan then passed the list to Peter, who read it and handed it back.

They sat in silence for a time then, lost in their own thoughts, possibly, like Dan, considering where they were and what had happened, perhaps just watching the dust motes in afternoon sunshine through the window, possibly thinking of the lighthouse and what such words could mean.

Lottie broke that silence. "Okay. It's getting on. Let me show you the lighthouse."

SHE DROVE THEM up to Tacking Point Light in her own car to give Dan a rest from driving. It was mid-afternoon on a brilliantly fine autumn day, the vast sweeps of sky and ocean filling the world, extending from the little white tower and service building on the grassy headland off to the north beyond Sea Acres sanctuary to Town Beach, and south to where the great line of Lighthouse Beach stretched off and away so it truly did feel like the edge of one world unravelling, forever unravelling, into another. Those long waves sweeping in couldn't help but remind Dan of Johnny Barrack's delta waves rolling through the sleeping brain, slow, steady, eternally replenishing, just like this.

The roar of that surf line was on endless repeat too, as were the sounds of wind around the balcony buttresses and the lamp rail of the tower, the cries of gulls as they came wheeling in. The air smelled of salt and sea wrack, and that other smell that the mind always insists can only be the wind itself, as constant and enduring as everything else on that miraculous shore.

Behind them, Port stretched off in the golden afternoon, still more brilliance in sunlit whites, grays, and ochers, with the rooflines of Port Central clearly visible and the haze of blue-green distances beyond.

"It's astonishing," Dan said, and Lottie smiled.

"See? Didn't need to be higher."

"The tower's off-limits?"

"Always are, unless they're decommissioned. The Sisters are all active lights."

"Four at least," Peter said, returning to it. It was more to provoke himself, Dan knew, than to remind them.

Lottie noted his intensity and matched it. "Right. Though the Yamba replacement is operational."

"But not a Sister."

Lottie glanced from Peter to Dan and smiled. "A stepsister surely."

But Peter was frowning into the distance, as if considering the thread of dazzling cumulus that sat out over the ocean. "One can only wonder what happened in 1956 when Yamba Light was replaced to build that reservoir. The Barnet original demolished."

Lottie raised her voice above the sea-wind. "The replacement would have been active before that happened. Some kind of crossover."

Peter kept at it. "But the string of pearls broken just the same. Unless the painting does serve as a stand-in."

Lottie looked at Dan again for some appropriate cue as to how to react. "You're right. Maybe Susan's father or grandfather did do something about that. Maybe the painting isn't so old after all. One of them might have painted it so the original Yamba Light still existed during the 1956 overlap. No one said, and Susan was never sure."

"Lottie, Peter looks distracted, I know, but that's his way. He has to guide this now. Johnny Barrack knew it too. That's why he told us about Susan and the *muselet*. Somehow they're related, in Johnny's mind at least. Would Frank and Joe mind if we spent the night in Susan's flat?"

"What? Sleep there?"

"Sleep. Sit up, whatever you can manage, whatever they're comfortable with. Just so we can *be* there a while."

"Both of you?"

Dan looked across at Peter, who nodded.

"If it's okay," Dan said.

"Well, sure, I guess. You're booked in at a local B&B around the corner, but there's still the bedframe. I'll phone the boys. We could bring in a mattress, maybe a trundle bed."

"Whatever you can manage."

ONCE AGAIN, FRANK and Joe had no objections, doubtless allowing that it was something else that Johnny Barrack needed done so he could settle. The B&B owner was another old family friend, it turned out, and, since she was being paid for Dan's booking regardless, happily provided a replacement mattress and bedding, as well as an overflow trundle bed that was set up along the wall below the painting.

By the time the room was ready, with the curtain drawn over the window and the Tiffany lamp throwing a soft rose glow over everything, it was after 5:30 on a cool, early autumn evening and well past closing time. Dan and Peter were given keys to the rear door Susan had used to save coming in through the shop, were shown how to disarm and reset its security alarm, and given appropriate contact numbers for herself and the brothers.

Then, as she had family commitments to attend to, Lottie gave them some local restaurant recommendations and left them to it, saying she'd call later to see how they were managing.

When she had gone, Dan and Peter just sat for a time as the premises became quiet around them. If they listened for it, they could hear the surf folding in along the nearby beaches, a great braided monotone that never quite went away, and, now and then, if they really listened, what were possibly auto parts turning and touching in the flow of air through the grilles. Inevitably, their attention went to the painting. That's when Peter said it.

"I'm being hunted by something, Doctor Dan."

"Tell me."

"I'm not quite sure yet. But my *muselet* is strong. Yours too."

"Good. But how does that factor in?"

"Still can't say. But it matters."

"We should go back to Everton."

"Doesn't work like that. It reaches out."

"What reaches out?"

Peter shook his head. *Not sure yet.*

"The lighthouse?" Which was the wrong thing to do, Dan knew, speaking it, shaping it, provoking like this.

"Yes, no. Both."

"The painting? *This* lighthouse?" He couldn't help himself.

"Yes, no. Both."

"Then we're protecting you. Everything we do."

Peter didn't comment, just went over and switched on the too-bright overhead light, and switched off the bedside Tiffany lamp.

"That certainly kills the effect," Dan said.

Peter nodded. "Kills the drama. Shows it starkly as just a painting. How we need it to be."

"What are you thinking? What are you seeing?"

"Doctor Dan, I worry about being tricked. Blindsided. I just need to see everything. We should go eat. Come back to it fresh."

WHICH IS WHAT they did, went for an early Mexican meal at Poco Loco at nearby Flynns Beach to the north, wanting to keep well clear of the lights and bustle at the center of Port itself.

But any kind of small talk was impossible now, so they ate mostly in silence, each alone with his thoughts. Something important was happening, still happening, culminating, revealing what else it did.

Only when their plates were cleared and they were sitting over coffee did Dan come back to it.

"Peter, as Johnny Barrack would probably put it, something is preying on anyone sleeping near that painting. He'd say that it preyed on Susan's *muselet*, weakened it enough to *push* her through, possibly did the same to other members of her family across the years. Gradually. Eventually. However it works."

"The painting? You really think so?"

"It certainly catches the eye. And getting it from down on the slope like that. Making it look taller."

Peter was frowning. "The seaward side too, did you notice?"

"How could you tell?"

"You can see the light shining head on. It's blocked off on the landward side so as not to disturb the locals. Has to be down the seaward slope."

"Masked, right. And that late overcast. Not what you'd expect."

"Hardly just an overcast, Doctor Dan. That was a fully-fledged storm."

"A storm? You think? Well, there was no one visiting the tower anyway."

"How could you tell? It was so gloomy. All that blue and green from Susan's lamp."

"Blue and green? Peter, there was plenty of light. But pink and white. Is that why you turned on the overhead light? You saw blue and green?"

"You didn't?"

"Pink and white. Well lit. Overcast, late evening. No storm."

"Then blue and green are the hunting colors," Peter said, almost to himself, as if confirming something. "Secret colors."

"Where'd you get that?"

"Just the old saying. Blue and green should never be seen."

"That has to do with clothing. Matching clothes by color and avoiding that combination."

"No. It's something much older, Dan."

And it was Dan. Not *Doctor* Dan. Peter had forgotten himself, how he usually kept it between them. Or was remembering something else. Something pressing in . . .

It told Dan everything.

The painting affects the light and no one mentions it, he realized. We're not meant to notice. That's how clever it is. Adjusts the mind first. Close seeing. First thing it does. Hides in plain sight.

"We need to go back now."

Peter pushed back from the table. "We really do."

They drove with the windows down. It was a cool night but quiet enough, with just the constant fall of waves along the Port beaches they passed on their way back to Lighthouse Beach, the onshore wind hissing through the sand ridges, working in the trees above the shore, getting down in the streets of the town and along Ocean Drive, Pacific Drive, and the other coastal boulevards, doubtless finding its way through the ventilation grilles at the workshop and setting the hanging parts to stirring.

When they pulled up outside Best Port Spares, they could see the wash of illumination from Susan's curtained window at the rear, the safe white light from the overhead fitting Peter had left on.

No blue and green.

No pink and white either, of course. The heirloom lamp had been turned off. Which had Dan remembering what the notes had said, what those unnamed observers had seen and reported on. The remarks stayed with him as he disarmed the security lock and they entered the premises, turned into Susan's flat, and faced the unlit Tiffany lamp.

At first glance, it really did look like any other variant of that celebrated style, even with the thickened stem below the shade: two swollen brass gourds between three narrower waistings, all set atop a flared base. Many Tiffany lamps came with heavier bodies like that, and this one looked truly old, very much the antique Lottie had said it was, possibly even one of a set.

"Such a pretty light," Dan said, with grim humor. "Those pink and white panes."

"Doctor Dan, it's switched off, but I'm still seeing blue and green."

"Peter, they're pink and white."

"Then it's a different light," Peter said. "Or a changing light. And it's not the shade. The shade isn't the lamp. That's a distraction too." And, without another word, he lifted the thing and hurled it to the ground. The shade and globe smashed on the concrete below the thin carpeting.

Dan said nothing, just picked up the ornate brass stem, found it warm to the touch.

But how could it be? Peter had switched it off two hours ago.

Dan felt a rush of alarm as he rotated the body of the lamp in his hands, examining it closely.

It isn't plugged in!

He kept turning the metal shaft, noting every detail. There was no power lead. No USB or battery port. No solar accumulator modification of any kind.

Where does the light come from?

Though he knew. As Peter knew.

Not the painting. Never the painting.

It's waiting to kill us, has to be working at our muselets even now!

"We dare not sleep here," Dan said.

Peter was already emptying out the old canvas shopping bag that held his travel things. "We know where to take it."

THEY GATHERED UP the pieces of shattered lampshade, dumping the larger, still connected leadlight sections into Peter's canvas bag, and using a brush and dustpan from the workshop to sweep up the remaining fragments as best they could.

Peter was right. The shade hadn't been the lamp, just one part of it, another distraction. The body was the focus, and whatever was held within those decorative brass gourds and waistings.

When they were done, they drove up to Tacking Point, parking close by the windy headland where the little tower sat casting its beams out across the ocean.

Susan's lamp stayed warm all the way. Peter kept reaching into the bag to confirm it, though Dan was hardly surprised. Minus the shade, switched off and disconnected, it still thrived on borrowed life. And Dan was sure that it was still reaching out too, questing for their *muselets* even now, eager to unpick their lives.

It was still early evening, and while there were two others cars in the parking circle, no one seemed to be about, no one to see them move down the grassy seaward slope fronting the tower, find their spot and send the bag and its contents hurtling into the sea.

It was the least that could be done, Dan granted, allowing more misdirection, more deflection, more skewed providence in all that happened. In all that *it* might have wanted to happen.

And, as Dan and Peter learned over the next few days from those surprisingly numerous late-night wanderers, taxi drivers, shift-workers and highway truckers who noticed and either reported it by phone or posted it online, at around 3:10 a.m., a handful of automated lighthouses along the coast from as far north as Fingal Head to Crowdy Head in the south each flashed pink and white three times, pink and white, pink and white, pink and white, while the one at Tacking Point on its lonely headland above Lighthouse Beach flashed blue and green, blue and green, blue and green.

And out there, all across the world, they knew.

DID YOU KNOW?

TERRY DOWLING has been called "Australia's finest writer of horror" by *Locus* magazine, its "premier writer of dark fantasy" by *All Hallows*, and its "most acclaimed writer of the dark fantastic" by *Cemetery Dance* magazine. The *Year's Best Fantasy and Horror* series featured more horror stories by Terry in its 21-year run than by any other writer.

Dowling's horror collections are *Basic Black: Tales of Appropriate Fear* (International Horror Guild Award winner for Best Collection 2007), Aurealis Award-winning *An Intimate Knowledge of the Night*, the World Fantasy Award nominated *Blackwater Days*, and *The Night Shop: Tales for the Lonely Hours*. Other publications include his debut novel, *Clowns at Midnight*, which London's *Guardian* called "an exceptional work that bears comparison to John Fowles's *The Magus*," and *The Complete Rynosseros* in three volumes. His homepage can be found at www.terrydowling.com.

TIKI GODFATHER

BY WILL VIHARO

T HE Contender is sitting in a tiki bar named Desire on the waterfront in Teti'aroa, an atoll in French Polynesia. He sips his third Zombie, staring drunkenly at a rotund tiki statue in the corner.

"I coulda been you," the statue suddenly says in a familiar rasp.

"Sorry?"

"Instead of a bum, which is what I am, let's face it."

The Contender looks around. The nude native girls don't notice.

"Are you really *him*? Superman's dad?"

"In spirits, so to speak. This was my vacation home in life, before I was entombed in this relic. I fell in love with these islets while making *Mutiny on the Bounty*, and bought them. I can no longer enjoy them, as you see."

"I've always dreamed of living here."

"Do you want it?"

"How can I refuse such an offer?"

"You can't."

A mist swirls, and they trade places.

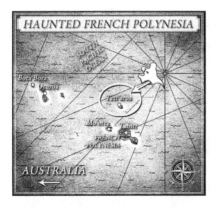

WILL VIHARO is the author of the *Thrillville Pulp Fiction Collection* and the *Vic Valentine, Private Eye* series. He lives in Seattle, WA with his wife Monica Tiki Goddess, PhD, and their cats, Tiki and Googie. www.thrillvile.net and www.willviharo.com.

* FILE UNDER: *Haunted Tiki Bar*

+ TINY TALE OF HAUNTED LOCALE +
FOSTER, VICTORIA, AUSTRALIA

THE WISHING WELL
BY JACK DANN

From Bellaires' *Compendium of Australian Oddities and Places*
(Melbourne: Osward & Co., 1931)

A SMALL and unusually deep doline pit can be found in the post town of Foster (Stockyard Creek) (38° 35' S lat., 146° 15' E long.). [See also *Seven Entrances to Hell* by Benedict Hekla (Melbourne: Longford & Gipps, 1919.]

Located in what is now called Pearl Park, upstream from the Stockyard Creek boat landing, this hellsmouth was initially enclosed by a capped circular wall of five feet high unmortared stone with a brick extension. The cap, however, was removed on Australia Day, 26 January 1918 when it was dubbed "The Wishing Well" by the mayor, Ebenezer Browne; and a stone perron was added so "tourists and lovebirds could climb up and throw coins into the pit for luck."

The initial wall around the pit was built in 1871 under the supervision of Lloyd "Larry" Townshend (1841–1886), a forester and gold miner who is credited with discovering the hellsmouth.[†] After witnessing four of his miners "getting sucked into the poxy hole," Townshend claimed it was the Devil himself who grabbed them.

As this edition goes into its sixteenth printing, there are plans to recap the well, as two children have been reported missing in the vicinity. A local clergyman claims that he saw "some hellish creature rise from the pit and suck them into its enormous mouth." The clergyman has subsequently been granted permanent non-pastoral sick leave.[‡]

[†] It might be noted that the traditional owners of the Gippsland shire, the Gunaikurnai People, claim to have known about the hellsmouth for 4,000 years and had no need of an enclosure to mark its location. [See songlines/dreaming tracks]

[‡] Note found in a succeeding edition: "Neither the children nor their remains have ever been found."

Foster's "Wishing Well". Caution: Stay back 6 feet from opening!

JACK DANN is a multi-award winning author who has written or edited over seventy-five books. His latest novel is *Shadows In the Stone*.

* FILE UNDER: *Haunted Well*

It was so cold down here compared to above ground . . .

WARP AND WEFT

FEATURE ENTRY 13

STRUCTURE TYPE: MINING CAMP

LOCATION: WITTENOOM (WESTERN AUSTRALIA), AUSTRALIA

LAT./ LONG: 22.4061° S, 118.4461° E

BUILT: CIRCA 1973

GROUND ELEVATION: 2,051 FT. (625 M.)

WRITTEN BY: KAARON WARREN

TRAVEL GUIDE NOTES

WHERE EXACTLY *DO* curses come from, and can we truly avoid them if unawares? In line with Dickens' *A Christmas Carol*, sometimes one may see the ghosts of what is to come as much as see ghosts of the past; unlike Dickens' masterwork, I view this as a particularly dreary form of curse, especially when knowledge of an unwanted future is unchangeable. Like ghosts, curses may manifest in myriad forms, haunting, life-altering, sometimes accidentally delivered, and even, sometimes, brought about by "the best of intentions."

Kaaron Warren, one of Australia's premiere horror and speculative fiction authors (and a comrade of the dark who is always a thrill to work with!) brings us this next tale of childhood friends who visit a relic of their parents' past, finding there may be no safeguarding against certain curses, especially when love, family bonds, and failing memory come into play.

And finding, too, that such are our lives—and afterlives—as a tapestry, woven together, filled with the twisting twine and strange overlaps of "Warp and Weft."

—Charlatan Bardot

OUR LIVES ARE WOVEN TOGETHER LIKE A PIECE OF cloth. Someone dies and there is a hole; too many die or leave, and the cloth falls apart. I looked at Dad, sitting at a fake bus stop in the care home I was paying a fortune for and wondered how strong the thread was that kept him tied to me.

He woke each morning as if the days before didn't exist. He still had enough brainpower to fake it though, stretching and rubbing his hands together while he looked around, trying to remember.

He was worse after six months into the residency. He barely knew me, although if I pressed items from home into his hands he'd raise them to his nose and sniff, as if smell was still a sense he could control.

A staff member came out to cajole him inside; they were doing some weaving and he needed to finish his, she said. Palm Sunday was coming up and they needed those crosses done, didn't they? She nodded at me, expecting me to support her. "They love their art therapy," she said, as if that would convince me.

Dad muttered to nobody, sitting alone on the bench. He saw ghosts all the time, and the staff indulged him, telling him *yes dear*, assuming he was imagining things.

I *hoped* he was imagining things. I wasn't keen to be visited by a ghost.

He'd had a fall, which is why he was in there in the first place, and since the fall, I'd seen him shrink by the day. He'd been a good father. Terrible husband, but a good father.

And it wasn't a bad place here; he always wanted to catch the bus, so the staff made him the fake bus stop, with a seat and everything. All the old people loved it. They sat there for hours, some of them, waiting, and chatting as if to strangers, just like they used to do.

Sitting at that fake bus stop, Dad's favorite tall tale was the one of the abandoned bus in the middle of nowhere.

"Behind a hill," he said, "over there." He pointed.

"The bus will be along any minute now," the staff member said. "You can catch the next one."

"Not just any bus," he said, although he'd sat docilely at the bus stop for months. "Is it, son? You know the bus I'm talking about."

DAD USED TO weave wonderful stories that stretched over many nights, filled with details he never forgot. I'd remind him with questions: *What did they have for breakfast? What did they find in the wall?* Things like that. He never got it wrong. He dropped out of Uni to go into the mine and I never

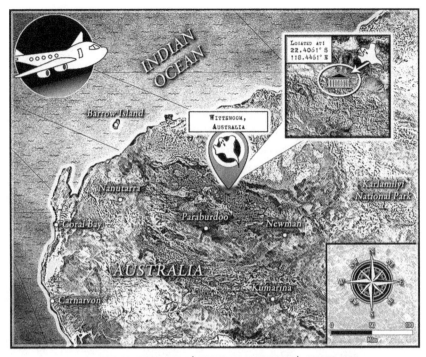

HAUNTED WITTENOOM (WESTERN AUSTRALIA), AUSTRALIA

knew why. Money, was the main answer. Shitloads of money, Mum had said. And the best mates a man could ever have, Dad had added.

When we were younger our parents had reunion parties. Drunken evenings, the wives either keeping to themselves or 'can't beat them, join them' blind-drunk with the men. My mum was one of those. She was a funny drunk, getting silly and carefree, then sick as a dog the next day, and my father nursing her and chuckling for weeks after. She was into arts and crafts, and she used to say the men were the warp and her family were the weft, and no one knew if she was being insightful or bitchy.

My friend CC's mum was a slutty drunk. No other word for it. She always had the boobs out and she'd laugh so loudly all of us kids, hiding in a cubby house, or behind the garage, smoking and drinking ourselves because no adult cared what we did on those nights, we'd all stop and listen. CC would roll her eyes, but they were kind of the same. CC loved to show off and she was good at it. How she became a doctor I don't know, but she did.

CC CAME WITH me next time to see Dad. Her own dad was long gone so she'd adopted mine.

We found him standing in the middle of a room at the care home. He said, "I forgot what I came in for."

"How long have you been standing there, Dad?"

He had no idea, but his coffee was stone cold.

He'd been a good father. Affectionate. A lot of the others weren't and we learned to avoid those ones, especially the girls.

All of the other fathers were gone by then. Some quick (accident, drunk), some slow (cancer, diabetes) some the living dead like my dad (dementia). CC's dad died in a pub brawl, apparently over whose turn it was to shout.

"This is shit," CC said. "You need to get him out of here for a while. I'll help you."

"We should get to the bus," Dad said. "Bus time. The others are waiting. We should get there." He waved his old motoring log book at us, the one he'd kept for years.

CC and I looked at each other.

We'd tried bringing out those crumbling memories by showing him old birthday cards, newspaper clippings he'd kept, and photos. These would register for a bit but then fade away. It was the complete opposite with CC's mum; once you got her started on the old stories she never stopped. The only thing that had really worked for Dad was this old log book, listing the places he'd been.

That night, I dropped CC at home, skipping the usual awkward moment where she wanted me to come in, and I didn't want to, by telling her I had to work. We'd had a series of one-night stands, was what I called them, over the last twenty years. In her mind, at least, this meant we'd end up together if nothing else came along. I tried not to be cruel to her because she'd been dumped so many times in her life. She didn't deserve that; she was a good person. But people didn't stick around.

SHE CALLED ME the next day, worried about Dad. She'd known him all her life; all of us called the other parents Aunt or Uncle, like some massive extended families. She said, "I wonder if we should take him to visit the bus? Maybe it'll help."

"It's in the middle of nowhere. I have no idea where it is."

"It's in the log book," she said. "It's written right there, if you follow in his footsteps."

CC was always the one who organized us. The miner's kids. As if our fathers' connections (and to a certain extent our mothers') meant our friendship was fate. There's always one person in any group who is in this position; they consider it more important than the rest of you do.

That week she gathered four of us together to talk about having a road trip. In her mind we should all go to the bus at the mine, see where our fathers had worked and slept all those years ago, see the place they bonded so closely they called themselves the Band of Brothers.

"We could do a bit of prospecting," DN said. He was the least of us then, to be honest, the one who never settled into a steady job, calling himself an artist but never actually making any art. "Find some gold if they left any behind."

Our fathers had told stories about how they'd beaten off intruders to keep their private mine safe. Sometimes they'd get out their tire irons and rocks and literally beat the person; other times they'd scare them away, pretend the place was full of malevolent ghosts.

"What about the ghosts, though?" JC said. We'd all gotten into the habit of calling each other by our initials and I can't remember why. I guess we were mocking JC, whose name was actually Jaycee. CC was Cora Cuthbert, but also she ate a lot of corn chips when we were kids, and she loved to boss us around and she would say, *See? See?* Anyway. "It's haunted," JC said. "The ghosts won't let you get near the place. They'll dry your eyeballs up. Shrivel your balls. They'll dry your skin till it cracks." Her dad (cause of death: suicide) was known as the scaredy-cat of the group.

The fathers were definitely the dominant personalities in each of our families, although with the exception of one or two there was no abuse with that. They were just strong in the mind and the character, and when they were together were like a great ball of energy. The mothers didn't seem to mind; certainly I don't remember any one of them being ignored. They stood clustered together, or they'd be in the kitchen gossiping and making food for us all, or sometimes they'd sit outside smoking and drinking if they were in the mood.

"Come on, JC," CC said. "It'll be an adventure. We'll take POQ's dad, and any of the mothers who want to come." POQ was me. Because Paul Quinn, and because they all said I'd piss off quick if there was any work to be done, and if any girl wanted some sort of a commitment. As the night progressed we talked about ghosts and our fathers. JC said she was haunted by hers. "He's long gone but I can smell that aftershave of his, mixed with the smell of beer."

DN said it was the spices lined up in the cupboard and the drawers pushed in when he'd left them open. He said, "My wife's too fucken lazy to do that." He hated his nickname, talking of lazy. DN for Dee Enn, Dean, his actual name, because we all said he was so boring he didn't deserve a more interesting one.

In the end, only DN wanted to come with us, but he wasn't bringing his mother, that's for sure. Or his wife.

CC AND I checked Dad out from the care home on a pass, and took him to my place in preparation for our trip across the country.

There was still evidence of my ex-girlfriend where I lived. She'd been gone a while but I'd never removed her little design touches, even though they'd annoyed me at the time.

CC's husband was long since run off. Long since *found wanting*, she'd say. She was married young, far younger than any of us, so she was in and out, done by twenty-two and no interest in marrying again. "You're all my husbands" she'd say to us, because she and JC were the only girls in our age group. The younger siblings did their own thing; somehow I think they were less influenced by the group than we were. Perhaps because by then the men were dying, and the group met less often.

I've never had much luck in love; I'm not one of those charming guys who people like. If I was charged with murder, like they found a dozen bodies buried in my backyard (there are no bodies in my backyard) people would say, *Him?* But he was such a nice man. But they wouldn't be able to tell you anything else about me. And they wouldn't protest in the streets for my release.

They'd believe I did it.

JC DROPPED ME, CC, and Dad off at the airport. The flight to Broome would take three hours, no snacks on board, so we had a quick meal at one of the cafés. She said, "I can't believe you guys are going to that place."

"You should come with. You can protect me," I said. We'd had our flirtations, too, but it never went far.

DN met us at the gate, late as ever, making it just before boarding, his belongings shoved into a half-split bag, his hair unbrushed, toothpaste on his cheek. "Bags sit next to CC on the plane," he said. I was hoping I'd get one of them to sit next to Dad, give me a bit of a break. He was repeating stories again, telling me about the buses and how he couldn't get one home after 9 p.m. *I had to get a taxi*, the story goes. *I called your mother and she told me to eff off.* He always sniggered at this point, the memory of my docile mother swearing at him pushing through the fog in his brain. She really had said this; before she moved away she'd confirmed this for me. She'd said, *those dreadful friends of his.* The meetings took place in pubs in later days; the women at last sick of them hanging around the house, I guess, although at the time I'd thought they'd enjoyed the company. The bravery it took for her to up and leave him once I was old enough to look after myself astounds me to this day. Dad couldn't cope with the betrayal; he told everyone she was missing. He put ads in the paper and everything. But I had postcards from her for a while and we talked on the phone every now and then, so she wasn't missing at all. Dad went to visit her once when she was in Perth but I don't think that went well. She didn't come back with him and we lost track of her for a while. I was glad to spend some time with her before she died, although she had no words of wisdom for me, nothing much to say. No warnings about the bus or anything else. I guess she knew less than I do; I guess she didn't know.

After we landed, we hired a car out of Newman Airport and started the long drive to Wittenoom.

Us kids had known for a long time about this place; it was part of our mythology, of our basic belief system. Long ago the men had parked a decrepit bus over a mine shaft, living there while they worked by day for the company in the gold mine, by night for themselves in the gold seam they'd found.

And in the town nearby (well, near for these parts. It was an hour's drive away), they told ghost stories to scare people off it.

Dad always promised to go back, to get more gold from their private mine, secure my future, he'd say. But then he'd also say, *Every last one of them on that bus a dead man walking.*

He was always talking about the bus. Obsessed by it. He'd threatened me as a kid when I misbehaved, only half-joking, *I'll put you on the bus and send you off into nowhere.*

Now, he had no idea where the bus was, but CC figured it out: his log book. It was meticulous. How far he'd travelled, how much spent, where he'd stopped along the way. So we retraced his steps, and that was heartbreaking in a way. There were times he'd show a glimmer of recognition (mostly he slept and farted) and it felt good to be heading to the place where he'd once been young and strong.

After a several-hour-drive, we passed a dirt track and Dad said, "You missed the turn-off, ya nong."

I laughed. That sounded like my old dad. He used to call everyone a nong and it made me feel a little bit superior not to be one myself. "Turn around ya nong," I said to DN. He winked at me; he loved Dad, too. DN and I were on the same footy team and it was Dad who'd taken us to every game, trained with us, told us we were the best on field even when we'd played like shit.

He remembered none of that now.

We drove over the bumpy road. Ahead, a low hill obscured the horizon. "Are you sure this is the way? It looks like a dead end," DN said, but when we pulled up, Dad hopped out happily and with great assurance.

An old battered sign stood before a bramble-covered pathway, reading, "Danger, Explosives," with a funny cartoon of a man being blown apart. The miners really didn't want anyone coming through here.

If ever I doubted the sanity of what we were doing, watching Dad stride ahead with his big walking stick put that to rest. CC and I walked behind, holding hands, and DN struggled farther back, complaining, whining, in a high-pitched voice that set my teeth on edge.

CC apologized for DN, as if everything was her fault, and I stopped her with a kiss, feeling more confident than I ever had.

The hill we had to climb was gentle, although I felt my thigh muscles complaining. It was a mild day for these parts but still hot; we stopped in the shade of every tree to rest and cool down. Dad marched ahead, thinking he was twenty-four years old or something.

I took a sip of the water in my backpack. As far as we knew there was a working pump at the site; we'd have to boil the water but we had matches and lighters so we wouldn't have to rough it to that extent.

"How'd they get a bus in here?" I asked. CC knew the answer to these things; she'd listened when the adults talked over the years.

"The long way around, like another three-hour-drive or something," she said. "And the road is closed now, washed away."

Another sign read "Quicksand" and another "Wild Dogs," both illustrated with the same poor cartoon man meeting his end. I wondered who it was modelled on. One of the bosses, I guessed.

"Come on," Dad said, and he called CC by her mother's name. She and I looked at each other, gossip faces on. There'd always been a rumor they'd had an affair; CC's mother was the prettiest of them all but also suffered from depression, so no one liked to talk to her much. It was one of the reasons CC became a mental health professional, to help her mother and others like her. Her dad was like mine; they must have been quite the pair when they were younger, quite the lotharios, the ladies' men, the sleaze bags. What a team. Her dad had left them for a younger woman years ago, leaving CC's mum there alone and lonely.

At the top of the hill, looking down we could see the bus. It really *was* there. Long, rusty, bits falling off it, but there.

Dad said, "They'll be waiting on the bus."

"You always said it was haunted," I said.

He nodded. "Ghosts can't hurt you, though. They can scare you because you don't know anything about them. That's all." It's as many words as he'd said in days, and his tone of voice was so familiar I choked up.

I said, "The last time you were here was for your second honeymoon, wasn't it? You and Mum." It had never seemed a very romantic choice to me. None of the other parents had done it. CC's parents went to Paris, I think. So Mum was the only one who'd seen this place. It was after this she'd moved to England and her little village. Sweet little place. They welcomed me when I flew over for her final days and funeral.

Dad didn't seem to remember this. He hesitated for a moment, looking at me, as if making a decision but not understanding what that decision would be. Then he headed down the hill.

We passed signs denoting where the toilets were. There was "Grand Canyon," which I assumed was the long drop for shitting, and "Yangtze River," for piss. It made the three of us laugh our heads off.

It was so quiet. The distant calling of a bird the only noise. And very still.

Outside the bus, seats were lined up around a campfire, many years since used. Bones in piles, and stacks of beer bottles.

There were shadows in the bus windows. Movement. DN pointed. "There's someone in there," but of course when we got closer there wasn't; it was cloud shadow, tree shadow, bird flying over shadow. DN found the water pump and asked if anyone needed a drink. Dad reckoned he wanted a beer. Just a distant sniff of the mine made him want to drink.

The door to the bus was off its hinges. CC squeezed through easily but my shoulders got caught until the two of us managed to shove the door further open. Dad wandered off. I hoped not too far.

Inside was like an oven but without the sun directly on me it was a relief. The smell was bad but not horrendous, a bit like an old man's shed full of rusty tools and ancient oil puddles.

The bus still had a third of its seats. The rest were the ones around the campfire, pulled out to make room for camp beds.

This was where our fathers had slept and eaten, where they'd formed the deep bond that meant all of us kids knew each other like cousins, that we in turn shared a kind of a bond. There was graffiti and jokes on the bus walls, crude stuff I wanted to take photographs of.

CC grabbed my hand and held it up to her eyes, as if she didn't want to see.

I looked for the secret trapdoor, the one that would open to their private gold mine, but found nothing. I couldn't quite believe it was all bullshit; had they really been having us on all that time?

DN squeezed through. "There's something up the back there."

He headed that way.

"Jesus," he said.

On the last seat, a body, preserved perhaps by that harsh dry heat.

Its head was forward, hands up to face, like a person deeply grieving, or ashamed, or regretful.

"It's fucken PP," he said.

PP. He'd hated that nickname, given to him because he'd wet his pants once. PP, who'd been missing for five years. It was clearly him; he wore a diabetic's bracelet alert, wore clothes that were familiar to us.

CC said, "He must have been there a couple of years at least."

"None of us have seen him for five. It could be that long," I said.

DN said, "What happened to him?"

CC took a closer look. "I can't really tell." She cast around, and in his lap found a bottle of pills and held them up.

"There you go." She pocketed the bottle.

DN stared at PP. "He's moving."

"It's probably rats," CC said. "Desert rats, looking for food or a cozy place to sleep."

PP's chest rose as she spoke. "Rats," she said again, but his head tilted back and forth and his face seemed to turn blue before . . . something pressed out of him. A mist, or a cloud, like a cloud in the sky and you say, *I see a rabbit*, and your best friend sees a sports car. This was him. A filmy, dark cloud, rising up out of him.

We backed out of the bus, DN screaming like a child in his high-pitched voice, CC panting, me . . . I just tried to breathe, just wanted to get out of there.

"Heat mirage," DN said as soon as we were out of the bus and standing by the campfire. "That's all."

I nodded, and CC did too. I heard her rattle the pills in her pocket.

My heart beat so fast I felt as if I'd run a race. Did it skip beats? Is this what it felt like to have a heart attack? I needed to find Dad. I called out for him but no answer.

A siren began to blare. The kind of thing they have in factories at the start and end of the day, and lunch breaks, and smoko. I had no idea what time it was but it was still hot; I could feel my neck burning.

I saw Dad, standing with his hands on his hips, and I walked toward him. Before I reached him, though, he folded back a rusty gate and disappeared into a hole.

Their mine.

We had to go after him.

I covered my nose and mouth; we all did. It was a close space down there, dark, so we used our phone lights as we went down. I could see Dad ahead, pressed against a wall of fallen rocks, reaching up with his hands as if he could claw his way through. DN held his light close to one of the walls, looking for gold. "Probably farther in. You can see it's been here, though."

The way farther in was blocked in one direction, so we headed the other. CC shivered; it was so cold down here compared to above ground, and I wondered why the men didn't sleep here. It must have been hellishly hot in that bus.

DN went ahead. "It's blocked up here too, I think," he called, then a shout and the sound of him falling over, a clatter of something, whatever he was carrying.

"DN?" CC called out. "Are you okay?"

Dad was the one to move toward him first, leading the way. DN pushed past us. "This fucken place," he said. "This fucken place." He waited by the mine entrance as Dad pressed forward, me and CC behind him.

What he'd found was a skeleton. Dad stood there nodding, as if this was no surprise. There was a wallet near where the person's left thigh would have been; I bent down to pick it up.

The men always talked about the arsehole boss who made them scrape their fingernails to ensure they didn't steal any gold dust. This was him. They'd murdered the boss. Hid his body down the shaft. Covered it up.

"Jesus, Dad," I said. As we watched, the bones shifted (More rats. Rats. More rats) and I stepped back, stamping on CC's toes, and she spun to get out of there and knocked over DN who'd crept in close again, useless bastard, and I had to carry him out. Whatever it was (rats), I didn't want to be stuck underground with it.

"Come on, Dad," I said. "Let's go," but he wouldn't come.

I didn't want to leave him, but he was stubborn, and DN was bleeding, so I figured I'd just give Dad a minute.

We climbed out into the sunshine.

CC took one look at DN bleeding from the head and had me carry him farther to the shade. I felt stupidly jealous as she began to tend to him, but all of us forgot everything, forgot to breathe, when we saw what emerged from that old mine.

Men.

Not men.

PP's red-haired father came out first, as tall as I remembered, and instinctively I stood in front of CC and she cowered behind because there was not one girl he hadn't grabbed at and worse . . . and the other fathers had done what? Too scared? Too blinded with adoration? DN was beside me, leaning into me, "That's PP's dad," he said, and I told him I saw it too, I saw PP's father's ghost dusting off his pants and heading for a beer.

PP had stood up to him once and ended up being beaten badly, not that day but a while later, when the rest of us couldn't defend him.

Then my dad, my dad, climbing out of that shaft and dusting off his trousers, sticking his head under the water pump (no water came out but that didn't seem to matter) and shaking his head like a dog, something he'd do to make us laugh.

The others came, too. CC's father was there, looking bruised and tired as he always did, and DN's dad, so incredibly handsome even in this ethereal sate. He mimicked closing the mine gate then joined the others around the campfire.

PP hovered nearby them. I couldn't tell if he was speaking to them or not. Dad glanced over at us. Did he beckon? CC started to walk toward him but I pulled her back.

"Fuck's sake," I said.

We watched them fade in and out of our vision. DN took off back to the car; he said he wasn't staying another second. CC said we needed to look after Dad; we needed to help him. She was so calm, though, as if she'd seen this before, and I thought about how easily we'd found the place, how well she'd directed us here.

Dad climbed on the bus and reluctantly I went after him, thinking of ways to trick him back up the hill, into the car, back home.

He sat there on a seat, and as I approached he held up a scrap of paper as a bus ticket. Not the slightest recognition or hint of humor.

I cried.

CC stood beside me. She said, "You've known for a while. I know you have. You know what the bus stop means. What catching the bus means. He wants this to be over, doesn't he? He's waiting to die."

She had a hypodermic needle in her hand. Insulin. "He'll fall asleep dreaming of sweets, of ice cream and pudding, of custard and fruit cake," she said. "It's painless. If you stay and watch you'll see."

"How do you know," I asked her.

She didn't answer.

There was a buzz, a feeling in the air and I looked out the window to see the men around the campfire, happy, stuck in place, released.

But what decided me is this:

My mother's ghost stepped onto the bus.

She didn't see me or Dad. She walked the aisle toward us and she looked just as I remembered her, smiling, loving, a bounce in her step.

Dad looked up but he didn't recognize her. There was nothing.

That's when I nodded at CC and walked off the bus. I wasn't brave enough to watch it.

If I seem calm now it's because all of this was a long time ago. I've never seen anything more terrifying, not before or since, but looking back I know those ghosts weren't the threat. They couldn't do any further damage than they did in life.

It was only later, when we were driving away, that I said, "That bastard killed her. He killed her and buried her bones. That's why she's there," I said. "Her bones are buried."

CC shook her head. "No, he didn't. He didn't have to. He knew she'd show up here, that she'd have no choice. It doesn't matter where you're buried. Where you die. If you've seen the place, this is where you'll come. You've got no say in it."

I shook my head. But what she said was true: Those men, they didn't all die there, nor even were they all buried there or their ashes scattered. And yet there they were.

"We'll be friends forever," she said. "PP is here. And you and me and DN."

She always did overestimate how meaningful our friendship was.

DN and I exchanged looks. He was driving, me beside him. He said, "There's a bit of time to figure out how to avoid it. We're young, mate. We'll work it out."

THAT WAS WHY Dad never took me there. He was protecting me. Saving me. Until he forgot how to do that. I hated to think of Mum stuck there with him, having run away, but maybe she'd realize he was a good man after all. She'd realize how much he loved her, how he wanted to spend eternity with her . . .

CC died in her forties, deliberate or not, I don't know, and she left me all her money, and so did the others, like we were in some kind of weird tontine or something. She had no one else to leave it to. We were it. She'd been alone for a long time but she didn't care, because she believed we'd all be together soon enough. Amongst her belongings were the pills she'd found on PP's body. Of course she'd prescribed them; I should have known at the time. I guess I should feel grateful she never rushed me along. She's happy to wait. She gave me the money on the proviso I'd take her ashes out to the bus and scatter them there. I'm not going to do it. Who's going to check? There's no one left to check. There's only me and DN left.

DN's as fit as I am, both of us in our nineties, doing our best to live forever, to help others do the same.

I'm not my father's son and never will be. He was a good man; I'm not. I know that. I don't really care. Enough money and it doesn't matter what sort of a man you are.

It seems heartless not to care, but I don't want to go back.

Not while I've got the choice, anyway.

DID YOU KNOW?

Shirley Jackson award-winner **KAARON WARREN** published her first short story in 1993 and has had fiction in print every year since. She was recently given the Peter McNamara Lifetime Achievement Award and was Guest of Honour at World Fantasy 2018, StokerCon 2019, and GeyserCon 2019. Kaaron was a Fellow at the Museum for Australian Democracy, where she researched prime ministers, artists, and serial killers. She's judged the World Fantasy Awards and the Shirley Jackson Awards. She has published five multi-award winning novels (*Slights, Walking the Tree, Mistification, The Grief Hole*, and *Tide of Stone*) and seven short story collections, including the multi-award winning *Through Splintered Walls*. She has won the ACT Writers and Publishers Award four times and twice been awarded the Canberra Critics Circle Award for Fiction. Her most recent novella, *Into Bones Like Oil* (Meerkat Press), was shortlisted for a Shirley Jackson Award and the Bram Stoker Award, winning the Aurealis Award.

THE FAIRY DOOR

BY ANGELA SLATTER

THERE'S a fairy door in the Addison Building (located next to the Commissariat Store on Brisbane's William Street). It's tiny, painted green and hard to see unless you're drunk and fallen over. The structure was the site of at least one harrowing murder. A dockworker, not known for his tenderness toward his wife and mistresses, was drowned in a barrel of brine meant for the preserving of fish. The rooms are haunted now by the self-same wife and two of those mistresses who'd had a free afternoon that fateful day.

Note: Fairies and ghosts can coexist in harmony

Occasionally, screams can be heard that turn into swallowing, and satisfied laughter soon after. The fairies and ghosts do not bother each other.

ANGELA SLATTER is an award-winning novelist and short story writer. She lives in Brisbane, Australia.

* FILE UNDER: *Haunted Warehouse*

THE MARTHA HOTEL: SUITE 101

BY LEE MURRAY

I WALLOWED in the tub. Snorted. Fifty bucks for a night in the bed of a murdered prostitute. It was my bus fare out of this dead-end mining town ...

A blurred figure thrust me backward, held me down. Submerged, I fought, thrashed, my feet slipping on the tub. Snatching the shower curtain, I hauled upward. Gasped.

The figure was gone.

Dressing, I quit the room. Flung the fifty on the bar.

"Scared, huh?"

"You said she died *in bed!*"

Vacancy at the Martha Hotel

The hotelier studied my dripping hair. Shrugged. "Rose was strangled in bed, yes. I never said nothin' about the one who was drowned."

LEE MURRAY is a multi-award-winning writer and editor of science fiction, fantasy, and horror (Sir Julius Vogel, Australian Shadows), and a double Bram Stoker Award®-winner. Recent works include short story collection *Grotesque: Monster Stories* and supernatural crime-noir *Blood of the Sun* (with Dan Rabarts). Read more at www.leemurray.info.

* FILE UNDER: *Haunted Hotel*

FASTEN YOUR

SAFETY BELTS...

NEXT STOP:

AFRICA

HAUNTED AFRICA

CAIRO, EGYPT

NIAMEY, NIGER

PLACE, NIGERIA

LAGOS, NIGERIA

MALAKAL, SOUTH SUDAN

PATIKO, UGANDA

NAIROBI, KENYA

ZANZIBAR CITY, UNGUJA (TANZANIA)

HARARE, ZIMBABWE

OKAVANGO DELTA, BOTSWANA

KIMBERLEY, NORTH CAPE, SOUTH AFRICA

0 100 200 300 400 500
Miles

AFRICA

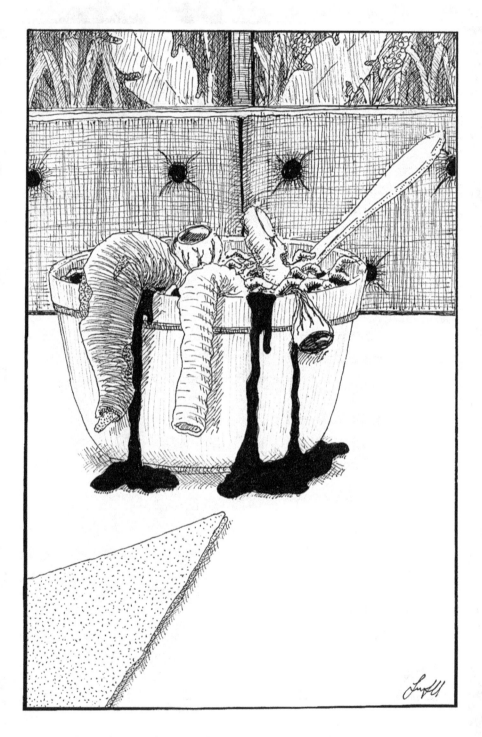

The chowder is a lumpy thing that tastes of hopelessness and despondency . . . Your mood plummets with every mouthful.

A TASTE OF UNGUJA

STRUCTURE TYPE: RESTAURANT
LOCATION: ZANZIBAR CITY (UNGUJA), TANZANIA
LAT./ LONG: 6.1625° S, 39.1916° E
BUILT: CIRCA 1970
GROUND ELEVATION: 36 FT. (11 M.)
WRITTEN BY: EUGEN BACON

TRAVEL GUIDE NOTES

A PERFECT TRANSITION from the geography and haunted buildings of Oceania into that of Africa, this next story straddles both, crossing a dark gateway between Melbourne to Zanzibar City. As does the author, Eugen Bacon, an African-Australian who's been rapidly rising through ranks of speculative, fantasy, and horror literature. I delight in Eugen's prose very much, the strange and often magical journeys that her characters take, facing fantasy and peril alike. As is this case for a certain grieved mother in a land and a relationship she feels has wronged her.

As a father myself, I understand intimately the bonds of parenthood, and the lengths one may go to see that their children are given every opportunity for safety and happiness . . . Yet for all my perspective and conviction, I speak as a male; I'm told—and I've seen—that no matter how strongly I may feel, a woman's maternal instinct can be a hundredfold more intense.

And so it is for this mother, facing entry at a peculiar restaurant, from where what is done here can never be *undone,* and woe be those who should ever get "A Taste of Unguja."

—Charlatan Bardot

NOT JUST ANY SON, HE'S *THE* SON. THE ONE, THE only. He loves fresh banana bread with a drizzle of maple syrup. Now you've lost him.

　　　　　The loss in your heart is desert dry. Your pulse is fast, loud in your ears. You languish in the scent of the impossible: how you carried something in your body a whole nine months, then misplaced it. Not by choice, taken. Because when love sours, emotion is bare. That Z, if he could . . . he has. Taken your son.

　　　　　You sit with a rock on your lap, not a metaphoric rock. It's a real rock, the size of Z's head. You lifted it from the botanical gardens where it guarded a new flowerbed. Z's name is written on every jagged facet of this stone—you chose it precisely for him, imagining the scatter of brain matter on the rock, the smashing soon-to-be. An ooze of white, or cream. A porridge of tissue, a spurt of blood.

　　　　　There's a girl in a bodysuit facing you two seats up in the tram. You wonder if—behind the quarantine mask—she's frowning. She looks at the rock, but you don't care. Time is a tricky memory, more so when masks float about. Most of them, like yours, are cheap disposables, pale blue outside, white inside. But there are people who maneuver the world with bandanas on their noses. There's a boy with a red cap. His mask is dusky. He's wrapped in a puffed-out jacket against the night cold. Then you see his eyes and realize it's not a boy but a grown Asian woman. There's a teen with a luminescent mask. A sheaf of curls on her head runs with the breeze through the slit of the tram window. Wind that starts anywhere, ends here.

　　　　　The tram is not a roomy one. Is there enough social distance between you and the other passengers? You distract yourself with colors. The tram is an ancient thing, green and white. Each yellow door has a red sign that says STOP. Its black face up the front, all glass. Its gloomy crown with a feeler, a tentacle reaching for the sky. The driver and their hi-vis, a screaming orange. The tram squeals and hums, groans, wobbles, rolls and jerks. *Ting!* It's off to the next stop, closer to your deed, where you'll follow your feet and wait in the dark.

WHEN Z TOOK your son, you felt hot and cold. But the system didn't care how you felt. The system said Z did what he could. It said you were an "other," your intentions unclear. Z was from here, a color the system knew. It trusted him, not you, with the safety of your son. You could hear their reasoning: *What's to stop you from stealing him, somewhere remote to the*

HAUNTED ZANZIBAR CITY (UNGUJA), TANZANIA

Sahara—where would we find the little one in that weird heat? Or Lake Victoria, islands everywhere—what's to stop you from hiding him in a crocodile? Or Mount Kilimanjaro, the tallest point in Africa—19,341 feet and then some. You could bury him in a glacier, we'd never know where to start.

They didn't care you were from none of those places.

A court order said you couldn't be within one hundred meters of your son. Someone called an ambulance for your collapse, but it was a hole in your heart no medicine could restore. You were alone, no one to help in your greatest need. Z's action—a man denying a woman her own child—was an apocalypse. It violated your culture: a child belongs to his mother.

TING! YOU STEP off the tram.

You stand there with your stone, you don't know how long. The sky bellows, it begins to rain. You still feel them together: heat and cold. A month of heat wrapped in a moment. An ice-covered mist submerging the essence of you until you're drowning.

Drowning.

You'd rather see the sun, even when its whiteness shimmers to blackness.

Tonight's rain is an unfurling of pins, twirling toward you in the shape of a cloak. Their pricks numb you from flying branches and debris succumbing to the deluge. You see the remains of a book, bushed and damp at your boots.

There's a nightjar. You wonder about it, calling, soft churring notes. It flaps slow wings in the rain, a beat that's almost hypnotic. Long wings you feel drawn to. A nightjar is the totem of your clan. And when it lands feet away, yours is a deep connection with the shine of its rubied eye. You draw near until you touch the bird, until the wet of its feathers turns to gold, black, and brown. But there's rain, more rain. You wish for the sun.

YOU REMEMBER THE caesarean, the soft pull almost a tickle, an epidural dulling your spine. He came out clean—how quickly they wiped him—eager for a tit. Three years on, he roared out his fear, but you held him. As the nurse pushed in a needle, you gripped the boy and your heart cracked over. You held him as if a vaccination was life and death, because it was.

A year on, Z took him to Mt. Martha—a boys' weekend with the cousins. First time you'd parted from the child for more than a day. You went near mad with longing, but couldn't reach your son on Z's smartphone, the signal so bad there. And finally, when the phone rang on that end, Z answered, and put your son on.

The boy said, "Mama." Your heart stopped beating. "What shall I do for food?" And you died.

Died.

When your heart came back, and breath floated in, you asked, "What about your father?"

And your son said, "He doesn't know."

Again you died.

So you drove all the way to Woolworths, swiped shelves into a trolley. The man at the checkout looked at you like you were nuts. A hoarder: Pasta. Pasta sauce. Chocolate. Iced tea. Vegetables and steak. Sausages. Chicken. Packs and packs of 2-minute noodles. Lots of milk. A clutch of canned tuna. The supplies all fit in the car, though the boot nearly didn't close. You drove an hour and five minutes all the way through the M1 on the Eastlink, the M3 and Mornington Peninsula Freeway, the M11 to Moorooduc Highway, the exit 19 to Mt. Martha, because that's what . . .

A mother does.

IN A CONFUSING arena of sin and struggle, pedophiles in masks demand protection as marginalized persons with an attraction to little people. Their expressions are fresh as snow, in a bible's name. They speak in a way that uses the creative process of a serpent to bring definition, no punctuation, to the term "freedom" and all shorthand modes that take or give, and dance with thunder. What's your confession, oh flesh and blood? Genesis 3: We may eat of the fruits of the garden, they say, fingers on their hearts. Story after story their words morph in shifts and changes, but each subject and predicate, noun, verb, or adjective, is a weapon of mass destruction complete with apathy. Nowhere is their weakness more dramatic than in each war of words. You think about this, standing in the rain. But Z is not a pedophile, and you're not sure it's a good thing. His act toward you is monstrous.

But there's no monster inside.

YELLOW-LIDDED BINS—it's collection night.

Love is not part of what you lost; you can't lose what you never had. Love never was. For your son, yes. For Z, no. How do you love someone empty?

Maybe it wasn't Z who was empty.

He's a creature of habit, is Z, that's how you'll get him. Tonight, it's yellow bins.

You stand outside his gate with your rock. It doesn't matter that curfew is looming—before long he'll wheel out the bin.

But the nightjar is calling, calling, soft churring notes, flapping, flapping in the rain. *Life is a bee*, sings a melody in your head to the nightjar's. *And a bee leaves a stinger inside you.* Something about the tune . . .

You drop the stone in a trance, follow the nightjar's singing. *Unlike the bee, life doesn't die. It never does, only you.* A discarded mail-van by a girl's school. Suddenly you're walking up a hill and it says Clowes Street. *Stay Safe, Stay Well*, a sign says. Red brick houses with ebony windowsills, shadowy garage doors. Gray posh houses with ivy climbing up walls, grilled gates. Manicured hedges a rich olive. Flats. Units. But the world is moving like a jigsaw, everything shifting.

There's a grandfather tree. What happened to Z's suburb, immobile cars lining its street, the ghosts of pay stations? Now you're in a botanical garden, not the one that gave you the rock. A low-flying plane rumbles overhead. Then you see it: *313 The Gateway*, next to an underground car park. Your sanity jars. How's this possible in the middle of a garden? Your feet push another inch. Without warning, you slip down a track, a noiseless fall. You sit up, bushed. The night is a rubbish tip. You've lost your face mask.

There's the nightjar beckoning you to follow and, like a fool, you do. You push past a sign that says: NO ENTRY.

Safe is the old limit, not a delta into the evening. *A Taste of Unguja*, says a blinking neon you've never seen before. Another sign says: WE'RE OPEN.

Karibu Sana, a wooden placard with its welcome, crooked on the entry before you step into the building's arcade, and into the soul of Zanzibar.

Sweet taarab music seeps gently into your space. It's music so full of want, you notice details in its notes: the vibrato and staccato of an accordion. The sweet wail of a reed flute. The rhythm of clapsticks. A hollow *click, click* in the claves. A fall of pebbles in the rattle and shake of the maracas. Lyrics full of poetry, adages and proverbs in a repeated phrase whose modulation is a funereal jazz eddying spice, ripples, and scales.

The walls have silhouettes of dhows and wild cats. A cheetah cocks its head in the savannah, scanning the horizon as if listening for something. It rises in a crouch, disappears in the grasslands. But you can tell from the sway of grass that the beast is stalking toward you. It bursts from the scrub in a sprint, nimble lopes in a shadow. You are the kill.

You stand rooted, helpless in fascination more than fear. You smell the cheetah's wet fur from its sweat, the rot in her breath as a paw lifts in speed to knock you down . . .

"Table for one?"

The voice startles you. The waiter has one leg, the other is a spade. His eyes are a sound, a howl that spills. His name is embossed on the breast of a ghost-white shirt: *Nungui*.

"What?" you say absently, as your eyes return to the cheetah, head cocked in pose in a painting on the wall.

"I asked if you needed a table for one." Nungui's voice comes and goes.

But, finally, you can relax—yes, a table for one.

There's something about the compilation of the restaurant, so hidden you fell into it. You wonder why it's open long after curfew inside a metropolis in a state of disaster. You look at the nothingness all about. Steamed-up windows, though they're broken. So cool inside, it's freezing. Like a spare bedroom in a winter cabin. Is that a black cat on the windowsill? And a red lizard? The place smells of lilacs and toilet freshener, the fake politeness of a wake. The walls, the chairs are shining, everything polished like a coffin. A trio of slit-eyed goats nibble at a curtain, right there near that table.

The menu is a party scene that ends in tears—*why did you think that?*

You place your order of potluck full of spice: cumin, turmeric, paprika, and cloves. "*Mchuzi wa pweza*," you say, mindless that your own voice is a sound falling, a clatter of pebble, a lone one, down a staircase.

"Octopus curry," says Nungui. "Fresh from a coral rock, best in the house."

He offers you a cocktail from a tray. You see the sun in the flute of tamarind, a sticky syrup, sweet and sour. You chew on the pulp that strangely tastes of coconut, before it sours.

Nungui appears as if in a blink. He holds in bare hands a steaming clay pot. Are those frogs and tealeaves? You're dissolving, the desert on your tongue. Nungui's plucked-off fingers rest on your table. Removed from his body, holding a plate of your lifetime, not many years left to run. You wonder if he knows that his leg is a spade. His skin is flaking, his muscles falling.

You fear for a moment that the fingers will climb into your chowder. But they skitter back to his now skeletal frame. You lift a spoon to your mouth. The chowder is a lumpy thing that tastes of hopelessness and despondency, a bird with broken wings, an elephant graveyard, a dead baby, stepping on a landmine, a slow erosion of the body by cancer. Your mood plummets with every mouthful.

"Don't you like it?" Nungui's voice is a nonvoice. His face is gone—in its place teeth and bone. A dent where eyes should be. The music is playing over and over. It's full of scales in your head. Your heart drops beneath the table.

You hear them before you see them. A murmur of sound. A fragment of senseless words and phrases floating above your head: *Pulpits. Cards. Horseshoes. Is that a flood or a fire? It's a bleed of basements, pools and spools filled with scratches and howls.*

You see them at a table together, near where the goats were. They're not looking at you. They're the only patrons beside you. Dead people, their eyes full of tar. But they're not just people or dead. They're *your dead people.*

There's your grandfather, ash-hair, wisdom eyes, half his body unclothed. A pale sarong made of batik is tied around his waist. He died of hopelessness. There's your grandmother, tiny, sweet-faced, her spine all bent. She's wearing a *chitenge* sprigged with sunflowers. She died of heartbreak. There's your mother, kind-lipped, the eyes of a fawn. She died early, killed her own mother with heartbreak. There's your father. A thousand suns in his smile. He's wearing a breasted safari suit the color of the Sahara. He died of heart, liver, and kidney disease. There's your sister, isn't she the picture? Tiny nose, fair skin, elastic hair falling to her knees. She died of anguish—there's the son she lost, the other son, the daughter just a bub.

You wonder if they're the same as you knew them. Your family. You fear you'll never know the answer. Your own son's face, once imprinted in memory, is now an unknowing. You can't bring yourself to look at a photograph, his photo, the apocalypse too devastating, each fading memory a fresh atomic bomb that disintegrates you anew.

They're playing a card game with the intensity of a fisherperson casting a net. But it's all reverse—it's the baby who's the dealer, shuffling, reshuffling the decks of cards, her hole card facedown as the others stand or hit. Everything is backward, even Nungui. He's facing wrong, a sly grin cast your way. You wonder at his posterior, his hands, the skeletal foot of his good leg . . . directed away from you.

The taarab music with its dhows and waves is loud, louder. Your grandfather stands, swaying to its tune. He loosens the batik wrapped around his waist, lets it fall. He turns, bends his knees and bares his buttocks. Your grandmother stands. She unknots the *chitenge* from the shoulders. It falls to her feet. Paper breasts, a gnarl of skin. She has no underclothing. She turns, bares her behind. Your father unbuttons, then unzips the khaki trousers of his safari suit. He peels it down his legs, steps out of his underwear. He turns . . . Your mother lifts her batik . . . It's a procession, an orchestra of motion. Silent music as your sister lifts her sunflower dress, pulls down her panties and bares her bottom.

It goes on, until the baby undoes the lilac- and pink-headed pins of her white nappy the texture of a towel. It's soiled. A smell of bad fish, dead rats hits you. She bends, bares her bottom. Only then do you cry out, a sound whose vehemence climbs from your stomach, falls out of your throat, and you're gagging. The expulsion is twisting, jolting. You convulse to the floor, your mouth foaming, failing in its pleas to your family that they don't, please stop. Because you know, yes you know, how a curse is summoned.

Oblivious to your appeal, the music now loudest in your head, a melody with the roar of oceans, your relatives begin a synchrony of dance. It abruptly stops with a throttle of the flute. The funereal wail of the Swahili jazz is gone. Your people straighten, reclothe, one by one. Now they look at you in silence.

The nightjar is flapping, beating at your face with his wings. He calls you, calls you, soft churring notes. He flies toward the exit, then back. Calling, soft churring notes.

He wants you to follow.

You climb to your feet, turn one last time to speak to your family, but see only three slit-eyed goats nibbling at a curtain. Your head is woozy. Nungui is whole again, the nametag on his ghost-white shirt. Your smile to him is an apology, the haste in your leaving.

"How much?" you manage to say.

"The Gateway," he says. "On the house."

You pass the cheetah, running backward in slow motion, a silhouette receding from your view. You hear Nungui's words behind you, in front of you, everywhere, as you stumble, fall out of the void and into the air of smoke at dawn: "You're welcome."

Karibu Tena, the placard's invitation now different, still crooked on your way out of the building's arcade. You doubt very much that you'll be coming back. Somewhere in your mind you know that, if you came back tomorrow, you'd find nothing of tonight here. Suddenly you get it. The message your dead were giving. You're not alone but cocooned in tradition, from one side of the world to the other.

Two coppers stop you. "Out and about? At this time?"

You blink.

"Ten minutes earlier, it would have been a fine. But we get it, curfew is over."

"Over?"

"It's 5:10 a.m., mate. What you need is a mask."

They hand you one, the cheap disposable one—pale blue outside, white inside.

Your legs are strings. You follow the nightjar down the hill. The world moves in jigsaw, everything shifting. Before long you'll reach Z's suburb, cars lining the street. Your rock is waiting for him to collect his bin. You have the rage to do it.

When he appears, you'll step into the light. He'll soften at the sight of you, sorry for what he's done. He'll think you've come to beg back into his life, even as he says, "The fuck are you doing here?"

Wasn't the separation your idea? It was meant to be temporary, something a marriage counsellor could fix. You just needed room to sort out your head, to face your fate in the grind of a loveless marriage. You never loved. It was Z who was enamored by you. The sight of you now will again swing the axe of his loss, the one that spilled cruelty out of him. There's no salve for it. Some bridges you eternally scorch, and that's that. He took matters to an unspeakable place.

You won't say, "Screw you, Z," the words you've thought over and over since that fateful day he took your son and filed an injunction. You cried narrow lanes and carved doors. You cried dhows. You cried to the Indian Ocean and to Mother Africa. The time for "Screw you, Z" is past. Instead, you'll walk on asphalt into the light, as a keening wail of taarab music fills your head. You'll spin and give Z your backside. You'll hear yourself say in a voice inside a voice, "You should see this."

The melody whirling in your head will be a sweet seduction, the croon of a violin pining for islands. There'll be nothing sexual or seductive about the ritual. You'll lift your skirt to the bass drone of drums. Pull your knickers to bare your black bottom, and sway, sway to the airy tootle of a flute, as the nightjar churrs, flapping overhead—the totem of your ancestors.

What Z will get is a taste of Unguja. You'll seal his fate to where no one, not even you, can undo it. Because what you have is the gift of a curse. You'll get your son back. You'll give him fresh banana bread with a drizzle of maple syrup.

As for your cursed ex . . . He'll set roaming, roaming, homeless on the streets of Melbourne. Nothing can save him.

Did You Know?

Eugen Bacon is African Australian, a computer scientist mentally re-engineered into creative writing. She's the author of *Claiming T-Mo* (Meerkat Press) and *Writing Speculative Fiction* (Macmillan). Her work has won, been shortlisted, longlisted, or commended in national and international awards, including the British Science Fiction Association (BSFA) Awards, Bridport Prize, Copyright Agency Prize, Australian Shadows Awards, Ditmar Awards, and Nommo Award for Speculative Fiction by Africans, and 2020 saw the release of two chapbooks, three collections, and a novella. In 2021 she has a prose poetry collection (with Dominique Hecq), and a black speculative fiction collection. Website: eugenbacon.com Twitter: @EugenBacon.

PATIKO

BY DILMAN DILA

A DEMIGOD, jok Adong, used huge rocks to build a palace in Patiko, but our ancestors stopped offering her sacrifice and so, saddened, jok Adong returned to her sky home. Patiko prospered into a very famous market until slave traders came and turned it evil. Our people fought back, but the slave traders were too strong and well-armed.

A cave leading to ruined Patiko Market

An old priest remembered jok Adong and offered sacrifice. Pleased, jok Adong shook the Earth, and rocks rolled off Patiko and buried the slave traders. Today, you can find the market inside the caves that formed after the rocks collapsed, and you can still hear echoes of the slavers' screams. And, sometimes in the dry season, you can see their blood, bright red on the white rocks, a reminder of jok Adong's power.

DILMAN DILA is the author of a collection of short speculative stories, *A Killing in the Sun*, and his works have been listed in many prestigious prizes. His films have won multiple awards and attracted millions of online views. More of his life and works at www.dilmandila.com.

* FILE UNDER: *Haunted Slavers' Market*

"Yes, he told me the marquee is haunted . . . "

THE CASE OF THE MOANING MARQUEE

FEATURE ENTRY 15

STRUCTURE TYPE: MARQUEE TENT
LOCATION: LAGOS, NIGERIA
LAT./ LONG: 6.4532° N, 3.5567° E
BUILT: CIRCA 2017
GROUND ELEVATION: 13 FT. (4 M.)
WRITTEN BY: SUYI DAVIES OKUNGBOWA

TRAVEL GUIDE NOTES

THIS NEXT STORY is fun. And smart. And a wonderful play on the world's most famous detective duo, set in modern time, reimagined if they were Nigerian, and also if they were a witch doctor and . . . a dog. The concept is more than elementary, my dear Watson.

National Public Radio recently gushed over author Suyi Davies Okungbowa's 2021-released novel, *Son of the Storm*, and rightfully so: Suyi's writing is crafted with complexity and perception, while building beautiful and imaginative worlds. Such as with this following selection.

Do ghosts have purpose in their emergence, or are they wrenched from afterlife domains, as unhappy to be in the realm of the living, as the living are at seeing them? Always there is a cause for such acts done, and subsequent root causes behind those, winding steadily backward through effects triggered by "other" actions, tangential ramifications that affect the world around us. The flapping of butterfly wings is indeed the truest analogy of Chaos Theory . . .

Although the choices of man tend to be worse.

Or decide for yourself: put on your sleuthing hat and come along to investigate "The Case of the Moaning Marquee."

—Charlatan Bardot

I T IS NOT OFTEN IN LAGOS THAT YOU FIND A MAN AND his dog by a street corner at 7:30 p.m. on a Sunday, idly regarding an ordinary marquee tent in a Lekki suburb. Or, shall I say, an *otherwise ordinary* marquee tent.

"It does look very ordinary," I say to Shylock, who sits on the ground next to me. "See—they haven't even cleaned up the place."

Shylock snorts, then says, *But we should be glad.*

Well, he doesn't *say* it per se because dogs can't talk, and only I can hear what he says, and only as thoughts in my head. But Shylock is not a dog, or not *just*. I haven't yet decided upon a word to describe his predicament: an Alsatian walking around with a once-renowned private detective's still-functional brain in him, with said brain telepathically connected to me, his once-best friend.

A dirty scene is a detective's best dream, Shylock expounds. *Cleanliness is bad for business.*

As with most things, he offers this information in flat affect, the subtleties of physical conversation lost when all you receive are words in your head, a phone call from the beyond. But I completely understand and am okay with this. If my consciousness of sorts was trapped in a dog, I wouldn't waste time parsing the nuances of human communication either.

I'm yet to fashion a retort before our client arrives, riding in the back of a commercial keke tricycle that comes around the bend. He gets down and pays the rider, who zooms off.

"Sorry for keeping you waiting," he says, flustered from the ride. He's a gentleman of stout stature, dark complexion, and languid comportment. He holds out his hand. "Olalekan Bashiru, but you can call me Lekan."

"You're the owner?" I ask, shaking his hand.

"Oh no, no, no," he says. "You spoke with my brother, Banky. He's CEO of Bash Tents & Rentals. I'm chief of operations." He looks me over. "And you must be the witchdoctor."

He says this without qualm. I don't look like much—not in this up-and-down brocade that has since lost its shine. I'm also forty-two, which is younger than most people expect for witchdoctor types. But again, most people have never had cause to meet one of us, and therefore have zero idea what we actually do and look like. The way this guy responds—no quips or comments—tells me he's probably already met with a witchdoctor in his life. I'm not sure if that says something good or bad about him.

"I'm Dr. John," I say, and angle my head toward the dog. "This is my associate, Shylock."

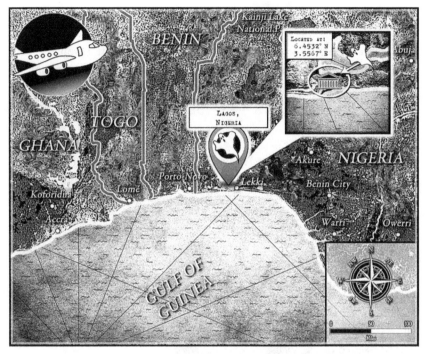

HAUNTED LAGOS, NIGERIA

"Ah, so *that's* the other half of Shylock & John Associates." He clicks the back of his tongue, as if he's just discovered something exquisite. A client's response to meeting Shylock often tells me a lot about them. Most are unsure if they'll be meeting two witchdoctors, and are often taken aback to learn that Shylock is not a person. Well, not a person *to them*. I often find it wise to hold back the truth that though I'm the witchdoctor, Shylock is the real brains of the operation. I'm just the tagalong who gets to sniff out any possible supernatural elements. Most often, there are none, and I do nothing but relay to the clients whatever Shylock has deduced. But sometimes, it turns out I'm needed more than expected.

Lekan's response to Shylock is attempting to pat his head. Shylock growls in a low register, baring enough teeth to set Lekan aback. The man retrieves his hand promptly.

"Doesn't like strangers, eh?" he says, chuckling. "Alsatian?"

"Human," I say, more truth in the word than I mean. "Nobody likes non-consensual touch." I point toward the marquee. "Would you mind?"

"Sure, sure," he says, taking out a key to open up the gate to the chain link fence surrounding the marquee. He swings it open and beckons us to go inside.

"You're not coming?" I ask.

"Inside there?" He frowns. "Didn't Banky tell you about . . . " He glances aside, as if checking to see if anyone is listening. "About . . . the event?"

"The ghost you mean?" I say. "Yes, he told me the marquee is haunted."

"It's not the marquee," Lekan says, assured. "Maybe the land. No matter how many times we've changed the marquee itself, every tent we put here gets . . . "

"Haunted?"

"Yes." He gestures inside. "Maybe you can see for yourself."

It's pitch dark when Shylock and I enter into the tent, so I turn on my phone's flashlight app. Shylock, who no longer needs as much light now that he has dog eyes, scurries off and gets about his business, sniffing every corner, making deductions that I can't help but overhear.

Crime, they always say, Shylock ponders. *Yet the grass smells nothing but ordinary, the floors simply unkempt. Bizarre events do not always mean criminal.*

He's referring to what Bankole Bashiru—or apparently as people know him, "Banky Bash"—had said when he'd made the call to me, informing me that he needed our services.

"Somebody buried, planted—I don't know—*something* on that land," he'd said. "I need someone with your . . . expertise to find it and dig it out."

I wasn't sure if he wanted us to find the person or the haunt, so I came along with Shylock just in case it was either. But now, standing in the dark, holding up the meager light from my phone, a coldness engulfs me, the kind that only I and my ilk know is not physical but spectral in nature. I realize that Banky might not have known this when hiring us, but he indeed needs both services.

There *is* something lurking here. Something cold and angry about being held back from fully crossing into its rightful place in the worlds beyond this one. This entity, whatever it is, is not in the land. It is *inside* the marquee— in the very cloth of the tent. And though the drawn, plaintive moan the initial spotter claimed to have heard is absent, I know exactly what it would've sounded like.

I lift my phone higher and look through the tent.

Nothing about it is spectacular. It looks like every other marquee-for-hire in Lagos for weekend weddings and other parties. All the lights are off, but silky orange draperies hide the tent's flaws and PVC walls. The roof, from which a few inert chandeliers dangle, is also covered in drapery. Attached to the walls, equally spaced, are fans and industrial-level air conditioners, all designed to combat the heat of packed bodies.

But that is where the ordinariness of the scene ends. Everything else present tells the story of the abandoned party the day before. Half-eaten plates of food and half-drunk glasses scattered about, stinking with a day's worth of decay. Microphones still attached to their stands, the band's equipment left behind. The decorated couple seater on the dais untouched, the cake pieces cut for said couple to perform the aged ritual of feeding each other still in the corner. Chairs congregated about tables, some with personal effects left behind in the rush to exit the party: shawls, handbags, slippers, suit jackets, a wig. Dusty shoe prints litter the red carpet leading from the door to the dais, feet facing every direction, demonstrating the nature of the panic that must have taken hold when the first scream of *Ghost!* had cut through the wedding reception.

The original screamer wasn't wrong. My ten years of witchdoctor practice are picking up the presence of a specter of sorts. The specter itself is already gone, but its telltale signs linger. The feeling of being watched even with no eyes about. The sudden draining of energy from the atmosphere, as if all color has been stripped away. The strange smell of sick, of rotting, which might in this case be the food, but not always. And the cold—*always* the cold.

But I'm not interested in the presence or absence of the specter. What I'm interested in are the two key questions to ask about specters: *Why here?* and *Why now?*

I wander over to the toilets, where the scream that brought forth the mayhem was understood to have originated. Shylock is already there, sniffing about for clues, literally. The original screamer in this case had reported seeing something fleeting in the mirror, as well as heard the moaning. The possibility of hallucinations had been floated, but this was sadly not the first time someone was reporting a haunted Bash Tents & Rentals marquee.

Is there one? Shylock asks. *I seem to find nothing of criminal import, so tell me there's a spirit here.*

"There is," I say, feeling the signs of ghostly presence intensify as I step into the cubicle. "And no, it is not in the land. It's in this marquee itself."

Okay. Shylock sounds unperturbed. *So we answer the questions.*

"You go first," I say. "Why here? Why now?"

Shylock sits and takes his time to ponder. Sometimes, I am astonished by how his actions can be so humanlike, how they can so resemble those of the man who was my best friend but now lives inside a dog. But I stop myself, remembering not to think about the circumstances that brought about this very predicament. I remind myself that what we have now is better than what the alternative would've been.

They did say they've changed the tent multiple times, correct? asks Shylock.

"They did. And the staff and equipment. Even this location—the land itself—is a new one."

So, we are to believe the business itself is haunted? That does not hold up to deduction.

"Indeed it doesn't," I say, holding up my light to the mirror, and that's when I see it.

A word, written on the glass of the mirror. Not written for the average eye to see. But the witchdoctor's eye is akin to steam on this glass, unearthing words etched by a dry finger. Especially if that finger does not sprout from a human hand but a ghostly one, scratching across the mirror, over and over, the only word that it knows, the same word that brought it here, that keeps it coming back.

The writing on the mirror uses no alphabet—it's all symbols and drawings, language from a time long before the arrival of English in this country. It is also one I can immediately connect to a specific person far away from here, the only person I know who might have an idea what this word is doing on the mirror of a random marquee in Lekki.

I bring out my notebook, draw the symbols as best as I can, and then next to it, note the best English equivalent of the word that I can muster. It reads: *GHOST WRITER.*

"Come," I say to Shylock. "We have an old foe to visit."

DR. FREDERICK LIVES in an estate in a half-industrial part of Lagos called Palmgrove. His real name is Ẹniìbùkún, but like me, no one calls him that anymore. There was a time when being a witchdoctor wasn't as customary or recognized as it is today. Changing our names to more Anglicized ones and attaching the honorific title of Doctor has always been the way we keep safe. Survival in this way is not quite as necessary these days, but true identities are still at a premium. It remains currency to know the true name of one of us, and can be traded in at any point. I aim to engage in one of such trades with Dr. Fredrick.

We arrive close to 8:30 p.m. His apartment is one of those four blocks of flats specifically built for families in a neighborhood specifically designed for families, tucked away in the heartland of a zone otherwise filled with factories and warehouses. I never pegged Dr. Frederick to be a family man, but I knew he'd been out of witchdoctor circles for a long time, after being associated with too many activities of a fraudulent nature. Perhaps he had truly decided to go clean and settle down.

We climb the stairs to his apartment and knock. There is a shuffle, and a young child opens the door, peers at me and Shylock through the gate and, wide-eyed at the prospect of a friendly animal, yells, "Daddy, there's a man with a dog!"

When this gate opens, Shylock says, *do not let that child near me.*

Dr. Frederick comes out. He's changed so much from the last time I saw him, a time I hazily remember involving a lot of chastising. Where he once was sprightly and animate, now he is portly and languid, channeling the air of someone who made a conscious decision to be just so. He is taken aback to see me, but especially Shylock, whom he immediately recognizes for who he is. For a moment, we stand there, looking at one another, him trying to gauge if this is a cordial visit or not.

"Dr. John," he says, declaring that he has decided this interaction is going to be businesslike. "Shylock."

"Fredrick," I say, nodding.

Nincompoop, says Shylock.

"We have questions," I say. "Perhaps we can take them outside, in the car, out of view of the family."

He regards me for a moment more, then shrugs, puts on a pair of slippers, shouts *I'm coming, let me see these guys off!* somewhere into the apartment, and follows us back to my '03 Corolla parked outside the compound.

Once in the car, I present him with the symbol in my notepad. His face shows little change, like the practiced conman that he is. Unluckily for him, the senses of witchdoctors are just so that the slightest shifts in a person, of a natural or supernatural kind, are reputably perceptible. And the fluctuations in Dr. Fredrick's breath and temperature are much too quick and panicky, betraying the disquiet he wishes to hide.

"What's this?" he asks.

"Let's not do this, Fred," I say. "Let's not pretend that I don't know that you know exactly what this is."

He eyes me, refuses to look at the paper.

"Look," I say, "nobody is dying or anything. I just need to find out who you wrote this enchantment for."

He looks at it for a while more, then sighs.

"If I told you I can't remember, would you believe?" he says. "It's been a long time. The memory grows old."

"Not for a scammer such as yourself."

"Don't—" he starts, then puffs his cheeks. "I don't know what you want from me, John."

"I want you to tell me who you wrote this mangled enchantment for."

"What do you mean *mangled*?"

"Don't play with me, Frederick."

Maybe just let me at him, Shylock says. *Take off a finger or two.*

"Not yet, Shylock," I say. "Frederick?"

"What d'you mean *not yet, Shylock*? Sorry, hold on—what's mangled about this enchantment? I looked up the translation directly from *The Witchdoctor's Guide*."

"So you *did* write it?"

Frederick puffs his cheeks again. "Okay, fine, I did. For one guy a few years ago."

"What was his name?"

"Name? Are you kidd—I don't remember the names of clients."

"Because you want to forget who you've scammed, right?" I tap the paper. "Who, Frederick?"

"I don't know, a guy—he was a disgraced academic or something. I remember because he had become a ghostwriter now and wanted some help—supernatural help—so that his clients would always accept whatever he writes and pay him good money for it."

"And you wrote him *this* enchantment for that?" I lean back in my seat. "Oh you stupid, stupid man."

"What? I translated it directly from—"

"Exactly, idiot. You translated it directly from *The Witchdoctor's Guide*, forgetting that that book is not a dictionary, not a *guide* in any sense of the word. It does not tell you what to do or what not to, and you wrote a stupid, broken enchantment out of that."

"Oh."

"Yes, Fred. Now, all you've done is give a man the power to bring ghosts to life."

ON OUR WAY back home, I place a call to Bash and tell him I'll be attending the next event scheduled at his marquee. I explain that his last ghost is long gone, but there'll be a new one at his next event.

"Whatever is there can be easily removed," I say. "But it has to be by the same person who put it there."

"And you have this person?" Bash asks.

"No," I say, looking to Shylock, who nods at me. "But he will be there, at your next event."

"Wait—what? As one of the guests?"

"No, he'll just be there, somewhere. My associate, who understands criminals and criminal intent much better than I do, has advised me this is a personal matter for this person. You're just a victim of someone else's . . . misguidance."

There's a long pause on the other end of the line before Bash says, "I don't know what all of this means, so I won't ask. Just set my marquee free."

He provides the details in sharp, short bursts. It's a weekend birthday party for a bigwig socialite who doesn't pay enough attention to the rumor mill to have heard about the last event. He hangs up without saying goodbye.

Clients, says Shylock. *Ungrateful bastards.*

WEEKENDS IN LAGOS are all the same. They start slowly and undergo swift metamorphosis, the untouched dew of morning suddenly assaulted by a flood of bodies, all decked out in their brightest before midday. The weekend of our event is not any different.

The Bash marquee looks transformed. All haphazardness from our last visit is gone, and new draperies have been introduced to reflect the event's colors of the day: teal and amber. The dais has been exchanged for a larger built stage, which carries the same colors with a large *Happy Birthday, Daddy* stacked in sparkly detail. An emcee paces in front of that, doling out jokes and raising a ruckus. Food of all varieties—traditional to continental, heavy to light—passes around. The music from the speakers, provided intermittently by both a DJ and a live band, each set up at either end of the marquee, booms through the structure.

A ghost would have to *scream* to be heard here.

I have been forced into a suit for the event and presented as a bodyguard because Lekan says it's the only role Lagosians would accept for a grown man walking around with an Alsatian. It would be a different case, he says, with a smaller dog—or as he calls them, *handbag dogs.* After walking around, I can see why he was worried. Half of the guests are frightened by the mere presence of Shylock, while the other half make moves to pet him, receive growls in return, and end up just as frightened. Shylock and I are eventually banished to patrol the periphery of the event.

Though I have a drink in hand to look like I'm partaking in the festivities, my eyes are mostly scanning. I'm not looking at the guests, no. These types don't visit witchdoctors themselves—they have people do it on their behalf. They also don't fit the profile of disgraced academics. People like these are never disgraced enough to lose anything. My eyes are on those who slip between these bodies unnoticed: servers, gardeners, security, cooks.

Between the emcee's bad jokes, the band and DJ struggling for ascendancy, and a ceremonial cake-cutting, I find nothing of import. Even the ghostly feeling is gone. Now, the event has moved into a new phase: a fully-clad cultural troupe performs a traditional dance on the stage.

"Are you sure he's coming today?" I ask Shylock.

Patience, says Shylock, nibbling on the meat left on a tossed-away bone. *He'll be here.*

"How can you be sure?" I'm barely unsure about these things, but this one has me befuddled.

Because this is about power, says Shylock.

"How so?"

He's a disenfranchised person with sudden unimaginable power, Shylock expounds, hacking at the bone. *This event is too good an opportunity not to use it. But not* just *use it. He wants to relish the results, the chaos.* He lets the bone go. *He'll be here.*

Just as he says it—or almost—a crawling settles upon the skin of my neck. My muscles stiffen.

"It's here," I say to Shylock. "*He's* here."

An ear-piercing scream follows, and things play out as expected. First, dismissal: a collective hope that this scream is a one-off event, a mistake soon glossed over. Then confusion, as the troupe stops performing to regard the screamer, who's tearing through the crowd, heading for the exit, his eyes wide saucers.

"Spirit!" the man, still in his waistcoat jacket, is saying, "Spirit!"

The confusion soon gives way to a second person, closely followed by a third, who jump out of the toilet area, screaming the same thing. There's more effect now because one of these is the daughter of the celebrating father, and the other is her aide.

"Spirit in the toilet!" the aide screams and tears for the exit.

A beat passes, then everyone else follows.

It should be hard to spot who I'm looking for with everything so helter-skelter. But rather than my eyes darting from body to body, I'm looking for who's *not* running. Who's standing exactly like I am: watching, waiting, taking it in.

That's when I spot him.

He's not as aged as I thought—not in the way many people think university professors to be. Perhaps five-ish years younger than I am. He's outside the chain link fence, posing as one of the people who loiter at the gates of big events to pester guests for money. But he has a book in hand, out of place with his raggedy clothing. He peers through the fence, his expression quiet and contained, but unmistakably gleeful.

Then he looks across the compound and his eyes catch mine. An understanding passes between us, and he *knows*.

Slowly, he reaches into his book and tears out a sheet. Then he puts it in his mouth and eats it. A group shuffles past the loiterers, and I lean aside to watch what the man does next. But when the bodies clear, he is gone.

THE SPECTER IS not even a well-written one.

It's what many people think a ghost *looks* like: a woman in a white dress, face painted white, teeth red with blood, no legs. Straight out of a Nollywood B-film. She floats around the tight stalls of the toilet, bouncing from cloth to cloth above, past the ceiling. She appears in the mirror sometimes. But mostly, she's just confused, wondering who has put her in this dress, painted her teeth so. And she's angry, which explains her hisses and moans. But I can't do anything about it, so Shylock and I just sit there with her instead. The person who wrote her here has destroyed the source, anyway, so she'll be gone soon. Like the last one, she'll fade away and return to whoever and wherever she was, leaving behind the cold and unsettling remnants of her once-presence. And like me and all of Bash Tents and Rentals, she will hope not to be pulled through that veil and back into this world again by some unruly person with a vendetta.

She passes a bit before dark. Shylock and I return outside. Lekan is the only person left, sitting in a chair outside the chain link fence, moping. He hands me a phone to talk to an enraged Bash. Bash wants to see the perpetrator brought to heel immediately.

"When you find this man—and you'd better find him," Bash says, "I want you to bring him straight to my office."

"What for?"

"You're in the business of finding, not of asking questions," Bash snaps. "I will do with him as I please."

"Contrary," I say. "Asking questions is literally my job description."

"Don't be smart with me," Bash says. "You know this person must be dealt with. Can't go free after destroying my business like this."

"Fair," I say. "So send him to the police station. Let the law take its due course."

Bash scoffs. "And what crime would I present at court?"

"Exactly."

There's a lull, and then Bash says: "Do your job, or I'll find another witchdoctor who will."

"Then maybe you should," I say. "I don't subscribe to jungle justice."

I toss the phone back at Lekan when leaving. "Tell your brother I'm not one of his thugs-for-hire. I don't know what he's been told, but witchdoctors still have a moral code."

IT TAKES ME two weeks to fail at shaking off the question of *why*. Why does a man, equipped with such power, partake in this near sadistic endeavor? And most importantly, *Why now?* and *Why there?* I'm not very comfortable with unanswered questions, and neither is Shylock. So, paid or unpaid, we set out to find our culprit anyway.

I go the modern route of computers for this one. Early on, I learned a lot of the job of Shylock and Associates would be the job of finding people, and I invested in an online course on finding information on the web—everything from social listening to parsing metadata to discovering archived content. As long as it has a digital footprint, I will find it.

It doesn't take me long to find the ghost-writing man. Few cases of academic misconduct ever attract a penalty of dismissal, if they attract a penalty at all. Between the few universities in Lagos and Twitter chatter from the last few years, I'm able to pinpoint the man: Aminu Rosunu, formerly Lecturer II at the Yaba College's School of Art, Design, and Printing. Dismissed for accepting bribes from students in exchange for them passing his class.

I find him on Facebook. Still in Lagos. No home address, but there's a business name for his now defunct ghostwriting business. Finding the business address is easy. I wager it's the same as his home.

We wait for the midday Sunday traffic to die out before we head to his place. It's surprisingly located in Lekki, but in the underbelly, where all the service people who power the posh locales live. Every road is untarred, and sewage water runs free with spirogyra. Worse, it's windy when we arrive, and the motley mix of smells do not make for great welcoming. Even Shylock the dog has misgivings.

The house is a rundown spectacle with no fence, no gate and a weak door that opens when we knock. A voice inside asks us to come in, and we do. It's a woman tying a wrapper, sitting on a low stool in a living room with no furniture except two plastic chairs. There's no electricity, and the only light is a lantern.

Without a word, she points to Shylock, then points outside.

Sorry friend, I say, as Shylock grumpily agrees. The animals-outside-the-house rule is one I'm yet to come up with ways to surmount.

I introduce myself to the woman as a witchdoctor and tell her who I'm looking for. She nods along.

"Is he here?"

"This na his house, yes," she says. "But his not here. If you want to talk, talk to the wife." She points to an adjoining room, dark but for its own solo lantern. "But she no too feel well."

I thank her and enter. A woman of similar age is lying in bed, covered in wrappers. The room smells of Aboniki balm and kolanut.

"You're looking for my husband," she says, waving me to sit, then sighs. "Don't worry, I heard everything. I knew somebody would find out one day and come."

I sit, worrying that I might've scared her a bit. "I'm not here to harm or arrest or even judge your husband. I just want to know . . . why."

She nods. "Hmm. I didn't understand in the beginning too. I still don't understand. But I've accepted it as my fate. Especially as I was the cause."

"You were the cause . . . of what?"

"He says they deserve it for what they did to me."

"Oh? You were wronged by Bash Rentals?"

"Who?" She squints to look at me in the dark. "I don't know who that is. I catered food and drinks for many different event centers here in Lekki. I can't remember all their names."

"I see."

"Did he do one today?" she asks. "Is that where he is now?"

"I don't know," I say. "But I'm hoping not. I'm hoping to tell him to stop, and hoping he'll listen." I shift in my seat. "Maybe you can help convince him?"

"You think I've not tried?" she says. "When we found out what the quack witchdoctor did, it killed Aminu's business. He couldn't write anything—he was afraid to even write his own name. That's why I became the breadwinner of this house in the first place. And if I wasn't working so hard, almost killing myself for these event centers, it would not have pained us like that when they owed us and refused to pay. Now I'm sick and we have nothing, cannot even afford the right medicine." She sighs again. "I don't know what exactly he does when he goes out there, but if it hurts them even just a little bit, I'm not going to lose sleep over that."

While she spoke, the light in the room changed. It's only when she's done I realize it's a shadow that has darkened the doorway. I turn around sharply to find Aminu Rosunu, taller-looking than when I last saw him, but every other bit the same. He wears glasses, which give him an air of calm, quite dissimilar to the commotion I witnessed him perpetrate. His cheeks, below the glasses, bear faint traces of good-looking tribal marks. In one hand is a bowl of food, which I figure is for his wife. In another, a pack of medicines.

We stare at one another, rabbits caught in headlights. I realize he's listened in on most of what his wife has said. He's waiting for my response, for me to make the next move.

So I rise, straighten my clothes, and ask him only one question: "Why?"

It takes him a moment to answer, and when he does, it's one word: "Joy."

"Excuse me?"

"Joy," he repeats. "They cannot continue to have joy, while we have none. If we must have pain, then so must they."

I nod, thinking.

"I am sorry for what you have been through," I say at last. "And I will not cast judgement on you. I will not tell you both what to do either, because you already know what that is. What I *will* tell you, though, is this: if the only way you seek joy is in the misfortune of others, then you can never find it in yourselves." I let it sink. "Also, you will get caught. Don't think the next person who Bash hires will be as kind to you as I've been."

I don't wait for a response before leaving. Outside, I regroup with Shylock and we head back for the car.

Will you be reporting this to Bash? Shylock asks.

I scoff. "Fuck Bash."

He snickers, as much as a dog can, then asks: *So you're just going to hope this man does the right thing? Heh. Aren't you just as foolish as ever.*

I laugh a full laugh from my belly. Always the drama king, this one.

"One of us has to be. Lest it just be two cynics running this business. Plus, what's a detective without a heart full hope?"

A good detective, says Shylock. *But I guess you'll do for now.*

DID YOU KNOW?

SUYI DAVIES OKUNGBOWA is a Nigerian author of fantasy, science fiction, and general speculative work. His latest novel is *Son of the Storm*, first in the epic fantasy trilogy, The Nameless Republic. His debut godpunk fantasy novel *David Mogo, Godhunter* won the 2020 Nommo Ilube Award for Best Speculative Novel by an African. His shorter works have appeared in various periodicals and anthologies and have been nominated for various awards. He earned his MFA in Creative Writing at the University of Arizona, and currently teaches at the University of Ottawa.

THE BRIDGE WITH NO MIDDLE

BY DEREK LUBANGAKENE

THE bridge with no middle towers over a dried river bed south of Malakal County in the Upper Nile Region, north of which lies the belt of the Sahel. Pastoralists settle one side of the river and, on the other, are farmer-folk and long-limbed fishermen, hoarse-voiced from driving herons away from their drying-racks. Both peoples speak the same tongue, though they have never shared words.

Legend says, if you walk long enough on this bridge, you'll not emerge on the other side of the White Nile, but come upon the end of the world. Only a farmer's boy has ever returned from such an excursion, and when he did, the rain poured for three nights.

The elders, plume-crowned and glaucoma-ridden, said the rain marked the sorrow of the gods. "The gods lament the ill that mortal hands have wrought," they said. They named the boy a messenger from the gods. But they couldn't divine the message. Their gods, like the White man's god, favored silence. The warrior caste, impatient to divine their own message, ventured bridge-wise. Only to become sacrifice to the stonework bridge, like the many who'd made the journey before.

The bridge, now sunken, still echoes with the screams of warriors tumbling down. Alas, you'll never hear their proverbial splash.

HAUNTED SOUTH SUDAN

SUDAN

Talodi

Malakal

Bentiu

Asosa

Nasir

SOUTH
SUDAN

White Nile River

DEREK LUBANGAKENE's work appears in *Jalada*, *Escape Pod*, *Omenana*, *Apex Mag*, Brittle Paper's *Afrofuturism* anthology, among others. He lives in Kampala, Uganda and online at www.dereklubangakene.com.

* FILE UNDER: *Haunted Bridge*

GHOST ROADS OF THE OUDE KIMBERLEYS

BY CAT HELLISEN

EVERY South African town has an Oude Kimberley Hotel, dust-whipped and waiting. All constructed from the same Art-Deco-in-Africa template of wrapped balconies, narrow columns, and fussy white trims. Even the font remains the same: hand-lettered, the red of slope-backed Sanga oxen.

Always open for guests:
The Oude Kimberley Hotel Chain

Ghosts gather at the doorways, passing from one room to another as they loop their final moments, and savvy travelers use their tracks as portals. Quiet deaths are too ephemeral. To hold a door, you need a murder.

And the Oude Kimberleys provide.

Follow the red hands, the weeping, the drunken screaming. Echo invitations.

The ways will open.

CAT HELLISEN grew up in various South African towns, and now lives in Scotland. Her story "The Worme Bridge" won Short Story Day Africa, and her latest fantasy novel *Bones Like Bridges* plays with class and magic to take on the end of a civilization.

* FILE UNDER: *Haunted Hotel*

You have a perfect example of a tomb
warning right in front of you . . .

HAUNTED TRAVELS

A TOUR OF THE RAMSES

FEATURE ENTRY 16

STRUCTURE TYPE: HOTEL
LOCATION: CAIRO, EGYPT
LAT./ LONG: 30.0722° N, 31.3488° E
BUILT: CIRCA 1925
GROUND ELEVATION: 292 FT. (89 M.)
WRITTEN BY: JACKSON KUHL

TRAVEL GUIDE NOTES

I LOVE STORIES where the past meets the present. In a way, that's what this entire anthology-tour guide is about, as hauntings must have a cause, something that's already occurred in order to affect those in the here and now; but this story, in particular, draws upon that, the confluence of Egyptian lore and the Hollywood-inspired, Deco-gilt, overindulgent craze of the early 1900s. Beauty and glamour and cultural appropriation for royalty and the elite, or anyone else who could afford it. But as with all things, it comes to an end, what was once highly sought now fallen to memories and crumbling relics: Those institutions reveling in mummy kitsch in a way become mummies themselves.

Author Jackson Kuhl writes smart fiction, quiet tales rich in historic detail. This is the third time my co-editor Eric J. Guignard has worked with him (my first), and all of Jackson's stories are carefully constructed accounts. The following is subtle, splendid, and tragic. Come along with this author and his genial caretaker, as they lead you through a closed and decaying hotel, giving its history for the final time, during "A Tour of the Ramses."

—Charlatan Bardot

T HANK YOU FOR COMING. SUCH A HANDSOME couple. Newlyweds? On your honeymoon? How romantic. Congratulations.

Well, here we are. Let's begin.

You see before you the façade of the self-styled jewel of Cairo, the Hotel Ramses. It was inspired, of course, by Howard Carter's discovery of KV62, more well-known as the tomb of Tutankhamun. When asked by Lord Carnarvon if he saw anything within, Howard replied with three words that became immortalized as surely as the mummified teenager whose eternal rest he disturbed: *Yes, wonderful things*. Note the fluted columns and black granite marquee, still intact, and how the bulky lintels and seated pharaohs could have been lifted straight from a Theban necropolis.

And yet even the glitter of the treasures Howard spied inside the boy-king's crypt were outshone by the magnificence of the Egyptomania that followed. The owners of this site here along al-Alfi had long intended to build a luxury hotel, which they believed would be attractive due to its close proximity to the Azbakeya Gardens, just around the corner. But when Carter struck gold, so to speak, they imagined a tourism boom to Egypt, and set to work immediately. The Ramses opened in 1925.

It was designed by Achille Marchant of the French firm Rouzet and Delacroix. The owners and Marchant quarreled from the very beginning. Marchant imagined a modern streamline affair inspired by airplanes and zeppelins, but the owners showed him photographs of Grauman's Egyptian Theater in Hollywood, which had opened in 1922, and insisted. Finally Marchant caved and created what the owners wanted, although not necessarily to anyone's benefit, as we will see.

Shall we go inside? As far as I know, I'm the only person in Cairo who has a key to the door.

Come in, come in. Watch your step. Allow me to close the door behind us, for our own safety. This neighborhood isn't what it once was.

True to the terms, Marchant presented his clients with an edifice designed in Egyptian Revival, although he stubbornly injected elements of the Heliopolis style into its floorplan. Guests were greeted outside by valets dressed in white galabeyas with red turbans and sashes. Once past its revolving door, now sadly boarded up, the guests entered this massive atrium, the rooms rising five stories above. They then marched down a corridor formed of ram-headed sphinxes to the front desk. To either side of the sphinxes was the lobby, where men in dinner jackets and women in silk dresses lounged on sofas, drinking gin and tonics and chatting merrily as if

HAUNTED CAIRO, EGYPT

biding the evening on an upriver journey to Luxor, with none of the malaria. Unlike the rest of the furnishings, the sphinxes were too heavy to move and so remain. Yes ma'am, it does look like they're smiling. Happy sphinxes, happy to see you.

What was that? Oh don't worry. Probably somebody yelling in the street. I wouldn't concern yourself about it.

In the hotel's prime, the lobby was decorated with potted palms and obelisks and statues removed from minor sites. The bartenders did their work atop actual stone sarcophagi taken from real tombs, and in the rooms above—now stripped and vandalized—smaller relics and dark gilded wallpaper imparted a sense of sophisticated exploration, where every guest could feel like he or she reconnoitered the Queen's Chamber or the Grand Gallery. There were several mummies. Marchant had sent his decorators to scour the casbahs and antiquity shops for the best items for their hotel.

Sounds a bit macabre, doesn't it? The atmosphere wasn't lost on the owners, I assure you. When they saw what Marchant had done, they worried all of it might frighten the guests. Imagine, for a moment, a Waldorf Astoria or St. Regis bedecked in funerary urns and gravestones and statues of weeping angels, and then consider the rather different appeal of such an establishment. But Marchant, with almost diabolic glee, reminded them that it was exactly what they'd requested.

In the end, the owners worried needlessly. The clientele of the Hotel Ramses regarded the furnishings with titillation—to them a set of authentic canopic jars, once used to house the organs of a mummified cadaver, raised the pulse; while a glass case containing embalming hooks and spikes, formerly employed by grisly priests to gouge brains from their pans, thrilled the spirit.

And so his work complete, Marchant collected his paycheck and returned to Paris. He did not live long to enjoy it. On the voyage he caught a cold which worsened into pneumonia, and died less than three weeks after disembarking.

As you can see, we've arrived at the front desk, where guests would sign their names upon the papyrus pages of the hotel register. To your right are the elevators; only the gates and metalwork remain.

It was here that Mr. Plummer first laid eyes on her.

Who was Mr. Plummer? He was the night manager of the Ramses. Formerly of the Ritz-Carlton in New York, the owners lured him to Egypt with the better title and a sizable pay raise. He was an attractive candidate, for he possessed the attribute prized above all others in the service industry: namely an unwavering loyalty to the hotel he served.

That included an attitude invulnerable to the ghoulish fixtures. The mummies erected in their coffins he greeted with nothing but cool disinterest, and his only regard for the shelves and displays loaded with bric-a-brac looted from desert sepulchers was that they not fall into the pockets of an overenthusiastic guest on his way to checkout. Plummer cared for nothing but the comforts and whims of his clientele. A good man to have about, in a place like . . . this.

If you walk with me this way, you enter what was once the hotel restaurant. Over there was the bandstand, now dismantled, where musicians played numbers like the "Egyptian Glide" or "Mummy Mine."

And here, standing directly opposite the front entrance, we've reached the centerpiece of the Ramses, an imposing spiral staircase that winds the full five levels of the atrium. Designed to awe the guest with its monumental scope as would a pyramid or titanic sculpture, it was the owners' sole concession to the contemporary tastes of Marchant. The more infirm guests preferred the elevators to reach their beds, but anyone with a flair for the dramatic took the stairs. They made everyone's exits climactic and anyone's entrances breathtaking.

Please watch your step as we ascend. The marble can be very slippery.

What's that, ma'am? Who's "her?" The one Plummer laid eyes upon?

None other than Asya Sevim. I doubt the name is familiar to you, you're too young. But take it from me, there was a time when everyone throughout Egypt knew the name Asya Sevim. Well, almost everyone.

I can imagine it now: a great bustle of confusion at the front entrance catching Mr. Plummer's attention as he stood at the desk. Flash bulbs pulsing and popping through the glass and suddenly, with an explosion of noise, a long parade of valets, bags, steamer trunks, and hollering newspapermen rushing between the ram-headed sphinxes toward him. Striding at the head of this river is a tall woman, her eyes shielded by dark glasses, the feather in her golden turban bobbing with every shimmy of her exaggerated gait. Upon reaching the front desk, how she must've coolly regarded the clerks and Plummer before slapping the service bell with a gloved palm.

"Good evening," says Plummer. "How may I help you?"

"I wish to take your very best room," says the woman between pulls on her cigarette holder. "The largest suite you have."

"My pleasure, madame," says Plummer. "How long will you be staying with us?"

"Indefinitely. As long as the Alhambra will have me—which, for their sake, should be a very long time."

"Certainly. And may I ask madame's name?"

At this, the woman lowers her glasses by a fraction of inch, and, peering over their top at him, says, "Do I really have to say it?"

And Plummer, who supposes he should know her identity but doesn't, responds, "No madame, you don't have to say it but you do need to *write* it." Then he slides the guest book toward her.

For a beat no one—the clerks, the valets, the newspapermen—utters a sound. Then the woman laughs. "Oh, I like you," she says. "We're going to become the very best of friends."

Asya Sevim may have been a name unheard in Plummer's New York, but she was well known in the shisha bars and cabarets of the Levant. She was a star of the *raqs sharqui*, the belly dance, and she performed—as she was fond of telling anyone—for presidents, prime ministers, princes, and paupers without discrimination, as long as they paid. Though the dance itself was original to the Land of the Pharaohs, Sevim's Turkish technique was more flamboyant and acrobatic than the conservative Egyptian style, making her a novelty outside her native Turkey and a celebrity throughout the Near East.

"My life is a long string of hotels, Mr. Plummer," she said to him one evening (I imagine) in the Nefertiti suite, the grandest in the whole hotel. After her nightly show at the Alhambra Casino, Sevim was fond of summoning Plummer to her rooms on some pretense, only to lure him into conversation which he, in his capacity of keeping his guests happy, obliged. "A blur of ugly lobbies and bad food and grimy, unctuous managers."

"Present company excepted, of course," said Plummer.

"You're very funny, Mr. Plummer. You should come see me dance, as my guest."

Sevim did not allow many into her suite, nor did she confide in anyone else beyond her manager, a thick-necked bull of a cousin through some convoluted lineage Plummer didn't even pretend to follow. She'd known many men, she said. Sevim enjoyed chronicling her life and travels, and her stories included a *dramatis personae* of lovers, admirers, and suitors; and Plummer could tell by her slight sarcasm and distaste that she considered them all beneath her. Yet she clearly did not lump Plummer with them. She intuited a certain truth about him, if I may say so, and when she asked why he left New York for Cairo, and he implied a failed love affair played a role, she tactfully didn't inquire into the particulars. She trusted him because, in his heartbreak, she held no temptation for him; and she confided in him because her loneliness was mirrored by his own.

"I take it you're unfamiliar with belly dancing," said Sevim. "Well then, you shall begin your education with the best. I will ruin all other dancers for you, though some wounds are worth the injury."

Plummer, incapable of refusing a guest's demand, put on his best suit and did so. I will summarize the effect: he fell in love.

It can be difficult for people like you and me to understand what it's like to be celebrated—to have money and acclaim, to be surrounded by admirers and flatterers. But Sevim distrusted it; she knew admiration quickly curdles into jealousy, and flattery is often simple obsequiousness. For those reasons she didn't like to linger at the Alhambra after her shows. On the nights she felt social, she invited guests back to her suite at the Ramses. Plummer was always present.

There was a particular night. Sevim's manager-cousin was there, along with his wife, plus several habitués of the Alhambra that Plummer didn't know. There was also an Egyptologist from America named Babcock and her husband, both downriver from Luxor.

Having an expert among them was too good a chance to pass up. Sevim soon brought up the Ramses' collection of esoterica—and, to the enjoyment of the party, whether any of it was cursed.

"The ancient Egyptians didn't believe in curses," said Babcock to her rapt audience, seated on sofas and arms of chairs around her. "Contrary to public opinion, there aren't any curses written inside Tut's tomb. I've seen it for myself."

"And Lord Carnarvon?"

"Thousands die from infections every week." Babcock sipped her drink. "Warnings inside tombs are commonplace but not curses."

"Fame is its own curse," said Sevim.

"The Egyptians would've argued otherwise. To them, the worst thing was to be forgotten and unremembered. They had a cultural obsession with fame."

Babcock nodded toward the wall. "You have a perfect example of a tomb warning right in front of you." As one, the eyes of the room swiveled to gaze upon a framed papyrus scroll, doubtlessly bought for a trifle by Marchant's decorators from some Valley of the Kings thief. Torn and ripped, it was still a remarkable specimen of art, depicting a number of supplicants kneeling before a woman of noble and scornful demeanor. Countless squiggles and scarabs surrounding the figures presumably captioned the scene.

"That scroll depicts Weret-Hekau, the goddess of magic," said Babcock. "A sorceress. Her power was often invoked to protect tombs."

"To curse intruders?" asked Plummer.

"To warn them. To inform them that Weret-Hekau would erase any and all defilers and thieves from history. To make sure they were *forgotten*."

"That sounds like a threat," said Plummer, "and very much like a curse."

Babcock shrugged. "The distinction may be lost on the layperson."

"Maybe she's who I hear talking at night when I go to bed," said Sevim.

"That's just you talking in your sleep, Asya," said the manager. "You cannot bear the absence of your own voice." And they laughed.

Plummer lingered until the other guests left.

"What you said before about hearing voices," Plummer said to her. "What did you mean?"

"It's just echoes from downstairs," said Sevim. "They're all garbled together, but the effect is very strange. It sounds like just one voice, speaking in the next room. And I can never understand the language."

Plummer knew his friend spoke five different languages. "None of the other guests have ever complained about voices."

"It's nothing, darling. Don't worry yourself."

But listen to how I digress. Keep up, keep up. We're nearly there—the culmination of our tour.

Here we are. You see around you the Nefertiti suite, the finest in the whole hotel. Sadly, much diminished, now full of garbage and fallen plaster. Tragic, really.

You will, however, surely note that one artifact remains, even though the rest of the hotel has been stripped to its nails. It is, of course, the same papyrus scroll featuring the goddess that the American archaeologist spoke of. It persists because no one dares touch it.

The fortunes of the Ramses plummeted not long after that night. There were fires and deaths. One man shot another in a jealous rage. A woman fell to her death. Stranger events happened too. Guests reported seeing unexplained lights late at night, floating through the hallways or rooms—

For the love of—! Don't be alarmed, ma'am, that surprised me too. I thought it was just a pile of trash. But as you can see, it's merely an old woman dressed in rags. A homeless beggar, squatting here. How she goes in and out of the building without a key, I have no idea.

No, it's fine. She asked us if we had any food or money. I told her in Arabic to leave us alone. You can give her some money if you want, sir. It's very kind, but you know how these beggars are in Cairo. It just encourages them.

What's she saying now? It's ridiculous. She's saying she used to be a guest at the hotel. Complete nonsense.

Where was I? Right—the decline of the Ramses.

There came a point when Sevim couldn't travel anywhere, not in Cairo, not in Egypt, without being swarmed by admirers. It was so awful she would only leave the Ramses to perform her nightly show at the Alhambra, then immediately return to her suite afterward. Room service brought up all her meals, and of course her friend Plummer made certain no one disturbed her. The front desk became the battle line he maintained in her defense.

Too much time alone is never good for anyone.

"Do you think the skin of my neck is looser?" Sevim asked Plummer one afternoon when he'd come to check on her, or so I'd like to think. She sat primping in front of her mirror.

"Of course not," Plummer would say.

"The lights are too harsh. I must tell the Alhambra to light me better during my routine. They exaggerate the lines around my eyes."

"I will have instructions sent over immediately."

"I've been thinking." She turned in her seat to face him. "Perhaps I should reduce the number of performances. I can't stand to keep doing shows every night. It's taking its toll. I'm so *exhausted*."

You can assume the rest. In her withdrawal from the world, Sevim soon became completely detached. First there were six shows a week, then four, then only one. Then came the week when Sevim refused to leave her suite at all. Still beloved by her fans, they clamored to see her, but she refused all indulgences.

I really must apologize for this harassment. Now the old wretch is babbling that she recognizes me. Of course you've seen me before, you old hag—I'm the tour guide. Who knows how long she's been living here. I must insist the authorities remove her.

What became of the hotel? Nothing but calamity and hardship. The great Asya Sevim wasted away here. Such a loss to the world—a tragedy. I don't even know how to describe it, really. I was told she simply vanished. It staggers the senses. Imagine misplacing someone as famous as Asya Sevim?

After that there was no shaking the reputation of a curse, and patronage dwindled. It was worse with the Depression. The owners sold everything that wasn't nailed down before selling the building itself. It changed hands a few times and the clientele became, shall we say, increasingly unsavory. There were a great number of murders and overdoses before the police finally shut it down.

Now the hotel is as you see it. Quiet. Lifeless. Except for this bag of bones.

Get off my arm! I tell you I don't know you, you old witch. Leave me be.

Come my friends. Let's go immediately. I'm sorry you had to witness that. I assure you, you're perfectly safe from her. She's never been this aggressive.

Yes, you've guessed correctly, ma'am—Plummer was my grandfather. He could never bear to return to New York, even after the hotel closed. Something rooted him here to Cairo.

Part of him died with Asya's disappearance. He's buried not far away. One day the sands will cover his grave and perhaps in some remote future his dried-up corpse will be leaned against the wall of a hotel for the amusement of its guests. Egypt is a land of cycles. A land that never forgets.

There goes the old woman caterwauling again. What a racket.

Goodbye. I hoped you enjoyed yourselves and I apologize again for the interruptions. And sir, if I may? Hold your bride's hand tightly as you descend the staircase. Don't let go until you reach the street. Hold on. You never know when the sight of her face will be the last.

Congratulations again.

Did You Know?

Jackson Kuhl is the author of the Gothic mystery, *A Season of Whispers*, set in a haunted 19th-century transcendentalist commune. His short fiction has appeared in *Black Static*, *Weirdbook*, and several anthologies. You can find him online @jacksonkuhl or at jacksonkuhl.com.

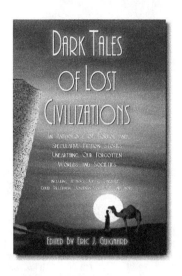

Seven doors stand at even intervals down one
wall. Each door is of a different design . . .

THE BROTHER

FEATURE ENTRY 17

STRUCTURE TYPE: CONVERTED HOTEL-OFFICE BUILDING
LOCATION: NAIROBI, KENYA
LAT./ LONG: 1.2776° S, 36.8178° E
BUILT: CIRCA 1921
GROUND ELEVATION: 5,466 FT. (1,666 M.)
WRITTEN BY: MAKENA ONJERIKA

TRAVEL GUIDE NOTES

HOW FAR WOULD you go to find reason or meaning in death of a loved one? Or, otherwise, what else would it take to attain closure in their unexplained absence? Even with tenacity, money, and time, Moses may find he has to go much further than he's willing, and only to uncover answers he doesn't want to learn.

Writing from Kenya, Makena Onjerika recently won the distinguished Caine Prize for African Writing, only the fourth author from her country ever to do so. There's good reason for her accolades: Makena's stories are beautiful multi-hued slices of life set to the dark caprices of circumstance. They're honest. Compelling. Reflective. And, most all, haunting. One of the last stories acquired for this anthology, it was certainly a gratification to be able to include the following.

An old adage says that a journey begins with a single step and, considering that, the "step" here crosses chasms, as Moses searches amongst memory, illusion, and dark whispers for "The Brother."

—Charlatan Bardot

T HE BUILDING IS THE PAST, THE PRESENT, AND THE future. This is what people say. Well, one person: Moses's Uber driver from last Friday. Another hoax. Moses's social media inboxes are full of messages from private eyes, witchdoctors, and seers (every possible type of Nairobi con man), each offering his services—at a reasonable fee, of course. Moses had done just about everything to find his brother, and this is the last.

The building was once a Whites-only hotel with a façade of Corinthian columns and leafy capitals—colonial pretensions lost soon after Independence. Now it's just another building in the hustle and bustle of downtown Nairobi. Still, Moses, at six feet and some tall, feels diminished before it. He is making a mistake, but he cannot bring himself to turn back.

Earlier this year, when he appeared on the country's 40-under-40 list of entrepreneurs, one article writer described him as "sharp minded," "aggressive," and "unshakably confident." He is all these things but he is also a fool in pursuit of a ghost because of a half-baked story told by an Uber driver on a drunken night—an Uber driver who watched him cry and drip snot in the back seat of a Toyota.

The time is now 11:56 a.m. and the day, although sunny, has a certain haze to it, as if veiled. Moses must enter the building at exactly 12:03 p.m. His phone is set to ring at that very moment.

"No earlier, no later," the Uber driver said.

Moses is certain he will get robbed, or worse, in the building that now houses a second-rate college on its seventh floor and a multitude of struggling businesses in the micro-partitioned floors below. But he is desperate and has been for the four hundred and forty-seven days since he found out his younger brother was missing.

When his phone buzzes, he lifts his chest with a deep breath and walks past flirty college students to the oversized reception desk behind which two harried guards sit checking IDs. The building has the characteristic rundown look of downtown Nairobi—dust-dulled glass, off-white walls, cobwebs in a high corner, a feeling of too much space, and tile seams as black as a beggar's nails.

"Wapi?" asks one of the guards, pen poised above the visitor's book.

"You say Wachira and Kamau's on the third floor, but that's not where you will go," the Uber driver instructed.

Having clipped the visitor's badge to his shirt collar, Moses asks the guard about the stairs. The woman gives him a quick survey and shakes her head. After all, the building has four operational lifts, standing like portals

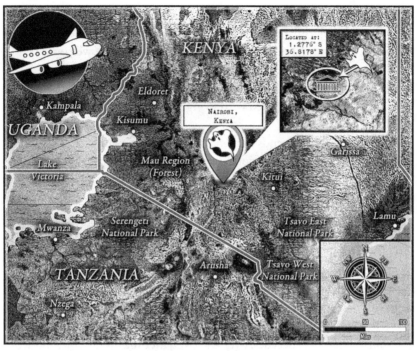

HAUNTED NAIROBI, KENYA

to other worlds, just opposite the desk. She points over her shoulder dismissively.

"Climb forty-seven steps, and the first person you meet, say, 'I have come to see the Giver,'" said the driver.

"Anyone I see?"

The driver ignored the question. "Before you go there, be very sure."

Moses carries his doubts up the white marble stairs, and they echo back at him in the wide, unhurriedly spiral stairwell. What is he doing? The Directorate of Criminal Investigations closed his brother's case five months ago. "Disappeared without Trace" was the best they could do. But Moses remembers his mother and the way her face could hold disappointment, muscles slack, mouth downturned at the corners, her eyes unable to make contact. For a split second, he thinks he is seeing her again, a younger version of her, coming down the stairs in a peach, chiffon dress. But it is only a college student with books pressed to her chest and the smallest, most useless bag slung across her body.

Only when the girl has gone past, and a flight down, does Moses realize that they have encountered each other on the forty-seventh step.

You can't be serious, he thinks, but calls out, "Excuse me."

The girl looks up and smiles in a manner that suggests she thinks he is about to proposition her and that such advances would be welcome.

"I am here to see the Giver," he says.

Her laughter erases all the meekness her slender body suggests.

"Oh, you are not satisfied with living so you have come for death?" she asks.

Before he comprehends that she has spoken in a language he does not know and that he has mysteriously understood her, a large group of young men come down the stairs with voices bouncing off the walls like attempts to grasp empty futures. Moses is resentful toward them. Their stupid confidence. They have no idea just how much Nairobi will grind them down when they graduate and start seeking jobs. And the fools have given the girl an escape.

"The Giver will see you," says one of the young men, startling Moses. He points toward the top of the stairwell, then grips Moses's forearm and leans in. "There is a price to pay, and you will not afford it."

Moses shakes as he climbs. Each step feels familiar, as if he has travelled the stairwell all these decades, over and over, lifetime on lifetime, and worn soft grooves into the marble. The stairwell is now his life, rising, changing, tedious, and yet circumscribing the same ground. It is never ending. He does not know why he is here.

"Nyaera," he whispers and tastes the bitterness of regret.

He pushes open the door he is certain leads to the roof of the building, all the while thinking it is best to go home, pour himself a whiskey neat, and forget all this. Instead, the door yields onto a white corridor.

Fluorescent tube bulbs glare at him. Seven doors stand at even intervals down one wall. Each door is of a different design. One a Lamu door, intricately carved and studded with brass protrusions—from a trip with his ex-fiancée when he proposed. Another door leads to the toilet at a bar Moses has patronized too many times this last year and a half. And yet another, imposing in black wrought iron, the door to his childhood home, now long sold off.

Instinctively, Moses knows he must choose but also that whichever door he chooses does not matter. Something will come to an end in this building, today. He feels this in his chest—the density of an iron ball right behind his sternum.

"Is He God?" he asked the Uber driver, last Friday.

The man laughed. "You must decide that for yourself, brother."

Moses chooses the fifth door on the corridor, the only one he does not recognize. It opens without his touching it.

An abandoned office. Dark shapes stand geometrically to each other in the darkness. Moses's body tells him that terrible things await within.

"Hello?" he calls.

In response, the room draws him in, one mighty pull, and casts him back through all he has tried to forget.

Four hundred and forty-seven days ago. His brother's university hostel room. An unmade bed and underneath it a used condom. Moses gags and remembers a rat he once cornered and bludgeoned in his uncle's home. Looking at the bloody mess then, Moses recognized himself as hideous. The feeling has never left him and is now clay in his mouth as he looks around his brother's room.

He is alone, but there is a voice.

"You know . . . young people . . . you know."

The manager of the hostel who had overlooked reporting Nyaera as missing for almost two weeks.

Moses pushes the voice aside with a wave and also Nyaera's lingering and aggressive cologne whose bottle sits on a shelf above his study desk, labelled "Adventure"—the same kind of cheap crap Moses used to purchase from stalls in downtown Nairobi when he was at the University.

"Hello?" calls Moses as he tries the door.

"Not unusual . . . Happens sometimes," comes the same voice.

Moses knows he has been drugged somehow. He is hallucinating as someone empties his pockets and perhaps slices up his body for organs. He rattles the door knob. He pulls the whole thing off its hinges and falls.

A familiar fall remembered from his childhood—the moment just before sleep swallowed him, when he tumbled into a black, star-studded sky. He was at peace then, now he is flaring.

"He needed your help, you know," says the girl seated across from him—Stella, Nyaera's would-be-girlfriend who called Moses to say Nyaera was missing. Something was off about her. Moses tries to remember what. "Hey, look," he says.

She does not hear him or does not want to. "You could have just talked to him. He messed up, but you guys always treated him like shit. Sometimes, when he was really high, he'd cry about you and your sister. Asking what he did. Why you hated him so much. He was stuck. A little boy who could never grow up."

"What do you want?" yells Moses.

Almost as though his words were a gale, the girl disintegrates into powder and with her all the light.

"Why did you come?" asks the darkness.

Moses cannot see his hands. He doesn't feel them either.

"My brother."

"You killed him."

"No. No. He's lost and someone said you could help me find him. Look, why don't we talk?"

"You cannot pay the price."

"Please. Listen. Please help me. He's just a kid."

A sharp pain bites Moses in the neck. Teeth. He screams.

"Remember."

He does. He remembers the two years he did not take any of Nyaera's calls, only sending him his monthly allowance via mobile money.

"I had to teach him a lesson... he ended up in a police cell... he wouldn't listen," he stammers as his throat rips apart.

He falls.

He is five years old and crouching. The Giver is beside him, as a wavering of the air, speaking words that are an urgent torrent in his ear. Moses's attention is elsewhere, watching himself in a group of half-naked teenage boys. But he is also the crouching five-year-old, and that child is Nyaera hiding behind a pile of rocks, neck elongated to watch Moses bellow and leap off a ledge into a pond at the bottom of a quarry. The day is hot, and the clouds are in tatters behind the outstretched wings of a hawk. Large flies buzz around a turd that Nyaera ignores determinedly. There is longing in him, making him itchy under his skin. He can taste the laughter swirling in the throats of the teenagers.

"It's the mouse," someone says, and he is suddenly being dragged from behind his shelter, being manhandled, and tripping over the rocky ground.

Then a slap and his ears ring. He is both Moses slapping Nyaera and Nyaera shrinking in pain.

"I told you not to follow me."

"You tried to drown him," whispers the Giver.

"No," says Moses who is now himself, watching his brother struggling in the pond of water, laughing with the others.

"No. That was an accident," he says. "He wouldn't go away. He wouldn't listen. He tripped."

Water rushes into Moses's open mouth, up his nostrils, and into cavities he did not know he contained.

"No, please," he screams and many eyes turn to look at him.

A room full of White colonialists in ridiculous dress at tea and biscuits. On the wall a sign "Africans Not Allowed." They growl at him, turn into dogs, and snap at his heels as he runs toward his brother. Nyaera in a waiter's uniform, with a tray in hand, and a cap on his head. He is as dull as an old photograph. His skin sepia.

Nyaera says, "He is toying with you, brother. Run. Save yourself."

"No. Wait," gasps Moses.

He stumbles into a wind-blown room. Windowless. The ceiling has caved in, electrical wires and water pipes hang loose, exposed veins, and the crows that have taken up residence in various nooks and crannies caw at him.

"They call him the Giver, but he is really the Taker," says Nyaera from far far away.

Moses runs on. His dead mother is in his mind. She will never forgive him and neither will Heaven.

Nyaera is not in the next room, which is not a room at all but the open plain, the hills, the distant acacia tree in its diagonal stance and a herd of donkeys grazing. To the North is a shimmering of water, a swamp, and beyond it, forest. Moses senses something stalking him in the tall, yellowed grass and runs. But it is the sticky kind of running one does in a dream. His limbs do not obey; he cannot get away. He is swallowed.

"I found him kissing some girl at Blue Longue. He is like that. Unable to see what is right before him," says Stella's voice. "His dick is always looking for new pussy, and I, I was stuck on him." She begins crying. "He called me all sorts of things. But I couldn't stop wanting him. That night I tried. I left. I ignored his text. He said 'Help me' and I ignored it."

Her wails grow louder.

When they met all those months ago at the student canteen, Moses thought her pathetic. But now her voice invades his body and distills him down to one fact: he is alone; there is no one to tip some of his sorrow into; he has lost them all—Nyaera, his mother, his sister Nyakio who won a scholarship to France fifteen years ago and emails him only once a year, and even the girl who he thought loved him.

"You destroy everything. Nothing is safe from your selfishness," his ex-fiancée says in the darkness.

She explained nothing. One day, she simply left and changed her phone number.

"Stop it. Why are you doing this? What do you want?" he yells.

"He is toying with you," warns Nyaera's voice.

"I think, but I can't be sure, I think this guy fought with someone that night," says the bouncer from Blue Longue.

"Yeah, yeah, I remember," pipes up a waiter. "Yeah, he was caught tonguing someone's girl and got slapped around."

"He is dead," they chorus.

"What will you do with the dead?" asks the entity called the Giver. She is the girl from the stairwell, and the young man who pointed toward the top of the stairs, and the old Uber driver from last Friday.

They stand beside Moses at a large window, Nairobi's city-center spread before them, its skyscrapers as insignificant as its smaller buildings and crow-infested empty lots and beflowered roundabouts.

"What is your price? I will pay it," begs Moses.

"Don't listen to him, brother. I gave him everything. Don't." Nyaera is suddenly standing with them in the room with a window and no doors. "He will—"

The Giver cuts him off with a lazy gesture.

"Do you know how many decades it has been?" they ask. "You talk of loss, but you do not know what loss is, what *we* have lost. We will teach you."

Nyaera is seemingly stretching. As Moses liquifies with fear, his brother's arms elongate; his neck thins; his eyes swell in his head. He is reshaped like clay. And Moses—oh he is a coward, he always was—he sees the price that he must pay for Nyaera, and he flees.

The Giver's voice pursues him. "So you will betray him again, after all."

"You have stolen my happiness," Moses's mother says in one of the rooms of his childhood. The walls are off-white, the floor of red oxide, and the sofas clothed in bright flowers.

Moses's mother whimpers in Nyakio's arms. Two-year-old Nyaera is wailing at their feet. Moses stands with the machete in his hand. He has just chased off Hesbon, Nyaera's father, their mother's second husband. She found him in a vision as she knelt in prayer, fasting before God. She saw herself climbing a hill and he descending it. This is the testimony she gave in church, as he stood by her side, her prize, years after Moses's father boarded a bus to Kampala and vanished.

"You have taken everything from me," she says. "From us."

"He was kicking you," Moses says. He does not yet know that she has withdrawn working capital from her supermarkets to finance a very big and very vague deal Hesbon swore would make them rich.

"He was going to kill you, mum," Moses insists, but she does not hear him. She lies in a mahogany coffin, like a gift among soft things. She is herself again now that she has begun to bloat and the funeral home has given her a wig for the hair she lost to her breast cancer radiotherapy.

"You killed her," accuses Nyakio.

Her face contorts and loses form. Underneath it is the Giver.

"Can you live with it all?" they ask.

They bring Moses into a room with a high window that looks out at a sliver of moon. There are two double-decker beds in the room. As the slumbering lumps in them take shape, Moses realizes he is not in a room but rather a large boarding school dormitory that extends into darkness: Nyaera's school dormitory.

"Nyaera?" he calls to the body in the lower bed on the right.

Whispers. Figures emerge from the depths of the dorm. Faceless and evil. They crowd around Nyaera's bed. A hand reaches for Nyaera's mouth. He startles awake, and Moses sees that he is screaming behind the hand over his mouth. He fights but they are too many.

"We told you we'd deal with you," says one of the figures.

They carry Nyaera into the darkness beyond Moses's range. He runs after them and finds nothing.

"No, no. He never said anything about abuse. I would have helped him," he says to the Giver.

"You would not have believed him." The Giver stands very close. "But now you can do something. You can save him."

"You will let him go?"

"I will let him live."

Moses nods and puts out his hand, but something crashes into him and he falls again. Nyaera lies sprawled on a mattress on pallet crates. Chest bare, arms crucified on the tangled sheets, eyelashes spangled with sunlight. A blunt between his fingers.

"I never told you this one," he says, eyes still shut. "Man, the things I've gotten myself into."

"Nyaera?" says Moses.

"This time, this chick comes and tells me she is pregnant and it's mine. I go into a serious panic, man. I mean, I'm twenty, first year in campus. What am I supposed to do with a baby? I can't eat. I can't sleep. It's like my body is wearing me. I try talking to her. Let's get an abortion. I'll even pay for it. With your cash, of course," he chuckles here and opens his eyes. "But the chick is throwing religion at me. Which makes no sense, because you should have seen her in bed with me. Chicks, you know. So what do I do? Leave uni to find a job?"

"Nyaera?"

He offers the blunt and shrugs when Moses shakes his head.

"What do you think I did, bro?"

"Nyaera, listen. We have to go."

"No, you listen before you go doing stupid things. I'm not some good guy. I made my decisions. I wasn't going to let that bitch destroy my life. I had asked her if she was safe and she'd said, yes, let's do it raw. So I called her, "Mwende, come we talk about this." I cooked up something. She was all impressed. She felt loved. I put the abortion pills in her coke and watched her take it sip by sip. She almost died from the bleeding. I did that to someone."

"I'm sorry."

"I know, bro. I know."

"We can fix this . . . "

"That's not how it works, Moses. Those guys at Blue Longue hurt me bad. And I was afraid of dying. So when he came and knelt over me and asked me what I would give to live, I said everything. He said he did not need everything, only that I remember him. I didn't understand what remembering would cost. It would have been better to die."

"No, Nyaera. Come with me. Let's go home."

"I gave him my life freely, bro. I cannot let him have yours too. You understand?"

And Moses falls again.

Surrounding him are curious Nairobians, gawking.

"Give him space. Let him breathe," a woman says.

Hands catch him under the armpits and raise him. He feels his phone leave his pocket. His shoe returns to his foot.

"I'm okay. I'm okay," Moses yells at the hands beating dust off his clothes.

He elicits glares, and several tongues click in disgust at his thanklessness. He pushes his way through the crowd and faces the building. Its door is a wide mouth. It dares him to enter again. He cannot. He turns and enfolds himself back into the world of the living. But he does not forget.

The DCI traced Nyaera's phone to Dandora at the tail end of the investigation. The officer who took Moses's small gift of ten thousand shillings to focus on the case declared a visit to the dumpsite a waste of time.

But many months from now, Moses will drive there anyway, just to stare at thirty acres of trash. The smell of it, the heat of the day, and the purr of a plane headed elsewhere will collide and push vomit up his throat, and he will swallow it down. He will not desecrate his brother's grave.

He will seek anything by which to mark Nyaera's presence in the four decades-worth of garbage that has become a mountain range on which lorries drive and upend their backs. He will find only the scavengers—human, canine, and avian—picking through the trash as smoke drifts off multiple fires as though souls escaping bodies. The offals of Nairobi's four million lives.

Standing there, he will consider the nature of transgression and the fact that even after forgiveness, transgression has its consequences and someone has to absorb them; they do not merely evaporate. Transgression leeches heavy metals into the soul; it funnels toxic air into the spirit; it cuts or pierces through flesh then bone.

An agitated, wheezing garbage truck will roll into the dumpsite, and a flock of marabou storks will take flight like a mysterious awakening. When the birds settle again, they will tuck their wings behind their backs and return to the business of supervising the decay, pink pouches hanging like sickness at their throats. The cycle of life beginning and ending simultaneously.

And Moses will accept that Nyaera is gone.

DID YOU KNOW?

Makena Onjerika won the 2018 Caine Prize for African Writing, was shortlisted for the 2020 Bristol Prize, and was a 2020 Best of the Net nominee. Her work has appeared or is forthcoming in *Adroit Journal, Granta, Johannesburg Review of Books, Fireside Quarterly, Wasafiri, Jalada, New Daughters of Africa,* and others. She founded and teaches at the Nairobi Writing Academy (@Naiwacademy). Find her on twitter as @onjerika.

BOSS MADAM KADUNGURE'S EXTRA-DELUXE IMPORT AND EXPORT INTERNATIONAL LTD

BY T. L. HUCHU

SEGMENTS of a rusty fence with sections torn down and posts stolen for scrap. An unkempt yard overrun by elephant grass. A fire in 2003 gutted the main workshop, killing a dozen employees, including the heiress who ran the business, Boss Madam Kadungure.

The administrative building, which remains structurally intact, is now boarded up. The Zimbabwe Republic Police's community relations office recently issued a statement to unemployed youths in Harare, urging them to stay away from this derelict structure in the Southerton industrial district.

It's rumored that unsolicited job offers arrive via WhatsApp, email, or other social media platforms—an irresistible proposition in a country with a ninety-percent unemployment rate. The youths who visit this business come back affected and afflicted, unable to speak, displaying novel mental deficiencies.

Inquiries are currently ongoing.

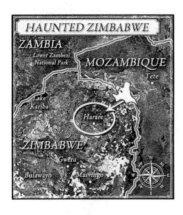

HAUNTED ZIMBABWE

ZAMBIA
Lower Zambezi
National Park
MOZAMBIQUE
Tete
Lake
Kariba
Harare
ZIMBABWE
Gweru
Bulawayo   Masvingo

T.L HUCHU is the winner of a Nommo Award for African SF/F, and has been shortlisted for the Caine Prize and the Grand Prix de L'Imaginaire. His fantasy novel *The Library of the Dead*, the first in the Edinburgh Nights series, is published by Tor.

* FILE UNDER: *Haunted Import/Export Office*

THE SOCCER FIELDS OF ABETE, IWAYA

BY DARE SEGUN FALOWO

DOWN on the mainland, under the simmer of Lagos, away from the market zones of Yaba and Sabo, you can feel it pull, calling you. You sink deeper into Onike, off in the distance glimpsing the back gates of the University of Lagos as cars and okada zoom mad around you. You're seated atop one taking you down a narrow street that reduces to a neck. The neck ends at a rusted gate behind which they play.

Entrance to a soccer field in Onike

On the fields, they are running. The boys are circumambient around the ball. Soccer burns between their feet and they kick, rumble. Plumes of almost-white sand from a distant beach, fine enough to lie in, to want to fall in, fly off their feet, and they dribble and sweat, turn dog and lion, attack defense: *Goal!*

The sunset catches them there. Its ochre gleam on their sweating backs. Their cries of victory echoing across the city and bouncing off the sky.

Our players go home to flat dinners, watery soup, bile.

In the absence of light, the boys who died in their sleep emerge from the sands to mirror the living, kicking chattering skulls between their toes.

DARE SEGUN FALOWO is a queer writer of speculative fiction rooted in Nigerian wahala. Their stories have appeared in *The Magazine of Fantasy & Science Fiction* and *The Dark Magazine*. They are currently working on a debut novel.

* FILE UNDER: *Haunted Soccer Field*

We welded ourselves into its woodwork, its
decks, its walls—we breathe through it . . .

THE BIOPHILIC-DESIGNED HAUNTING

FEATURE ENTRY 18

STRUCTURE TYPE: SAFARI LODGE
LOCATION: OKAVANGO DELTA, BOTSWANA
LAT./ LONG: 19.1193° S, 22.5304° E
BUILT: CIRCA 2021
GROUND ELEVATION: 3,189 FT. (972 M.)
WRITTEN BY: TLOTLO TSAMAASE

TRAVEL GUIDE NOTES

THE CONCEPT OF sustainable ecotourism for safari lodges is relatively modern. There was some early groundwork in the 1980s, but the great conflux of luxury and environmental ethics becoming these community-conscious tourist camps runs mostly from the last fifteen years. Which means a lot of the development is still new, encouraging innovative yet untested ideas, contemporary and experimental designs, a willingness to push boundaries while perhaps not yet fully understanding consequences... For what "else" is being included in the rushed construction? What might be overlooked? What else was already part of the land now being hurriedly developed to cater to rich tourists from the world over who want to experience exotic locale guilt-free, as long as their Rock Shandies are still ice cold?

Motswana author Tlotlo Tsamaase has some ideas, and they are not pleasant...

Tlotlo is killing it lately (in a good way!) with a litany of top stories releasing through prominent markets such as *The Dark*, *Apex*, and *Strange Horizons*. Consider this next inclusion a "Plus One" to her literary canon, and to her guest list, as she takes us on her own tour of the latest sustainable safari lodge, in "The Biophilic-Designed Haunting."

—**Charlatan Bardot**

WE NEST IN THE RAFTERS, THE NOOK OF DARKNESS when they come. We didn't arrive by foot, boat, or flight, but rather we boarded the sternum of a sixteen-year-old boy (a son of one of the mokoro gondoliers) who traversed us from Gabs city to a remote island in the Okavango Delta.

The people who've come: an architect of some sort, a journalist of some sort. The others, who have remodeled our abode, a safari lodge with a cuisine of culture, as most of its visitors come from various backgrounds and cultures to treat our palates: travelers, backpackers, corporate team-building trips, honeymooners, those ones are surely tastier. Personality at times can make them spicy, or sweet, or with no taste at all. The lodge sits comfortably in a private concession like a wood-ribbed animal preparing for flight; it has a biophilic and sustainable design that is culturally intuitive. The building is permeable to the nature surrounding it, feeling like one is the animal cocooned into the land. We've sprawled ourselves over 10,000 hectares of land as they built the structure, we welded ourselves into its woodwork, its decks, its walls—we breathe through it. It's our perennial holiday. We spend our days drifting through the lagoons, the channels, the reeds, galloping on antelopes, gliding through the air on the backbone of herons. Lagoons, lily-filled. Crushed scent of foliage smeared into the air. It's peaceful here even for ghost standards.

I was murdered, killed at an orphanage with a primary school built in a postcolonial style in a village near the city. I was killed by a young female teacher. Put aside in the earth and forgotten. Missing and forgotten. I rose through the earth, like a sapling, and avenged my death over a blood-soaked year. Others came, like me, joined me, and it was the new intake of teachers who suffered to the point that no one was desperate enough to be employed by the school, such that it closed down, remained barren, never reopened, to now sit as a heritage site because of the history in its architecture.

Seeing then that our food source was gone, that people were afraid to even step foot into the site, we had to move. So we rode that sixteen-year-old boy as legion, northwest, for eight hours. Not a comfortable trip, but even then we collected more. Other spirits, killed, wronged, or merely vengeful, joined us. We merged, grew, an aggregate of retribution, hunger, lust . . .

If I tell you the name of our home now, I doubt you'd come visit, which would leave us famished. Of course, if you're one of those paranormal investigators that is enticed by our spirit-energy, it matters more that you know our location, except paranormal investigators are not part of our diet.

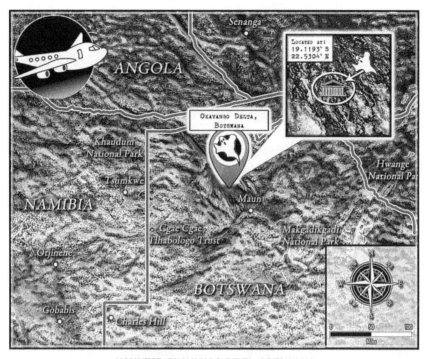

HAUNTED OKAVANGO DELTA, BOTSWANA

In this new place, we heard them rumbling through the gravel in their 4x4 vehicles, spitting dust and gravel.

The architect, Pearl Mosiame, dons a chandelier of iridescent earrings, and each time she moves her head, smiling, the earrings sing against each other. "Welcome, welcome. Come, come." She has a tasty, crunchy personality.

"Thanks for having us," the journalist, Akanyang Kgotso, says, shaking her hand by the entrance to the reception desk. He's here to write a review, we later discover. He has a devilish smile, dons chino pants and a tailored white shirt speckled with sweat. Oh, I'd love to shear his sex with the blade of my tongue.

Of course, those names are pseudonyms. Even such details could identify our house of terror. I know what you're thinking—we'll make it into the newspapers, sensationalized and all. But news always die, and the fascinating thing about people is they flock to the mecca of crime scenes regardless, hoping to see something and revel in the fame of the site. Of course, the locals may not want to later talk about it, bad for business, you know. But I'm certain we'd still have a tourist who knew nothing of what happened.

258   TLOTLO TSAMAASE

That is, if we choose to stay here afterward.

Akanyang's hand rests on the banister made from the branch of a tree, and he stares up at the towering trees, the dewy air that hangs like a fabric of spiderwebs. To the eastern side of the site, a field of solar panels bask in the sun, shimmering. The rest of the surrounds are trees and lagoons. "This is all just magnificent," he says.

Now they've come to ogle at us, with their cameras. We are one body in here. The structure and us. We've been ruffled far too many times during the construction phases (honestly, those construction workers *had* to die), though it all was cited as site accidents. Some fell from obscene heights. Some were trampled by tractors. Death, all the same; it was fun. We love it here, far more than we did life. And sure we must feed on them. Pearl, architect and concessionaire extraordinaire, a rare find in this landscape dominated by foreign-owned safaris, has a smattering of lodges. She laughs gleefully at his comment.

Pearl, a peacock of a thing dressed in flair and boots, steps into the vestibule of the reception area, explaining to Akanyang the feat it took to build without disturbing the environment. She is articulate with her hands, dancing them through the air so that we can almost taste them.

"This way," she says, gesturing to the direction of the accommodation. They step out and down onto a decked walkway woven from the forest-ground, in bark with tusk-like columns; it is glass-roofed and flanked with foliage as if one's walking on the extended branches of trees.

We pass the gift shop filled with sculptures, artifacts, hand-woven bags and paintings and benches made from fallen trees. Hanging onto his shoulders, we come upon one of the twenty-two freestanding suites that are nestlike, conceptualized after the numerous nests of birds found here. The stilts are uprooted from the ground like the legs of a wattled crane.

The suite we step into, roughly 90-square-meters, is where we'll be spending a warm-welcoming night with the journalist. This will be our most difficult night: we must restrain ourselves, otherwise this will ruin what we may receive from his successful review. For one, it could turn away interested tourists. We don't care about the money, we just want a variety of people, spiced with differing flavors of histories, genders, nationalities, experiences, languages—you just can't tell how that versatility alone influences the taste. We are artisans, we are chefs, and we make do with what ingredients of humans we have. But we're seriously bored of consuming the same old tourists infused with cliché and dull thoughts, bitter as blackstrap molasses, though just as nutritious. You have no idea how some shocking and inventive thoughts can offer a tangy flavor, just a pinch of that is an art of seasoning.

"This is where you'll be staying," Pearl tells him.

The room is decked in soft-pale wood, bleached and ready for the volcanic blush of blood; door knobs, sheer black, curving walls. Pops of teal in the scatter cushions. Cultural motifs clad the façade.

In the lounge sits complementary coffee steaming into the air, driving our adrenaline high. The journalist doesn't waste time to drown his system in espresso. At the ready, two assistants procure a shiny tray from a chafing dish sitting on the kitchen island. They move the food onto a new tray onto the set dining table. It dazzles with sliced madombi, seswaa, and grilled vegetables.

"This all looks very tasty," he says.

The architect leans in with an air of secrecy. "Trust me, you haven't seen anything yet. This was just a quick meal the chef prepared before our game drive tonight."

We are gossamer-thin on the mosquito net as she shows him around. "Our premium suite is decorated in furniture and sculptures and paintings from local artisans. It's fitted with one master bedroom, an open kitchen plan with a dining room, a fireplace—" then noting how tired the journalist looks, steps quickly into—"the secluded outdoor shower adjacent to the enclosed ensuite luxury bathroom. Oh right, our power's sustained by the PV systems, which reduces our carbon footprint, so you have your energy-efficient air conditioners," she adds, pointing in the eastern direction of the shimmering panels glinting. She's really laying it on the journalist for a couple of rating stars. She leans forward into the outdoor shower, swipes the sleek handle, runs her fingers through the warm water, and we slip and swirl around her ringed fingers, swarming into her pores. "Thermodynamic geysers provide your hot water." We follow her out into the lounge as the suite's spatial design gracefully curves around the existing trees. At this, she mentions, "We worked closely with an arborist to ensure preservation of the site's ecosystem of flora and fauna."

"This is all rather lovely, but let's save it for the following days' interview and tour guides."

"Of course," she says, approaching the door. "The inauguration of the lodge is slated two weeks from now. Several suites have already been booked."

We'll feast on them with the exception of one, who we'll instead board to whichever country he or she came from—in the same way we arrived here, by way of that sixteen-year-old boy—hopefully sunny and off the continent for a little bit of experimenting; after all, we can always come back home.

"How wonderful," Akanyang says, eager to have some alone time.

"We'll be keeping to the itinerary," she continues. "This evening, we'll be taking you on a game drive. It's nice out here when the city lights aren't obscuring everything. Our stars are our city lights."

"I do need a detox from the city life," he says, laughing.

"Our assistants are here at your beck and call. And we look forward to your review of our resort." She claps her hands. "Now I'll leave you to get settled." Taps her watch. "See you in two hours."

He nods, smiles. She leaves.

Silence enfolds. Peace at last since the humdrum of the last few days at work, finalizing written pieces and last-minute interviews. We follow him to stand on the verandah that overlooks a lagoon, the sunset is a tinge of calmness. He leans against the balustrade, watching a lechwe within the shoulders of the water reeds. Jackalberry trees shield us. He exhales, jetlagged. His breaths fume the air with an undeniable punch of anxiety and confidence, and I have to hold the others back from tearing him apart. The air continues to fill with his thoughts, his two-days-ago late-night sojourn at his girlfriend's Cape Town apartment that his blood is still saturated with the sex, his six-days-ago alcohol binge—the contents of his life deliciously packaged in him. Just one sip of him—but, no we must not touch. Not a hair. Not a bone. His feature article is very important. It will attract tasty affluent visitors. For, two weeks from now, the inauguration of this beloved safari lodge will be serenaded by an opus of their screams we'll binge-drink until early morning.

Some of us come from far. We never reached the sea, our rivers settled here in this private concession, in the soil, in the delta. The trees breathed some of us in. You can say we are strategically placed throughout the site for those who will flee, screaming and cursing. People are unwittingly paying obscene amounts of money for a horror-fueled night. We aim to please.

Welcome, to our safari lodge, we look forward to your stay . . .

Did You Know?

TLOTLO TSAMAASE is a Motswana writer of fiction, poetry, and architectural articles. Her work has appeared in *Clarkesworld*, *The Dark*, *Terraform*, *Apex Magazine*, *Strange Horizons*, and other publications. Her poem "I Will Be Your Grave" was a 2017 Rhysling Award nominee. Her short story, "Virtual Snapshots" was longlisted for the 2017 Nommo Awards. Her other work includes a novella, *The Silence of the Wilting Skin*. You can find her on twitter at @tlotlotsamaase and at tlotlotsamaase.com.

HOUSE OF MOUTHS

BY OSAHON IZE-IYAMU

UNDERNEATH Precious Learning Boarding School, there are teeth.

The teeth spring up at midnights in July, hungry and razor sharp, chattering underneath the soil. The teeth are clear-water white, as distracting as a car's headlight cutting through the darkness of an empty street. The teeth are said to be bones of the former students who lived in the

Make new friends at Precious Learning

school—students who mysteriously disappeared. Students who never graduated. The teeth whisper words to those who pass by the abandoned buildings . . . if you listen close, you might hear them.

The teeth might say "we are hungry, come and feed us" or the teeth might say "you're next."

But the teeth of Precious Learning School really are just lonely, and what they want most is a new friend.

OSAHON IZE-IYAMU is a Nigerian writer of speculative fiction. He has been published in magazines such as *Clarkesworld* and *Strange Horizons* and you can find him online @osahon4545.

* FILE UNDER: *Haunted Boarding School*

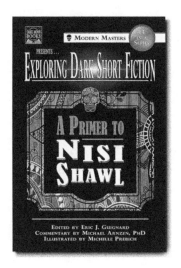

FASTEN YOUR

SAFETY BELTS...

NEXT STOP:

UNITED STATES

AND CANADA

HAUNTED UNITED STATES AND CANADA

GARNET (MONTANA), USA

HUNTSVILLE (ONTARIO)

OTTAWA (ONTARIO), CA

CROW ISLAND (NOVA SCOTIA),

PORTLAND (ORE

GOVERNMENT CAMP (OREGON), USA

JOHNSON CITY (NEW YORK), USA

WILLIAMSBURG (VIRGINIA), USA

HOLLYWOOD (CALIFORNIA), USA

GLADEWATER (TEXAS), USA

NEW ORLEANS (LOUISIANA), USA

0 100 200 300 400 500
Miles

UNITED STATES AND CANADA

I knew something was wrong a quarter
mile up the block before I got there . . .

THE LAST BOOTH

FEATURE ENTRY 19

STRUCTURE TYPE: DINER
LOCATION: JOHNSON CITY (NEW YORK), USA
LAT./ LONG: 42.1049° N, 75.9549° W
BUILT: CIRCA 1941
GROUND ELEVATION: 886 FT. (270 M.)
WRITTEN BY: JEFFREY FORD

TRAVEL GUIDE NOTES

T HERE ARE CERTAIN authors I read and think of their writing: *This person can do no wrong.* Jeffrey Ford is one of them.

My co-editor Eric J. Guignard wrote a Primer book on Jeff (*Exploring Dark Short Fiction #4: A Primer to Jeffrey Ford*), and if I may lift a passage from that, I'll quote: "Jeffrey Ford's stories manifest looming peril, heartache, excitement, and intrigue in beautifully wrought structures of stories within stories . . . his writing works on multiple levels—you can 'feel' it and feel *in it.*"

You might say that commentary was written presciently for this next selection.

If ghosts seem more likely to appear at the darkest hours of the night, perhaps it is indication of something greater at play, an allegory for their emergence instead during the darkest times of one's *life.*

For when circumstance and loss collide, sometimes calamitous effects unfold. Sometimes you're the subject of the effects, and sometimes merely the bystander. Sometimes life just inexplicably drives you to "The Last Booth."

—**Charlatan Bardot**

B ACK IN THE DAY, BEFORE I EVER PUBLISHED A STORY,
I'd stay up all night writing. Lynn would be off in the bedroom,
under the comforter, sawing wood, and I'd be at the kitchen table in
a straight-backed chair, leaning over a legal pad, pen in hand. Outside the
apartment windows the leaves of the oaks that surrounded the old house
scraped against the second story at the insistence of an early autumn wind.
It was like white noise for me. In that glowing bubble cast by the overhead
fluorescent ring, pushing back the dark, I'd mutter to myself in the voices of
the characters, rub my hands together, scheming, laugh out loud.

No matter how halcyon my recollection of those early days and nights,
I still do vividly remember times when I'd lose the thread. What usually
came so easily, spilling out across the pages, reels of bad sentences and a
steady parade of crazy plots fucked to their rotten cores, would occasionally
dry up completely. I mean nothing would come, no words. So, I'd put on my
sneakers, my old camel hair overcoat that had been bequeathed to me by a
dead uncle, and I'd wander the night, looking for the loose end of the thread.

I'd sit outside the locked-up carousel at the park and have a smoke or
two, walk the dismal streets of that long dead factory town unaware of its
own demise, stop in at the Oasis just before closing and have a beer with old
Mr. Kesmai, the owner. Sometimes I'd pass through the cemetery on Floral
Ave. and rest on a bench amidst a thicket of concrete trees, a strange
memorial to someone named Cake who'd died in '42. None of the things
I'd passed or places I'd visit were in my thoughts. Instead, it was just the
chaos of pitiful newborn stories dragging themselves toward consciousness.
I believe you could really have called it a hypnotic state and it left me hyper-
unaware. Far better than sullying my spot at the nighttime kitchen table
with cast-off frustration and the effluvium of failure, I spread the bad vibe
all over town, diminishing its potency.

By the end of the night, I'd usually wind up at Buddy's All Night Diner.
It was down by the railroad tracks, between two monolithic red brick shoe
factories that had been abandoned and sat empty since 1938. The place was
in the style of a chrome train car with yellow trim. There was a neon sign in
the window that flashed electric blue and read, *Pies Pies Pies*, and a hand-
painted one in the Egyptian style over the entrance that read, BUDDY'S
ALL NIGHT DINER in faded red letters. The yellow trim was peeling, the
chrome was tarnished, but the blue pie sign shone like a sacred presence in
that sketchier end of town.

Buddy's had three basic shifts of customers. From 6 p.m. to about 9
p.m., you had the sad sackers, those forced to eat by themselves for lack of

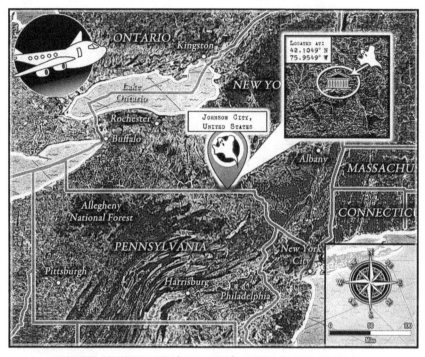

HAUNTED JOHNSON CITY (NEW YORK), UNITED STATES OF AMERICA

friends and family, afflicted by age or loneliness. Things picked up after the movie house in town let out around 10. Couples, partiers, weird dates, could wind up at Buddy's. This period was the most fun and the most volatile. A lot of the patrons had a bag on board, and there was often slurring and high-pitched laughter. A lot of shouting. Roughhousing might break out, but Buddy always put the kibosh on it, reaching for the sawed-off shotgun everyone knew was hidden beneath the counter. The gun never made an appearance except for once when a biker gang stopped at the diner late on a Sunday night. They harassed a customer just minding his business at the counter, and that gun came out and Buddy said, "I'll kill every fuckin' one of you." There was stillness. There was silence, and then she asked, "Who's having what?" All Buddy really wanted to do was make breakfast and hamburgers for burn-outs all night long.

By dawn, she'd have the place cleaned up, stocked for the next night, blinds pulled down against the impending day, and locked with a big chain. It was as if she was a vampire and had to get home to a coffin before the sun came up. She was a thin, wrinkled sixty-plus-year-old with a dirty blonde fright wig of hair, bag-laden, big gray eyes, and a heart tattoo on her miniscule but diamond-hard bicep. On the banner that wrapped around the inked organ, in vein blue, were the words "I love Moachie." One night I asked her who Moachie was, and she told me it was her kid, who ran away when he was seventeen, and she hadn't seen him since. "It was a long time ago," she said, and stood there looking like she'd been squeezed through the end of a whiskey bottle.

In addition to the two shifts of customers I've mentioned, there was a third, and that was my shift—after the lonely hearts, after the revelers, later in the night, between the Jesus hour and sunrise. That shift was a limited clientele—cops, junkies, and wayward writers. The stillness was only broken by the bacon sizzling on the grill, the occasional blink of the fluorescent lights. Usually there'd be maybe one other person on board by the time I landed there. Sometimes it would just be Buddy and me, and we'd smoke and bullshit. I'd told her once I was a writer, and she always asked what I was working on. I had to remind her that if she saw me, it was only because I wasn't working on anything.

Then, if there was no one else to cook for or serve, she'd tell me a story about something to do with the diner—the customer who always came in and took his fake leg off and put it on the counter next to him before eating his mushroom and barley soup, or the guy with the enormous hair wave. "He must use six fuckin' cans of spray to keep that thing aloft," she'd said. I told her maybe she should be the writer and I should cook for late-nighters. She patted my hand and laughed, saying, "Give it time. It's all there. You just have to realize it."

One night after a pretty good couple of months' run of non-stop writing, I hit the proverbial wall and instead of trying to push it, I surrendered, donned the camel hair overcoat and hit the dusty trail. Of course, I wound up at Buddy's around 3:15 a.m. and took my usual spot at the end of the counter. She came over and poured me a cup of coffee. I asked for a corn muffin buttered and grilled. She put the muffin on and then came back to stand in front of me. Leaning over, she whispered, in a voice that smelled like vodka, "Don't look right now, but do you see that guy sitting down there in the last booth?" She backed slowly away from me and as she did, I cautiously turned my head to look.

There he was, leaning over his meal, long greasy hair covering his face, his hand trembling as it lifted the coffee cup. I turned back to Buddy and shrugged. "Looks like an upstanding citizen."

Still sticking to a whisper, she said, "He's been in every night for the past half a week. Comes in at 3 a.m. Orders S.O.S. and coffee in a voice duller than a hammer pounding frozen dirt. The only thing is, he never looks at me when he orders. His complexion is a pale yellow, like bad chicken, and he's skin and bone. His clothes are torn, and his coat has no buttons."

"Are you scared of him?"

"Not the way you're thinking," she said. "You know, I've seen all kinds come through the diner. Plus, I got the shotgun. It has nothing to do with that. The thing that scares me is that I never see him leave. He never pays, he just seems to disappear around 4:00. I want you to watch him till he leaves. I need to start cleaning. When he gets up to go, call me."

She served my muffin and poured me another coffee before going back behind the grill. Every few seconds, I'd nonchalantly turn my head slightly to make sure he was still there. And he was. I sat over my coffee, had a smoke, and checked up on the fledgling story ideas in my head. Things were a dizzying jumble there. The sight of it put me in a trance for a minute until my addiction snapped me out of it and told me to take a puff. As I inhaled, I remembered the guy in the last booth. I looked and caught sight of him standing, wearily adjusting his green jacket. Buddy had been right about the state of his get-up. Lots of shreds and holes in shirt and pants, and the jacket had been repaired with duct tape. I called out for Buddy, and then stood to block the stranger's way. I took a position in the middle of the aisle, and said, "Don't forget your bill."

He looked up and his pale, mournful nature startled me. Looking through my head, he staggered forward. Behind me, I heard the safety come off the shotgun. I braced in case he lunged. Fear was hiding in the beat of my heart. And then he just disappeared. For a mere instant I saw him disintegrate into something like dandelion fuzz. An instant more and there was no trace of him.

"What the fuck?" I said.

"I saw him do that the other night," said Buddy. "I just wanted to make sure someone else saw it, so I could be sure." She asked me to describe what the guy looked like. I'd gotten a good look at his face and told her, "My guess is he's early forties, a nasty scar above the left eye, five o'clock shadow, needs a haircut and a bath, maybe jaundiced, maybe mental health issues, drugs, has a tendency to disappear."

"Fuck," she said. "The diner's haunted. Now what? It's not like bugs where I can just call the exterminator."

"How often do you do that?"

"You'd be surprised," she said and I went no further with it because right then, Officer Hernandez stepped in and set the bell to ringing over the door. All the denizens of the dark knew Hernandez, a short guy with bushy eyebrows and a disarming smile that could stop a homicidal maniac in his tracks and actually once had, as far as the story goes. Six nights a week, he patrolled down around the tracks and the decrepit remains of the old warehouses. Once I asked him what the cops were afraid might happen back in the old ruins. "Good question," he said and smiled. "I just follow the orders from the high command." As far as cops went, not that I knew many, Officer Hernandez (or Carlos, as Buddy called him), seemed about as chill as you could be in a job where you had to carry a gun. He'd spend a good hour at Buddy's every night over a stack of pancakes and sausages. He smoked the cheapest cigars with fruit flavored tips and always eventually got around to telling about the mystery books he read in the patrol car on slow nights.

"That guy was in again tonight," Buddy told him as he took a seat at the counter. He took off his hat and set it in the empty chair next to him and put his portable radio on the counter.

"Did you tell him you were calling the police?"

Buddy laughed as she brought him coffee. "He blinked out before I could get a word in." She set the cup down and snapped her fingers. "Like that."

"You want me to come by earlier tomorrow? What time?" he asked.

"Three," said Buddy. "I've got a plan. I talked to Mrs. McCarthy. She stops in for dinner every other night. She said to come over to the church tomorrow and get some holy water. She'd have the father bless me a gallon. Then I should put it in a plant mister and spray the whole area of the booth. When the creep comes in, I'm supposed to spray him too. She said that's how she got rid of her late husband, who'd materialize for a piece every night at two. She said his dick was like an icicle."

"You know," he said, as he put away pancakes like a guy three times his size, "my grandmother practiced some of the rituals of Santeria. I know for protection against bad spirits she used black salt. I have a couple packets left from when she lived with us. I'll bring them tomorrow night."

Each of us speculated as to what this apparition could mean. I asked Buddy if she knew if there'd ever been any deaths on the premises.

"Just the corned beef hash," she said.

Hernandez said that if you had a ghost it either meant the place was haunted or someone in the place was haunted. That seemed to make sense, but neither me nor Buddy took the idea any further. A few minutes later, I said my goodbyes, split, and headed home across town. It was kind of stupid to take the old Civil War tunnel that cut under the highway, a long black throat of a structure that was dark as the pit and sometimes littered with insensate junkies, but I was tired and needed sleep. The whole journey I thought about that spirit I'd seen, coming up the aisle at me. By the time I made it home and got into bed, I was shivering. Without waking, Lynn put her arm around me and said, "You're freezing."

Even if I had something to write, I wouldn't have stayed home the next night. I got to the diner at 2:30 a.m. Buddy was just sending off an old couple, both with canes. They paid at the register and, after the exchange, she hugged them both and saw them to the door, which she opened for them. I was in my seat already. She got me coffee and I ordered two eggs over hard with buttered rye toast. As she cooked, she called over the grill, "You here for the exorcism?"

I nodded. "Do you have the gallon of holy water?"

"I could only get a quart. Supposedly the priest wasn't capable of blessing more than that."

"That sounds screwy," I said. "What's the difference between blessing a quart and blessing a gallon?"

"Beats me," said Buddy and flipped my eggs.

At ten to three, Officer Hernandez came in. He sat at the counter two seats from me. He put his hat on the stool between us and his portable on the counter. Then he reached into his uniform pocket and pulled out what looked like two large tea bags and threw them on the counter. "I'm not sure this is really black salt," he said. "It's black and my grandmother left it behind when she passed. I know she mentioned black salt, but this stuff looks more like a powder."

"What does it do?" I asked him.

He shook his head and said, "I'm not really sure, but it has something to do with protection. From your description of this poor guy, what good is a gun gonna do if he gets stupid? This is just the kind of weird event that required all our ancestors to have to cultivate magic. They needed protection from the nature of reality."

"What's that mean?" I asked.

"The world dishes out some weird shit, whether you choose to believe in it or not."

Buddy came out from behind the grill at precisely three o'clock. Bingo, the door opened, the bell rang, and in stepped the spirit, looking worse than ever. We three froze as the stinking thing moved past us, reeking like a man-sized turd and staggered down the aisle toward the last booth. Hernandez was the first to break the paralysis by taking his gun slowly out of his holster and laying it on the counter. He put his hat on and stowed the black salt packets in his jacket pocket. Buddy then came to and retrieved her plant mister full of holy water and a menu for the customer. I couldn't believe she was going to him. He sat there, hunched over, part infernal landscape, part eternal loser.

As she moved down the aisle, Hernandez leaned his arm on the counter and put his hand on his gun. We heard Buddy say, "Havin' the usual, hun? Cream chipped beef? Home fries? What kind of toast do you want?" The strange figure merely grunted and bobbed forward in answer to her questions. It didn't make any sense that she took his order before spraying him, but that's what she did. Then she lifted the mister and commenced pumping. As the soft holy rain fell on her customer, she said in her convivial waitress voice, "The Lord compels you. Be gone to Hell." The figure twitched, and she sprayed some more. The twitches quickly developed into tremors. Hernandez lifted his gun off the counter. Buddy kept spraying and then I heard a low growling coming from the figure, who reared back on the bench. We saw his face full-on, a skull covered in a thin scrim of pale-yellow flesh. His teeth were more pronounced than the last I'd viewed him—big rotten chompers that snapped amid the growling. Any liquid still existing in his desiccated body leaked from scabbed lips. Buddy backed against the wall as whatever the fuck it was rose out of the booth, howling like a dog in pain. Still, she kept spraying, which didn't seem like the best idea to me.

It stood to its full height, and turned like it was going to pounce on her. Hernandez left the gun but reached into his pocket for the packets of black salt. As he ran down the aisle, he ripped the tops off the two of them at once, and when he reached the last booth, he swept out his arm and sent the contents of black powder spraying all over the scene like he was casting seed in spring. The instant the salt made contact, the spirit cried out in worse agony, and tiny fires sparked in its hair, across its face and the length of its neck. I picked up the gun, never having shot one before. The cop grabbed Buddy by the arm and pulled her back up the aisle with him. She seemed in shock, and he was having a hard time dragging her away. The entire figure caught fire and it reached out toward her. In a voice that was like a distant cry in a dream, came the desperate screech, "Mama, Mama . . . " The flames were to the ceiling and it still tottered toward us, now reduced to infernal weeping. Hernandez deposited Buddy on the first counter stool and took the gun out of my hand. It was only a few feet away when he turned and fired two shots. Before the second bullet reached its target, the figure had vanished.

I tried to apologize for having been so useless but my words came out stuttered and out of order. Buddy put her finger to her lips and shushed me. Hernandez sat at the counter with one hand to his forehead and the gun in the other pointing at the floor. "Are you okay, Carlos?" Buddy asked him. He nodded and said he was just thinking about how he was going to write up the discharge of his service weapon. "I'm gonna have to make something up," he said. "Who's gonna believe this? I don't even believe it."

"My hat off to your grandmother," I told him. "That black salt is something."

Buddy went behind the grill and brought out a fresh bottle of vodka and three glasses. She poured and we each threw one back. She poured again, a fuller glass, and we sipped and stared back down at the last booth, the floor next to it still steaming, and at the twin bullet holes in the mirrored wall behind it. Somewhere in the middle of that tall drink, Buddy came out with, "Could it have been my son? Could it have been Moachie? Carlos, did you hear it say, 'Mama'? It called to me."

"I'm not sure," said Hernandez. "I'm not sure it said anything. Might have just been screaming."

Buddy looked at me. I know Hernandez heard that word, just like I did, but I took his lead and said I didn't catch anything I could swear to. She shook her head and bummed a cig off me. Hernandez pulled out a fruit tip crap cigar and we smoked in silence. That quiet brought with it a bad feeling. In my bones, I felt it was time to split the scene. Buddy broke the silence. "He left when he was seventeen. We had nothing. My husband died and I was a mess, strung out on the flea powder. When I got myself together, I went to look for him but he'd vanished like he never existed. When he was a kid, he loved to go to the diner. So I bought this place, hoping against the impossible, that he might some time, just by chance, tumble in out of the dark."

Hernandez had to get back on his shift. Against my better judgement I asked Buddy if she needed me to help her close up. She shook her head, took another cigarette off me, and shooed me out the door. I looked back over my shoulder once as I walked across the parking lot to the sidewalk and caught the outside lights of the diner go out. I couldn't take the Civil War tunnel home and had to walk way out of my way to get past the highway. There was no chance I was going underground after that evil madness. Buddy seemed dazed by the thought it might be her son's ghost. I told myself, *There's a good chance it wasn't. How many millions of lost spirits do you think are crying "Mama" throughout eternity?* After the first mile and a half, my mind turned to stories, and I figured I had enough whim-wham stored up after the events of the night to write for six months. I obviously couldn't tell this story as it happened. Who'd believe it?

Six months passed before I ran dry again. The incident at Buddy's was much on my mind and had infected my dreams for a few months. But by the time I had to wander the night again in search of my words, the memory of it had faded. Don't get me wrong, if I really concentrated on it, the incident still scared the crap out of me. But, you know, life rolled on as it does, and I needed to ramble. Out I went to all the old haunts, and at 2:45 a.m. I wound up at Buddy's. I knew something was wrong a quarter mile up the block before I got there. I couldn't spot the blue neon *Pies* sign. As I stepped onto the parking lot of the place, it was clear the lights were out, there were no cars, the chain and lock were on the door. I went up the steps and peered in through the glass. Everything was dark except there was a tiny night light on somewhere behind the grill. As I walked away, I distinctly smelled the scent of frying bacon. It was present everywhere.

Two nights later, I was sitting amidst the concrete thicket of Cake's memorial in Floral Avenue Cemetery, smoking a joint. It was an early spring night and the wind was raucous, branches creaking and tapping together, the new leaves rustling. I was high and recollecting being in the cemetery one night a year earlier. There was a young woman then passing among the gravestones. She startled me and I jumped off the bench a foot or two when she wandered in amid Cake's memorial. She apologized for scaring me. Under her arm, she was carrying a big old portable tape recorder. She was short and blonde and pretty with pig tails but probably crazy in a kind of slow simmering manner. I could see it in her eyes by starlight. She told me she went around to the graves at night and set up her recorder and recorded voices of the dead.

My response? "Get the fuck out of here with that." We both laughed. But she told me she'd play one for me and I'd be convinced. So she cued something up on her recorder, brought it over and put it to my ear. "Listen carefully," she said and hit a button. I heard leaves blowing above the sound of the leaves blowing at that moment around us. Out of the recorded night I heard a very faint male voice say, "Claire, don't forget to feed the cat." It definitely sounded like the voice had been recorded elsewhere and then inserted in that spot amid the wind in the trees.

There was more to the memory, but now someone was actually moving through the dark. I hit the joint and held it so as not to give my position away. It didn't matter, a flashlight beam came on and found me. "I've been looking for you," said a voice.

"Who is it?" I said.

"It's Officer Hernandez," he said.

"Am I in trouble?"

"No, I've been trying to find you for months. Have you been to the diner?"

"Yeah, a few nights ago. It was closed."

"Right," he said.

"Still smelled like bacon."

"I know," he said. "The night of the exorcism, after we'd left, Buddy stayed till dawn. After seeing the sun one last time, as she put it in her suicide note written on her waitress order pad, she then apparently blew her brains out all over the grill with the sawed-off shotgun."

"What?"

The cop nodded. She wrote that she knew the entity was the spirit of her son come back to her, and instead of helping him find peace, she'd sent him back to the torments of Hell. She took full responsibility for whatever her boy had done in his life and went to join him, stating that she hoped suicide would send her to perdition."

"Jeez," I said. "She seemed like such a nice lady."

"She was," said Hernandez. "But guilt, you know, not even the black salt can protect you from it."

"I suppose."

"Well, there's more. A few months later, I was showing a citizen one of our books of likely suspects to see if they could identify a perpetrator. As I flipped the pages, I caught sight of the face of that fucking ghoul that showed up at the diner. Granted it was worse for wear when we encountered it, and there was all the chaotic bullshit of the evening, but I know it was this guy. There was no mistaking him. So, I looked up that suspect's name and had the file pulled on him. Arnie Fryse. The guy lived with his mother in the old Windemere Hotel, which was right across the street and a few yards down from the diner. I'm sure he'd eaten at Buddy's at some point. Anyway, he drowned his mother in the bathtub. She was in her eighties and he was forty-something. She took care of him because he had mental problems—hearing voices, seeing things, the whole nine yards. In the file there was a newspaper article about his story, and I remember the first line of it was, "Arnie was always worse the days it rained." A couple of cops found him down by the lake, dead. He dosed himself with all his pills at once. By the time they found the mother in the tub, she came apart like pulled pork."

"The ending is rarely what you think it's gonna be," I said.

Officer Hernandez, nodded, got up and headed out of the memorial. Before he disappeared into the shadows, he called back, "For a new place, try Mickey's Blue Haven. Not the same relentless dirty charm as Buddy's but decent coffee, a nice cream chipped beef, and no ghosts."

Any time after that, whenever I was over in the neighborhood at night and I'd pass Buddy's abandoned rig, I still smelled the scent of frying bacon. As far as I know, it's still there, serving infernal burn-outs till the sun comes up.

DID YOU KNOW?

JEFFREY FORD is the author of the novels *The Physiognomy*, *Memoranda*, *The Beyond*, *The Portrait of Mrs. Charbuque*, *The Girl in the Glass*, *The Cosmology of the Wider World*, *The Shadow Year*, *The Twilight Pariah*, *Ahab's Return*, and *Out of Body*. His short story collections are *The Fantasy Writer's Assistant*, *The Empire of Ice Cream*, *The Drowned Life*, *Crackpot Palace*, *A Natural History of Hell*, and *The Best of Jeffrey Ford*. Ford's fiction has appeared in numerous magazines and anthologies and been widely translated. It has garnered World Fantasy, Edgar Allan Poe, Shirley Jackson, Nebula, and other awards. His collection *Big Dark Hole* will be out from Small Beer Press in July, 2021.

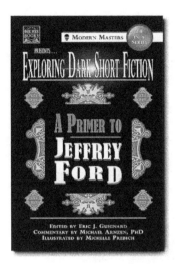

THE NORGE THEATER

BY ELIZABETH MASSIE

**WILLIAMSBURG, VIRGINIA:
NOVEMBER 12, 1947**

The Norge Theatre in Williamsburg

GEORGE Norge bought and converted a dilapidated Colonial-era barn into a movie theater. His last $157 went to purchasing a 16mm camera, and he directed, starred in, and filmed his very own comedy. After all, the war was over; Americans needed to laugh!

He gave out one hundred free tickets for opening night.

"When over, please review me in the *Gazette*!" he said as movie-goers took their seats. The film started. It ran. It ended. No one had even smiled.

Infuriated, George shot all one hundred, shrieking, "Laugh, damn you!" and then slashed their mouths into bloody, gaping grins.

He was arrested and executed the following year. To this day, the ghosts of the eternally-grinning movie-goers are occasionally seen and heard in the theater late at night. And at times their screams sound a bit like laughter.

ELIZABETH MASSIE is a two-time Bram Stoker Award-winning author of numerous horror novels and short stories. The novels include *Sineater*, *Desper Hollow*, *Hell Gate*, *Wire Mesh Mothers*, and the middle grade series, *Ameri-Scares*, which was optioned by Warner Horizon for television.

* FILE UNDER: *Haunted Theater*

HITCHHIKER

BY POPPY Z. BRITE

I CLIPPED the disused tollbooth doing ninety. This place, this no-place, sucked me in. My atoms soaked into the broken glass and shattered steel. A traveler might glimpse my face in the sheen of oil on blacktop, hear my voice in the doppler rush of traffic through the lonesome night. I rode in one man's back seat for ten miles before our eyes met in the rearview. He screamed, skidded, rolled, burned. I watched him die in hopes he would stay with me, but I snapped back to my concrete purgatory alone.

Perhaps the next wreck will bring me companionship. I'll keep trying.

Stop for toll at this haunted booth

POPPY Z. BRITE, also known as **BILLY MARTIN**, is the author of *Lost Souls*, *Exquisite Corpse*, and many other novels and shorter works. Brite is currently working on a nonfiction book about religion and spirituality in the works of Stephen King.

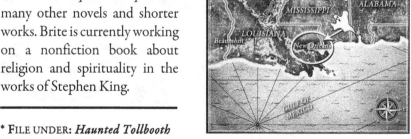

* FILE UNDER: *Haunted Tollbooth*

"You'd do well to remember that this place is cursed."

THE LIGHTHOUSE

FEATURE ENTRY 20

STRUCTURE TYPE: LIGHTHOUSE
LOCATION: CROW ISLAND (NOVA SCOTIA), CANADA
LAT./ LONG: 45.8662° N, 60.0600° W
BUILT: CIRCA 1824
GROUND ELEVATION: 20 FT. (6 M.)
WRITTEN BY: D.R. SMITH

TRAVEL GUIDE NOTES

THE VERY EXISTENCE of lighthouses is built upon death. Or, at least, the *prevention* of death, of horrible watery demise by way of sinking ships during monstrous midnight storms. Lighthouses are erected in places known for vessels to strike reefs, to overturn, to break apart. After enough disasters, a lighthouse goes up, and is born a symbol of hope, the proverbial flame in the darkness gallantly aiding future ships along their hazardous course.

The lighthouse and its safeguards are not, however, infallible. There still exist a litany of perils related to the environment, the equipment, and the human element itself—that vigilant lighthouse keeper. Noteworthy is that this occupation has historically proven to be one of the most dangerous in history, as the sole caretaker must contend with all-consuming storms, ice floes, drowning, contamination from toxic lead and mercury, and extreme isolation, often leading to all sorts of batshit insanity.

So when D.R. Smith submitted through open call the following story, and of its subject building, I was certainly excited to read it, and I was not let down, especially with its quiet, Gothic tone. For herein, even the dead find need of "The Lighthouse."

—Charlatan Bardot

Nova Scotia, 1869

THE FOG SAT LIKE A HEAVY VEIL ON THE COLD, steely waters of the North Atlantic. Every now and then a stiff breeze stirred the mist, sending hazy phantoms twirling toward our boat, their damp fingers reaching down the back of my thick wool coat to chill my spine.

Shivering, I blew on my hands and looked at the oarsman, a rugged-looking sea dog named Wharton, who propelled our skiff with great earnest and not a little terror as we approached the fog-shrouded coastline of Crow Island. The island, situated less than a mile off the northeast shore of Nova Scotia, brooded in eerie gray silence. Although its isolation in infamously treacherous waters gave many men pause, I looked forward to my duties as the new lighthouse keeper. I grew up in the small Maine town of Kennebunkport and spent my youth on wharves watching shipbuilders create some of the mightiest vessels in the world, later serving on some of those same vessels as a midshipman and second lieutenant. Upon receiving the offer for the keeper's job by a Mr. Condon, Nova Scotia's Supervisor of Lighthouses, I eagerly accepted. I wanted nothing more than to spend my life at sea and protect the brave mariners from the shoals and rock ledges that threatened every passing ship.

"You're sweating profusely," I noted of the oarsman.

"'Tis not the effort that dampens my brow, Mr. Abbott," he replied in a gravelly voice.

I followed his gaze and noticed the dark silhouette of the lighthouse slowly emerging from the fog. "I see our destination awaits." I glanced back at Wharton. "You don't like the place?"

"I prefer it better from a distance, sir."

I frowned. "Surely an experienced mariner like yourself doesn't believe the tales?"

"I believe what happens at the Crow ain't natural."

"So you've told me."

Wharton expressed to me over ales the night before that former Crow Island keepers didn't keep their jobs for very long. Many turned up dead of unnatural causes, or disappeared altogether under mysterious circumstances. Indeed, the island got its name from the superstitious folks who lived in the nearby village of Wolfes Landing. A flock of crows was called a murder, and not because of their tendency to feast on the dead. Instead, according to folklore, crows would gather to decide the fate of an injured or sick member of their flock.

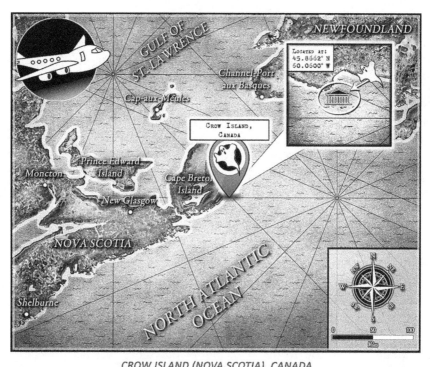

CROW ISLAND (NOVA SCOTIA), CANADA

And usually that decision was death.

I was not surprised that Wharton shared this opinion of the island. Its history of shipwrecks, drownings, and other untimely deaths was well established in these parts. However, my own experiences and education in the science of naval vessels fortified me against absurd beliefs in the supernatural, but I wouldn't hold it against Wharton, whom I liked very much.

The old sailor's ruddy face turned pale as he guided the skiff up to the island's wooden mooring.

"You'd do well to remember that this place is cursed," Wharton said after we'd docked. "There've been suicides here. The last keeper to stay here went mad and attacked his own family. Blood was found on the walls and floor of every room, as if he hunted them down like prey. When it was over, he threw himself from the top of the lighthouse. But his wife and children . . . they weren't so lucky, sir. Their deaths were slow and brutal."

Wharton crossed himself before continuing.

"Not a seaman from here to Halifax ain't heard somethin' afoul about this place. If it weren't for your generous payment and my missus needin' nice things, I wouldn't have brought you here."

"Your interest in my well-being is duly noted and appreciated," I remarked as I grabbed my two bags and stepped off the skiff.

"You're a good man, Mr. Abbot," Wharton commented. "Your rise from midshipman to second lieutenant on board the *USS Chesapeake* is well known. I'm sure you know more about the sea than most men alive. But the Crow ain't like most places, and the sea 'round here has its own way of draggin' men down."

"I hope to see you again soon, my friend," I said, touched by his concern.

"Aye." With one last anxious glance up at the towering lighthouse, Wharton pushed off without another word. I watched him row away quickly until he vanished into the fog.

After Wharton's departure, I turned my attention to the woefully dilapidated lighthouse. After many years of brutal treatment by the sea, its stone edifice was missing chunks of rock and had been stained black with mold. The wind and waves had, over the years, shifted many of the large boulders on the small island, giving Crow Island a wild, reckless appearance.

A small skiff lay beached next to the lighthouse. Upon closer inspection it appeared to be in good working order, for which I was grateful. Tomorrow I would need to row to the mainland for provisions, weather providing. Satisfied to know I had means of transport, I started up the gravel path to the surprisingly commodious house attached to the back of the lighthouse tower. As I walked, I stole a glance up at the lantern room and noticed a shadow lingering behind the glass. I stopped.

The shadow slid to the left, and I could distinctly make out a head and possibly the torso of a man. Startled, I dropped my bags. The dark form moved swiftly from side to side, as though searching for something—and then it vanished!

I took a few deep breaths to calm my racing heart. The light was surely playing tricks with my eyes. There were a hundred natural explanations for what I'd just seen, and one surely would present itself when I climbed the steps to the lantern room and inspected it for myself.

I continued along the path to the back of the house. It, too, needed repair; but what sank my spirits was not the condition of the house but the size of the island.

Crow Island was a tiny spit of land. There was neither tree nor shrub, and hardly a single blade of grass. The surface was rocky and irregular. My hope for a vegetable garden and a self-sustaining lifestyle were immediately dashed. It appeared I would be making frequent trips across the bay to Wolfes Landing for supplies and provisions.

Sighing, I entered the house. The door opened to a spartan but otherwise comfortable communal area. On the right stood a small wood stove, cupboards, and a modest table. Ahead was a living area consisting of a faded green davenport and a reading chair set on a threadbare rug in front of a stone hearth. To my left a steep wooden staircase led to the second-floor bedrooms. Next to it a narrow entryway opened to a set of steps spiraling up to the lantern room.

As soon as I got myself settled in, I would see at once to the lamp, which was no doubt in serious need of repair.

I wandered over to a large picture window behind the davenport and stared out at the vast expanse of sea. The sun had come out, lifting the fog. The sea was calm, its sun-dappled surface at rest. But to the north an ominous stack of dark clouds caught my eye. A storm would be here by nightfall, if not sooner. I needed to get the lighthouse functioning before then.

Without further delay, I carried my tools up the twisting stairwell to the lantern room, a cramped, iron-framed space surrounded on three sides by thick panes of glass. It smelled of mildew and decay. The condition of the lantern was as I expected: the wick needed to be trimmed, the oil refilled, and the lantern panes cleaned inside and out.

I set about at once to my duties. Fortunately, all the supplies I needed were well-stocked: oil, cleaning tools, additional lamps, and a vast array of brushes. The lamp was encased in a Fresnel lens of the sixth order called a *lanthorn*. I cleaned the lanthorn thoroughly until it sparkled. Satisfied, I then inspected the mechanism that burned the oil and pumped it up from a reservoir below by means of weighted clockworks. Salty sea air tended to erode the metalwork if not properly maintained, and I could see it was already taking its toll on the mechanism.

As I finished up my work, I heard a noise near the bottom of the stairs. The floorboards creaked as though someone were pacing back and forth inside the house. This was followed by a scraping sound dragged along the walls, and then the loud crash of a heavy object striking the floor.

My mouth turned dry as a sanding sponge and my throat sealed with dread. Remembering the shadow of a man I'd seen earlier crossing the lantern room, I reached into my toolbox for a hammer before going down to face the intruder.

I rushed down the steps and quickly scanned the living room. If someone had been there, he was gone now. Finding nothing amiss, I rushed upstairs to the bedrooms.

I stood on the landing and listened. All was calm and quiet. A quick check of the two drafty bedrooms revealed no intruder.

Damn peculiar, I thought as I returned to the main floor. I was sure of what I'd heard and that it was coming from inside the house.

I did another sweep of the house. Somehow I had missed a small wooden writing desk toppled over on its side. A ledger lay splayed open like a crushed bird under the desk.

I righted the desk and picked up the ledger. It was the former keeper's record of happenings at the lighthouse. Usually, these were mundane records of daily lighthouse duties. In this case, however, I was astounded by the detail, the meandering thoughts, and the vivid observations of the sea. I was eager to begin reading, but first I prepared a simple meal, and then set about making a blazing fire in the hearth. It was well into the afternoon and approaching evening, and the storm I'd spied earlier was beginning to darken the sky.

Though I was aware of the variability of Nova Scotia's weather in early spring, the penetrating cold I felt in the house unnerved me. An unseasonably bitter chill squirmed through the cracks in the walls and seeped into my bones. It wasn't until I sank into the reading chair by the blazing fire and opened the ledger that I felt my first moment of comfort in my new home.

Scrawled in a shaky hand, the old lighthouse keeper introduced himself as Saul Langston. He was married to a woman named Sarah and had two children, Thomas and Eve. They settled at the lighthouse last summer and by all accounts seemed happy in their new surroundings. Friends and relatives visited from the mainland. Birthday parties were thrown for the two children. Accounts of beautiful full moons, a lunar eclipse, and the Northern Lights were described in brilliant detail.

All seemed to be going well for the keeper and his family until things changed. The weather turned bitter cold and the Atlantic more aggressive. Winter's long string of gray and miserable weeks could corrode a man's soul, and it was during this time that Saul's writing became more erratic and he appeared ill at ease with the isolation on Crow Island.

And then the stranger arrived.

Part of the duties of every lighthouse keeper was to watch the sea with a perceptive eye and help any sailor in need. Despite the beacon, every now and then inexperienced seafarers struck a shoal or ledge, and men needed rescuing from the sea. On one evening in early December, Saul wrote of a ship entering the harbor . . .

A winter storm was raging, and through the whipping snow I watched the clipper sway and teeter on the restless ocean. Next, a colossal wave came out of nowhere and struck the vessel on its starboard side, throwing men overboard and capsizing the vessel.

Over my wife's objections, I rowed my skiff out to where I'd seen the men fall overboard. When I arrived, I found the bodies of dead sailors floating like driftwood everywhere. I shuddered at the horror on the men's frozen faces as they gaped at me from the black waters. Their deaths had been quick but not painless. I called out for survivors, but nobody called back—until, that is, I sighted a man waving desperately for help. I dragged him on board and wrapped him in a blanket and rowed at once for Crow Island. Each time one of my oars bumped a body, I crossed myself and said the Lord's Prayer. I knew a proper Christian burial was not in any of these sailors' futures; the Atlantic would become each man's cold, watery tomb.

Saul described the man he pulled from the sea as having a haunted expression with a disconcerting intensity about the eyes. His skin was mottled gray, blue around the fingertips and eyes. He looked dead already, in Saul's estimation, but the fact he still drew wheezy gasps spurred the old keeper to put his back into his rowing and get the young man to safety before the elements could claim him.

Once back at the lighthouse, the sailor spoke nary a word. He merely sat on the davenport and stared bleakly into the fire. He took a few sips of broth but appeared to neither care for the taste nor the comfort of the food. Despite the heat of the fire, which Saul claimed he stoked to a roaring blaze, the stranger's flesh remained stippled and blue. His wife crossed herself more than once as she kept her distance from the stranger in their midst.

Then, a most unusual occurrence. Without warning, the stranger stood and wandered to the window. His eyes, still sunken and black, gazed upon the roiling sea with fascination. Then Sarah screamed. What caused the woman such dismay was the knife in the sailor's hand, a long steel blade he produced from an inner coat pocket.

The stranger looked upon the weapon as though he'd never seen it before, and then proffered it to Saul. "I . . . I cannot keep it anymore," he said in an odd cadence, his voice filled with sorrow. "It is cursed."

Saul quickly snatched the weapon from his morbid guest's hand. It was icy cold. Stunned, he dropped it with a clatter and kicked it away. The stranger had turned back to pondering the winter storm again, an expression of relief settling on his face, as if a burden had been lifted.

Saul ordered his wife to take the children upstairs to their bedrooms and wait for him there. I could only imagine the dread the old keeper must have been feeling.

There was much more to Saul's tale, and while curiosity gnawed at me to continue reading, I had to see to my evening lighthouse duties first.

Dusk had arrived. The sky rumbled with thunder as I ascended the steps to the lantern room on shaky legs, unable to get the image of the forlorn sailor and his knife out of my mind. I threw myself into my work; a keeper's duty went beyond merely lighting the wick. In the evening, it was necessary to check wind direction and adjust the vents to allow just enough draft into the lantern room. This created the necessary vacuum to draw the fumes and soot up the glass chimney attached to the top of the lamp and out of the lantern room. Then, during the course of the evening, I would need to return to properly trim the wicks, clean the chimney, adjust the vents, and wind the weights once more.

Once the work was completed I returned to the hearth, but my heart still galloped. Each crack of thunder caused me to jump and glance about, expecting to discover a presence in the house with me. Eyes pressed in on me; perhaps the figure I'd seen earlier in the lantern room had returned. But when I searched the place again, all the shadowy corners, rooms, closets and hideaways were empty. With a fresh fire ablaze, I settled in my chair and returned again to Saul's account of the mysterious shipwrecked stranger.

A day had now passed, and still the nameless sailor brooded restlessly by the fire. And his physical condition was deteriorating rapidly. He was losing weight. His skin had turned sallow, almost translucent, and he stunk like a beached carcass. He would not speak of the knife or the circumstances of the shipwreck no matter how many times Saul urged him.

His continued presence in the house affected Saul's mood. The keeper's fascination with the knife grew to obsession. The children hid in their rooms, afraid to come out and face the stranger or their own father. Perhaps it would have been better, Sarah suggested, if the sailor had gone down with the rest of his shipwrecked crew.

Saul would hear none of it, however. It was his duty as keeper to save lives as well as keep the wick burning. He would care for this man, no matter how peculiar his mannerisms, until he was well enough to go home.

I appreciated Saul's sense of duty and honor, yet he seemed to be losing his grip on sanity. What hold did this mysterious guest have over Saul's mind? Judging by the last journal entry, Saul's thoughts were growing increasingly erratic. And violent. The desolation of the island and the stranger's presence were no doubt taking its toll on the poor man.

> *I know what madness feels like now, its creeping sensation over the body, its heat in the limbs. I stared at the knife all day as if it beckoned me to pick it up, and I thought of my dear Sarah and the children, the little lambs, stashed away upstairs.*
>
> *What does the stranger want of me? Why won't he SPEAK to me of the knife, for God's sake!*
>
> *I watched as he sat by the window staring out at the sea all day. Sometimes I heard him mutter as though another were there beside him. He called out from time to time in a wretched voice for a man named Bannerman, but when I inquire as to the fellow's whereabouts, the sailor drifted into another fugue and ignored my entreaties to help.*
>
> *Finally, in a fit of ill-temper, I accosted the stranger over the knife. "It is cursed," he told me with gut-wrenching anguish. "Be rid of it at once, or its blood will be on your hands." I snatched up the knife from the mantel, meaning at once to fling it out to sea, but a power I could not describe resonated within the metal. I resisted with all my will, but it was too great. I weighed the knife in my hand, flexed my fingers around its hilt, and called for my lovely family*

The last sentence ended abruptly with no punctuation, the letters streaking down the page as if Saul's hand had grown too weary to hold the pen anymore. I was left with the chilling certainty that I had just read the final thoughts of a murderer.

A sudden blast of wind rattled the house. Waves crashed like cannon balls against the island. I knew I should check the lantern to make sure the wick was still lit. Relieved to have something to do to occupy my mind, I prepared to attend to my duties in the lighthouse when a glint caught my eye.

There, sitting on the mantel, was the knife described in Saul's journal. How had I missed it before? Bewildered, I couldn't take my eyes off it. It was waiting . . . but for what?

My heart pounding madly, I picked up the knife and examined it from all angles, recalling Wharton's words from earlier:

The last keeper even went mad and attacked his own family. Blood was found on the walls and floor of every room, as if he hunted them down like prey. When it was over, he threw himself from the top of the lighthouse. But his wife and children . . . they weren't so lucky, sir. Their death was slow and brutal.

As I held the knife, I saw it all as Wharton had described, in a grisly tableau racing through my mind:

The children's bodies bloodied and crumpled in the corner of their bedroom . . .

Sarah, pressing her hands against the wound in her stomach, blood leaking around her fingers, as her husband came up behind her and shoved her down the stairs . . .

Saul, blood-stained hands trembling, climbing the stairs to the lantern room . . .

I cried out and dropped the knife, and at that same moment a loud bang echoed upstairs. Startled, I spied a shadow gliding along the stairs.

An impulse to flee overwhelmed me, but I held fast and waited for it to pass. Besides, where would I go in a storm? I *must* confront the horror residing in my own house, lest I meet the same fate as Saul Langston. I steeled myself for what I might discover in the upstairs, and though my body quaked, I scooped up the knife and climbed the stairs slowly, keeping alert for any sign of the intruder.

When I reached the landing, I was struck by an unsettling cold. A rank odor filled the house: briny sea air mixed with decaying flesh. Shivering, I probed ahead to the open door at the end of the hall. To my great surprise and horror, a ghastly apparition stood before the wide-open window, gazing out at the storm-tossed sea!

The phantom turned to me as I stood there gawking, and I recognized the apparition at once from the description in Saul's journal. He wore a midshipman's uniform of first lieutenant rank: a red navy frock coat, white lace around the sleeves, and a band of white around the top of the coat. The sailor looked to be no older than twenty, though his corpse-like pallor made him appear ancient. His eyes were black as inkwells, and they fixed on the knife I held out before me with despair.

My fear of the apparition quickly faded. His grief and suffering were evident, and I wanted nothing more than to help.

"Who are you?" I asked.

By all accounts, I expected no answer, but suddenly the apparition frowned, and the words he spoke were twisted with pain.

"It wasn't meant to happen this way," he said, turning back to the window.

"What wasn't?" I edged into the room. "Tell me, so I may help you."

"So much killing," he mourned.

I followed his gaze out the window and saw, to my astonishment, the dark outline of a sloop foundering on the raging sea. Was it even there? Or was I imagining this as well, like I did the deaths of Saul and his family when I held the knife downstairs?

I waited and watched as the ocean battered the small seafaring vessel until its rigging broke apart and its mast collapsed. Something felt wrong to me, however. I thought of Saul's account of the sinking ship. He described it as a clipper, an entirely different class of ship. What, then, was I witnessing now?

"We went down in the storm that night," the phantom continued, as though sensing my bewilderment. "Pirates boarded our vessel just before the storm hit, killing our officers and throwing their bodies out to sea. We never saw the attack coming. So much killing," he repeated.

"You mean, you . . . ?"

He turned to me. "There were no survivors."

"But Saul, he rescued you."

The apparition's stare dropped to the knife in my hand. "They sliced Captain Bannerman's throat and cut the hands off anyone who got in their way. I tried to stop them. I grabbed the knife and wrestled it away from one of them, but I was overpowered. They tossed me overboard. Then . . . then . . . "

Utter confusion wracked the tormented spirit's face.

"Saul rescued you the night the clipper sank," I interjected, "only you weren't a member of her crew."

"I was still so angry."

Realization dawned on me. "You didn't mean for Saul's family to die! But your rage at your own death infected him, and he was already so close to the edge of insanity."

The apparition's grim features softened, perhaps due to the empathy I projected on him. "What year?" he asked.

"1869."

"Ten long years at the bottom of the sea," he said with a sigh and a resolute shake of his head.

"What can I do?"

Again, his eyes flicked to the knife. "Throw it away or I shall never find peace."

Immediately I understood; the murder weapon bound him to this plane. Without further delay, I left the lighthouse and walked to the edge of the island. I waited for the right moment and flung the knife as far as I could into the sea. With the task completed, I returned to the house to assure the distraught spirit that all had been set right again, but to my disappointment I found the apparition had vanished. The chill in the air and the foul odor were gone too, and the house felt truly empty.

I gazed out the window where the spirit had stood and watched the waves crash against the rocks below, pondering what Wharton had said about how the sea had a way of dragging men down.

It would seem, on occasion, it could dredge them up too.

DID YOU KNOW?

D. R. SMITH lives in Livonia, NY with his wife and two children. He is a special education teacher in the Canandaigua City School District by day, and a writer of the grim and gruesome by night. Ever since he was a boy he's been besotted with dark fiction—to the horror of his parents and teachers—and favors the work of Ray Bradbury, Stephen King, Neil Gaiman, Clive Barker, and Richard Christian Matheson. He's published short stories in the anthology *It Calls from the Forest VI* and the magazines *The Dread Machine*, *DarkFuse*, and many others. He is also the author of three story collections: *Let 'Em RIP: 13 Tales of Horror*, *The Dead of Night*, and *The Edge of Midnight*.

A SHINING VACATION

BY JOHN M. FLOYD

THE traveler entered the Timberline Lodge in Oregon. A red-horned desk clerk said, "You're in the wrong place."

"What?"

"Look into my eyes."

Timberline Lodge, where fiction crosses reality

When he did, the traveler saw a film reel of images: a frozen maze, blood-gushing elevators, a bald Black man, a typewriter, a kid on a tricycle, orange hallways, a grinning man with an axe.

The traveler shook his head. "Only the exteriors were filmed here. The movie's based on the Stanley Hotel in Colorado." He paused. "*You're* in the wrong place."

The devil-clerk gasped, then vanished in a puff of smoke.

The real clerk smiled. "Name, please?"

The traveler smiled back. "Stephen King."

JOHN M. FLOYD's short fiction has appeared in *Alfred Hitchcock's Mystery Magazine*, *Ellery Queen's Mystery Magazine*, *The Strand Magazine*, *The Saturday Evening Post*, and three editions of *The Best American Mystery Stories*. A former Air Force captain and IBM systems engineer, John is also an Edgar Award nominee, a four-time Derringer Award winner, and the author of nine books.

* FILE UNDER: *Haunted Hotel*

There're no hard and fast rules about contacting the dead . . .

BLUSTER

FEATURE ENTRY 21

STRUCTURE TYPE: SALOON
LOCATION: GARNET (MONTANA), USA
LAT./ LONG: 46.8253° N, 113.3387° W
BUILT: CIRCA 1897
GROUND ELEVATION: 5,909 FT. (1,801 M.)
WRITTEN BY: NORMAN PRENTISS

TRAVEL GUIDE NOTES

SÉANCES, HAUNTED OLD West towns, and toxic masculinity—the perfect trifecta for horror of both the supernatural *and* societal kind. Celebrated author, poet, and editor Norman Prentiss takes us on a tour stop to the Old West ghost town of Garnet and one of its *thirteen* saloons.

What is it about patronizing know-it-alls who seem to sadistically relish needling people? Is there delight found by inciting reactions in others? Or is there some intrinsic need to bolster their own low self-esteem? Or perhaps they just don't have a clue. It's true sometimes others' personalities are simply grating without intended malice. Sometimes people speak without a "filter." Sometimes they say the wrong thing at the wrong moment, and sometimes those things and moments coincide in a haunting.

Cautionary tale? Passing anecdote? Or just a strange occurrence in the weird, wild world of haunted buildings? Be it as you may decide, a word to the cautious: Be not "Bluster."

—Charlatan Bardot

T HERE'S ALWAYS SOMEONE IN THE TOUR GROUP
that you end up hating.

For Hadley, the fellow traveler she had privately nicknamed as "Bluster Mansplain" filled that role. He loved correcting the petite tour guide, such as when he shouted over her quiet explanation that the town once featured nearly a dozen saloons.

"Thirteen in its heyday," Bluster announced. "A quick look at Garnet's town records would tell you that, little lady."

Wow, "little lady"? Maybe he was aligning himself with the time period, emulating language and outdated attitudes to fit his research about the past. Or, more likely, quoting cliché dialogue from B-movies he'd watched as a kid. The latter would explain his outfit: he was the only one among the guests who'd arrived in costume, complete with spurred boots, leather vest, and a cross-chest ammunition belt with a six-shooter toy pistol holstered at his right hip.

The guide turned her head with a dismissive cough, then continued. "This particular saloon is the best preserved *of the thirteen.*" She motioned to the bar with a three-paneled front, an empty frame behind it that would have held a mirror. "We kept original materials, when we could. The only modern addition is electric lights, which helps for nighttime showings."

"Electric lights aren't ideal for a séance," Bluster said.

"That's the thing about electric lights. They have an off switch."

Ouch. Score one for the guide. Bluster probably didn't even realize she'd nicked him.

How tiresome, though, that he felt free to opine on spiritualism as well as old-West history. After his frequent interjections about the founding date of the town, or the value of gold in the late nineteenth century converted into modern dollars, or how a 1912 fire essentially emptied Garnet and made it the ghost town attraction it is today—as if he should be the tour guide rather than the expert the rest of them had paid good *modern* dollars to hear—she thought he'd at least shut up when things shifted from facts to phantasmagorical.

There're no hard and fast rules about contacting the dead. Every medium has their own strategies. On rare occasions, Hadley had actually seen a spirit materialize over the séance table, or heard a long-gone voice speak through the medium or even through one of the other

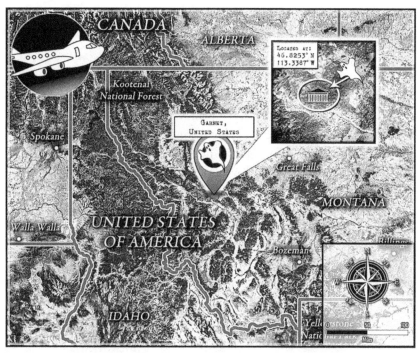

HAUNTED GARNET (MONTANA), UNITED STATES OF AMERICA

participants. In all those sittings, however, she'd *never* heard one of those participants try to explain procedures to the expert.

"There's ten of us here, including me," our guide said. "Let's push these two round tables together so we can clasp hands during the session."

"Holding hands isn't necessary." Bluster was technically correct here: in the history of spiritualism, hand holding suggested that no trickery was involved, since the medium or other guests didn't have freedom to sneak away from the table in the dark, turn on a projector or tape player. Still, it was an indelicate remark—and the idea of an unbroken circle, of a physical connection among all participants, seemed a logical way to channel the group's energy.

In all the successful séances Hadley had attended, everybody held hands.

The tour guide walked behind the saloon bar to retrieve a wooden box. It wasn't clear if the box was related to the town, but it had scorch marks as if it had been rescued after the 1912 fire. She lifted the hinged lid, took out a small, tarnished candlestick, and placed a fresh white candle in the socket. She set the candlestick on the uneasy balance between the joined tables, then lit a match.

"I'll turn out the overhead lights," everybody's-friend offered.

"Let me finish setting up." The guide's teeth were clenched, lips unmoving the way they'd have to be if she was throwing her voice—a skill she might employ later in the tour. Here, she was just letting some of her irritation show. She could have done more, Hadley thought, since the rest of the group was clearly on her side.

The guide reached back into the box and scooped up what looked like an assortment of rocks. On closer inspection, Hadley realized they were crystals. She watched the guide spread them across the tables quickly, almost like she was rolling dice.

"A crystal ball works better."

As much as he annoyed Hadley, she wondered how their medium/guide was able to keep her cool. If she really had spiritualist power, she'd need her fullest concentration to be effective.

Then again, if she was a *fake* medium, Bluster might be her perfect suggestible subject—the way a stage hypnotist identified an audience member easy to manipulate, willing to chicken cluck or otherwise make a fool of himself. Another possibility: he was actually her assistant, with his jabs at her ability calculated to divert suspicion.

One of the other tourists pointed at Bluster's holstered pistol. "Hey, is that real?"

"Don't worry. I got something better than an open-carry permit." Bluster tapped the plastic "Sheriff's badge" pinned to his vest.

Hadley wondered if it wasn't just toxic masculinity that made this guy so confident. He walked around like this toy gun had live ammunition, play-acted like he really was a sheriff—or some mall cop, daring little kids to question his authority. He thought he was intimidating everyone.

Wouldn't it be funny if that was a real gun?

The guide signaled for everyone to gather at the tables. Hadley decided she'd get the best experience sitting next to the guide, but Bluster had the same idea and beat her to it on the near side. From the remaining seats, Hadley ended up with the spot nobody else wanted—right next to Bluster.

The guide clapped her hands, and the electric lights went off. The saloon, which had a high wood-buttressed ceiling, seemed smaller in the glow of a single candlelight. Their faces practically floated in the dark around the pushed-together tables.

"Clasp hands."

Hadley held an older gentleman's hand on the left, then reached reluctantly for Bluster on her right. His grip was overly firm.

Their guide shifted fully into spiritualist mode, working to establish the proper atmosphere for a séance. She described the saloon they'd just toured, asked everyone to imagine fresh wood, unbroken fixtures, a room full of people. People who drank and laughed, gossiped and gambled, and sometimes got rowdy and fought.

"Consider the threads connecting us over time," the guide said in her quiet voice. "The people are like us, with similar emotions: mixtures of love, petty jealousies, selfishness, or mistrust. And we exist in the same building as them, with a bar and tables and chairs, a roof over our heads, and above that roof the same stars circling in the sky."

And then the crystals on the table shone like stars, those crystals she'd apparently thrown down randomly but now flashing to outline familiar shapes: Orion, the hunter; Ursa Minor, with the north star crystal shining brightest; then Taurus the bull, its head and horns outlining a bright "V."

It was an impressive effect, Hadley had to admit, even if it was probably computer-assisted.

A more impressive effect followed: the voice that emerged from the spiritualist's mouth.

"You cheated." A full throated, masculine voice from their petite guide. It filled the room. People around the tables looked alternately at her, then at other participants to gauge their reactions.

Bluster squeezed Hadley's hand, hard. His hand was sweaty, a sponge wringing itself out.

"I can't stand a cheat. A loud-mouthed cheat." The guide stood, her head seeming to float higher. It floated almost beyond the candle's circle of illumination. A hand lifted into view, gripping a six-shooter pistol.

"That's my gun." Bluster had the soft voice now, lacking his usual confidence. "I'm still holding her hand."

But it was only a trick. The gun was a toy.

"You'll never cheat again."

In the glow of the single candle, Hadley tried to interpret the expression on Bluster's face. The poor guy actually looked scared.

A single shot fired. Someone clapped their hands to trigger the overhead lights.

Did You Know?

NORMAN PRENTISS is the author of *Odd Adventures With Your Other Father*, *The Apocalypse-a-Day Desk Calendar*, and *Life in a Haunted House*, and he won the 2010 Bram Stoker Award for Superior Achievement in Long Fiction for *Invisible Fences*. Other publications include *The Book of Baby Names*, *The Fleshless Man*, *Four Legs in the Morning*, *The Halloween Children* (written with Brian James Freeman), and *The Narrator* (written with Michael McBride), with story appearances in *Black Static*, *Dark Screams*, *Blood Lite 3*, *Best Horror of the Year*, *The Year's Best Dark Fantasy and Horror*, and in five editions of the *Shivers* anthology series. His poetry has appeared in *Writer Online*, *Southern Poetry Review*, *Baltimore's City Paper*, and *A Sea of Alone: Poems for Alfred Hitchcock*. Visit him online at www.normanprentiss.com.

THE COLD HOUSE

BY SIMON STRANTZAS

THERE are no ghosts in the former home of Captain George Hunt, founder of the small Canadian town of Huntsville, Ontario. Stricken with a paranoia regarding all things otherworldly, Captain Hunt hired the infamous occultist Hieronymus Slant to perform a cleansing ritual that forbade all things ectoplasmic from crossing the threshold. Many visitors to the dilapidated landmark today report being overwhelmed by a deathful chill upon entering followed by little else. It's only long afterward they report a profound sense of loss, coupled with the memory of their autonomous bodies as though seen from a great distance. Or perhaps they recall the sound of their muted screams and of their spectral hands as they bang and claw at the building's walls, desperate to be reunited with their flesh. These are the lucky visitors. More tragic are those that report no such memories and what that might suggest.

Entering the house in groups is not recommended.

SIMON STRANTZAS is the author of five collections of weird and strange fiction, including *Nothing Is Everything* from Undertow Publications (2018). His work has been reprinted in various annual best-of anthologies, nominated for awards, and translated into other languages. He lives with his wife in Toronto, Canada.

* FILE UNDER: *Haunted Landmark (historic home)*

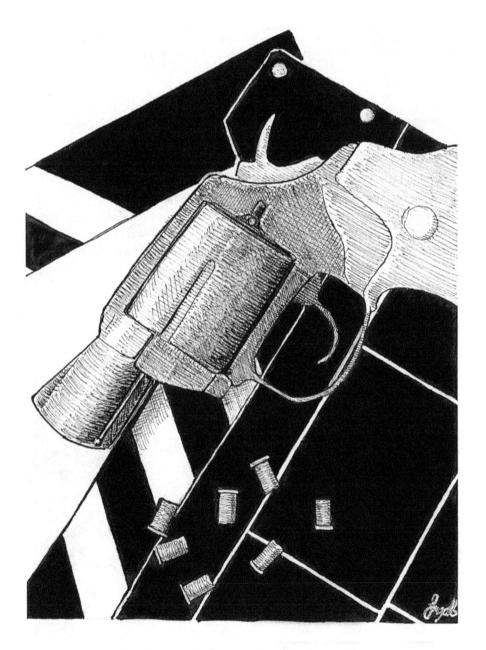

So this is Hollywood, she thought.

THE GULCH

STRUCTURE TYPE: SOUNDSTAGE
LOCATION: HOLLYWOOD (CALIFORNIA), USA
LAT./ LONG: 34.0903° N, 118.3321° W
BUILT: CIRCA 1921
GROUND ELEVATION: 292 FT. (89 M.)
WRITTEN BY: LISA MORTON

TRAVEL GUIDE NOTES

THERE'S AN EXPRESSION that for someone who's well-experienced in a task or situation, they've "been around the block." In the case of Lisa Morton, she's been around just about every block there is in the writing industry: Fiction Author, Essayist, Screen Writer, Mentor, former (and longest serving) President of the Horror Writers Association, and considered such an expert on Halloween that she was made consultant to the first-ever U.S. Postal Halloween stamps.

A native Angeleno (as is my co-author, Eric J. Guignard), Lisa's background ties in nicely to the following story, as she's also a former Hollywood special effects model maker, and has been involved in a number of indie and major production films. If there's ever something dark or ominous, sordid or shocking, eerie or foul, to be found in back-lots of sound stages, Lisa's probably seen it.

There are ghosts on-screen and there are ghosts at hand, and sometimes the realms of their existence cross, such as at HFP Studios, located in the heart of Hollywood at "The Gulch."

—Charlatan Bardot

A S NESSA LEANED AGAINST THE RUSTING CHAIN
link gate, she put a hand on the wooden frame to steady herself and
found her thumb sinking into wood that had the consistency of
sodden newspaper. Fascinated, she pushed farther into the pulp several
inches; when she withdrew her thumb, it was covered with a filigree of dank
gray mold. Peering into the hole she'd created, Nessa saw something white
squirming away from the sun.

So this is Hollywood, she thought.

Just then the gate began to rattle back. Nessa looked up to see Todd
waving at an elderly, bent man on the other side.

"You must be Mr. Fleming," Todd called. The gate stopped, and instead
of answering Todd, the old man cursed and tottered off to the side, out of
sight. Todd turned to Nessa. "Guess we know why the place is so cheap."

Nessa tried to smile, but she found both the decrepit Mr. Fleming and
the ugly, decaying buildings around them oppressive.

"Dude," she remembered Todd telling her, "it'd be the perfect place to
make our movie. You're the one who said we had to shoot with real cameras
in a real soundstage, so this is a real soundstage with *history*. I mean, you can't
get more Hollywood history than Gower Gulch." He hadn't bothered to
add that it was dirt cheap.

Nessa didn't see much history now. Instead, she saw graffiti-covered
ruins with boarded-up windows, dying trees whose tops rustled with rats,
and a crack pipe discarded in a nearby gutter. A few blocks away squatted
the urban desert of souvenir shops and bars that was Hollywood Boulevard.
In front of Nessa stood Todd's idea of cinematic history: "HFP STUDIOS"
read a peeling, faded sign over the gate. Finally the motor on the gate started
up again, and it rattled back more. Todd and Nessa stepped in as Fleming
waited for them.

If Nessa had found him repellant from the other side of the fence, up
close the man was nearly intolerable. He was at least seventy, with a few long
greasy locks fringing his pale head, no teeth, and a strange odor. Nessa tried
to place it, could only come up with something halfway between moth balls
and hot tar.

"Mr. Fleming," Todd started again, extending a hand. "Todd Marantz,
I'm the producer. This is Nessa Vasquez, the writer and director."

Mr. Fleming briefly shook Todd's hand before leveling his squinting
gaze on Nessa. "A woman director, huh?" He snickered.

Nessa felt a small surge of anger, but she pushed it down and answered,
"I've got a Masters in Film from USC."

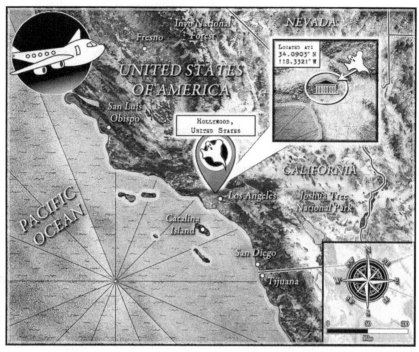

HAUNTED HOLLYWOOD (CALIFORNIA), UNITED STATES OF AMERICA

Fleming ran his eyes over her, making Nessa's skin crawl. She was relieved when he turned away. "Lemme get the gate, then I'll show you around the lot."

He paused long enough to close the clanking old gate, then turned and motioned to Nessa and Todd, who followed him. "How'd you say you found us?"

"The Action Hollywood e-mail list," Todd answered. Looking around, Nessa understood now why her housemate Steve had tried to tell her not to rent HFP: "It's *totally* haunted, you know." At the time, Nessa had laughed.

"Those'd be your offices," Fleming noted, gesturing at a small bungalow off to the right. "It's hooked up for Wi-Fi and power. Your crew can park here."

They were crossing a dirt lot, heading for a warehouse-sized old wood-and-plaster building. Nessa saw dead weeds and empty cans around the edges of the lot, and when she turned to glance back at the gate there was a filth-encrusted homeless man glaring at her from the other side. While she watched, the man unzipped and began to urinate through the gate. "Do you think the car's safe out there?" she asked Todd. Todd quieted her with a look.

"How long you thinking of renting the stage for?" Fleming asked.

"Four weeks," Todd responded.

Fleming stopped and eyed them; Nessa felt him judging her again. "Not much time to prep and shoot a whole movie."

Todd gestured at the tablet he carried. "We've already got everything planned out, so we don't need more than a week of prep. We're already cast and rehearsed, the sets are simple . . . a week of prep, three weeks to shoot, and we're done."

Fleming scrutinized Todd for a while before asking, "You never made a movie before, have ya?"

"What does that have to do with—"

The old man cut him off. "'Cause if you had, you'd know you can't do it in four weeks, even on digital." He chuckled, more of a grating hiss than a real laugh, and turned back to the soundstage before them. Prying one key apart from the others on a huge ring he carried, the old man unlocked a door leading inside. "This'll be yours," and then, with another of those horrible rasping grunts, "the Redd Rossmore stage."

He reached inside and flipped a switch, flooding the interior with weak fluorescent glow. Todd and Nessa stepped in behind him, and Nessa immediately felt a pressure around her chest, a strange sensation she'd never experienced. She wondered if there was asbestos in the walls, or some gas leak.

Fleming had moved to the center of the soundstage and was gesturing up. "You got thirty-foot ceilings and a lighting grid, you got catwalks with the stairs over to the side there, you got your loading doors back there and dressing rooms out that door to the back."

Nessa and Todd followed Fleming, trying to peer into the murk. Somewhere Nessa heard a loud *crreeeaaakkk*, and for a second she shuddered as she imagined the crossbeams overhead having the same solidity as the gate frame outside. *No telling what could be crawling around up there.*

Nose wrinkling as he looked around, Todd asked, "What was that name you used for this stage?"

"Redd Rossmore. You *do* know who Redd Rossmore is, don't you?"

Something tickled the back of Nessa's brain, but both she and Todd shrugged. Fleming actually spat something thick and green into the dust before going on. "Figgers. Well, if you knew anything at all about movie history, you'd know that Redd Rossmore made the first Hollywood silent comedy right here, on this land, back when Hollywood was still Horace and Daeida Wilcox's little religious commune, and they were still giving land away free to churches and the like. 'Course this soundstage wasn't built at that point 'cause they shot right under the sun for the light."

Fleming led them to a far corner of the stage where he bent over, his joints popping loudly, and wiped away some of the grime on the floor. He straightened up and pointed down at the clean spot he'd made. "Take a look at that."

Todd and Nessa had to crouch to make out anything in the gloom, but when they did they saw a concrete slab with writing embedded in it. Though worn by the years, they could make out *REDD ROSSMORE 1921*, and two footprints.

"On the day the crew finished building this stage for Redd, he put his footprints in there along with his name 'cause he was famous for the oversized boots he always wore. Some folks say that's where Sid Grauman got the idea for the footprints in front of the Chinese Theater." Fleming creaked as he straightened, adding, "Redd Rossmore was the greatest clown in silent movies. He taught Chaplin how to throw a pie and Keaton how to duck a falling building. He was a huge man—weighed north of three hundred pounds—but could move like a teenage ballerina. He *made* HFP Studios."

Nessa and Todd straightened up, and Nessa had to reluctantly admit she was intrigued. "So what happened to him?"

"In 1925, he got himself into a little trouble—started diddling the girlfriend of the studio boss's son. One day the kid, whose name was Max, found out, came in here with a gun, and shot Redd six times at point blank range. Redd was dead before he hit the ground."

"What happened to Max?" Nessa asked.

"Daddy bought off the entire crew, fed the papers a story about little Maxie needing a rest. He kept the kid out of jail that way, although Max spent the rest of his life in a loony bin."

The old man walked a few feet, stopping at a large stain in the cracked concrete. "Right here's where Redd was gunned down." He paused before adding, "Some folks claim they've even seen his ghost here, walking the stage in those boots of his. Even had one fellah swear he found fresh blood once at midnight."

Todd made a mocking, ghostly wail, but elicited only a wan smile from Nessa.

Fleming frowned, apparently not amused. "Look, you gonna take the place or not?"

Todd looked around. "We need to think about it a little. It *is* pretty rundown."

"You're not gonna get a better deal anywhere. I take plastic, and I'll even throw in an extra week for free. You'll need it."

THAT NIGHT, NESSA finished a final rewrite on *Odds Are*, the script they'd soon be making into their feature debut, then she Googled Redd Rossmore. There were some of his old one-reel movies on YouTube, featuring the behemoth comedian stumbling along in his comically large boots while engaging in perilous slapstick and (unsettling, given what she already knew) chasing female co-stars; there were shrill items at gossip sites about Redd's depraved history of scandals that had finally climaxed with his murder; and there were the stories about Redd's ghost haunting his soundstage.

Nessa clicked on a few of the latter, and felt a stab of unease: actors, directors, and paranormal investigators all reported knockings, temperature drops, unseen presences that poked and groped, and (twice) full-body apparitions of a "huge man dressed in an old-time suit." One producer said he'd left the stage with his show unfinished because his lead actress would no longer work there. A man who'd been on a shoot there as a technician was nearly killed by a falling light he'd just positioned, and that he'd *known* was secure.

Nessa texted Todd about what she'd found; he texted back to tell her he'd just signed the contract with HFP Studios and he'd give them the first payment in the morning. *Maybe*, Todd texted next, *we should make a horror flick.*

Taking a deep breath, Nessa hoped her gut instinct was wrong.

THE NEXT DAY they met with Fleming to pay the deposit. When Todd handed a credit card over, Nessa was surprised to see it had Todd's father's name on it. "Don't you need him here to sign it?" she whispered to Todd.

"He doesn't even know I have it," Todd confessed, smirking. Fleming hadn't objected to the name on the card. Later, Todd and Nessa argued about the ethics of charging their entire production to Todd's dad without his knowing, but Todd averred that he "could handle it."

"Besides," he added, "we already used it."

Two days later they were supervising a construction crew in the soundstage. Fleming had thrown in, as part of the deal, access to the studio's set and prop storage. This turned out to be another tottering wooden building behind the soundstage, filled with flats leaned up against walls, chairs strung overhead from unraveling ropes, and moth-eaten sofas and tables littering the floor. Todd and Nessa had discussed the sets for *Odds Are* with their art director, an enthusiastic carpenter named Gil, and Gil had agreed that the script's simple comedic story of the romantic entanglements of three queer couples would easily lend itself to the available flats.

As they pulled out flats needing less repair work than the others, they uncovered one that left them stunned. Although it was built as a flat, with 2"x4" construction and muslin covering, it was painted like something by a Dutch Master who also happened to be a pornographer. It showed, in detail, a vast orgy, raw pink flesh intertwined with brown, black, and olive, limbs and heads and genitals all rendered with chiaroscuro realism, taking place in what looked like a twentieth century mansion; there was even a door leading through the center of the writhing bodies. Gil and his crew had laughed, but Nessa stared at it, perplexed and disturbed—why had it been created? It was too explicit to be used in a mainstream movie, and too complex to be tossed off in a porn film. She knew she could probably ask Fleming, but the less she had to do with him the better.

She stared at the flat longer than she'd intended, her gaze fixing on one large figure at the center of the carnal cluster: a rotund man with red hair. He was naked, except for a pair of huge boots. Nessa was wondering if it was Redd Rossmore when the figure's visible eye winked at her.

She staggered back as if struck, then caught herself. No—the painting was still, nothing moving. It had been a trick of the light. *Isn't that what they always say in ghost movies?* Nessa thought, before turning away, trying to ignore the chill at the back of her neck.

TWO DAYS LATER the cast was brought together for on-set rehearsals. There were seven characters, and the cast had been assembled from ads in the trade papers and friends of friends.

Ariana Mills was a twenty-two-year-old blonde Midwest beauty whom Nessa had chosen for the role of Heather, a sweet-natured airhead. Although Nessa had truthfully been very impressed by her audition, she knew that, deep down, there was another reason she had hired her: Ariana was the most beautiful woman she'd ever seen in person. She was a young movie goddess in the making, and Nessa wanted to be her Pygmalion.

Todd had, in his typical way, reduced it down simply to sexual attraction on Nessa's part; after all, Todd had admitted, he'd like to get into her pants, too. But that was (*fortunately*, thought Nessa) unlikely to happen, given that Todd had a girlfriend, Carrie, who had been cast in the other female lead.

They held a final rehearsal on the sets the Sunday night before the start of shooting. One of the actors, Zach, was concerned over the "bad vibes" in the stage; he told Nessa he was sensitive and that there was more than one spirit here. "At least two, and neither of them very happy," he'd told her, before asking if he could stay after the read-through to smudge the place with sage. Nessa agreed, mainly to keep her cast happy; besides, she liked the thick smell of the burning herb.

After Zach had finished and gone, Nessa was alone on the set. In less than twelve hours this space would be filled with bustling cast and crew, working on the first day of principal photography of *Odds Are*; but now it was just her, by herself in a world she'd previously only imagined. She felt a deep satisfaction, but also an inexplicable separation; soon this world, that had been hers alone, would belong to everyone.

She suddenly had the sense that she was *not* alone. She'd been seated at a kitchenette table when she heard the creak of leather from a couch in the living room set. Hairs bristling, she rose and walked to the empty couch, where the imprint of a large and heavy body was plainly visible. Nessa tried to tell herself that someone big had sat there earlier and the leather had retained the shape—except that as she stood over it, it *moved*.

In that moment she accepted all of it. "Hello, Redd."

No response.

Because there was no one else around, and because she *knew*, knew that it was all real, that Redd Rossmore had never left this place where he'd lived and died, she felt emboldened by her new knowledge. "Look, Redd," she said, not feeling embarrassed or amused, "let's make a deal, okay? You had your time making movies here, but this is *my* film, so just leave it alone."

The temperature around her dropped. Her courage started to disappear, as if it were being siphoned off.

When she left, she almost thought she heard laughter.

THE THIRD DAY of shooting called for Ariana's nude scene. In the script, she and her ex-girlfriend had gotten together for a last fling, and Nessa wanted the shots to be sexy without feeling gratuitous. Their crew was so small that there was no need to clear the set of nonessential personnel (everyone there was essential), but Nessa still found the twenty-two-year-old novice crying in her dressing room before the scene. She spent an hour with her, talking about art and film and beauty, and at the end of the hour Ariana thanked her, strode onto the set, and dropped her robe while smiling at Nessa.

That was when she fell in love.

Later, she realized that wasn't exactly true; she'd fallen in love during the hour in the dressing room, when she'd spoken to Ariana of her talent and knew no one else ever had, when the young actress had listened carefully while Nessa told her why she loved movies and wanted to make them.

The next evening, she and Todd watched the dailies of the scene. Ariana looked, if possible, even more luscious on film, and Todd blurted out, "God, I totally want to fuck her now."

Nessa struggled to retain her composure, and suggested, "I don't think that'd be the best thing for the film."

Todd laughed and added, "I'll be the judge of that."

The morning after, Nessa ran into Fleming on the lot, and Fleming laughed in that hackle-raising way. "Redd says he's taken a liking to that nice little piece you kids got there," he sniggered at Nessa.

"What . . . I'm sorry . . ." Nessa stammered.

"The little blonde. Redd says he could make her a star." Then Fleming chuckled in an especially obscene way and walked off.

Nessa made a mental note to keep an eye on Ariana, especially if Fleming was around.

TWO NIGHTS LATER, filming wrapped at 10:30. The weary crew had left, and Nessa was in the office going over her shot list for the following day when she glanced out and noticed Ariana's car still in the lot. Concerned, she left the office and walked across to the stage. The night was warm, with a Santa Ana wind blowing desert dust.

Nessa poked her head into the stage, and when she saw the lights were off she was about to leave, until she heard it: The unmistakable sounds of moaning, of bedsprings . . . of sex.

She knew she should leave, but her feet seemed to carry her forward instead of back. She made her way carefully past light stands, apple boxes, and odd pieces of furniture until she saw a tiny light ahead. It was a flashlight placed on end, so that it pointed upward. It stood on a table next to a bed, a bed that formed the centerpiece of airhead Heather's bedroom. In the bed were Heather—or Ariana—and Todd.

Nessa's stomach clenched, her head swam. She clamped her jaws tight and stumbled back. When she did, she heard Ariana's breathy voice: "I think someone else is in here. We should stop."

Todd: "We're alone, baby. Don't stop. C'mon I'm gonna make you a *star*."

Ariana giggled.

Nessa stumbled to another part of the set, crumpling against a wall that shimmied behind her. Eventually she heard Ariana and Todd leave, and some impulse directed her to her feet, to the bed the others had left. Nessa buried herself in a pillow, inhaling the sweet scent of Ariana's hair. After a while she fell asleep there, but soon awakened from a dream in which Redd Rossmore, oversized boots clacking, had walked up, handed her a gun and uttered the phrase, "Go on, go crazy—you know you want to."

When she sat up, there were tiny pieces of rotted wood and dust on her face; she ran hands through her hair, shivering when she felt something moving. She shook her head wildly, until a large and many-jointed thing fell to the ground and skittered off into the murk. Nessa looked up and saw that part of the catwalk overhead had fallen apart during the night, and she knew that the corruption would spread very quickly now.

WHEN NESSA APPEARED for work on Monday morning, she found Todd already there, snorting a line of cocaine off his desk. "When did you start doing drugs?" Nessa asked.

Todd sniffed and grinned. "Since we became official citizens of Hollywood. Join me?" Nessa declined and returned to the set.

That afternoon they found the corpse.

Nessa had sent Gil to the set storage to find a better chair for one of the sets. Gil returned five minutes later, breathless and plainly scared.

"I think there's somebody dead back there," he shouted.

Todd and Nessa immediately went out with Gil, followed by the curious crew. The door to the storage building was still open; inside, the smell hit them before they saw the body. The interior was gloomy, and Nessa asked Gil to raise the loading doors. All she could see for now was a dark bulk nestled into a corner—and then there was that overpowering stench, of rotting meat, unwashed flesh, sickness. Death.

Gil rolled up the big loading door, and as light fell on the human shape Nessa felt a new horror penetrate her numbness. "I know this guy," she told the others.

Todd was gagging. The thing before them looked to have been dead for months, although that was impossible—they'd been in the scene storage just days ago. It was male, already oozing liquid decay and surrounded by buzzing gnats. "You know him?" Todd gasped.

"I saw him outside the fence one day." Nessa knew he was the homeless man she'd seen that first time ... except he'd been alive then.

"What happened to him?" Ariana asked. Nessa noted coolly that she wasn't crying; somehow she thought she would have, a week ago.

"He was homeless. Probably crawled in here for shelter and then just died," Todd commented. He gently nudged Nessa. "I've gotta go get Fleming."

Nessa nodded and Todd left, taking most of the crew with him. Nessa bent down to look closer, saw that the man's eyes (now milky and sunken) had been open when he'd died. Nessa knew what he was looking at.

She made sure the flat painted with the orgy scene was covered before she left.

DURING THE COURSE of that week, one actor passed out on the set and required hospitalization; they lost a half day's shooting when the main camera they'd acquired stopped working; a flat collapsed when its rotten timbers finally gave way; and Gil was sent to the emergency ward, where twenty-two stitches were required to repair the head gash he'd gotten when a rope in the set storage building had split and dropped a large framed mirror on him. Gil gave them his hospital bill to pay and informed them he wouldn't be back. "Zach's right," he said, "there *is* something wrong with this place."

Todd's father, meanwhile, had received the first credit card bill, and Todd took a day off to meet with him, confident that thirty minutes of rough-cut footage would convince Dad to continue their financing. It didn't. Todd returned from the meeting and delivered the unwelcome news that, although their bills were covered through shooting, they'd have to come up with some other means of financing the post-production. To console himself, Todd snorted three more lines of coke.

Nessa knew the film was rotten within, too. She'd labored for months on the script; she'd crafted witticisms and plot twists and climaxes that she'd believed were truly new; but now, when the words were actually being spoken and the twists being spun, she saw them for the clumsy constructions they really were. Every night she watched the footage from the previous day, and she saw *Odds Are* as nothing but a feeble, clichéd attempt. Todd, high on coke and his most recent sexual escapade with either Ariana or Carrie, applauded and whooped and declared it the best new film since *Paranormal Activity*.

That was when Nessa knew what she had to do: rewrite.

She stayed up all night, working. In the morning she handed Todd the new pages—because Todd would be an actor in the movie now. *Odds Are* would no longer be a romantic comedy; now it was a tense drama with film noir overtones.

Nessa found new energy in the film's revised direction. She drove the actors with sudden ferocity, and both the pace and passion of the shooting increased. She saved Todd's scenes until the last day. Then, after she called "Cut" for the last time, after champagne was passed around with tearful hugs and phone numbers, Nessa told Todd she had a final scene she wanted to shoot. By this time Todd was so drunk and high that he just giggled as Nessa led him to the set, and started rolling.

It was a suicide scene. Nessa gave Todd a prop pistol, and then stepped behind the camera to frame the shot.

"Who's gonna run the sound?" Todd asked, slurring badly.

"No one," answered Nessa. "We'll add it later in post. We're alone right now."

"No, we're not," Todd said, squinting at something past Nessa's shoulder.

"You're right, we're not." Nessa adjusted a light, then returned to the camera, leaning over the viewfinder.

"So whatta I do now, Nessa?" Todd asked.

"Nessa's not here."

Todd snorted. "Neither is Todd, I guess. So what do we do, whoever we are?" Somewhere in the distance, another piece of timber could be heard collapsing.

"It's the movie's climax. The tragic suicide."

"I don't feel very fuckin' tragic right now."

"It's okay," the voice cajoled from the other side of the camera, "you don't have to be tragic. Suicide isn't always tragic. Sometimes it can be pretty comic."

"Yeah, right—like throwin' a pie. Whatta I do?"

"The gun's empty, so just put it to your head and pull the trigger. We'll add the 'bang' later."

Todd laughed again. "I'll add it now—*BANG!*"

"C'mon, we're burning film here."

Todd tried to compose himself. "Right. Serious now. Okay?"

"Good. *Annnnd*—action!"

He pulled the trigger.

TODD'S DEATH WAS ruled a suicide, with complications involving alcohol and cocaine, to say nothing of his serious financial trouble. Nessa gave a properly-tearful speech at the funeral, and vowed to finish the film in Todd's memory. She managed to crowdsource the movie's remaining costs.

Nessa did finish *Odds Are*, and it even won minor prizes at two film festivals, where it was acclaimed for its "daring segue from comedy to tragedy." It never found a distributor, though, and even Todd's father never saw it. Only one person who did—Ariana Mills—ever questioned the suicide scene, but she never voiced her question to Nessa. In fact, after the screening of the film, she returned to her small midwestern town and never saw either Nessa or Hollywood again.

Nessa tried to make a second film, but crowdsourcing failed this time. Not long after, she developed her own drug problem; her housemate Steve found her dead one day of an overdose. Near her hand was a slightly-crumpled old headshot of Ariana Mills.

HFP Studios enjoyed a brief renaissance after *Odds Are*, since news of Todd's suicide invited some media attention. Fleming gave more tours to young filmmakers, speculating that now Todd's ghost walked with that of Redd Rossmore... among others. A few of the filmmakers believed Fleming when he told them the facility was safe and sound, and they rented it; most didn't.

What he didn't tell them was what he'd seen that last night, secretly spying on the production of *Odds Are*—the dialogue followed by the gunshot. No, he didn't give that away, because he treasured that moment, as a vital and darkly gleaming secret from the Gulch in the black heart of Hollywood.

Did You Know?

Lisa Morton is a screenwriter, author of non-fiction books, and prose writer whose work was described by the American Library Association's *Readers' Advisory Guide to Horror* as "consistently dark, unsettling, and frightening." She is a six-time winner of the Bram Stoker Award®, the author of four novels and over 150 short stories, and a world-class Halloween expert. Her recent releases include *Weird Women: Classic Supernatural Fiction from Groundbreaking Female Writers 1852-1923* (co-edited with Leslie S. Klinger) and *Calling the Spirits: A History of Seances*; forthcoming in 2021 is the collection *Night Terrors and Other Stories*. See more at www.lisamorton.com.

VANPORT SPEEDWAY

BY CODY GOODFELLOW

WE heard engines and squealing tires roaring over Vanport. The speedway shut down, no underground action for weeks, and the cops tied up downtown. Me and Tug jumped in my Mustang.

We cruised Columbia, Fessenden, the wetlands. It got louder but no closer, howling on the straightaways, shrieking on the turns. Tug saw lights on Marine, and we floored it.

The crossing at Vanport, OR

Up through the gears, a mile to the finish line at the train crossing. Top speed, but they passed us like we were parked. Tug opened the nitrous. The headlights fell away. In the rearview, vintage Chevy hot rods with flame paint-jobs, exposed four-banger engines and nobody behind the wheels.

Tug screamed, "Train!"
We beat them all.
We still lost.

CODY GOODFELLOW has written nine novels and five collections, and eaten many Pringles. He lives in Portland, and likes it a lot.

* FILE UNDER: *Haunted Speedway*

"Look inside the car. That blood on
the seat covers, that belongs to you."

DEAD CAR

FEATURE ENTRY 23

STRUCTURE TYPE: JUNKYARD
LOCATION: GLADEWATER (TEXAS), USA
LAT./ LONG: 32.5520° N, 94.9334° W
BUILT: CIRCA 1963
GROUND ELEVATION: 380 FT. (116 M.)
WRITTEN BY: JOE R. LANSDALE

TRAVEL GUIDE NOTES

T HERE IS LITTLE that "Champion Mojo Storyteller" Joe R. Lansdale hasn't done. Besides being an Award-winning, Bestselling, Genre-pushing author, Joe has some of the most diehard followers in author fandom, myself (and co-editor Eric J. Guignard) included. Joe writes horror, he writes crime, he writes pulp, and he writes literary beauty. His stories are being increasingly made into film (*Bubba Ho-Tep*; *Cold in July*; *Hap and Leonard* series, etc.). He's a speaker, a teacher, and, besides writing, he's founder of the Shen Chuan martial arts system, and inductee into the U.S. as well as International Martial Arts Halls of Fame. He's one of the three founders (along with wife Karen and author Robert McCammon) of the instrumental Horror Writers Association. And he's just a nice guy.

Forgive the gushing. It's always a thrill to be able to work with Joe, and this time around was no exception. Although Joe is often known more for his outrageous, action-packed works, I personally prefer his "quieter" writing, which always strikes me as the most natural of human elements placed in scenarios that are just slightly off-kilter. Which is what follows in a simple conversation around a "Dead Car."

—Charlatan Bardot

THE CHEVROLET SAT IN THE JUNKYARD. IT WAS A wad of blue metal with silver scrapes, and the windshield was gone and the side windows were webbed with safety glass cracks. The steering wheel had been bent on both sides. There was still blood on the seats. The sun was going down so the blood looked like dark drops of a soul dripped loose from its hosts.

Bill and Janey arrived. Bill touched the car, bent down and looked inside.

"What a mess," Janey said.

"Yeah."

"Way it hit that tree, there was no chance."

"None at all," Bill said. "You and I were lucky."

"We have to convince them for sure, tonight."

"I know. We've been careful, but now, we need to be a bit more forceful."

"Stay kind," she said. "It has to be hard."

"Of course," he said. "It should be about time."

Janey checked her watch, then turned her head to see the other couple had arrived at the trunk of the car and were standing there.

Jim was tall and handsome, wearing his cocky smile like an ornament. Claire was as pretty as the feel of nostalgia. Her hair was silver as the moon.

"Man, that looks bad," Jim said.

"It is," Janey said.

"What was it, last night it happened? I've been a bit confused since the wreck. It's like things aren't quite yet in focus."

"It's been four days," Janey said.

"Go out for a ride, something goes that wrong. I never considered such. All that booze we had. Stupid of us."

"We were fools," Claire said. "We could have all been killed."

"That's right," Janey said.

"But we weren't," Claire said.

"I was driving," Bill said. "It was my fault."

"What ends well, ends well," Jim said. "We all learned a lesson."

"What happened to you guys after the wreck?" Bill said.

"What do you mean?" Claire said.

"After the wreck. Where did you go?"

"Home," Jim said. "We went home."

"You went off in an ambulance," Janey said. "Same as us."

"Yeah," Jim said.

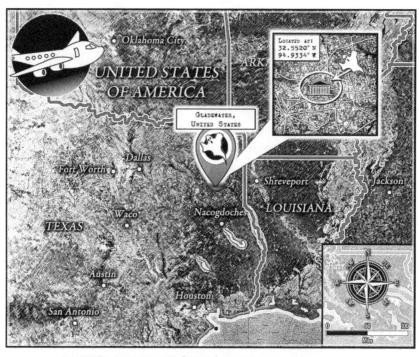

HAUNTED GLADEWATER (TEXAS), UNITED STATES OF AMERICA

"And then what?"

"Went home," Jim said.

"What did you do when you got home?" Bill asked.

"Well . . ." Jim paused. "That's funny. I don't remember exactly. I think I had a mild concussion. Still do, I guess. Can't quite put it all together."

"Think a moment. What did you do when you woke up?" Bill said.

"I guess I just got up."

"But you don't remember exactly?" Janey said.

"Must have hit my head harder than I thought."

"Must have," Janey said. "Claire, what did you do after the wreck?"

"I don't remember either."

"There's a reason," Bill said. "I want you to really listen to us this time. Neither of you made it."

"Made what?"

Neither Bill or Janey responded. They let their comment float about.

"What do you mean?" Jim said. "Made what? You're making me nervous. Made what?"

"You're here, all right, but you're not here."

"Sort of double talk is that?" Jim said.

"Last place you were, when you were alive, was this car," Bill said.

"Alive?" Jim said.

"You keep coming back here, every night," Bill said. "You and Claire."

"But we're talking to you," Jim said. "We're looking right at you. Don't be daft."

"Yes, you are," Janey said. "We see you, me and Bill. Because you were with us. In the wreck. We came here next night after the wreck, saw the car out of curiosity, and you two showed up. Right on time, at nightfall. We could tell right away . . . That you weren't right."

"I don't accept that," Claire said. "That's ridiculous."

"It doesn't matter what you accept," Bill said. "You haven't let go yet. Haven't accepted it. We first saw you, we thought you were alive, and then we saw you weren't."

"I don't understand," Claire said.

"I feel plenty alive," Jim said.

"Do you?" Janey asked. "We just want you to let go, find peace. Quit coming back nightly to look at the car. We're going to quit coming to see you, so, it'll just be the two of you showing up here looking inside the car until you decide to let go. We want to help, but we can't keep doing this. We truly are sorry."

"Look inside the car, at the backseat," Bill said. "That blood on the seat covers, that belongs to the two of you."

Realization landed on Claire like a grand piano. "It's true. I know it now. It's true."

She held out her hands and looked at them.

"The starlight shines through them," she said. "I read somewhere we're all part of the stars."

"That's right," Bill said.

Jim felt the weight of the truth as well. He said, "What do we do?"

"Don't know exactly," Bill said. "You could climb in the car, sit there, close your eyes, and maybe it will come. Whatever it is. I think you just did the hard part. Accepted that you're not living anymore."

"I'm afraid," Claire said.

"I'm thinking it'll be easy," Janey said. "You're already dead. Past pain. My guess is you'll just slip away."

"And if we don't?" Jim said.

"I don't know," Janey said.

"I remember now," Claire said. "I never went home. I was awake in the ambulance a little, and then I wasn't. Next thing I remember, we came out here."

"Yeah," Jim said. "I remember the hospital though, and then I felt sleepy. Next thing I know, we were together, coming here."

"And you've been coming for some time," Janey said. "You come, and then before daylight you walk off and disappear."

"To where?" Claire said.

"Limbo, maybe," Janey said. "I don't know. Some place that holds you until you decide to let go."

Jim reached out and touched the car trunk. He pushed, and his hand went right through it. He pulled his hand back.

Jim walked around and looked inside the car through the back window, then he bent forward and sat down inside on the back seat by sliding right through the door. Claire followed, sat beside him. They held hands.

"She feels so solid," Jim said.

"On your plane, she is," Bill said.

"So, this is it," Jim said.

"I feel it," Claire said.

Bill and Janey watched as Jim and Claire slowly faded away like morning mist on a warming pond.

"They've accepted," Bill said. "They're gone."

"I'm glad," Janey said. "Now we can go home."

They started away from there, but when they got to the edge of the wrecking yard, near the gate, they paused.

"Strangely," Janey said. "I don't know where to go."

"Home."

"I can't seem to do that."

They stood for a long moment. The cosmos clicked. The stars seemed different.

"I can see the moonlight through you," Bill said. "I know now I always could."

Janey said, "The four of us. We all ... "

She let that hang as if on a hook.

"We thought we came here to help Jim and Claire pass over," Bill said, "but I don't remember anything but this place after the wreck. I saw the tree. Threw my hands in front of my face, and then we were here, and Jim and Claire came up."

"We found a reason to be here that made more sense than the truth. We hadn't accepted it either."

328 JOE R. LANSDALE

Bill didn't answer. Starlight and moonlight crawled through the air. Bill took her hand. They turned and went back to the car and climbed in the front seat and held hands. They looked through where the windshield had been.

"I'd been drinking," Bill said.

"We all had."

"I swerved for a shadow in the road. Something that wasn't really there. And there was the tree."

"It doesn't matter anymore."

They sat in silence, then the cosmos clicked again. They slowly faded, leaving silver moonlight lying on the seat.

The car motor hummed soft and distant. The car remained, but a misty shape that looked like the car started to move away from it, out across the wrecking yard, passing through the tin fence that surrounded the yard, down the hill and onto the highway, gliding like a bird on an air current.

Back in the junkyard, some of the cars hummed and shimmered, waiting for the return of those who had died in them, those who still wandered. The rest of the cars were just cars and had not housed the dead or dying. The light of the moon and the stars lay flat against them.

The spectral Chevy that carried Bill and Janey, Jim and Claire, rolled along. Then it became thin and pale. Finally, it was an outline, and in short time, a shadow of a shadow.

And then it was gone.

DID YOU KNOW?

JOE R. LANSDALE is the author of over four hundred short pieces, fifty novels, screenplays, TV scripts, and comic scripts. He has received numerous awards for his writing, and his work has been filmed for TV and film. He is a member of the United States Martial Arts Hall of Fame.

GREENBELT BUS SHELTER

BY LISA L. HANNETT

ABOUT two clicks up Moodie Drive out of Bells Corners, past the Hunt Club intersection but before Jack Pine trail, there's a tiny open-front hut sagging by the roadside. Forty-odd winters have stripped the pitched roof of its shingles, but the split-log sides are still standing, still dovetailing at the corners, some still with knot-holes big enough to poke a mittened thumb through. Inside, a single plank is propped on hand-forged nails, the bench barely wide enough for two people.

No bus has stopped there in decades. Traffic is steady enough, but the 416 carries much of it elsewhere these days. Mostly it's family wagons and long-haul trucks whizzing way too fast along this long straight stretch of old highway, though the pavement's always slick with ice in winter, always treacherous with potholes in summer, always at the mercy of the surrounding Greenbelt and the wild-eyed deer bounding dangerously out of it. This forest is a real drawcard for locals and tourists alike; a government-sanctioned conservation park in the heart of our nation's capital. A trail-trekker's paradise.

A place best approached warily, and on foot.

Every so often, weary hikers pause at the bus shelter to adjust their backpacks or reapply moleskins on their blistered heels. They plunk their bags down on the bench beside the child in her gingham dress and little white boots. No matter the season, her plump legs are always bare, always happily kicking. No wind ever ruffles her.

What are you doing here, sweetie? (They all ask the same thing, these city-born hikers, or variations thereof.) *Where's your mother?*

Find Mamma, the girl replies and hops down from the seat. *Hold my hand.*

And as she reaches up, it's impossible to resist: she's so small, so alone, so vulnerable. Yet her pudgy grip is cold and firm as eternity. It's impossible to let go as she runs for the highway, dragging with a toddler's unholy strength; impossible to yank free as she runs, calling *Mamma! Mamma!* while tires screech across ice or pot-holed asphalt, the cars on that deadly stretch of road forever going too fast.

Be leary talking to strangers here, even small children

LISA L. HANNETT has had over 75 short stories published in venues including *Clarkesworld*, *Apex*, *Weird Tales*, and *The Dark*, and her first collection, *Bluegrass Symphony*, was nominated for a World Fantasy Award. You can find her online at www.lisahannett.com and Instagram @lisalhannett.

---

* FILE UNDER: *Haunted Bus Shelter*

FASTEN YOUR

SAFETY BELTS...

NEXT STOP:

LATIN AMERICA

AND CARIBBEAN

HAUNTED LATIN AMERICA AND CARIBBEAN

Mexico

Havana, Cuba

Chiquibul Forest Reserve, Belize

Port Royal, Jamaica

San Juan, Puerto Rico

Lopinot, Trinidad and Tobago

Corrientes, Argentina

São Paulo, Brazil

Blumenau, Brazil

Colonia del Sacramento, Uruguay

0   100 200 300 400 500
Miles

LATIN AMERICA AND CARIBBEAN

"Did you mean to make him that big, cariño?"

THE HAUNTING OF THE PLAZA DE LA BENEFICENCIA PINKBERRY

FEATURE ENTRY 24

STRUCTURE TYPE: FROZEN YOGURT RESTAURANT
LOCATION: SAN JUAN, PUERTO RICO
LAT./ LONG: 18.4672° N, 66.1195° W
BUILT: CIRCA 2011
GROUND ELEVATION: 118 FT. (36 M.)
WRITTEN BY: GABRIELA SANTIAGO

TRAVEL GUIDE NOTES

T HIS FOLLOWING SELECTION is amazing. It's socially conscious, relevant, funny, weird, breathtaking in its beauty and depth, and bilingual, while also building upon Shirley Jackson's literary triumph, *We Have Always Lived in the Castle.* I'd be hard-pressed to point to another story in the speculative genre that packs so much humanism and emotional layers into only 6,400 words.

Author Gabriela Santiago is talented in numerous creative endeavors (see her bio, at story's end), not least of which, certainly, is penning dark tales of uncommon acumen in leading horror and fantasy publications.

ADVISORY: Be careful of the homelands you travel and of the baggage you may bring, and consider your privilege, culture, and pride, or it may be time to face your own ghosts, a curious self-reckoning akin to "The Haunting of the Plaza de la Beneficencia Pinkberry."

—Charlatan Bardot

T HE COLOR OF OLD SAN JUAN WAS BLUE: THE ROBIN'S egg blue of the sky and the brightly painted walls, the darker blue of the sea just out of sight, and the scuffed blue of the brick streets, jewels worn down to dullness.

And I was looking at all of it from inside a Pinkberry.

I had resisted. I'd spent the first couple of hours after the taxi dropped me off in Plaza de la Beneficencia wheeling my suitcase through the adjoining streets. I'd looked in shop windows, tried to pet stray dogs. I had made my way back and bought a piragua. I'd found a spot on the steps that didn't absolutely kill my spine, across from the weird statue of the guy with a bunch of kids on his arms, and struggled through five pages of my Spanish translation of *We Have Always Lived in the Castle*.

I admitted defeat at 11:21 a.m.

And so there I was in the Pinkberry, trying to find out how slowly I could eat a salted caramel frozen yogurt.

I should have been able to eat it more slowly; besides the piragua, I had compulsively consumed all the cookies my mother had packed for me, and three of the very fancy chocolates from the box of Abdallah Candies I'd gotten for my tía as a last minute thank-you-for-picking-me-up-in-San-Juan-when-I-only-told-you-three-days-ago-I-was-planning-to-be-in-town-to-put-flowers-on-my-abuela's-grave gift.

But I had walked into a Pinkberry with a very pretty girl behind the counter.

She had wide cheekbones and skin two shades darker than mine and cute bangs and wore red capris made out of the same material as a shirt I'd bought last time I came to Puerto Rico, which I wore once and never again because it didn't make me feel the way I had wanted it to make me feel because it had been a crop top and I'd gained ten pounds and I didn't know how to be the kind of person who didn't care about those two things together.

The nametag just below the orange collar of the girl's uniform shirt, which I had tried not to notice was much tighter than any uniform shirt I'd previously seen on a Pinkberry employee, read HELLO MY NAME IS ATABEIRA.

And then she had spoken to me in Spanish, and before I had gotten three words out, she switched to English, and her English was as perfect as my Spanish would not have been, and I had chosen a flavor I didn't like and that I now couldn't stop eating because eating was something I could do with my hands and my mouth that didn't immediately mark me as out of place, which I shouldn't have been, but I was.

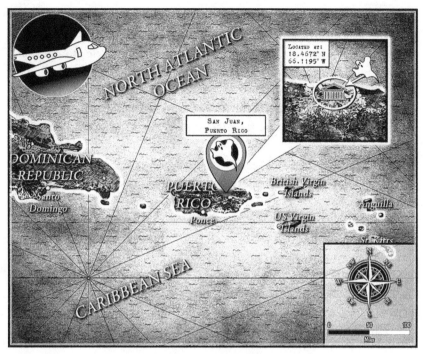

SAN JUAN, PUERTO RICO

The entire Pinkberry smelled like sugar. I was the only customer, which made my every movement feel like it was happening center stage.

"So, you visiting San Juan?" HELLO MY NAME IS ATABEIRA asked.

I blushed, even though the suitcase would have made it obvious even if my hesitation before ordering had not. "Yeah. Well, sort of. For a day. Then visiting family out in Ponce."

I couldn't think of anything else to say, so I looked down at my yogurt, and then I thought maybe that was rude, so I looked up again. She had a beautiful smile.

"Doing anything fun?"

"The art museum, probably," I said like a complete dork. "Maybe go hiking? Visiting family," I repeated, needing to say something to establish my bona fides. "I had a free week—" and I hadn't wanted to go home—"and it had been a while"—and I felt guilty watching random Lin-Manuel Miranda clips on YouTube, like this guy could take time out of his schedule and I couldn't?—"and my dad said he would pay for it if I put some flowers on my abuela's grave . . ."

"Ah." Atabeira didn't stop smiling, but she pressed her lips together and nodded seriously. "Maria?"

"Wha . . . ? Oh. No." It had taken weeks before we had heard from our family during Hurricane Maria, but they'd been fine. Firmly middle-class enough that it seemed to have erected a transparent bubble around them, only minor damage to the roof and the gate, though I would be seeing for myself for the first time on this trip. "Cancer. A long time ago. There was some trouble with the drugs, I think, the hospital getting them, I mean . . . "

"*Pairdon*," a voice came from behind me, and I almost knocked my yogurt off the table.

I had thought the Pinkberry was empty when I'd entered, but a man stood there, holding a phone. He had a sunburnt nose and a little forked brown beard.

"Oh, this guy," Atabeira said.

This was weird. It was weird both from a customer service perspective and from the perspective of me, a person from the Puerto Rican diaspora, who had never returned from a trip to the island without two dozen hugs and at least three gifts, and had presumed a certain level of near-pathological generosity and overall welcomingness to be the norm.

"*Pair-don!*" the man boomed again. "Estoy—looking for—" He waved his phone up and down.

"It's okay," I said. "We speak English."

"He's more trouble than he's worth," Atabeira said. "He'll be gone in a minute, if we don't engage."

I could feel my forehead creasing as I looked over at her. I glanced back at the man, who—

Was gone.

"So yeah, that's the ghost," she said.

I was pretty sure she was making fun of me. "The ghost."

"You didn't know you brought him with you?" she asked. "That's okay, a lot of people don't. He looks a little different each time, but after a while you start to recognize him."

Definitely making fun of me. "Right," I said, looking down at my hands. "Well. I have work. For school. So. I should. Well."

She gave me another brilliant smile then, wide enough that I thought maybe I had misjudged her. "Let me know if you need anything."

I picked up my copy of *We Have Always Lived in the Castle*, turning the cover ostentatiously so that if HELLO MY NAME IS ATABEIRA wanted to look up from where she was scrubbing the counter, she could see that the front read *Siempre Hemos Vivido en el Castillo*. I turned to where I'd left off:

"Nunca toco las bayas," Costance dijo; *ella miró directamente a Señora Wright y dijo seriamente, "Rara vez tomo azúcar en algo. Aún ahora."*

Oh, right, this was the part where Constance didn't take sugar, and it was super sketch. Something-something the trial—

"Qué ella no usó el azúcar, yo quiero decir. Pero fue estrictamente una cuestión de principio—mira, yo admiro el principio mucho. Fui capaz de ilustrar, por mi colección extensa de artículos de los periódicos en el subjeto mismo—

A long history of—was that word 'slavery?' It looked like 'slavery'— something-something islands of the Caribbean—

—simplemente para que podemos disfrutar una pizca de dulzura sobre lo que es ya dulce."

Something-something scandal—

"¿Qué relación tenemos con las islas? ¿Qué relación tiene Constance con la esclavitud? ¿Que va a pensar Lucille de ti?"

I didn't remember this passage in the original. It seemed a little wordy for Shirley Jackson. I flipped to the front to see if there was a translator's note, or at least a date of translation, but all I got was the original copyright date, 1962. The year my father was born in New York City, one year after his mother and father and older two brothers had moved from the island. There were no more jobs; the mill had closed, and those that remained had more than enough workers ...

"Esta preocupación con el pasado no es sana; la pobrecita ha sufrido suficiente."

Who was she saying had suffered ... of course, Constance. Or was it Merricat? I regretted not rereading the book in English first, but I had wanted to make a point, even if it was only to myself. I'd wanted to prove that I was not coasting through on remembered plot, not sneaking a peek at subtitles and fooling myself into fluency. But now—I wished I had brought the English edition. I wished I could look at them side by side, see the choices the translator had made, agree or argue with them . . .

"No lo ocurrió realmente?"
"Por supuesto que lo ocurrió realmente."
"Tengo los retazos de los periódicos. Tengo mis notas. He anotado todo. No borrarán todo, ¿verdad? No van a olividar—"

"Don't forget this," Atabeira said. I jumped, not expecting her so close to me. She slid a little paper rectangle across the table at me, smiling brilliantly. "I gave you a few extra stamps. Ten and you get one free."

"Thank you," I said.

She still stood there, smiling. She had such cute bangs. Was she flirting? Oh God, maybe the air conditioning had frozen her brain and she didn't realize I was too pale and too fat in an uncurvy way and deeply unsexy in cargo shorts and a shapeless *Doctor Who* T-shirt, and she was flirting with me?

"I should go," I said, standing, almost tripping on my own feet. My book fell and hit the floor with a thwap, spilling open next to her feet. "I have to go, my tía will be here soon, I shouldn't keep her waiting—"

"You didn't finish your yogurt—"

"That's fine, I wasn't really hungry—" Great, now she was going to think I was white *and* wasteful, and it shouldn't matter because I was never going to see her again, I was fleeing—I grabbed my suitcase handle. "Keep the book, I don't need—"

"Don't forget the ghost," the girl said, which was weird, but I was already stepping outside—

—and saw an impossibly tall tower that had not previously been in Plaza de la Beneficencia.

This was physically impossible. No one could build a tower like that in twenty minutes. Where was the statue with the kids on the guy's arms? This was the same door I had stepped into. There had only been one door, which, come to think of it was maybe a fire code violation so there might have been a second door in the back, but I hadn't gone out the back—

The tower was built of white stone, and for a second I thought I was in El Morro—equally impossible; El Morro was at least a ten-minute walk, but maybe I had blacked out? Could you black out from too much sugar and gay panic?—before I saw the smoke from the tower and realized it was a chimney. I followed the line of it down and saw a building that, while it loomed impressively in the same white stone with white-washed tin roofs, was inescapably not a fort or a castle or anything of that kind, but a factory.

The air smelled like burnt caramel.

There was an official-looking placard in front of me.

I looked back, and there was the cheerful pink and green sign of the Pinkberry above a Plexiglass window. Atabeira waved at me from inside.

The rest of Plaza de la Beneficencia was gone.

I read the placard.

> *Durante la epoca del año conocida como "la zafra," los campos de La Caña de las Memorias estaban llenos de caña de azúcar madura. En el calor cegador, los esclavos—*

—okay, yes, that word was definitely 'slave,' but then—something-something cutting something-something liberate, something-something before the arrival of electricity, iron wheels—

> *—La fuerza y la presión son requeridas para liberar la dulzura. No vamos a ser liberados. El mundo tiene hambre por el sabor. El mundo tiene hambre de olvidar. Bienvenidos, azucarera, bienvenidos bienvenidos—*

"Donde esta the tour guide?" came a voice next to my elbow, and I jumped.

It was the man from the Pinkberry. I knew him immediately, even though he'd gotten rid of the stupid hipster beard. He had gone all Teddy Roosevelt instead, with a thick mustache and little glasses over his nose.

"Do you know where we are?" I asked.

"Indeed I do!" He removed his hat and waved it enthusiastically over the view. "Bought this lovely little place with my special budget. The natives will howl, but look, we won the place fair and square. Going to feed the nation, we are." He winked. "And make a tidy profit too, I don't mind saying. It's all going to fall like dominoes."

He was wearing a full suit in the heat, a black tie firmly around his throat, and this more than any of the rest of whatever battershittery was going on, convinced me that Atabeira had not been teasing me, and he was actually a ghost.

There was the little tinkle of a bell as the Pinkberry door opened, and Atabeira joined us. Her mascara made bright red circles around her eyes, and there was another circle, sticky with something like cherry topping, painted on top of her uniform shirt. "I tried to tell you, you brought him with you."

"Sorry," I said. "I was distracted by—it doesn't matter what I was distracted by. But okay, yes, obviously a haunting is happening. Does he know he's a ghost? Are *you* a ghost?"

"You're funny," Atabeira said, with a smile that could have powered the entire factory if they'd put in solar. "Me, a ghost? It'd hurt my feelings if you weren't so cute."

"And why aren't you at work?" the American said, turning on Atabeira, his face going red. "We gave you admission on the understanding that you were to work, not laze around looking for handouts."

"What is going on?" I asked.

"No di testimonio en el juicio, ¿entiendes?" Atabeira said to me. "Mi salúd no fue capaz, antes or ahora, de tratar de las preguntas groseras de extraños."

"Of course we were acquitted after all," the American said. "Most certainly we were acquitted."

"Ya nadie piensa en eso," said Atabeira.

"Nobody ever thinks about it anymore."

"Yo admiro una mujer decentemente curiosa, Señora; pude ver inmediatamente que usted estaba devorada con una passion por ver la escena de la tragedia."

"Wait," I said, "what tragedy?"

"That's what I say!" the American interjected. "No tragedy at all, but an opportunity! You know, the Chinese word for crisis—"

Atabeira rolled her eyes. "He doesn't like to talk about it." Her gaze softened. "You don't like to talk about it either, do you?" She touched my temple; her fingers burning. "So many funny things in your head! So many ways to say it and not to say it. We tried to choose something recent, something you would understand."

Her eyes were smiling, like I had said something funny, and they were sad, like she knew something she was going to have to tell me. I didn't want to look at her eyes anymore.

I looked back at the factory and saw its outline waver for a moment, become that of a castle on a hill.

I could feel the panic, delayed like its flight had been canceled, finally arrive, building up in the back of my throat and clamoring to be let out.

"Why me?" I asked. "Why is this happening to me? You said I brought him—but there can't be a connection—my family is from Ponce, I think they worked at a sugar mill but it would have been there—"

What had they done at the sugar mill? Workers, I'd thought—but in the stories, had anybody actually said?—they'd immigrated after the plant had been forced to close down, the strike—

If they had been workers, would there have been enough money, a generation later, to buy my tía's house? She was a medical technologist; how much did medical technologists make? Enough for a two-story house on a hill, air conditioning and a kitchen bigger than my apartment, bright pink paint and an expansive courtyard, lush vines over one side of the terrace and the other looking down a hill of equally big houses, not a tin roof in sight—

I didn't want to think about it.

Atabeira's fingers closed gently over mine. "We have always lived in the castle."

The tourist snorted indignantly. "*We* have always lived in the castle!"

Atabeira snarled, baring her teeth. "Nobody thinks about it anymore! The tragedy!"

"We were acquitted!" The tourist thumped his chest. "Most certainly, we were acquitted!"

I broke away from both of them, my suitcase thumping awkwardly over the rocky ground. I ran toward the tower, because it was the only landmark and because it was away from them, maybe if I just ran away from them—

"View the scene of the tragedy!" the tourist bellowed, and when I cast a look behind my shoulder I could see him growing in size, eight feet tall now, no, ten, no—

My foot caught on the wheel of my suitcase, and I shot out my hands to break my fall. They hit the hard brick of the tower and kept going, the stone exploding into fine dust that coated my skin, sticky and sweet as I coughed it out of my lungs—I threw up a hand to protect my eyes, my ears ringing with the blast—

The roar softened, became the shrill whine of fluorescent lights.

I rubbed the dust from my eyes, and looked up to see myself in a mirror that reflected back the gleaming stalls of the Pinkberry bathroom, and my abuela.

She was black-and-white like the only picture we had of her, the one that ended up on every school project family tree that me and my cousins ever made. But she was real, down to the wrinkles in her face and the oxygen canister clanking next to her ankle.

"And which one are you?" she asked. Her voice was quavery and thickly accented, like she needed to pluck up each of the English words with her thin and trembling fingers and set them into place. "Who has she woken me up for now?"

"I was supposed to bring you flowers," I said stupidly.

She looked around the bathroom, concern creasing her forehead. "Did you lose them? Well, that's all right, cariño. You've been having a busy trip. And that plane, ay dios mio, I don't know how you get on those things! We took a boat in my day." She touched my arm, her skin soft and papery. "Ay, I remember you now. Rafe's youngest. You liked to look at my saints and hear their stories."

I remembered her room, so dark when the sun dipped below the horizon, a house meant to deflect light and heat. The great dark wardrobe, looming in shadow, with tiny paintings of men and women torn and stabbed, set neatly in gilt frames glinting through the glass. Beautiful and terrible and tantalizing all at once.

I had gone there when the glare of the sun and the shriek of my cousins playing had become too much, and there had been Abuela's voice—English? Spanish? It hadn't mattered; I had understood.

"You're dead," I said.

She broke into a deep laugh that hit me like an electric shock—I knew that laugh in my bones. Deep and warm and carrying with it the smell of arroz con guisantes and tostones, of water dripping off great green leaves into the dirt.

She had been dead a month after my last visit to Puerto Rico. On my last visit, when I was too young to know how bad my Spanish was, and no one at school had called me a coconut yet, and my baby fat was still considered cute.

Back when going to the island still felt like a homecoming, and the idea of home was still uncomplicated.

"I'm sorry I wasn't at the funeral," I said.

"Ay dios mio, I wasn't there either!" That laugh again, still strong despite the wheeze. "You had your education. You know we were always so proud of all of you and your education."

I wanted to hug her, but something held me back. Something always held me back—from reaching out, from speaking. I always felt like there was a glass pane between me and everything I should be able to do.

There was a thud, and the entire bathroom rattled.

I clutched at the edge of the sink.

"What's going on?" It came out as yelp.

A shadow settled over her face. "Ah, cariño, I wish I could explain."

The room shook again, the stall doors creaking on their hinges. I staggered, and her arm caught mine. Her fingers were just as I remembered them, thin but strong. "Why can't you?"

"You know I never was so good at English." Her mouth pursed, so rueful. "And the words keep changing! Ay dios mio, you like the tricky books, don't you?" She stroked my arm gently. "Siempre hemos vivido en el castillo." Her tongue skipped lightly over the S in 'castillo.' "But some things change as they are passed down. Or maybe some things, we just see the different sides of them. We wanted only good things for you. But we are"— a shrug—"who we are."

The room shook even more violently than the last time, dust falling from creaking supports where the wall met the ceiling.

"We have to get out," I said.

Abuela laughed. "Out?"

I tugged at the door; it stuck for a second in its crumpled frame and then pulled open—

The tourist's hand filled the Pinkberry.

I knew it was his instantly, the light hairs ruffled in the wind of the air conditioning, an immense hairy fist knocking against the counter, knuckles squeezing the frozen yogurt until it spilled over the floor, the air itself sticky with the scent of sugar. The fingers scrabbled at the doorway, cinderblocks ripping out as they caught on his nails; I sprawled back and tripped again— Abuela's hands caught me, not nearly as frail as they looked.

She regarded the hand with mild interest. "Did you mean to make him that big, cariño?"

"Did we do something?" The words were spilling out of my mouth now, high-pitched, uncontrollable. "Our family, did we do something, what did we do—"

"Was there anything we didn't do?" Abuela neatly side-stepped the grasping fingers, pulling her oxygen canister along with her. She squatted on the floor next to me, her eyes shining. "So proud! Your father with his big job in the government and his cousins in the hospitals. Our name on the wall in the art museum—we donated that painting, you know that big one, the lady in orange? That was us. We've always been something in this town."

Her words seemed to arrive in my brain on a delay, like messages relayed from a distant star. My heart hammered in my chest as the fingers in the doorway swelled even larger, a single tobacco-stained fingernail now scrabbling at the brilliant white tile. "I made him big? You said I made him big. And the girl said I brought him—is he one of our ancestors? Is Atabeira? Why is this happening, did our family do something, did I—"

Abuela cupped my face. Behind her, the giant's fingernail gouged a furrow in the floor a foot deep.

"Not one person. Not even one family. The island." The finger withdrew, and the roof shook, something gleaming like bone shearing through the ceiling—"The island and the mouth around it, always biting down."

The tooth took out a string of fluorescent lights, and I screamed.

"Ssh." Abuela gestured toward the mirror. "Ve la escena de la tragedia."

I staggered to my feet.

For the moment, I only saw myself, sweating and wild-haired, my hand still gripping the handle of my suitcase like a lifeline my brain hadn't told it yet meant nothing. No one behind me, as if Abuela were a hallucination. Was I going crazy? Was I—

Atabeira smiled over my shoulder. "Por supuesto que lo ocurrió realmente."

I jerked my head around; neither she nor my abuela were there.

I whirled back to the mirror. They were still gone; I was still there. I was—

I was changing.

Deep brown stole across my arms like a spill of caramel sauce; my summer tan faded away from my face like I was turning to snow. No, not snow, but still granular—sugar, my entire body was becoming sugar, and I opened my mouth to scream but my lips crumbled and my nose crumbled and my fingers disintegrated around my suitcase handle—

The monstrosity in the mirror grinned, and reached out to pull me through just as the giant teeth bit down where I had been.

LA ESCENA DE LA TRAGEDIA

Antes de la construcción de la fábrica, este lugar fue hogar a algunos centrales diferentes. Operado por los esclavos, muchos Africanos fueron importado despues de los Tainos se—

Died.

The words swam before my eyes. There was something about the difficulty of work, the skill required, how highly valued was the—what was that word—

—*azucarero*—

Something about fire—

    ¿Por qué estás buscando solo una tragedia, azucarera? ¿Por qué estás buscando solo un momento? ¿Por qué quieres una sola historia, solamente un comienzo, un medio, un final? ¿Es el fin qué más anhelas? Pero no hay un fin, azucarera, y no hay una sola historia, solo esta la historia en qué tú estás dentro ahora y todas las historias qué están dentro de esa historia qué han sido olvidadas pero aun gritan—

I lost my place in the words as soon as I saw my hands were framing each side of the placard. *My hands.* Shaking but solid flesh, no longer sugar. My hands, light brown, on the plaque. Which meant I was—

I looked up, and saw the castle.

The sugar mill. Of course, yes. It was a sugar mill. Not a castle.

The tourist towered over it. He was in modern clothes again, I noted dimly with the part of my brain not going *giant giant giant holy fucking shit he's a fucking giant.* He rested one hand on the high chimney, and I heard the squealing protest of stones.

At the base of the factory, Atabeira leaned against a wall. The wall she leaned against looked pockmarked, run-down, but I was distracted from looking too closely by Atabeira, who seemed to have—not flattened, but simplified, as if instead of flesh and blood she were made of solid implacable lines, spare but radiating energy.

"You break it, you bought it," she said with a grin.

"What?" I croaked.

"Sorry," she said. "Customer service humor."

The ground shook, the giant's feet sinking into it as he inhaled the burning sweet scent of the smoke.

"Please tell me what to do," I begged Atabeira. "I don't know who you are or what is going on, but please just tell me, and I'll do it."

"Why do you assume you need me to tell you?" She asked. She was still smiling; she'd never stopped smiling since I met her. Every one of her smiles was a riddle, even this one, which was only two ovals in the air, slightly larger than her eyes. The line-mouth and line-eyes went wide and delighted. "You brought him with you, remember?"

"You keep saying that!" I tried not to scream. I could feel the hysteria wrapping like a strangling vine around my throat. "You keep saying that, and I don't know what it means—"

"Don't you?" she asked. "¿Siempre has vivido en el castillo?"

The chimney became my tía's house. The chimney became my father's house. The chimney rose and fell and became my abuela's house, and the chimney again.

Around it the land rose and fell, and with it people, some with my nose and some with my eyes, some of them black and some brown and some white, some nothing like me at all, men and women and—

Their voices swelled like a tidal wave, so many voices that I could not have deciphered the words of any one person even if I could have been certain I spoke all their languages, and above them, the voice of the giant, booming—

"*We were acquitted! Most certainly we were acquitted!*"

A sob rose in my throat. I couldn't do this—I didn't even know what 'this' was—I had come to lay flowers on my abuela's grave, and I hadn't even been prepared for that, hadn't been prepared for a pretty girl in a Pinkberry, hadn't been in any way prepared for anything my whole life and now I was in the middle of a maelstrom of magic shit, like I'd stumbled into a churchyard and picked up Excalibur without ever taking a single fencing lesson.

Through the blur of my vision I saw the giant stop, start, and look down. He had seen us. Me.

"*It counted strongly against her at the trial!*" he roared, and reached for me.

I watched his hand descend. *Run run run,* screamed my brain, but I knew that if I ran, my legs would only crumble again.

I had never been enough.

"You brought him with you," Atabeira said, pointedly this time, like she was trying to give me a hint on a test.

The fingers closed around me, crushing the air from my chest. The wind whooshed as I hammered at his palm with my fists.

"What are you trying to do?" asked Atabeira. She was a tattoo on the back of the giant's hand now.

"Fight—him—" I wheezed. "Destroy—him—isn't that . . . what you want . . . what I'm—supposed—"

"Destroy him?" Atabeira asked. "Whatever gave you the impression that you were supposed to do that? That you *could* do that?"

"Wha—"

And then he swallowed me.

I HIT STOMACH acid with a splash that sent rancid liquid shooting out to splatter against the walls of the stomach, dripping back down into my hair. I spit and spit, the sour-sweet taste coating my mouth, and flailed until my arms hit a slippery, sandy slope—sugar, or earth like sugar, mixed with rocks and leaves that looked like they had been through a hurricane. I clambered on top of it and spat some more. Bits of litter, paper cups and bowls, were scattered there too; a jagged plastic spoon dug into my hands as I braced myself against the shore.

Atabeira sat cross-legged next to me, human once more. Her Pinkberry uniform was spotless.

"So I'm *not* supposed to destroy him?" I asked.

"Did anyone ever say you were supposed to?" Atabeira asked, curious. "How would you even do that? He's huge now."

"I don't know." I dug the heels of my palm into my eyes. "I don't know, and no one's helping me—"

"There are rules," Atabeira said gently. "I am much reduced. Mi salúd no fue capaz, antes o ahora—"

"To the rude questions of strangers," I finished, recognizing the quotation. *We Have Always Lived in the Castle.* I looked back up at her.

She smiled. "Or of family."

I felt so close to understanding, like the words were lingering just outside a door in my mind.

"But why is this happening now? To me?"

Atabeira raised an eyebrow. "Who said it was only happening to you? Who said this was only happening now?"

That feeling, like reaching in a dark room for something that had to be there, in a second the light would come on—

—*bienvenidos, azucarera*—

"People have fought him before?"

"People are always fighting him."

"But no one's destroyed him?"

"No. It might happen someday. But not yet."

I threw up my hands. "Then what do they do?"

Atabeira hesitated, and for a maddening second I knew she was going to quote another Shirley Jackson line, and I was going to *scream*.

Then she reached down into the pool of bubbling stomach acid and drew out my suitcase, the plastic warped and buckling as bile streamed down the sides. A wheel popped off and rolled away as she placed it in front of me.

"They learn to carry him."

I looked down at the suitcase, and back up at the gargantuan stomach walls around us.

Atabeira's eyes crinkled at the corners. "They find a way to make him small enough to carry."

"How—"

But she was gone.

—make him small—

I stood and walked over the angry pink wall, and placed my hand on it. The anxiety hit me like a truck.

Fourth grade, and we're all filling out the bubbles on our sheets of paper before Mrs. Carter hands out the test. I make sure to shade mine all the way in. The teacher leans over my desk. "Oops!" she says brightly, tapping next to Hispanic. "That's not right. Erase that and fill in this one—"

—senior year of high school, Mr. Forrest's class and we're debating homeland security policy, and I'm eviscerating Rory Evans who hasn't even looked at his textbook all year. All my friends are laughing into their hands and his face is getting redder and redder, and he snaps, "I'm just saying, if you don't like this country, you should go back home," and my stomach drops out of me because where do you even start with that? That this is my home? That Puerto Rico is part of this country? That—

—freshman orientation career fair at Carlton and I approach the Latina Students' Association table and I stand there, and I stand there. This beautiful girl with hoops is talking loudly about how 'Latinx' is cultural erasure, and the girl she is talking to smiles at me, but is she really smiling at me or is she smiling through me, smiling beyond me at some girl who also has strong negative opinions on the word Latinx instead of kind of liking it, who grew up speaking Spanish and didn't grow up in a suburb with all white friends, who deserves to be there, so I walk away before anyone else can notice me—

I almost yanked my hand away. My heart pounded in my ears. My whole body shook. I wanted to run, but there was nowhere to go. I wanted to tear everything to pieces, but Atabeira had already told me that that would be futile.

—*they learn to carry him*—

I didn't want to carry this ghost. I wanted to destroy him. I wanted to rip him into tiny shreds, blow him up, crush him to bits.

But I couldn't, because he was me.

I wanted him to have never existed. But if I tried to believe he never existed, that would mean staying away from all the things that were not him, that reminded me of how I was him, his power, his privilege. I would pull away and away, and he would only grow.

I took a deep breath.

—HELLO MY NAME IS ATABEIRA on her name tag and she switched to English when she saw me, and I wanted to die. I wanted to flee. I wanted to never have to see her again.

But no one had asked me to flee. I didn't need to start packing up. I could have smiled back at her, and talked to her, in English or in Spanish. I could have treated her like a person, and not a judgment.

"You didn't know you brought him with you?" she asked. "That's okay, a lot of people don't. He looks a little different each time, but after a while you start to recognize him."

"So you work at a haunted Pinkberry, huh?" I said. "Who haunts a Pinkberry?"

I let my breath out.

They find a way to make him small enough to carry.

I OPENED MY eyes, and I was outside the sugar mill again.

It had clearly been abandoned for decades. Chunks of the chimney had fallen away, and trees grew up through holes in the tin roofs. The ground was littered with Domino sugar packets and broken Coke bottles.

I was clenching something in my right fist. I opened my hand to see a small green army soldier.

My left hand held the handle of my suitcase, once more pristine.

I bent down, and put the toy soldier into its front pocket.

I stepped into the door of the castle.

I STEPPED OUT into La Plaza de la Beneficencia. There were the stone steps, descending to the statue of children dancing on a man's shoulders. There were the palm trees, sheltering the piragua man calling out his wares. There were a profusion of flowers at my feet, my abuela's favorite, maybe I could pick just one? There was—

I looked behind me for Atabeira in the window of the Pinkberry, but the Pinkberry was no longer there. There was a Starbucks. The barista did a double take as he looked up and saw someone exiting the store that he hadn't seen inside.

There was no Pinkberry anywhere in sight.

There was a girl several feet from me, finishing a Frappuccino.

"Disculpe," I said haltingly. "Esto—esta tienda fue ser un Pinkberry?"

"A Pinkberry?" she repeated in unaccented English. "But... that burned down *years* ago!" She held that pose for a second and then broke, grinning. "I'm just shitting you. There's one two blocks down that way." She pointed to the left. "There did used to be one here too, though. Fucking corporations, am I right?"

"Right," I echoed. "Okay."

It was done. I had done it. What it was... that was something that would take longer to figure out. And to sustain.

She frowned at me, probably wondering if I was just going to stand there all day. "Are you not going?" She gestured at my suitcase. "Do you need help carrying that?"

"Wha—oh!" I blushed. "Oh no, I'm not hungry. I, I just thought I remembered one here, from last time."

"Not hungry, huh?" She raised an eyebrow, and I only wasted about half a second admiring how sculpted it was. "What about thirsty?"

Was... was this flirting?

"Uh, maybe? I'm waiting for my tía, but she's not supposed to get here for a few hours, so ... "

She grinned, and for a moment I thought I saw the bright lines of Atabeira's essential self radiating through her mouth, but no, that was just her lipstick, red as a stop sign that I was going to ignore. "Can I buy you a drink?"

I said yes.

DID YOU KNOW?

GABRIELA SANTIAGO is a Clarion graduate and member of Team Tiny Bonesaw whose work has previously been published in *Clarkesworld*, *Strange Horizons*, *The Dark*, and *Lady Churchill's Rosebud Wristlet*, among others. A performer with such Twin Cities institutions as Patrick's Cabaret, Raw Sugar, OUTspoken, Gadfly, Queertopia, and Mother Goose's Bedtime Stories, she is also the founder and curator of Revolutionary Jetpacks, a science fiction cabaret centering futures imagined by BIPOC, queer and trans, and disabled artists. She is writing three novels and needs to be persuaded not to start a podcast. You can follow her @LifeOnEarth89 on Twitter. She would like to thank Alicia Alarcon for her assistance with the Spanish.

LOPINOT PLANTATION
BY R.S.A. GARCIA

. . . an' see.

No, not over dere. Not de house where de old Count still wander. Looking fuh wife an' chile. Looking fuh forgiveness.

(He never getting forgiveness.)

Here. By de spreading banyan tree. Here, in de dark under de branches.

An' yuh don't 'fraid? With yuh motor cars an' electric lights? Phones an' cameras?

(No lights out here. Jus' me. Burning hot. Burning slow.)

I by meh friend. He hanging here below. Waiting tuh come down an' deal with de Count.

Waiting fuh you.

(Fuh fresh meat.)

So come nah.

Come an' see de soucouyant.

The slave dey hang.

Come. Come . . .

R.S.A. GARCIA lives in Trinidad and Tobago with an extended family and too many dogs. Her debut science fiction mystery novel, *Lex Talionis*, received a starred review from *Publishers Weekly* and the Silver Medal for Best Scifi/Fantasy/Horror Ebook from the Independent Publishers Awards (IPPY 2015). She has also published short fiction in international magazines, including *Clarkesworld*, *Abyss and Apex*, *SuperSonic Magazine* (Spain), and in several anthologies. Learn more about her work at www.rsagarcia.com.

---

* FILE UNDER: *Haunted Plantation*

LAST NEWS

BY CARLOS ORSI

"Today Dies Today"

THE building remains, a skeleton, the ground floor an empty skull full of echoes, stained with soot. The bomb that burned down the print shop of the *Hoje* (*Today*) newspaper in São Paulo was thrown at 12:01 a.m. on August 1, 1975. The flames took to the paper reels, eight men died, the company folded. *Hoje* was no more, another victim of the dictatorship that would last ten more years.

Nonetheless, that day's front page, never written, never printed, can sometimes be seen, but only after midnight, hanging, framed, on the wall of the pub across the street. The headline, "TODAY DIES TODAY."

CARLOS ORSI is Brazilian journalist and a writer of mystery and speculative fiction. Nowadays he lives with a wife, a kid, and two cats.

* FILE UNDER:
Haunted Print Shop

They used to come at night to descend my
stone stairs to the well of Juan Clemente . . .

JUAN CLEMENTE'S WELL

FEATURE ENTRY 25

STRUCTURE TYPE: CHURCH
LOCATION: CORRIENTES, ARGENTINA
LAT./ LONG: 29.0154° S, 56.5762° W
BUILT: CIRCA 1686
GROUND ELEVATION: 226 FT. (69 M.)
WRITTEN BY: H. PUEYO

TRAVEL GUIDE NOTES

INSIDE AN ARGENTINIAN church nearly 350 years old, there are secrets only the walls and wells may know. Memories of atrocity carried out, awareness of confessions, of sins effected and still persisting—sometimes the offering given is for blood rather than atonement.

Heartbreaking and truly haunting, H. Pueyo speaks from the soul of Paróquia de la Virgen de los Dolores, lamenting the corruption of human life, and the political violence of military powers witch-hunting for "detractors." It's a short piece, but no less impactful than something five-fold its length; H. Pueyo makes every word count.

Visit here, if you dare—not many tourists do. And make a wish as you descend through its painted brick vaults, below the sanctuary and nave, through the cold cellar, and then down, down into this bottomless pool, filled with coins, blood, and bones, that is "Juan Clemente's Well."

—Charlatan Bardot

T HERE IS A WELL UNDERNEATH ME, AND IT GROWS bigger every time I breathe. It was first built in 1689, three years after my construction, a small hole in the cellar caused by the water that dripped from the humidity underground. Many things have changed since: the brick walls have been covered with gold, the sky blue paint of the ceiling has lost its color, the Ionic columns, the statue at the center of the altar, and even my name, but not the well. The hole grew, alone, until it became deep enough to bring the attention of the priest who found it and decided to make it a wishing well.

Today, its exterior is made of marble, eerily similar to the holy water font of the floor above, with an embellished wrought iron water pulley holding a bucket that is never used and a cross above. THE VENERABLE FATHER JUAN CLEMENTE'S WELL, says a small bronze plaque, describing how the angels came to Father Clemente in a dream to show him the well that would proceed to cure maladies and save souls, connected directly to the Guarani aquifer.

I exist for more than three hundred and thirty years, and yet I know nothing of lost souls; I know only what is thrown inside the well.

THEY USED TO come at night to descend my stone stairs to the well of Juan Clemente. Most of them brought coins and bills: fifty cents in nuevos pesos, ten pesos ley folded in a dirty banknote, a silver coin equivalent to one Chilean peso, a pile of guaraníes, several ever-changing cruzeiros and novos cruzeiros. To them, the money paid for whatever they did; to me, their offering fed my open mouth.

Isn't it a little too late to pray? an officer would ask another. The question came in Spanish, Portuguese, and occasionally in English, but it echoed in my chambers: *pray, pray.* The older soldiers never bothered to explain, not in my presence; perhaps they waited until they were inside their cars, safe and far from my realm, as if my mortar could suffocate them if they stayed too long in my inner walls. *You'll see, when you're used to this job,* they would simply say, believing, maybe, that there was any soul left to save.

Sometimes it was only one man. Sometimes it was two or three, but never more, never at the same time. They glanced at the painting of Venerable Juan Clemente, darkened by the shadows of the night, they inhaled the damp aroma of my cellar, and looked into the hole in the ground. *It's for you now,* they would claim.

Whatever fell into the water became mine.

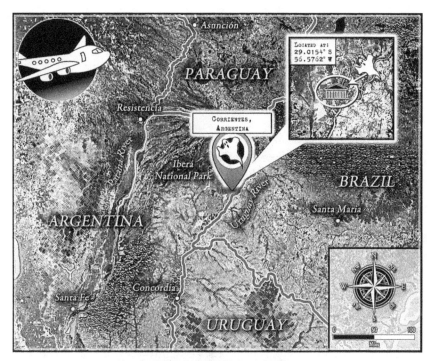

HAUNTED CORRIENTES, ARGENTINA

THE COINS NEVER reach the bottom of the well because there is no bottom. They plunge into the water, but the water is also mine, and my blood irrigates the soil, maintains the pillars, holds the gilded walls. The statue that stands in my middle, the spectacle of my altar, holds her own chest, a thin dagger crossing her exposed, immaculate heart.

Tears drip from her carved eyes to her chin, salty and crystalline, a fact that has brought local attention to me in my last one hundred years. It happens when the coins flutter in my bowels every now and then, making me feel what their previous owners made others feel. A neck squeezed, knees suspended and restricted, blood that leaks from the ears. Forgotten cells, erased names. Rats in closed rooms.

Her tears are my tears.

The parish trembles.

Pain is water, and it floods. My well deluges, my walls weep, my ceiling gutters. Waves engulf gold and wood, inundating me with the memories the visitors who come here wish to disappear. How easy it is for them, who only need to drop a coin down my throat, how difficult it is for me.

The aching that swamps me also drenches those who are inside me. In 1969, it took Father Eustácio Menezes, who had come from Brazil half a year before. In 1971, solicitous Father Anastasio Videla. In 1974, Sargent González, from Encarnación. In 1999, two Italian nuns who worked in an orphanage in Argentina. All shared the misfortune to be in my company when the flood began.

When it starts, it's overwhelming—images and names come to life, from the mothers who never find their children to the men hanging from metal posts. They invade me; I become them. The corpses were found damp, their lungs filled, their eyes teary. *Aid us all*, my chambers whisper, *who are the children of thy sorrows*, the voices urge me, *in our last agony*.

The statue is the one who cries, but I answer their prayers.

PEOPLE COME TO Paróquia de la Virgen de los Dolores every once in a while. My parish is located between the towns of Santo Tomé and Paso de los Libres, in the northern province of Corrientes, Argentina, and is frequented by visitors from here and other nearby countries. Some stay at an inn in Yapeyú before passing by the church to pray or throw a coin or two in the well, while others cross the Ibicuí bridge and visit Guaviraví, a small but charming river. The prairies of the pampas that surround me have been here for a long, long time.

Today, Father Antonioni is in charge of the maintenance of my body. He's a young man, quieter and far more gentle than his predecessors, but he cleans my stained glass, wipes my pews, and dusts my altar with incessant devotion. Sometimes, when he comes from one of those towns, he brings white chancel flowers for the statues and lights new candles for me.

"Just one more thing," said Sarita, one of the followers, when he first arrived. She lives two kilometers from here, and has seen many priests come and go in her eighty-nine years—more often come than go, she seems to tell me when she eyes my walls. "You should not stay here at night."

"Is the road any dangerous?"

Sarita arranges the mantle around the Virgin's shoulders. "The problem is not the road."

It takes him a while to hear of the rumors. He knows of the miracles, but not that many have died inside of me. *Don't you worry, Ms. Sarita*, he tells the old woman time after time. *The deaths have been because of the mold and the humidity, but we have already fixed those issues in the underground.* Her wrinkled hands touch the surface of the holy water near the entrance. *The holiness we see above cannot be found under the ground,* she says, but he won't listen.

Sarita has warned many before him. I have seen her, first as a little girl, then as a young woman, an expecting mother, a housewife. *The military, Father,* she whispers, looking around as if anyone could hear. But she's inside of me, and I always listen. *The military has tainted the well,* continues Sarita. *And the Spanish, the Portuguese, all of them have ruined it too. You must know. You must understand.*

Father Antonioni smiles at her.

"I appreciate your concerns, Ms. Sarita," he repeats every time, a broken record that plays itself. "But there is nothing wrong with the well."

GROUNDWATER BATHES MY floors, washing away the burning feeling in my roof. It slices my terracotta tiles and draws blood that drips from my walls, transparent and water-like, turning the gashes into scars. They are just lines in my structure, fragments of a past that I turned mine. Father Antonioni has not yet met the strangers that come at night, but my pain sometimes suffocates him, forcing him to go outside.

A wallet full of reais floats on my surface. I swallow and it blazes, fire taking everything in its wake, until it turns liquid again. Coins glitter under candlelight. *No,* a voice tells me, her echoes leaving the hands of those who brought her. *No.*

Father Antonioni is coughing when a group of tourists arrive. The guide asks his permission to enter, and turns to explain my history to the newcomers after receiving his blessing.

Can we see her? My insides rumble hearing the question. *Can we see the Virgin?*

"Mater Dolorosa cries again," says the guide, following the runner rug toward the altar. They don't see the water, but they feel the pressure, drowning under me. *No,* the voice continues, *no.* "The processional statue was commissioned in 1875, and has attracted many followers to the region ever since."

Tears run through her sculpted face, and her eyes keep looking at the same place. *How beautiful,* one says. And maybe it is beautiful to see her sorrowful eyes, her furrowed brow, her parted lips. The tears that fall from her chin. A pleading voice makes my water gurgle, and I remember again: *no more, please, no more.*

"But that is not all," the guide continues. The attentive eyes of the visitors follow her, and I can already feel myself hungry. "There is also Juan Clemente's well downstairs, if you have a coin to spare."

Come, my voice sounds like the wind as they descend the stone stairs. The floor of the cellar is wet, and their shoes splash water as they surround the well. Come, and let me eat.

Did You Know?

H. PUEYO (@hachepueyo on Twitter) is an Argentine-Brazilian writer of comics and speculative fiction. She's an Otherwise Fellow, and her work has appeared before in *Magazine of Fantasy & Science Fiction*, *Clarkesworld*, *Strange Horizons*, and *The Year's Best Dark Fantasy & Horror*, among others. Find her online at www.hachepueyo.com.

CUARTO FRIO (COLD ROOM)

BY ALVARO RODRIGUEZ

The old gas staion between Camargo and Miguel Aleman

OFF the old road between the northern border towns of Camargo and Miguel Aleman, in Tamaulipas, Mexico, you will find a long-abandoned gas station whose pumps have not run since 1978. Direct your attention west. Sun-bleached paint flakes off the 10x10' cinder-block structure, once a cold storage that local hunters used for deer. Broken hinges hang in the frame, but the door is missing; the opening juts like a maw into darkness. Step inside. Though the cooling unit is absent, the temperature drops. A groove runs the length of the floor to a drain in the center. At the base of the walls, rough holes the circumference of a snake mark the four directions. A scent persists, blood and fear, and a far-off sound like the bleating of a deer, or a child. Her name was Marina.

Born and raised on the South Texas border, **ALVARO RODRIGUEZ** is the co-creator and executive producer of the original Netflix animated series, *Seis Manos*. His short fiction has been nominated for a Pushcart Prize and his story, "Boy, 7," appears in the Bram Stoker Award-winning *After Death*.

* FILE UNDER: *Haunted Cold Storage*

It was only in this moment that he
considered he had made a mistake . . .

XTABAI

FEATURE ENTRY 26

STRUCTURE TYPE: OBSERVATION POST
LOCATION: CHIQUIBUL FOREST RESERVE, BELIZE
LAT./ LONG: 17.0783° N, 88.6904° W
BUILT: CIRCA 1991
GROUND ELEVATION: 1,145 FT. (349 M.)
WRITTEN BY: JO KAPLAN

TRAVEL GUIDE NOTES

HOW FAR CAN behaviors be legitimized while claimed to be in "the pursuit of furthering science"? Certainly, there's some grand case file on the science of lechery, although generally speaking, a hard line is drawn at philandering... especially when it involves the supernatural.

Jo Kaplan (or as she's alternately known, Joanna Parypinski) is building an admirable reputation of literary-genre excellence, with publications in the last year alone from HarperCollins, *Nightmare Magazine*, *Fireside Magazine*, and more. She writes now from her experiences in Belize, of the geography and vast legends of this jungled land.

Consider the following as a cautionary tale involving lust, consent, and hubris: Follow not ghostly women in unfamiliar jungles, especially one by the name of "Xtabai."

—Charlatan Bardot

MACAW RESEARCH STATION SITS IN THE HEART of the Belize jungle, an hour's drive from the nearest airstrip. On the day the visiting professor arrived, a young scientist of sustainable ecosystems drove out to pick him up.

Rain beat down when she ushered him into the car, jacket pulled over the professor's bald head. They tore off beneath the green canopy where the downpour quieted and the road became dirt.

He introduced himself with hesitant politeness, and she introduced herself with easy good humor. The visiting professor's name was Elison. The driver's name was Jana.

He asked how long she had been a driver for the station.

"Today's my first day driving," she said. "But I do have my PhD."

Elison raised a surprised, perhaps disbelieving eyebrow, which deepened the grooves of age in his face. His granite eyes found the midnight-dark hand clutching the stick shift and darted back to her round smiling face and corkscrew hair.

"Of course, everyone here has their PhD," she continued. The car bumped violently over deep welts in the dirt road while she swerved around worse ones. Brown puddles splashed each time a tire sank into the depressions. "PhD—Pot Hole Driving!" She laughed over the gunshot rattling of rough terrain.

Elison grabbed the handle above the door. "Shouldn't you slow down?"

"Then we'll never get there. Anyway, don't worry. There are no speed limits in Belize."

This only seemed to make the professor even more worried. He gave a small, embarrassed laugh. "I've faced bushmasters in Costa Rica, white caimans in Trinidad and Tobago, and hordes of scorpions in Huatulco. I suppose a few potholes won't kill me."

Even so, he was green by the time they arrived at the research station campus. Jana slowed, so she could point out the different buildings: the kitchen, the thatch-roofed open structure with hammocks for relaxing, the bunkhouse, laboratory, library, composting toilet, and the new observation post for rangers. As they went the long way around to the cabins, Elison glimpsed a vine-tangled building through the twisted branches of a Ceiba tree. "What's that?"

"The old observation post. It's no longer in use."

"How come?"

She told him that the building was falling down. "See how all these buildings are elevated? The floor of the old observation post began to rot in the damp, might collapse if you tried to walk on it."

HAUNTED CHIQUIBUL FOREST RESERVE, BELIZE

"Will they make some other use of it?" he asked, frowning, as it shrank out of sight behind them. "Leaving it there to rot seems a bit pointless."

"No one likes to go in there," she said as they pulled up to the cabins. "Here we are. Why don't you go put away your things, and I'll take you to the dining hall."

When he was ready, they headed to dinner, swatting mosquitoes. His smile was thin but congenial. "I look forward to meeting the other scientists. I'd expected to be greeted by one, actually, but you've been very helpful for a driver."

Ignoring his dismissiveness, Jana opened the door to the dining hall. Dr. Diali—a short, dark woman with an infectious smile—waved them over to introduce Elison to the station's director. They served themselves rice, beans, and *hudut*, a traditional Garifuna dish of fish with coconut milk and mashed plantains, followed by chocolate. When Jana handed Elison a can of Belikin beer, he took it ruefully, having discovered his earlier mistake.

"So you *do* have a PhD? An academic one, I mean."

"Of course," she said. "I told you today was my first day as a *driver*."

"You drive like a pro," said Elison. "Never would have known you were just a simple scientist."

She found herself charmed by the awkward, pinched way he smiled, the mark of a man who spent more time in nature than with people, and whose social skills reflected it. Here was a man pushing middle age who had dedicated his life to traveling the globe in the name of science—a life of adventure that also courted loneliness.

Jana was no stranger to loneliness. Life at the research station was not conducive to exploring relationships. Except for several aborted flirtations among the staff, Jana had been single for almost two years.

She grabbed two more beers and strolled into the humid night with Elison, the darkness spraying stars overhead like speckles of white paint. He told her he was recently divorced; his wife had no longer been able to sustain his frequent absences without resorting to infidelity. Not that he had been entirely loyal on some of his longer trips. A sense of lonesomeness just always seemed to find him.

They wandered to the edge of the light spreading out from the dining hall behind them, to the line where it met the black wilderness. He leaned in first, or she did; it was hard to say. They kissed.

When they pulled back, his eyes widened over her shoulder. "Who's that?"

Jana turned but caught only the shape as it slunk away into the darkness. "Let's go back to the dining hall," she suggested, but he held her by the shoulders. A ripe smell like carrion flowers wafted over them, thick and putrid and sweet enough to choke. "It's dangerous out here," she tried again. "There are jaguars all over this forest. It's really not safe to be out after dark."

"That was no jaguar. That was a person," Elison said, eyes still searching the distance.

As his attention slipped away, Jana tried to suppress the opening wound that threatened to bruise her heart. "It's no one."

"It was a woman." He took a step away from Jana, trying to catch sight of the person. "Beautiful. With long black hair. A white dress, it looked sheer. And her feet were bare. She's not someone from camp, I can tell. But you know, don't you?"

"She's a ghost," said Jana, her voice hardening. The kiss was already forgotten, grown cold on their lips. "Forget you ever saw her."

"A ghost?" Elison laughed. "Is that supposed to be a joke?"

"No joke."

"Right. So what does this ghost want?"

"To seduce you."

He laughed. "Are you jealous?"

Jana shoved him hard enough that he stumbled. "Fuck you. You want her? Go and find her. But you won't like what you find, *fu tru*." She marched back to the dining hall.

Left alone, Elison felt the gleam of mystery at hand. Ghost or not, he knew there was more in the jungle still beyond the reach of science, species utterly unknown to man. It was what drew him to these wild places. The woman in the trees was yet another mystery he felt compelled to solve. And he definitely did not wish to return to the dining hall now, where a love-scorned associate waited.

He set out to pursue the mysterious woman into the trees, feet squelching in muck the afternoon rain had churned up. He could not imagine what a beautiful young woman was doing out in the jungle alone, least of all to have elicited such a reaction from Jana. He couldn't help but smile; the woman's solitude also excited him.

He had always enjoyed the hunt.

He followed the campus floodlights from one dark patch to the next. The night chirped and buzzed, thick with crickets and the calls of pauraques. Spider monkeys slept in the trees, and fruit bats foraged for nectar, flapping like airborne shadows. He was far from alone.

When he spotted her again it was beside the creek, in a field of mangroves. Where her feet should have sunk into the flooded ground, she instead seemed to float above it. Her eyes were like gleaming obsidian when they found him, and she beckoned him to follow with an alluring curl of her finger.

Perhaps a ghost, indeed, as Jana had said? Or a trick . . . but he was never one to quit at the first sign of challenge. The accolades Elison has won were not done by floundering at the lip of uncharted chasms—one must leap such obstacles with a running sprint.

So patiently he did follow her, as he would a particularly rare bird spotted in the canopy. Once, he had pursued a Quetzal for six miles through a dense, humid forest in Mexico, simply to claim it as his own—to learn its tricks and watch without being watched and snap his photos. There was a deliciousness in chasing.

Elison tramped through dirty water, into the dark. The smell of rot met him on the breeze—a smell like death.

He sneered.

He followed her to the abandoned observation post, where she climbed the ladder, giving him a tantalizing view, and disappeared inside. Despite the strangeness of the entire situation, he felt compelled to continue after her. Testing the soft ladder, he climbed up into the warm, dark interior. Floodlights shined eerily in the distance, while moonlight filtered through the canopy and into the structure's barren windows.

Perhaps the floor was rotted, but he could hardly tell. Bougainvillea climbed up the walls, flowered pink; vines and creeping plants burst up through soft patches of floor, overtaking it. Moss furred the ceiling. Mushrooms sprouted in damp corners.

The woman set down a comb of cactus spines she had been using to brush her long black hair and smiled at him. It was a smile that he recognized, one filled with promises. It was like not just finding the bird in its natural habitat, but capturing it in a cage to present as a trophy.

He drew closer but the smell overwhelmed him, and he began to wonder gravely at the sense of something rotten lying just underneath the heady vegetal odor that suffused the overgrown outpost.

Time seemed to slow, and Elison suddenly couldn't bear the silence any longer; if only he could hear her voice, he'd know any thought of supernatural menace would be laughed away. "What are you doing out here? I heard it's not safe."

To underscore his point, the floor gave a threatening groan where he stepped. He looked at her feet to see if the floor beneath her was solid and found not two human feet but one the taloned claw of a bird and the other a cloven hoof like a pig's foot. Neither one touched the floor.

Elison froze.

It was only in this moment that he considered he had made a mistake.

Yet each time before he had wandered off on his own into the wilderness in search of finds that no one else was privy to, he managed to come out unscathed. It was a measure of grace and good luck that seemed to follow him. As deadly as it could be, Nature had always looked out for him in his pursuit to track it down and catalogue it.

The woman who approached him, however, was like nothing of nature he had ever seen before.

In spite of his dread at her inhumanity, he could not deny her beauty as she leaned in to press her lips to his. The foul odor overwhelmed him; her lips were cold and slicked as with algae; the tongue that prodded him seemed barbed with tiny spikes. Riddled with horror, he tried to pull away, but vines enwrapped his ankles and held him in place.

As the ghostly woman urged him on, kissed him, stroked him, took from him, he wondered with cold fear if any of his own conquests had ever felt like this: rooted to the spot, unable to escape or to say no, as he brought them to his hotel room to assuage his loneliness. Tender young things impressed by his credentials or stories of his adventures. Beautiful women he had pursued down darkened hallways, thinking of them all as quests, to catalogue, to conquer.

When she was done, the woman vanished, but the plants continued to hold him where he stood, hopeless and violated, until the rotten floor finally collapsed beneath his feet.

THE NEXT MORNING, the visiting professor was found cold, wet, and half-dead not far from the creek. He had dragged himself, both legs broken and weeping blood, from where he had fallen at the old observation post, until he could go no farther. Mosquitoes and fire ants had ravaged his arms and face with blistering pustules.

Someone else drove him to the closest hospital, though Jana imagined how much every bump on the potholed road would jostle his injured body. Before beginning her work for the day, she trekked out to the old observation post and looked up through the ragged hole where Elison had fallen.

"Xtabai," she said, and though she could not see her in the daylight, she felt her presence: the beautiful Mayan woman who haunted the forest—the forest that belonged to her. "You shouldn't have done that."

The breeze blew her hair like a caress. Try as she might to feel something—anything—with the other flesh-and-blood people around her, Jana could not help but look forward to embracing her jealous lover again when the sun went down, and the nocturnal forest, with all its mysteries, came alive.

Did You Know?

JO KAPLAN is the author of *It Will Just Be Us* and other works of horror and suspense. Her short fiction (sometimes under the name Joanna Parypinski) has appeared in *Fireside Quarterly, Black Static, Nightmare Magazine, Vastarien, Haunted Nights* edited by Ellen Datlow and Lisa Morton, and elsewhere. She teaches English and creative writing at Glendale Community College. Find her at Jo-Kaplan.com.

HARKON TAVERN

BY JULIAN J. GUIGNARD

Harkon Tavern, always open . . . for the dead

DURING the time of American colonization, there were many pirates living at Port Royal, Jamaica, and many of those pirates died there.

On quiet nights, you can hear things there, faint songs and laughter. Listen close, there's echoes of a gunshot, sometimes more. All along the city's docks and the ocean's shore, and amidst the ruins of taverns and dark quarters, you can hear such things and more besides. But few know what these sounds really are . . .

They are those lost souls who died long ago: whether deaths from the deep, deaths from sickness, from violence, from worse—they are the pirates who died at Port Royal.

And now they sing, dance, and laugh.

But they didn't always do just that.

JULIAN J. GUIGNARD is a middle grade student with aspirations to be a veterinarian. He fills his days with reading, soccer, drawing, Boy Scouts, and spending every other spare moment with his dogs. Additional work can be found in *100 Word Horrors Book 2* and *Book 3*.

* FILE UNDER: *Haunted Tavern*

THE DOOR AJAR

BY MALENA SALAZAR MACIÁ
TRANSLATED BY TOSHIYA KAMEI

Fabled entrance of San Nicolás Cathedral

IN the Parque Antonio Maceo, children's laughter filled the late-afternoon air, jeering their friend Manolito for his poor ball-handling. Manolito batted away tears and chased the dropped baseball as it rolled through the ancient San Nicolás turret's half-open door. As his squinting eyes adjusted to the gloom, a soldier wearing a sharp uniform and many medals emerged in the penumbra. The ball rolled to a halt at his booted feet. Manolito timidly inched closer. He crouched down to pick up the ball, and the soldier smiled.

When Manolito returned outside, the park, his friends, and all signs of baseball had vanished. Church bells rang, warning against a pirate attack on Colonial Havana.

MALENA SALAZAR MACIÁ is an award-winning Cuban writer of science fiction and fantasy. Translated by **TOSHIYA KAMEI**, her short fiction has appeared in *Clarkesworld*, *The Future Fire*, *Mithila Review*, and elsewhere.

---

* FILE UNDER: *Haunted Cathedral*

The main street of the town had become a river of its own . . .

INTO THE RIVER

STRUCTURE TYPE: MAUSOLEUM
LOCATION: BLUMENAU, BRAZIL
LAT./ LONG: 26.9221° S, 49.0585° W
BUILT: CIRCA 1947
GROUND ELEVATION: 66 FT. (20 M.)
WRITTEN BY: CLARA MADRIGANO

TRAVEL GUIDE NOTES

I'M GOING TO say it: Nazis make horror stories better. Assuming, of course, that bad things happen to them. Nazis are natural villains, and it's not a great tug at the heart strings to see them offed by bullets, bombs, or horrible monsters. Or, in this case, a cursed river. There are ways to humanize Nazis, make them tragic figures—somewhat necessary for well-rounded characters—but ultimately if there's a Nazi in the story I tend to root for the force opposing it, even if it's diabolically worse.

So I'm very happy to include the following story related to such matter by Brazilian author Clara Madrigano. I first read Clara's work in *The Dark* magazine, "Driving with Ghosts" and then "Mother Love," and looked her up for further writing in *Clarkesworld*. I fell in love with her candid, haunting voice, which she delivered perfectly for this inclusion.

For it matters not how wealthy or powerful you are in life, how influential or imperious; the afterlife has a way of balancing out karma for choices made, whether by reward or by punishment. From that, there is no escape, just as there is no escape from the inexorable clutches that drag you "Into the River."

—**Charlatan Bardot**

MY MOTHER WAS THE FIRST TO TELL ME ABOUT THE river. When we arrived in this town, she went to a bookstore and bought herself a little book about the place's history—as we were strangers to Southern culture, and the way my mother tried to make herself acquainted to something was through books.

The house we lived in, at a dead end street, didn't provide many neighbors; our gate was mostly visited by capybaras, who would stretch on the sidewalks during days of mild temperature, and then disappear during spells of long, crushing heat—into the creek that ran at the dead end of the street, a long arm of the main river.

How hot that place was, how merciless summer imposed itself upon the town—that was something the immigrants who built their first houses here didn't know about. And they didn't know about the river, also. Coming from Germany, trying to escape poverty, trying to find rich lands they could name after themselves, not knowing that these lands already had owners, natives, the Bugres—as my mother's book called them—who were killed and chased away, as if they were weeds; as if they were the invaders, they, the ones who understood that earth, that river, that sun burning over their heads every day—and not the newcomers, arriving with guns and a strange language, a language that never meant to speak of peace. As the German immigrants settled, they thought the river a blessing—one could easily reach other parts of the region by boat. Goods would come in, goods would come out. They'd have water, water would never be in need anymore. They raised their houses with the wood from the trees they brought down, massive trees you wouldn't have found in Germany; they saw the spectacle of monkeys jumping tree from tree, monkeys baring their teeth at them, at their presence, monkeys they shot at for both fear and fun. But they didn't know about the river: that the river was anything but kind, and that the river was hungry, and that what man wanted, what man built—those things meant nothing to the fury of the waters.

Natives had tried to warn them—before being fired at and having their villages burned down by the German immigrants. They'd tried to warn them that the river was no friend; they knew well enough to stay away from those waters; they knew that the river gulped men down when the floods came, took bodies to the deep of those dark waters, where they'd be lost forever.

"So, a killer river?" I'd asked my mother, as I opened boxes and took our clothes out—mine and hers. We shared the same body type, giving or taking a few pounds, and we shared too a lot of the clothes we had. Our new house wasn't big, but it was more than enough for two uprooted women.

LOCATED AT:
26.9221° S
49.0585° W

BLUMENAU,
BRAZIL

BRAZIL

SOUTH ATLANTIC OCEAN

HAUNTED BLUMENAU, BRAZIL

"There were great floods, so they had to make up something. Make up intention to what is just nature." My mother flipped through the book. "Did you know they hid Nazis here? After World War II ended?"

"Oh, that's great. That's just great. Nazis and a killer river."

We came to this town because my Aunt Eliane had been living here for a few years; she said we should stay until we could get back to our feet. Now, imagine us: creatures with no feet; water creatures, shaking our fins and tails, trying to get out of dry land and back into the water. My mother, unable to stand after surviving cancer; me, after surviving divorce.

My aunt worked with native tribes; she worked at a Xokleng reservation not that far from the town whose founders had shot and burned the ancestors of those same Xokleng, only to claim their land, to claim the river. She would sometimes ring in; wearing her khaki shorts, her dirty boots; her white skin—as white as ours—now perpetually tanned, to have coffee with my mother and take us on little tours around the town. She was the one to show us the square where they had built a mausoleum—for the first immigrants' families, for the town's founder.

"Funny thing. He actually lived here most of his life, but then went to die in Germany. It was quite a struggle—between the Brazilian government at the time and the German government, to have his body shipped back, buried in Brazilian soil."

That mausoleum, that building made of modern lines, gray granite—that was the first place I felt cold since arriving in town. I had my arms around me as we walked through the decorative tombs that bore names engraved in gold, of the founder and his family; his wife, his sons, a daughter that died at young age. "Oh, don't worry. They're not actually buried at this level; they're deep in the ground," my aunt had said, as if she'd sensed something just by looking at my face. My mother had described the river as a thing of haunt—but at the mausoleum, that was the first time I actually felt spooked, thinking about the corpses hidden under the floor I so casually stepped on. Outside the mausoleum, a bronze monument had been raised as another *memento mori:* also to those first White immigrants, not the natives, not to the Xokleng. A list of German names, lives taken by the first great flood they'd had to endure.

"And did that stop them? No. They went and rebuilt the whole settlement again," my aunt said, dryly.

"How many great floods so far?" I asked.

"I think five. Five catastrophic floods, I mean. If we were to number every little flood, every time the river rises . . . well, we'd be counting forever."

We stopped to eat some cake—*cuca*, as they said in here. My aunt went on:

"So, before all that, everything here was named after some big-time German. But now everything has native names. Itajaí, Itoupava," she used her fork to emphasize the names. "Or they're named after dead presidents." I asked what she meant by "before all of that" and she said, "World War II, of course."

"Oh, the hidden Nazis."

"Much more than that," Aunt Eliane said. "They actually had Nazi parades. Even after many generations, they didn't think of themselves as Brazilians—they wouldn't even speak Portuguese. An act of defiance. Imagine that. Well, then the war ends, Germany loses and the government decides it needs to do something about this place—make an example out of them. So they forbid German names—the streets needed to be renamed, and fast; the squares, public parks, everything . . ." She squinted for a moment—and just like that, I realized how much she looked like my mom. "Actually, one of the great floods—one of the big ones—hit just a little after the war ended."

"Maybe the river demanded a cleanse," I suggested.

"Maybe," my aunt said.

"Oh God. I can't take this talk about Nazis anymore," my mom whispered. She was trying to drink her coffee, but the cup was trembling in her hands. "I can't believe you made us come to this place."

"Oh, the town is fine now, Leila. It's not like there are Nazis walking around today," my aunt said, and smiled at me. I smiled back, but my lips felt tense, forcing to put out that smile—to show my mother that, somehow, things would be okay. At night, I'd check her breathing. The way her chest would slowly rise, slowly fall. I'd gently caress her hair, just the few inches of it that had grown since chemo ended. I'd go back to my room and try to sleep. But behind our dead end street, the creek would keep me awake. I thought I could hear it, even from the distance: the water rising fast, hungry for another cleansing.

My boss would video-call me most mornings. She wanted to know how I was doing.

"Barely making it," I'd say. "The heat is unbearable."

"Really? I thought the South was supposed to be cold."

"Not *this* South. It's like living inside a pressure cooker." I was fortunate enough to be able to work remote. But as much as I liked my boss, as much as she liked me, the money just wasn't enough to allow me to keep living in São Paulo and looking after my mom with one solid income only. Here we were, then: Naziland.

"You know, the people who live there probably wouldn't like you to call their town Naziland," my boss said.

"I know. It's just between the two of us."

Right after we moved in, we had to deal with our first house problem. Not a Nazi invasion, but a cockroach infestation. When the sun went down, the heat still burning the streets brought the cockroaches out and right into our garage, into our kitchen; I had to squash them against the floor, broom in hands, while my mother screamed in panic much like the Final Girl in a horror movie. Finally, I had to call a pest control exterminator. The guy who showed up identified the nests with surprising easiness. After he'd sprayed the poison, I asked what else should I be on the lookout for. Snakes? Rats?

"November," said the man, simply. He couldn't have been much older than I was. Certainly not forty yet. But his face had been deeply marked by the sun. He carried the wrinkles of those who rarely ever took shelter and knew the ways of a certain land; so I took that advice, as cryptic as it may have been, as a piece of wisdom. November, I kept repeating inside my head. *November.*

My mother wanted more books about the town, so I took her back to the bookstore and she thoughtfully browsed the short story section, a finger lifted, as if she was about to call someone's attention at any minute—a child, maybe, were she a teacher. But the finger meant only to help guide her eyes, and so it levitated above the spines; she'd pick a book, read a bit, put it back. Outside, the sun was scorching. Even with the air-conditioner of the bookstore on full blow, I felt the nape of my neck sweaty and sticky. I made a quick ponytail. A young man at the cashier stared at me with no particular expression. When my mother finally picked her book, he registered it, I paid for it, and he put the book inside a smelly plastic bag. "Thank you. Have a nice day," he said. Just as we stepped outside, it started raining—as if the boy had unconsciously cursed us. We took a cab home.

Night descended, and once I was sure my mother was sleeping, breathing in a good rhythm, I'd do the work I'd been pushing back through the whole day; or I'd scroll my ex-husband's Instagram profile, grit my teeth at the picture of every new restaurant he was going to—back in São Paulo, our city—and trying to guess which of the many smiley girls that appeared on his posts he was banging now. Had I the power of foresight, I should have known our marriage was doomed to end. I'd insulted him on the very first day we met. That rarely bodes well to a blissful union.

"That's not really a job," I'd told him, when he informed me he worked as a marketing consultant.

But he was paying his bills. He could afford a big apartment, in the city we'd loved, and I could not, not alone. And was being a designer better than being a consultant, in the end? I'd started wanting to be an artist—to draw, to paint. And I did that; digital pieces I'd make for my boss, who ran an advertisement agency. I'd sold out, but selling out didn't pay enough, in the end. Selling out was just surviving.

After doomscrolling for a while, I finally turned my phone off and tried to get some sleep. I closed my eyes.

I woke in a wild panic some time later—maybe hours afterward—to my mother's screaming. She was sitting on her bed, eyes shut, her fists clenched and half-raised.

"Mom. Mom," I shook her for a moment—and then she opened her eyes, saw me and grew immediately relieved. She hugged me, grasped at my old t-shirt with her bony fingers.

"Oh, Luísa. It's you. Thank God." She could breathe now.

"What happened?"

"A nightmare. I saw him. I saw *that man*."

"What man?"

Her hands rushed to her nightstand. She grabbed her most recently purchased book, opened and then stabbed a finger over one page: the page had the reproduction of a centuries-old photograph of a white-bearded man, skinny and with hollow cheeks, thick dark eyebrows.

"That's him. The founder," my mother said. "I dreamt he was rising from that mausoleum—and I knew he was coming for us, coming to this very house..."

"Mom..."

"I know. It's silly. I'm sorry I woke you up." She closed her book, put it on the nightstand again. But her heart was racing. I could feel it through her camisole, through her frail body. *How could such a man—such a benign-looking man, dead for more than a century—cause that much fear?* Eventually my mother calmed down enough to get back to sleep. I was the one who couldn't rest.

A few mornings later, I went on a walk with my aunt. She asked about my mother and I told her the truth—my mother spent most of her time in bed. Not sick, but reading. And, occasionally, having nightmares that jolted me out of sleep.

"She's just very..." My aunt tried to find a word. She settled for something else: "Well, it's part of the recovery."

I wanted to say I didn't think that was the case, but the heat over our heads was so strong that I had trouble formulating sentences.

"No more Nazi stories," I told her, and my aunt laughed.

Without realizing, we had wandered to the square the mausoleum was located. I put my arms around my body—for all the heat I felt, a cold draft still seemingly came out of the mausoleum. On another occasion, I would have welcomed the cold. Now, however, it sent chills through my spine.

"It's haunted, you know," said my aunt. "Or so they believed."

I remained silent. The news, even if just silly superstition, didn't shock me.

"Why didn't he want to be buried here? The founder." I asked, after a while. From my mother's book, I'd learned the founder had once written a letter to one of his brothers, begging him not to let them take his body back to Brazil—not to let them bury him and his family in that land. That same land that had made him a rich man, had made a home for his compatriots—the town that proudly bore his name. I imagined him, the face I'd seen in that same book, even thinner than before; I imagined him scrawling the letter, feverish, knowing there was nothing he himself could do; that, once

death came and took him, his body would be of other people's concern—
and he couldn't, simply couldn't let them take him back.

"Damned if I know," said my aunt. "Maybe he regretted it. All the blood
he had on his hands."

I chuckled at the thought of any man of his time regretting his crimes.
My aunt looked at the sky. The sun had been quickly covered by a giant
cloud of terrible gray. It happened, I'd already come to learn; in that town,
the sun could be out for a moment, and then dark clouds rolled over the sky
and a storm announced itself. That's the price you pay for that much heat,
nature simply trying to balance things, make everything even. For every drop
of water evaporated, another was sure to fall.

"It's going to be bad," my aunt said.

And rain *was* bad—rain was as bad as the heat.

For days, my mother and I would stare out the windows as the rain fell
and the sound of thunder stifled the rest of the world. We drank coffee, we
talked, mother read. I tried to work. I slept badly; even with the rain pouring
outside, the heat was still oppressive, and I'd wake during nights soaked in
my own sweat. I had started having my own nightmares. Lively nightmares
about the muddy water of the river enclosing me and taking me under. I
would scream, and only water would get inside my mouth; I could taste it—
the mud, the dirt, the flesh of other bodies . . .

There was the night I woke up trembling, sweating, and saw him: the
skinny man from my mother's book, standing right there, on one corner of
my bedroom. He opened his mouth. Just a black hole that made no sound,
and yet: the sorrow, the fear I could feel, the horror . . . as if I could listen to
him only inside my head.

I screamed. I took a pillow and threw it on the apparition, but there was
nothing there. Only shadows, and my coat hanging from a rack.

Rain came for days, rain went away. And then the sun would come out
and punish us again. When November arrived, the rains intensified.

November. I remembered the exterminator's warning.

"Flood season," my aunt called to tell us—as if we couldn't read the
signs. "Stay put for the next week. If necessary, we'll come down and get
you."

"I think we should pack a few things," I told my mother. "Just in case."

But my mother was adamant about not leaving the house. "We'll
drown, Luísa."

"Mom, nobody is going to drown. Aunt Eliane will be here before the
water starts to rise." I made my best to keep my mom calm and put. I packed

her few clothes, the few jewelries she still had, my father's wedding ring, which she kept with her even after his death; I made her bed, for reasons I can't even explain; if water was to take all of it, or to keep the house unreachable for a few days, who would have known? About tussled sheets, about pillows mounting over each other? But I did her bed anyway—and then I got to the book. The book with that man hiding on one of the pages. I tossed it inside a garbage can. I didn't tell my mother. We watched, for the next few days, the TV informing us that the river was reaching an alarming level; we switched for stupid cartoons. During the nights, I'd observe our street through the window and register the lack of sound. A few neighbors had already packed and left, but the silence of the animals was what struck me the most. I couldn't hear the birds singing; I couldn't spot the capybaras.

"Capybaras are water creatures," my mother assured me. "They know how to survive floods."

"*Half*-water creatures," I said, in a low voice. But, again, weren't we all, in a way? Didn't we spend the first nine months of our life floating in liquid, and wasn't our first breath, our first cry outside our mother's womb the sound of loss? Loss of a home, the warmth of the liquid, our lungs having to adjust to the land of the dry. We had once belonged to that darkness, we had once been creatures of water, too.

My aunt came the day the stream behind our house rose enough to start flooding the street. She came with a jeep, a young woman of darker skin and big, black eyes driving it. Sonia, said my aunt, introducing us. A Xokleng woman who worked with her.

"C'mon, we don't have much time," Sonia said, as we put our things inside the jeep. I could sense her uneasiness near the water, the way she sweated not from the heat, but because of some ancestral fear of the floods.

I carried my mother on my arms to the jeep. She hid her face under her cardigan, as if ashamed to find herself in that position. She felt light and little, more so than a child probably would. She sat on the jeep and cried silent tears, and I put my hand over hers. The main street of the town had become a river of its own, the brown water running furiously, covering everything knee-length. "Can we make it?" I remember asking. And Sonia saying, *yes, yes*, her hands tense on the wheel. But when we passed the mausoleum, she stopped. At first, caught in a panic, I didn't understand what she looked at—but I followed her stern gaze, and then my aunt's petrified look.

Out of the mausoleum doors, the dead came.

The town founder, the skinny man with the long beard—who had haunted my mother's dreams and my own. The other dead followed him—women with centuries-old dresses, with lace bonnets, a young girl holding what I presume to be her mother's hands, their skin blueish and veiny. What an ugly parade they made, coming down the mausoleum steps as if in a daze, walking into the water and—into the arms that stretched out of that muddy water, dark arms that pulled then down, that grabbed their trousers, their skirts. And the dead opened their mouth to scream, but they had no voice—as the man didn't have in my nightmare; all they had was the act of going under, of disappearing into the violence of the water, into the arms that wanted revenge. My mother covered her eyes, whimpering in fear. To say I was horrified would be a lie: I simply had no reaction.

Once the dead had been dragged into the river, Sonia, without a word, pressed the pedal again. If she was satisfied, her face, immovable as stone, showed nothing. But her eyes, the shine inside them, almost as if tears were about to drop . . .

My aunt had been right; I could now understand why that man didn't want to be buried here. Not in a mausoleum built on land he had never really owned. He must have imagined the price to pay—the price of the blood he had shed and that others had shed in his name. He must have imagined the river would take him again and again, the hands of his victims pulling him down every time.

My mother and I didn't stay in town for much longer after that first flood, after what we'd witnessed—and what we refused to speak about. But sometimes, during the nights, safely tucked in my bed, back in São Paulo—in a smaller apartment, but far away from the water—I would still feel the cold of that mausoleum creeping under my skin. I'd still wake up and search my room for the man's pale face. But there would be nothing there to see. That dead man—those dead people and their sins—belonged to another place.

DID YOU KNOW?

CLARA MADRIGANO is a Brazilian author of speculative fiction. She publishes both in Portuguese and in English, and you can find her fiction in *The Dark* and in *Clarkesworld*. Two of her stories were recently selected for the 2020 Locus Recommended Reading List.

COLONIA DEL SACRAMENTO'S LITTLE TAILORING SHOP

BY DANTE LUIZ

THE shop never closed, even after its seamstress passed away. She mends, right now, a wedding gown she's unfamiliar with. Artificial silk, an embroidered hem, and a long row of fabric-covered buttons on the back, passed from grandmother to mother to daughter in a line of ever-prickly marriages. It's rare for such a well-

The shop that never closes

worn piece to not have been trusted to the seamstress' ghostly hands—the town is small, her work reliable—but the great-granddaughter has decided she won't mend it herself. *It's cursed*, she tells the empty shop. *But I have to wear it.*

There are no curses, the seamstress responds. *Only hurt wives.*

There is, however, a little pin, long forgotten, inside the bodice. The ghost carefully removes it, and cushions the interior for a bride who will be far more comfortable than the ones before her, one week from now.

DANTE LUIZ (@dntlz) is a Brazilian comic artist, editor, and occasional writer, with prose pieces published by *Constelación Magazine* and *Mafagafo Revista*.

* FILE UNDER: *Haunted Tailoring Shop*

FASTEN YOUR

SAFETY BELTS...

NEXT STOP:

ADDITIONAL

MATERIAL

Additional material (for your safety and/or amusement).

ADDITIONAL MATERIAL

SUPPLEMENTAL NOTES, KNOWLEDGE, AND ASTONISHMENTS:

Many, many lesser known haunted locales . . .

LESSER KNOWN LOCALES ("TINY" TINY TALES)

THE WORLD IS A MYSTERIOUS PLACE, AND THIS travel guide (as comprehensive as it is) may alight upon only a small number of haunted buildings. Know ye intrepid discoverer, there are many, many others.

Following are but a few more of such, being a selection of lesser known locales, subject to appearance, disappearance, movement, mimicry, or any other supernatural effect(s) that may mask perception of the ghost-infused world we live amidst.

Included are domes that float; igloos that mystify; schools that never end, and more: For as you surely know by now, buildings are not occupied only by the living...

—Charlatan Bardot and Eric J. Guignard

SMITHY OF WOE

Augsburg, Bavaria, Germany

The revenant of Johannes Hohner resides here. It is said the echo of his hammer on anvil sounds whenever an atrocity is committed. The echoes have never ceased.

GROUND ELEV. 1,621 FT. (494 M.)
48.3705° N, 10.8978° E

WHARF STREET HOTEL

Saint-Marc, Haiti

Haiti is renowned for its Voodoo; so is this hotel where Mambo priestess Cécile Champagne still resides, after dying in 1793. Pay your bill in blood to sustain her.

GROUND ELEV. 227 FT. (69 M.)
19.1049° N, 72.6949° W

ITINERANT IGLOO

Arctic Ocean

Built on top an ice floe, and always adrift. Has never capsized. Those who see it report beautiful, beckoning figures, shortly before suffering severe psychotic breakdown.

GROUND ELEV. 0 FT. (0 M.) (SEA LEVEL)
RANGE CIRCUM. 65.2482° N, 60.4621° W

PRISIÓN DE LA INQUISICIÓN

Seville, Spain

The terrors at this site are well documented: medieval torture, mass genocide, demonic maelstrom, etc. A wonderful day trip for the family.

GROUND ELEV. 23 FT. (7 M.)
37.3891° N, 5.9845° W

NIGHTMARE SCHOOL
Perth (Western Australia), Australia

Classes never let out. Algebra, chemistry, grammar forever. Visitors find themselves giving impromptu reports, while unprepared and inexplicably lacking clothes.

GROUND ELEV. 95 FT. (29 M.)
31.9630° S, 115.8274° E

SIMEON'S FORT OF SKULLS
Southeast of Pucallpa, Peru

Skulls used for construction are mostly animals, with minimal sacrificed humans. Removal or destruction of any skull releases devastating curse. Souvenir-taking forbidden.

GROUND ELEV. 505 FT. (154 M.)
8.3929° S, 74.5826° W

JIUGUAN EAST STAR INN
Yulin, Guangxi, China

Its sign reads: *Huānyíng lǚkè,* meaning: *Travelers Welcome.* The translation bears note, "welcome" is not as implied. Travelers may be beheaded and served as dumplings.

GROUND ELEV. 3,556 FT. (1,084 M.)
22.6540° N, 110.1812° E

PARAMOUR'S PAWNSHOP
Ptolemaida, Greece

Location is vexing. Curiosity seekers get hopelessly lost. Jewelry, clothes, and other spurned gifts abound within. The price is heartbreaking.

GROUND ELEV. 2,000 FT. (600 M.)
40.5130° N, 21.6785° E

THE DESOLATE DOME

Blantyre, Malawi

Alone, brooding, desolate. Its origins are unknown, its purpose more so. Locals claim it floats, spherically. Kudu migrate here.

GROUND ELEV. 3,409 FT. (1,039 M.)
15.7667° S, 35.0168° E

LA ROOM DE ROUGE

Toulouse, France

Once it was umber. Then azure. For a brief occasion it was mottled gold and celadon. Now it is red. Always red.

GROUND ELEV. 495 FT. (151 M.)
43.6047° N, 1.4442° E

GATEWAY TO ETERNITY

East border of Republic of San Marino

Take three steps through and turn west. Along the stony lip the wind blows warm. Take two steps more. No one has lived to step farther.

GROUND ELEV. 2,457 FT. (749 M.)
43.9424° N, 12.4578° E

HOUSE OF SILENT TONGUES

Haima, Oman

The mystery is more in this feudal estate's name, for the tongues here are never silent.

GROUND ELEV. 400 FT. (122 M.)
19.9535° N, 56.2873° E

NECROMANCER'S OUTHOUSE

Baku, Azerbaijan

Do no enter under any circumstance. Just nope. (Also avoid the adjoining luncheonette.)

GROUND ELEV. -92 FT. (-28 M.)
40.4093° N, 49.8671° E

LIGHTHOUSE OF THE LIFELESS VALLE

Death Valley, California, USA

Shimmering, it marks passage through the hottest desert in America for lost ships navigating ancient rocks and sand.

GROUND ELEV. -282 FT. (-86 M.)
36.5323° N, 116.9325° W

CRUMBLING EDIFICE OF SELF-REFLECTION

Reported multiple locations

The shell of its office remains, weathered by strange elements. Nearing, you hear it still: The whispers of what could have been . . .

GROUND ELEV. AND LOCATION
VARY GLOBALLY

FALLOUT SHELTER #37X

Ulyanovsk, Russia

Sealed airtight since 1952. On cold winter nights, passersby report hearing pleas to be let out, followed by a sharp, echoing, *"Nyet!"*

GROUND ELEV. 490 FT. (150 M.)
54.3187° N, 48.3978° E

So many books to read about haunted buildings (that are not houses).

A SELECT READING LIST OF NOVEL-LENGTH FICTION WORKS SET IN HAUNTED BUILDINGS (that are not houses)

HAUNTED HOUSE BOOKS ARE A CLASSIC TROPE IN the horror genre. Spooky manifestations within one's home is a powerful device, representing the inability to extricate a paranormal force from your personal living space. There's a sense of invasion, a loss of privacy, an impression of inescapability.

But ghosts haunt so much more. Cold spots and orbs, poltergeists, ectoplasms, echoes, wisps, and memories, manifested in countless manner of forms—these specters may make their own home in any other manufactured structure besides a single-residence domicile.

For those interested in reading ghostly haunting books that are not about houses, consider the following, which are a small sampling of (general adult) fiction novel-length works set in other structural forms of haunted buildings.

Apartment 16 by Adam Nevill (haunted apartment building): The mysteries of a haunted apartment are unraveled by a night watchman and the young American girl who inherits the apartment.

Beauty and the Beast (French: *La Belle et la Bête*) by Gabrielle-Suzanne Barbot de Villeneuve (haunted castle): The youngest daughter of an indebted merchant must go to live in the enchanted castle of a rich though beastly creature who falls in love with her.

The Booking by Ramsey Campbell (haunted bookstore): A bookshop's new employee must contend with the owner's paranoia and the store's strange oddities he discovers while bringing the shop into an "electronic" age.

The Broken Girls by Simone St. James (haunted boarding school): A journalist uncovers the dark secrets of an abandoned boarding school and the mystery of her murdered sister.

The Cabin on Souder Hill by Lonnie Busch (haunted cabin): A couple attempting to repair their failing marriage vacation in a remote cabin, which converges on an alternate timeline of their parallel lives that have undergone different circumstances.

The Castle of Los Angeles by Lisa Morton (haunted artists' loft building): The new tenant of an artists' loft finds herself involved in the lives of her neighbors, along with madness, stalking, and murder.

The Castle of Otranto by Horace Walpole (haunted castle): Generally regarded as the first Gothic novel, an evil lord seeks to avert an ancient foretelling by marrying his dead son's fiancée Isabella in order to attempt birthing another male heir.

The Catacombs (World's Scariest Places Book 2) by Jeremy Bates (haunted tunnels): Upon finding a video camera with mysterious footage, a group of friends travel down into Paris's crumbling catacombs to investigate, only to discover an evil thought to have been merely only fable.

Catherine House by Elisabeth Thomas (haunted university): A young woman enrolls into an experimental school that requires isolation of its students from the outside world for 3 years, and comes to learn about herself, and that the school may have other plans for her.

Chaos by Mary SanGiovanni (haunted apartment building): A young couple move into a new apartment that they soon discover was built on a gateway to another, horrible and monster-filled, world.

Creepers by David Morrell (haunted hotel): A group of people break into a famous abandoned hotel to learn its secrets before it is demolished, only those secrets become a trap, meant to keep them from ever getting out alive.

Cursed Casino by Sara Brooke (haunted casino): A group of friends hold reunion aboard a floating casino on the Mississippi river, only to encounter the ghosts who died there before.

Dark Choir by Paul Melhuish (haunted asylum): The small town of Scarsdale is haunted by the ghosts of those abused and murdered at a local asylum.

Dark Matter by Michelle Paver (haunted whaling cabin): A small Arctic expeditionary group camp on a remote island, where one of them is forced to remain in a small cabin, along but for his dogs and the ghost of a crazed recluse.

Devils of D-Day by Graham Masterton (haunted monument): An abandoned WWII tank-turned- monument, houses more than history, and a surveyor who opens it unleashes a demonic entity.

The Drive-In trilogy by Joe R. Lansdale (haunted drive-in theater): The epitome of weird horror, this trilogy of books follows a group of survivors who are first mysteriously trapped within a Texas drive-in theater, and then let out to an equally strange world.

Earthblood by James Kisner (haunted warehouse): A warehouse built on the site of an ancient Indian burial ground brings prosperity to locals, but it also summons an unspeakable evil.

Eidolon Avenue: The First Feast by Jonathan Winn (inter-related collection of a haunted apartment building): A haunted apartment building where the guilty go to die, feeding the dark things that live there.

Five Nights in a Haunted Cabin by Tamara Thorne and Alistair Cross (haunted cabin): A pseudo-account in the manner of *The Amityville Horror*, in which the two real-life authors meet for the first time in order to investigate a haunted cabin.

Ghost Mine by Hunter Shea (haunted mine): A couple of adventurers travel to an abandoned mining town searching for lost gold, only to discover ferocious things coming out of the mine pit.

The Ghosts of Hexley Airport by Amy Cross (haunted airport): A horrific plane crash at an airport leads to the victims' ghosts remaining, along with something darker, in this horror mystery.

The Graveyard Apartment by Mariko Koike (haunted apartment building): A young family move into an apartment building built next to a graveyard and encounter culminating terrors.

Halfway House by Weston Ochse (haunted halfway house): An eclectic cast of characters interact and suffer from the curse of a soul-devouring halfway house.

The Haunted Bookshop by Christopher Morley (haunted bookshop): A mystery story set in the world of books in which an assassination plot is discovered.

Haunted Bookshop Mystery, volumes 1-7 by Cleo Coyle (AKA: Alice Kimberly) (haunted bookstore): A series of detective whodunnits revolving around a bookstore, haunted by the ghost of a hardboiled private investigator.

The Haunted Halls by Glenn Rolfe (haunted inn): Two inn employees get caught up in the sinister legends swirling about their workplace.

The Haunted Hotel by Wilkie Collins (haunted hotel): A recently-married wealthy lord dies amidst a scandal of disappearances, insurance fraud, and ghostly apparitions, while his jilted ex-lover seeks the truth.

The Haunting of Briarwych Church by Amy Cross (haunted church): Two adopted children, recently moved to a new town, sneak into a church reportedly haunted by an ancient evil . . . only the discover the reports as true.

The Haunting of Cabin Green: A Modern Gothic Horror Novel by April A. Taylor (haunted cabin): A non-believer of haunted houses—while in mourning and suffering a family history of insanity—goes to stay alone in a distant cabin.

The Haunting of Maddy Clare by Simone St. James (haunted barn): A young temp employee assists a ghost hunter in investigating the powerful ghost of maid who committed suicide in a barn.

The Haunting of Thackery School by Skylar Finn (haunted school): A new teacher must face ghosts and the mistakes of her past, when she is hired on to teach as a prestigious school in Vermont.

Horrorstör by Grady Hendrix (haunted IKEA store): A group of employees at an IKEA-esque store investigate at night a series of apparent vandalisms, only to uncover a slowly shifting reality of a darker side of the store.

Inferno Park by J.L. Bryan (haunted amusement park): A man returns to his dying home town, drawn to the condemned amusement park where he'd witnessed a horrible tragedy when a child.

The Keep by F. Paul Wilson (haunted castle): A battalion of elite Nazi soldiers are slowly murdered while occupying a castle in Transylvania, and they initiate a showdown between two mythical beings.

The Keep by Jennifer Egan (haunted castle): Two cousins work to turn a European castle into a haunted attraction, although the ghosts in their own lives prove worse than anything they might fabricate.

Last Case at a Baggage Auction by Eric J. Guignard (haunted apartment building): A gambler wins an old suitcase from a baggage auction, and releases an entity into the apartment building he lives, which turns it into a cursed portal to a frozen realm of eternity.

The Little Shop of Found Things by Paula Brackston (haunted antique store): A young woman who takes over an antique store has a special power to "connect" with the history imbued into items, which also can send her back in time.

Mercy by T. Fox Dunham (haunted hospital): A cancer-ridden patient is sent to an ill-omened hospital that feeds on sickness.

Mischief (The Harrow Series, Book 2) by Douglas Clegg (haunted boarding school): A young boy is sent to a private school that is haunted by many things, including the boy's older brother who recently died.

My Bones and My Flute by Edgar Mittelholzer (haunted plantation): Four people who have come into contact with a cursed manuscript are haunted by the sound of an approaching flute in the forests of Guyana.

Needful Things by Stephen King (haunted shop): A mysterious shop opens, in which the proprietor "knows" what each customer needs, but the cost for the purchase is much more than just money.

Night Shift by B.R. Myers (haunted department store): A young man takes the job of night security guard at a high-end department store, only to fall in love with a co-worker who is more than she seems, and to discover the ghost stories about the store are true.

The Other Side of Her by K. Hari Kumar (haunted cabin): After a car accident, a successful romance writer moves to a quaint cottage to recuperate and finds herself embroiled in a murderous ghost mystery.

Our Lady of Darkness by Fritz Leiber (haunted apartment building): A horror author, recovering from grief and alcoholism, begins to see a brown specter that is watching him, leading the author on a quest exploring ancient books amidst a modern, urban landscape.

The Overnight by Ramsey Campbell (haunted bookstore): A strip mall bookstore is found to be a doorway to Hell, but too late for the staff locked in overnight.

The Phantom of the Opera by Gaston Leroux (haunted opera house): A deformed and bitter man known only as the Phantom lives underneath the Paris Opera House where he falls in love with an obscure chorus singer and privately tutors her while terrorizing everyone else.

The **Red** *Church* by Scott Nicholson (haunted church): Something lurks in the bell tower of an abandoned church, harkening back to the deranged former pastor who sacrificed a child in order to summon a Child of God.

Reign by Chet Williamson (haunted theater): Retiring from the stage after starring for years as the character of Emperor Frederick, an actor learns that someone like the Emperor is threatening his friends and associates, and worries that he is undergoing some kind of nervous breakdown.

Ringu by Koji Suzuki (haunted well): A mysterious videotape warns that the viewer will die in one week unless a certain, unspecified act is performed.

Sacred Heart Orphanage by Patrick Logan (haunted orphanage): A ghost hunting accountant and his team battles evil entities while he deals with a haunted, tragic past.

Sanford Hospital by Ron Ripley (haunted hospital): After suffering serious burns, a ghost hunter is sent to a mysterious hospital, where he must battle the undead head nurse.

The **Seance** *in Apartment 10* by Ambrose Ibsen (haunted apartment building): A young woman moves into a slum apartment that, besides its leaky faucets and broken air conditioning, also is inhabited by a malevolent presence.

Seven Cleopatra Hill by Justin Holley (haunted hotel): A blizzard bears down on a historic hotel where a Romance Writers' convention is occurring, snowing in the guests, and bringing with it a ritualistic evil entity.

The **Seventh** *Ward* by Patrick Logan (haunted hospital): A team of ghost hunters is called in to exorcise a psychiatric hospital that's haunted by multiple malevolent entities.

The **Shining** by Stephen King (haunted hotel): A caretaker and his family move into a snowed-in hotel during its "off-season" only to suffer a growing malfeasance that affects them all in different ways.

So Cold the River by Michael Koryta (haunted resort): The family of a dying elderly millionaire hire a producer to make a documentary of the man's life, and to solve the mysteries of his past, steeped in a hometown with a dark evil at its heart.

Steam by Jay B. Laws (haunted bathhouse): Amidst the fading glory of San Francisco party days, a vaporous presence slowly targets selected gay men for revenge, revolving around a once-thriving bathhouse.

Stranded by Bracken Macleod (haunted/ alternate reality oil rig): The crew of a disabled Arctic ship find sanctuary on an ice-bound oil rig, only to discover what awaits them is worse than what was left behind.

Summer of Night by Dan Simmons (haunted school): After one of their friends vanishes, a group of 12-year-old boys fight forces of evil that begin to develop at the grade school they'd just completed.

The Sun Down Motel by Simone St. James (haunted motel): A young woman visits the motel her aunt vanished from thirty-five years before, only to find the motel has not changed in all that time, nor has its secrets.

Tales from the Gas Station, volumes 1-3 by Jack Townsend (haunted gas station): In this horror comedy series, an eldritch horror (and other monsters) are drawn to a small town gas station, as documented by its employee who keeps a blog of the strange occurrences and deaths.

Those Across the River by Christopher Buehlman (haunted plantation): A troubled veteran and his wife move into a plantation home he's inherited, only to encounter the malevolence that has been building, waiting to strike.

Transparent City by Ondjaki (haunted apartment block): A group of Luandans live in a crumbling apartment block in unstable Angola in this series of vignettes in which the hauntings are more metaphorical than literal, but revolve around strange and tragic events of magic realism, social commentary, and political satire.

What Was Lost by Catherine O'Flynn (haunted mall): A young girl goes missing in a mall, only to be sighted on the security cameras twenty years later.

Widow's Point by Richard Chizmar and Billy Chizmar (haunted lighthouse): A struggling author spends a weekend locked in a haunted lighthouse as a publicity stunt for his new book, only to become a target for powerful supernatural forces.

A glimpse into the domain of Charlatan Bardot.

A BRIEF AND ILLUMINATING INTERVIEW WITH PROFESSOR CHARLATAN BARDOT

CONDUCTED BY ERIC J. GUIGNARD

ERIC J. GUIGNARD: Hi Charlatan, and great to chat with you here. You've led an extraordinary life as a paranormal investigator of haunted buildings around the world. What drew you into such calling?

CHARLATAN BARDOT: Please, call me Charles, as all my friends do! And thank you for your time and indulgence herein to give platform for my humble voice.

Anyhoo, regarding commencement of my career, a number of years ago I was recruited by certain covert operatives to investigate an uprising of Orang bunian at Malaysia's Kapong Theater. The theater has since been torn down, and my findings were classified as confidential and ordered sealed for seventy-seven years by an emergency government mandate. But! I can go so far as to say that the experience was unequivocal proof of man's centuries-long quest to find definitive confirmation of the afterlife.

EJG: Wow! What did you discover?

CB: Confidential, my good man. I said that already.

EJG: Ah, of course. Why were you initially recruited for such a role?

CB: At the time, I was studying law in the occult and had just published a highly regarded paper examining historic precedent and how it had been unjustly applied in Sweden to someone in my family, Lasses Birgitta, who was executed for being a witch.

EJG: My God, execution for being a witch? I'm so sorry to hear that happened. I had no idea countries still prosecuted over such archaic measures contradictory to concepts as intrinsic as religious freedom.

CB: They don't. This was nearly 500 years ago to a grandmother of mine, twenty or thirty generations distant. But the implication, you see, still nettles my family legacy. It was emphatically unjust when she was decapitated in 1550, after being found the first witch in Sweden's history, regardless of her widely exalted and lavishly illustrative (and accurate) instructions on how to "raise the dead." So as long as I can utter, write, or sign, I proclaim, "Exonerate the name of Lasses Birgitta!"

EJG: It certainly seems a cause of social injustice. I can understand your indignation.

CB: What can I say? The occult runs in my family. I was raised in Taunton, Massachusetts—the geographic center of the Bridgewater Triangle, the foremost vortex of unsolvable paranormal activity in the American northeast.

EJG: I've never heard of that before.

CB: Look it up. It's quite the rabbit hole of unexplainable supernatural events. Of course, I can explain it all, should you ever be interested.

EJG: Okay, speaking of the unexplainable, you've been investigating haunted buildings for over four decades. You've been named as "The most sophisticated man, in manner and in mind, in the field of International Architectural Paranormal Investigations," and you have won awards and accolades in almost every subject and category from accrediting bodies, organizations, and ruling parties of nations around the world in consideration of your work. Most people are not aware of the supernatural world around us, nor the prevalence of these haunted buildings. In brief, what do you tell the average reader about this?

CB: That there is nothing beyond the bounds of possibility, and we truly live in a weird, wild (and ghostly) world. Time is fluid and non-linear. Echoes of the past cross events of the present with whispers and bleeding scars. Ghosts surround us, although it is the rarest confluence of events that we actually perceive them, or, they, affect us. But I digress: Buildings may be haunted for any number of reasons—often an unfavorable event occurs within the structure or the land the structure has been built upon; or perhaps there is appearance of a malfeasant entity, or else the haunting (most often) is brought about simply by the poor decision or calamitous circumstance of a person in distress, or even by happenchance to someone passing innocently through. Spirits may be caught there, or memories, cycling through in perpetuity around a defining event. Or sometimes buildings are just built "bad."

EJG: I can imagine some terrifying building types. What's one of the most fearful or memorable experiences you've encountered?

CB: A post office in Detroit, Michigan. One of the sites, in fact, that inspired the phrase "Going Postal," due to a rage-fueled employee who brought a pistol there and killed six co-workers in 1985. He left behind a manifesto, explaining that he couldn't take the ever-increasing amount of mail coming in, piling up higher and higher, all needing to be sorted. Well, the facility has since been shuttered, but developers have done nothing to repurpose the building or land, so there it molders, its security cameras still somehow running, and showing, occasionally, glimpses of this employee— his revenant—eternally, frantically, sorting mountainous volumes of mail. And sometimes, on mornings after the anniversary of the shooting, mailbags are inexplicably found outside the building filled with letters to be delivered, all sorted and stamped, written to random households across the nation. The envelopes have no return addresses, and the messages within . . . I'll say simply that his manifesto is in ways contagious.

EJG: I fear I've received something like that once or twice before. So, speaking of haunted buildings, when people think of such, invariably the image of a decrepit Gothic-appearing mansion comes to mind. Yet you have famously said that haunted houses are the least of haunted structures. Where or how do you think this misconception originated?

CB: From authors. Storytellers. In the old days, ghost stories were told around the communal fire, late at night, as ceremonial oral tradition. Spirits and monsters and otherworldly forces are actually more likely to be found in nature, among trees and cave passages that lead beneath the crust of earth we habitate. But for greater sensationalism, storytellers would speak of ghosts existing where we *live*, the most invasive and personal scenario possible. Also, therefore, the most terrifying. The most memorable. But these creatures of the *métaphysique* prefer not the company of us living. Should they find their way into structures, it is always places where, at times, they may be alone. Shopping malls, offices, churches—all such have dark corners and dark hours.

EJG: What's the strangest building type you've ever found haunted?

CB: The abandoned stadium in Beijing, China from the 2008 Olympics, haunted by dashed dreams and googly-eyed cartoon mascots who wonder why they remain.

EJG: Do you enjoy your work?

CB: Of course. Love what you do, and it will reflect back to you with 10,000 faces . . . although that phrase may only apply advantageously to my own calling. I suspect it might be a bit jarring to find 10,000 faces reflecting back, should you be in the midst of toiling while as a clerk or mechanic, ha ha.

EJG: In closing, what's next for Professor Charlatan Bardot?

CB: I'll carry on in my ways, investigating architectural paranormal phenomena. I'm available for speaking engagements, consulting work, or demonic manufactured-structure exorcisms. And if people should have enjoyed this book, and shout loudly enough for an encore publication, perhaps I shall return another time with further (fictional) tales to the most haunted buildings in the weird, wild world!

EJG: Wonderful to chat with you here.

CB: Exonerate the name of Lasses Birgitta!

(Friday, August 13, 2021)

LA FIN

With sincerest thanks . . .

EDITOR'S REQUEST

DEAR READER, FAN, OR SUPPORTER,
It's a dreadful commentary that the worth of indie publications is measured by online 5-star reviews, but such is the state of current commerce.

Should you have enjoyed this book, gratitude is most appreciated by posting a brief and honest online review at Amazon.com, Goodreads.com, and/or a highly-visible blog.

With sincerest thanks,

Eric J. Guignard, co-editor
Professor Charlatan Bardot's Travel Anthology to the Most (Fictional) Haunted Buildings in the Weird, Wild World (2021 edition)

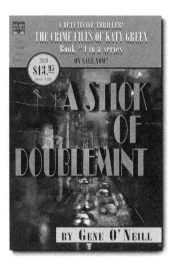

INDEX

ABOUT EDITOR PROFESSOR CHARLATAN BARDOT, PHD, EDD, EJG

CHARLATAN BARDOT is a revered excursionist célèbre of the paranormal and author of the phenomenal.

He has travelled the globe investigating preternatural occurrences for over forty years, becoming the most beloved worldwide travel documentarian in the realms of the spectral and incomprehensible.

He is an esteemed professor with multiple academic, legal, and/or honorary degrees relating to metaphysical applications; spirituality; law in the occult; and global culture and influence as it pertains to the afterworld (and to the living).

Named as "The most sophisticated man, in manner and in mind, in the field of International Architectural Paranormal Investigations," Professor Charlatan Bardot has won awards and accolades in almost every subject and category from accrediting bodies, organizations, and ruling parties of nations around the world. Additionally, he's a universally recognized and bestselling author (under pseudonyms).

Follow him at: www.darkmoonbooks.com/charlatan_bardot.html and on Twitter at @CharlatanBardot.

ABOUT EDITOR ERIC J. GUIGNARD

ERIC J. GUIGNARD is a writer and editor of dark and speculative fiction, operating from the shadowy outskirts of Los Angeles, where he also runs the small press, Dark Moon Books. He's twice won the Bram Stoker Award (the highest literary award of horror fiction), been a finalist for the International Thriller Writers Award, and a multi-nominee of the Pushcart Prize.

He has over one hundred stories and non-fiction author credits appearing in publications around the world. As editor, Eric's published multiple fiction anthologies, including his most recent, *Pop the Clutch: Thrilling Tales of Rockabilly, Monsters, and Hot Rod Horror*; and *A World of Horror*, a showcase of international horror short fiction.

He currently publishes the acclaimed series of author primers created to champion modern masters of the dark and macabre, *Exploring Dark Short Fiction*. He is also publisher and acquisitions editor for the renowned *+Horror Library+* anthology series. Additionally he curates the series, *The Horror Writers Association Presents: Haunted Library of Horror Classics* through SourceBooks with co-editor Leslie S. Klinger.

His latest books are *Last Case at a Baggage Auction*; *Doorways To The Deadeye*; and short story collection *That Which Grows Wild: 16 Tales of Dark Fiction* (Cemetery Dance).

Outside the glamorous and jet-setting world of indie fiction, Eric's a technical writer and college professor, and he stumbles home each day to a wife, children, dogs, and a terrarium filled with mischievous beetles. Visit Eric at: www.ericjguignard.com, his blog: ericjguignard.blogspot.com, or Twitter: @ericjguignard.

ABOUT ILLUSTRATOR STEVE LINES

STEVE LINES is a musician, artist, editor, and occasional writer, and runs Rainfall Records & Books with John B. Ford. He lives in England in darkest Wiltshire just a few miles from the Avebury stone circle and Silbury Hill. He has been illustrating books and magazines since the mid '70s and has worked for Centipede Press, Lindisfarne Press, Mythos Books, and Rainfall Books, amongst others. With John B. Ford he wrote *The Night Eternal*, a dark Arabian fantasy. He is active in several bands including The Doctor's Pond and The Ungrateful Dead. He is currently working on a new CD album by The Ungrateful Dead titled *Dali's Brain*; putting together a new line-up of The Doctor's Pond; editing a book of sketches by Bruce Pennington; and generally keeping himself busy.

About Illustrator James Gabb

J AMES GABB is an avid sketcher living on the south coast of the UK. He can usually be found drawing, working, with his family, or on the computer. Heavily into fantasy of all sorts, especially loving everything architecture, he likes nothing more than sketching or building things. Having previously only done illustrations and drawings for family and friends, these are his first published illustrations and he is excited to see his work alongside Steve Lines and hopes you enjoy them as much as he did drawing them!

For more on James's work, visit: www.sketchingdaily.wordpress.com.

CPSIA information can be obtained
at www.ICGtesting.com
Printed in the USA
BVHW042345271021
620116BV00006BA/15/J